OMINOUS ODYSSEY

OVERWORLD CHRONICLES
BOOK THIRTEEN

JOHN CORWIN

ISBN- 978-1-942453-07-9

Printed in the U.S.A.

RAVEN
HOUSE

To my wonderful readers, my amazing editors:

Thanks so much for all your help and input!

Books by John Corwin:

The Overworld Chronicles:
Sweet Blood of Mine
Dark Light of Mine
Fallen Angel of Mine
Dread Nemesis of Mine
Twisted Sister of Mine
Dearest Mother of Mine
Infernal Father of Mine
Sinister Seraphim of Mine
Wicked War of Mine
Dire Destiny of Ours
Aetherial Annihilation
Baleful Betrayal
Ominous Odyssey

Overworld Underground:
Possessed By You
Demonicus

Overworld Arcanum:
Conrad Edison and the Living Curse
Conrad Edison and the Anchored World
Conrad Edison and the Broken Relic

Stand Alone Novels:
No Darker Fate
The Next Thing I Knew
Outsourced
Seventh
Mars Rising

Join my VIP Club at
www.johncorwin.net

SHIVER ME TIMBERS!

The mysterious new leader of the Brightlings is after a secret weapon. The catch? It's hidden somewhere in Voltis, a forbidden place where violent elemental forces will slap you around like a red-headed stepchild. Naturally, Justin can't let that happen and convinces Elyssa, Shelton, and Adam to tag along, because who doesn't want to ride a flying ship into hurricane-force winds and certain doom?

Chapter 1

I was about to meet with a dead man.

Primarion Arturo was a blast from the past, and not in a good way. I thought I'd killed him in the final boss match on Eden between me and his beloved empress, Daelissa. Apparently, he had roach DNA.

Here on Seraphina, accompanied by a squadron of thirty of his flying archangels, Arturo glided on blazing white wings to a smooth landing atop Mount Ulladon. He wore a dark blue robe over sparkly blue armor, and a golden circlet around his head. He looked so damned magnificent with his thick mane of hair and chiseled jaw, I just wanted to punch him.

Showing no signs of surprise or anger that he was meeting with Justin Slade, the guy who'd killed his empress, Arturo strode across the open ground to the simple white canopy and took a seat at the table beneath it.

How in the hell are you alive? The Brightlings had specifically requested my presence here and I wondered if Arturo had been behind it. What if this entire meeting was a ruse so he could exact revenge on me? If it was, he was in for a hell of a fight even though I was alone.

I gave Arturo a few seconds to speak, but he remained stubbornly silent. It was all the more annoying because the Brightlings had requested the meeting. "Well?" I said. "Shall we get started?"

"Of course," he replied, voice calm and lacking the pomposity that instantly made me hate him the first time we'd met. "As crown ambassador for the Brightling Empire, I am prepared to negotiate peace."

His statement shocked me into silence. It took a few blinks before I could respond. "You want peace?" It was the last thing I'd expected from the Brightlings. If anything, I'd expected a long hard fight just to get them off Pjurnan soil.

If he was truly here to negotiate peace, I had a chance to make Nightliss's dream of a unified Seraphina come true. Her death sat heavy in my heart, but making her wish a reality would do wonders to lighten that load.

Arturo nodded. "I see no reason to continue a bloody war that might consume our entire realm." He clasped his hands and gave me a steady look. "I cannot deny that I despise you for murdering my empress. But after I crawled away from that battle, life barely intact, I was forced to live for a time among mortals. They shed blood without reason, prosecute war without faith, and have spread like a blight throughout Eden."

I raised an eyebrow. "Your point being?"

"Seraphina is paradise." Arturo gestured at the towering mountain peaks crowned with golden clouds. "Seraphim should be as wise as they are ancient and do whatever possible to preserve that."

"I wish Daelissa had believed that."

His gaze sharpened. "My empress would have set Eden to rights." He held up a hand to ward off a response. "Further conversation on this matter would only dampen my enthusiasm for a treaty. Let us move on to the details."

Thankfully, Commander Borathen had prepared a list of demands just in case. That man really knew how to plan for every eventuality.

"It just so happens I already have the details worked out." I pushed a small blue gem into the middle of the table and charged it with Murk. A holographic list of our terms appeared.

Equal rights for all Seraphim under the law.

Equal representation for all Seraphim in the government.

Free travel and trade between the Darkling Empire and the Brightling Empire.

I'd wanted to add some spiffy graphics and a video of cats cuddling with dogs to get my point across, but Elyssa and her father had nixed the idea.

Arturo read the short list and deactivated the gem. "Our terms are much simpler. Both sides sign a non-aggression treaty and we remove our troops from the Pjurnan borders."

"And continue to treat the Darklings in the Brightling Empire like second-class citizens," I finished. "I think it's time to be wise and unite all Seraphim. I have it on good authority that in the old days, there were no Brightlings or Darklings, only one people."

"Perhaps, but those days are long past." He leaned back and regarded me for a moment. "Why should we dilute our purity? If we allow Darklings the same privileges, then the two species will mate and produce inferior offspring."

"Do you know Fjoeruss?" I asked.

Arturo's lips tightened. "I know of the Trickster, yes."

"Is he powerful?"

The regent paused warily. "Nearly as powerful as Daelissa herself."

"Actually, Fjoeruss is far more powerful than she ever was," I said. "He's an ancient, one of the first Seraphim, and can channel both Murk and Brilliance equally. I believe uniting the Seraphim will once again restore the powers of old."

Arturo shook his head. "I cannot and will not endorse such madness, Minister Slade. My own people would rise up against me."

I wasn't a minister, an ambassador, or even remotely qualified to negotiate a peace treaty, but I was the face of the Eden army that had defeated Daelissa. Now I knew why Arturo had specifically requested to meet with me. He hadn't beaten me in battle, so he wanted to watch me squirm at the negotiating table.

I maintained a stony exterior and looked him dead in the eyes. "Are you willing to risk war over outdated ideals?"

He didn't flinch. "The question you should be asking, Minister Slade, is whether peace in our time is more valuable than a protracted war even you cannot hope to win." He folded his arms across his chest. "Tarissa is naught but rubble, her people scattered to the winds.

You have only two legions at full strength, and the Eden army is far weaker than the last time I fought you."

How in the hell does he know all that? My straight face slipped into shock, because, damn it, I just wasn't trained for this sort of thing. "Where did you get that information?"

"We have four full legions, Minister Slade." Arturo produced a gem and projected a flat map of Seraphina. Though the continents bore similarities to their counterparts in Eden, there were enough differences to make it look like an alien world.

Here, North and South America were known as Azoris and Sazoris, their land masses much smaller due to the larger oceans and aether vortexes claiming thousands of square miles. A mountain range occupied the ocean where Florida should have been, and there, a star atop Mount Hein marked the capitol of the Brightling Empire, Zbura.

Across the Altean Ocean sat the land of Goleaad. This version of Europe and Asia had lost the landmass of Russia and half of India to the Frigean and Castigean Oceans. Ijolica neighbored it to the south, its outline bearing a slight resemblance to Africa.

Solid white shaded nearly every continent except for gray Ijolica, while a lonely little continent in the far southwestern corner resembled a deep purple bruise on the world's ass. This place happened to be the same continent whose fate Arturo and I were discussing.

Pjurna resembled Australia, and Tarissa, the capitol city of the Darkling Empire, sat right about where Sydney would be in Eden. It was a small speck of land compared to the Brightling holdings, which was exactly why Arturo showed me this map. He wanted me to feel small, insignificant, and purple compared to the pure glowing white of the Brightling Empire.

I raised an unconcerned eyebrow to let him know I wasn't buying it and wished I could leave a fist-shaped bruise on his face. That was the bad part about being an ambassador. I couldn't just punch people whenever I wanted.

Arturo spread his hands grandly. "As you can see, our empire stretches across most of the globe. What you faced in Eden was but a sample of our true might."

I counted down from three to think of a response, and to resist the mighty urge to shove the gem so far down his throat he'd shoot holographic images out of his ass every time he farted. "If that's true, why didn't you invade Pjurna already?"

"The empire is weary of war." Arturo's voice sounded heavy with regret. "There are those who wish to crush Pjurna and rid the realm of Darklings altogether. Be glad I do not condone such action." He deactivated the gem and the map vanished. "Is it not better to live and let live than force ideals on one another? Is it not grander to start with peace rather than fight a hopeless war?"

Try as I might, I couldn't fault his logic. I desperately wanted peace, but I'd made a promise to Nightliss that I would unite Seraphina into a realm with equal rights for all Brightlings and Darklings alike. Right now it was looking like an awfully hard promise to keep.

"Like it or not, Minister Slade, you are trapped in this realm." Arturo leaned forward as if to drive home his next point. "None of the Alabaster Arches are working and there is no return to Eden." His voice softened. "Seraphina is your new home, so I suggest you take some time to get to know her before wounding her with another war."

Arturo had me back on my heels, but I wasn't completely helpless. "Don't tell me you haven't crushed Pjurna simply because you don't want war." I motioned at the Vjartik Mountains. The peaks reached far into sky, making them nearly impossible to traverse by air. "Overcoming the mountains here in the north or the aether vortexes and boiling sea to the east and west while fighting our legions would decimate your army."

"Perhaps." The crown ambassador of the Brightling Empire turned back on the holographic map then stood and turned toward his guards waiting outside the canopy. "Please, think about our offer. I will return at dawn for your answer."

I wanted to grab him, spin him around and slap some sense into his stupid head. "Why do you despise the Darklings? Why do you think they're inferior?"

Without turning around, Arturo answered, "It has always been so." He began walking so I got up and followed.

An imperious-looking archangel in shiny blue armor stepped in front of me as if he thought he could scare me. "You should consider our offer carefully," he said in a cold voice. "Do not squander our good will."

I gave him an equally cool look. "I'll do what I think is best."

"That is enough, Gravuss," Arturo said, and motioned for the other seraph to come with him. "Good day, Minister Slade."

As they walked toward the other archangels, Gravuss leaned in and whispered something urgently. I'd done such a poor job of negotiating, I figured it wasn't beneath me to eavesdrop for an advantage since I had supernatural hearing.

"Urgent…cannot afford to worry…Voltis must come first." Whatever else Gravuss said was lost to the wind. Blazing white wings spread from the backs of the archangels and they launched themselves off the cliff and glided north, probably toward the Brightling encampments on the northern shores of Pjurna.

I hadn't brought anyone with me, as per the agreement with the Brightlings, so I mounted a broom, whirled it around, and flew back toward basecamp in the military base of Kohvalla, named unoriginally for the Legiaros of Victrix Legion. Flying angry and distracted turned out to be a bad idea because I collided with a flock of white eagles and nearly oversteered myself into a cliff.

I shook my fist at the birds. "Watch where you're flying!" I smacked my forehead with my hand. "I'm an idiot. They never should have picked me to do something like this."

I reached the Northern Pass, a crack in the otherwise impassible Vjartik Mountains. Rising from the canyon floor below and into the mists far above, two towers inside the pass guarded the way into Darkling controlled territory.

A shimmering ultraviolet shield guarded against invasion, and massive aether gems embedded into the northern faces of the towers projected enough illumination at night to make it look like daytime. There was a nearly identical setup in the Northwestern Pass—the only other north-south route into Kohvalla.

I flew up to the section of the eastern tower where large red symbols strongly suggested I request entrance lest I be shot down immediately. Since I was the only weirdo on a flying broom—the Seraphim preferred flying on cloudlets—the guards knew who I was and deactivated a small section of the magical shield to let me through.

I smiled and waved cheerily, but the guards inside returned the dead looks of those who were either bored out of their minds, or wishing they could shoot me down for target practice. I hurried through the opening and raced down the rest of the pass.

Nestled in a valley of red grass and blue trees, Kohvalla resembled a small town more than a military base. The troops had been stationed here so long, they'd given up on going back to their homes and had made lives for themselves. I wondered if they'd be happy if I told them they could go home within a few days, provided I gave up on my ideals and signed the non-aggression pact.

Nightliss had fought for a unified Seraphina. She'd survived uprisings and the two Eden wars. I'd promised the people of Pjurna that I'd fight the Brightling Empire and bring lasting peace to the realm. Arturo had ruined all that by being a nice guy.

"How can I justify starting a war now?" I slowed the broom and hovered over the valley. People scurried below like ants in the civilian sector while rows of soldiers practiced drills on a wide field. Another group of Darklings took flying lessons so we could match Arturo's archangels if peace didn't work out.

I spotted a lone figure in black looking up at me. From this distance we were mere specks to each other, but I knew who it was and dreaded disappointing her with the news. I drifted down and landed atop the command and control center, a squat square building in the northern quadrant of town.

A smile couldn't hide my glum mood. Elyssa's violet eyes narrowed with concern. "Didn't go well?" she asked.

"On the upside, the Brightlings want peace," I said. "On the downside, they refused our terms and want to sign a non-aggression pact."

Her eyes widened. "They want peace?"

"But not equal rights for all Seraphim." I groaned. "I told you we should've used the video of the cat cuddling with the dog."

7

Elyssa's smile flickered and vanished. "Who negotiated for them?"

"Primarion Arturo," I started to say, then corrected myself. "Make that Crown Ambassador Arturo."

His name elicited a raised eyebrows and a jaw drop. "I thought he was dead."

"Nope, and he even got a promotion."

"We need to speak with my father." Elyssa hooked her arm in mine and led me inside the building. We took a levitator down several floors to the war room where we found Commander Thomas Borathen speaking with Legiaros Kohval of Victrix Legion.

The pair looked away from the holographic map hovering over the table between them and regarded me with uncomfortable expectancy.

I almost started with the good news, bad news line, but skipped the crap and laid it bare as a shaved cat. "Primarion Arturo of the archangels is the ambassador for the Brightling Empire now."

"I heard rumors he was back," Kohval said, his voice richer and deeper than any radio personality. "I'd hoped him dead."

"We thought he was dead," Thomas said. "Apparently, he survived and made his way back to Zbura." He drummed his fingers on the table. "What did he want to meet about?"

"Does he want peace or surrender?" Kohval asked.

I waggled my hand in a so-so gesture. "That'll be up to us."

Thomas and Kohval met that statement with raised eyebrows.

"Arturo wants to sign a non-aggression treaty and call it a day." I shook my head. "He said no to everything else. In my mind, that's like surrendering our ideals and putting off the war for another day."

"It is just as well," Kohval said. "Right now we could not win a war against the Brightlings, but give us time to rebuild and install a strong military government and then we will be the ones with the upper hand."

Thomas held his chin between thumb and forefinger. "How long would that take? Decades?"

"It takes as long as it takes," Kohval said. "With a non-aggression pact in place we could reduce the forces at the border and redirect them to Tarissa. A strong military force could have the city rebuilt in years. This time it would be built for function and defense."

"A strong civilian government is best," Thomas said.

"Civilians ruined our government and allowed Cephus to take control." Kohval made a fist. "We need a government that turns all citizens into productive contributors toward our common cause."

This was the same old argument Kohval had presented when we arrived yesterday. He certainly hadn't been happy to hear the Brightlings had wanted to meet specifically with me and he definitely didn't like Thomas's ideas about civilian government.

I forced the subject back to the matter at hand. "Somehow Arturo knows about our legion strengths, the destruction in Tarissa, and even that the way to Eden is closed." I let that sink in. "I don't know where he got the information, but since Cephus and Serena were running the show in Tarissa for months, it's safe to say one of them probably provided him with the intel."

"In other words, we can't bluff our way through this." Elyssa leaned on the table. "What do we do now?"

"An interesting question," Thomas said. "I believe there's more to this than Arturo is letting on."

I tilted my head. "How so? He seemed pretty straightforward to me."

Thomas stood and looked out the window as troops marched past, hands clasped behind his back. "I study my enemies. Arturo is not one who forgives and forgets, nor is a non-aggression pact the same thing as a long-term treaty."

"It was a bit odd," I admitted. "He told me he still despised me for killing Daelissa, but that living with mortals made him realize peace was for the best, yada-yada-yada."

"Doesn't sound at all like the Arturo we fought." Elyssa pursed her lips. "What ulterior motive could he have?"

"Perhaps, like me, he's merely tired of war." Kohval shrugged his broad shoulders. With his lean face and long nose, he resembled a war hawk, not someone to run away from a fight. "Though they lost a legion in Eden, they have far more troops than do we."

"Well, Arturo isn't going to tell me his reasons, you can count on that." I walked around the table and stood next to Thomas. "What answer should I give him tomorrow?"

Thomas looked me in the eye. "No."

"No?" Kohval jerked to his feet. "This is a golden opportunity to rebuild." He jabbed a finger at the soldiers marching in the square. "I have the best trained troops in the nation. I can rebuild the infrastructure and morale of our people, but I need the Brightlings off our soil."

Thomas turned his icy blue eyes on the seraph. "I don't intend to prosecute a war or sue for peace without knowing all the facts, Legiaros. For now, we buy time and try to discover Arturo's ulterior motives."

"Denied." Kohval set his large frame squarely in Thomas's way. "As Legiaros, I refuse to let you squander this opportunity based solely on supposition."

"Do you mean to commit treason?" Thomas said calmly.

"Treason?" Kohval scoffed. "Our government leaders are dead, and you outsiders believe you can come in and determine our destiny? I am more qualified to lead than any civilian."

Thomas ended his long silence. "If you do not wish to be part of the solution, Legiaros Kohval, you are free to resign your post."

"Who do you think you are?" Kohval rumbled.

"Would you like to find out?" Thomas said in quiet voice that sent chills down my spine.

Kohval bared his teeth, but instead of answering, threw up his hands and stormed out of the room saying, "If you destroy this opportunity, then you will surely find out who I am."

"Maybe we should have let the Void eat this realm." I found a basket of fruit and popped an olive-shaped quinto in my mouth. The tart juices made my eyes water.

Elyssa dropped into a chair, face glum. "I don't think anything has gone right since we got here."

Understatement of the year.

If things got any worse, I was packing up and moving to the country.

Chapter 2

I hadn't liked Kohval from the moment I'd met him, and I certainly didn't trust him. With him gone, I divulged the extra tidbit I'd been holding back about my meeting. "There's something else I didn't mention."

Elyssa narrowed her eyes. "Because of Kohval?"

I nodded. "One of Arturo's seraphs made mention of something called Voltis. He said it was urgent and couldn't wait."

Thomas pursed his lips in thought. "Odd. Cephus's language spell we used to help us learn Cyrinthian doesn't have a translation for that word."

Cephus had gotten inside my head when I'd first met him, though at the time I thought it was for a good cause. He'd basically uploaded the Cyrinthian language into my head with magic. He'd also poked around in my memories and used them in an attempt to control me. Though his motives had been evil, the actual language spell had proven useful for our troops.

The first time I heard an unfamiliar Cyrinthian term, my brain would fish out an image from memory and equate it to an English word. Voltis came back with an empty hook.

"It might be a place," Elyssa said. "Most of the city names don't have an English word."

"I wonder if this Voltis is the reason Arturo wants a peace agreement," Thomas said. He frowned. "Is Arturo staying at their northern beachhead?"

I nodded. "Judging from the direction they flew, I think so." The sliver of land north of Mount Ulladon was controlled by the Brightlings.

"It might be worthwhile to find out more." Thomas pulled out the holographic map.

"You want us to infiltrate their basecamp?" I said.

He nodded. "Any information on this Voltis could be vital, and we need it before tomorrow."

Elyssa pounded a fist on her chest in the Templar salute. "Yes, sir."

A smile flickered on her father's face before he saluted her back. "Well met, Templar."

I held up my hands. "Whoa, now. How in the world are we supposed to slip through enemy lines? There are hundreds of Brightlings soldiers guarding that beachhead."

Thomas shook his head. "Actually, the number of troops based there have been decreasing steadily over the past week, according to Kohval." He flicked the holographic map away and replaced it with a video recorded with the ubiquitous magic gems the Seraphim used for everything. In the video, dozens of soldiers at a time boarded cloudlets that rose into the air and floated away to the north.

"It seems as though the Brightlings are moving troops north to Guinesea and then due east to the continent of Ijolica." Thomas flicked back to the map and indicated the continent that in our realm would be called Africa. In Seraphina, the body of land was probably half the size of the one in Eden since the lower half had fallen into the ocean.

"They must be pretty confident that we'll accept the non-aggression pact." Elyssa traced a finger on the map. "Why would they go to Ijolica?"

"Kohval's spies haven't discovered the reason." Thomas stared at the map. "I would ask his spies about Voltis, but I don't trust them any more than I trust him."

"It's really sad to find out that the people you thought would help preserve Pjurna are just a bunch of jackasses." I sighed. "Well, if anyone could plan an infiltration, it'd be you two."

Just the thought of trying to plan the operation myself gave me a headache.

I ended up sitting around while father and daughter bonded over shop talk—namely how best to sneak into an enemy encampment without getting our heads chopped off. My girlfriend was essentially a ninja, which made her father the ninja leader. Elyssa had taught me a lot, but I couldn't hope to learn in months what she'd trained for since learning to walk.

We went over the plan until I started to go cross-eyed from boredom. There was nothing overly complicated about it, but Templars don't like leaving anything to chance. We wouldn't start until after dark, so that left us some time to kill. It was a good thing, because I was starving.

"I don't feel welcome here," I informed Elyssa as we walked outside in the warmer valley air.

Darkling soldiers cast suspicious glances and angry glares our way as we strolled through the training grounds. One of them spat, "Zhuka!" as she walked past with a group of other soldiers, and they burst into laughter.

My face burned with anger and heat blossomed in my clenched fists. Elyssa grabbed my arm. "Don't let them get to you."

"They just called us zhukas!" I growled.

Elyssa's eyes looked up as if trying to recall something. "I don't know that word."

Having spent more time in Seraphina than she had, I knew all too well what it meant. "They're these cute little animals that look like golden foxes."

"That doesn't sound so bad."

"A zhuka is the female," I continued. "Essentially, it's the Cyrinthian version of bitch."

"Assholes!" Elyssa bared her teeth and still managed to look beautiful while doing it.

I stopped her and ran my hand over her smooth fair cheek. "Don't let them get to you, babe."

She pressed her hand to mine. "You know, maybe we should concentrate on finding a way home and let the Seraphim sort out their own issues."

A part of me would have liked nothing better, but the other part was too stubborn to let go. "I promised Flava and Nightliss I'd see this through."

"How?" she asked. "We don't have the support of either remaining legion, we still have to rebuild the capital city and rehabilitate hundreds of citizens Cephus mutated into fighters. On top of that, our own forces are still recovering from the war and the shock of being trapped in another realm."

"We'll build a new army."

She put her hands on her hips. "How long do you think that'll take? A year? Ten?"

"As long as it takes." I'd spent nearly every waking moment thinking about how to fight the Brightlings, but I hadn't realized we'd get so much resistance from the very people we were trying to help. "I'm just worried that Kohval might do something stupid."

A phalanx of soldiers ran right into us, bouncing us between bodies and leaving us stunned and grabbing each other for balance after they jogged past, laughing.

My inner demon rattled the bars to its cage and demanded release. I almost let it. "Would it be bad if I roughed them up a little?"

Elyssa's face turned crimson. "Idiots! Can't they see we're here to help?"

"I think Kohval made it pretty clear we're unwanted outsiders." I pounded a fist into my palm. "None of these soldiers fought Cephus. None of them saw the sacrifices we made for Pjurna. If only they knew."

"Let's get out of here," Elyssa said. She took my hand and we hastily left the military zone and entered the village that had grown larger over the centuries as the soldiers of the Victrix Legion realized this valley would be their permanent home. Organically curved and twisted buildings were in the minority in this military town, rectangles and domes dominating the landscape instead.

14

A small blue dome was our home away from home away from home. We went inside and freshened up, then went back out for dinner.

Seraphim didn't kill animals for meat and relied on a diverse array of fruits and vegetables to supply their nutritional needs. As such, their restaurants didn't offer a stunning variety of meals, if you could even call the eating establishments restaurants. There were no wait staff, no chefs—just you, an array of edibles, and a preparation alcove.

"Glurk and panari, or panari and glurk?" Elyssa mused as she looked over the food lining the crystal shelves. "Or how about quinto-marinated cruna?"

I sighed. "I'm getting sick to death of glurk. I'm gonna try something new." I grabbed a white vegetable labeled *bruk*, and an ear of *chlub* because it looked exactly like corn. I chucked it in a small black crystal box—an angel microwave oven—and charged the gem on the side with aether.

A moment later, the box opened and the steaming entrée emerged, bruk neatly sliced, its insides moist and fleshy like chicken. Elyssa took the same items and relied on me to charge the gem to the prep box while she grabbed utensils.

The seating area was crowded with military types mingling with civilians and children, but we managed to find seats near the back.

"You have funny eyes," a little girl said in Cyrinthian as she stared at Elyssa. "They look like Murk."

Elyssa seemed uncertain how to respond. "Uh, thanks."

The mother grabbed her child by the arm and whispered angrily at her.

I exchanged an eye roll with Elyssa and dug into my food.

"Tastes like chicken," Elyssa commented as she ate a slice of bruk.

I chewed the bruk and agreed with her assessment. It was a nice change from glurk, but like everything here, something was off. "I want pizza and a hamburger."

"Then I guess we'd better find a way to get home." Elyssa's wary eyes studied the crowd. "We're getting a lot of looks."

"That's nothing new," I muttered. I finished off my meal and we left, strolled back down the pedestrium in the deepening dusk. "I hope Adam and Shelton are making progress."

"Somehow, I think decrypting the data gems Cephus and his researchers left behind is going to be a monumental task." Elyssa stopped at the seamless outer wall of our lodgings and waited for me to charge the gem. "I feel so helpless here. I can't even open a door without you."

I sent a spark of Murk into the gem and the outer wall misted away into an opening so we could enter. I took a step forward into the dark house and my senses tingled. Elyssa threw up her arms defensively and blocked a blow from an unseen assailant.

We tried to back up but a dozen masked people swarmed from hiding and surrounded us. Before I could come up with a witty comment, the soft whizz of projectiles caught my attention. I ducked and weaved, narrowly avoiding small crystal burrs.

One smacked an attacker in the face mask and they went down like a sack of wet dog poo. Elyssa reached over her shoulders for the sai swords she wasn't wearing. I tried to stop, drop, and roll my way past the burrs, but one of them stung my neck. The last thing I saw was Elyssa falling to the ground next to me, lips peeled back in anger, but her eyes slowly filling with hopelessness as the knockout agent dragged us into unconsciousness.

I jerked awake, a brilliant moon lighting a small glade in the forest as if it were daylight. Looking down, I quickly realized I was bound to a tree by a sheet of ultraviolet energy that hugged my body like shrink wrap all the way up to the shoulders. Elyssa was bound similarly against a tree to my left. Before me stood a dozen masked people. I felt certain they weren't Brightlings sent by Arturo to kill me, because I'd already be dead. Infiltrating a heavily guarded military town would also be nigh impossible for such a large group.

One of the masked people spoke, her gender evident from the sound of her voice. "You will accept the peace offer from Arturo or you and your mate will die, Slade."

I flicked on my demon vision so I could view the magical spectrum and saw golden halos surrounding each of the dozen Seraphim. More than half were female. Four of them were channeling the magic restraining me and Elyssa. I planned to say no, but first I let them know that I knew what was up. "Kohval sent you."

"We will release you and hold your mortal," the woman said. "When you do as we ask, she will be spared and released."

I gauged my audience. "Tell me, do you want a unified Seraphina with equal rights for all? By agreeing to a cease-fire, you'll be giving that up." They looked at each other—comical really, since they all wore facemasks and couldn't see expressions. As my query rippled through them, I took the opportunity to draw in aether.

Before I'd journeyed up here to meet with Kohval, I'd fed my demon and Seraphim side from the humans we'd brought with us. What these Seraphim likely didn't know was that human soul essence amplifies Seraphim magic. How or why, and if it would be enough to defeat a dozen Darklings, I didn't know. The only certain thing was that I wasn't leaving Elyssa alone with a bunch of hooligans.

I imagined a thin layer of Murk rising from the pores of my skin, slipping the energy beneath the enemy bonds.

"You will agree to peace," the sera—a female Seraphim— repeated stubbornly. "Sign the treaty and leave us forever."

I showed her my teeth. "How about you let us go right now, and I won't subject you to an ass beating?" The term didn't translate well into Cyrinthian, and several of our kidnappers looked at their backsides, probably wondering why I'd focus on their bottoms.

"You will not beat our asses," she replied. "You will submit."

"No," I said, and amped my power draw. "I won't." With that final declaration, I sent a burst of energy from my skin and against the barrier. Two Darklings cried out and stumbled backwards as I overpowered them. Before anyone could react, I knelt and fired off two fist-sized blasts of Murk at the pair holding Elyssa's bonds. She slumped to the ground, still unconscious.

I didn't have time to pause, so I rolled right to avoid return fire and dove right into the middle of our captors. As predicted, none of them dared fire magic or their sleeping burrs while they might hit their comrades. I relied on fisticuffs instead of magic, delivering a crushing uppercut to the closest masked menace, spinning and driving a foot into the solar plexus of someone charging from behind.

A sweep of my foot took down two attackers. I punished them with blows to the head to keep them down then focused a double-fisted blow to the chest of a third. Someone gripped my neck from behind. I flipped them over my shoulder and conked them on the noggin. There were still too many for me to take out, so I took the low road and grabbed the sera who'd threatened me.

Wrapping my arm around her neck, I dragged us out of the fray and channeled a thin spike of blazing white Brilliance, holding it near her temple. "Stop fighting or I'll kill her," I growled.

The conscious attackers backed off, hands up.

"Take him, you fools!" the feisty sera ordered. "Let me die if you must!"

"Nah, ah, ah." I jerked her back another foot as the others slowly came at me. "If you even try, I'll use deadly force on all of you." I nodded at their unconscious friends. "So far, I've been merciful."

The sera elbowed me hard. My breath oofed out and I nearly lost my grip on her, but I'd endured worse. Resisting the urge to punch her, I bound her in strands of sticky Murk and dropped her on the ground. My right hand heated as I forged a blazing sword of Brilliance. The cold of creation enveloped my left arm, forming a thick shield.

"Fight me and die. Surrender and live." I bared my teeth. "Your choice, zhukas."

"Fight him!" the sera screamed, bucking and writhing against her bonds. "He is our only chance to end this war!"

Thankfully, her friends didn't want to tangle and lowered their hands.

"Masks off," I ordered. "Take them off your sleeping friends as well."

They hesitantly removed the hoods, revealing the faces of strangers I only recognized because they'd nearly run us over on the way out of the military base. I released the sword and knelt to tug off the mask of the sera. Black hair spilled out and I nearly lost my crap when I saw her face.

I staggered upright and shook my head. It wasn't the first time since coming to Seraphina that I thought I'd seen a ghost. I'd met Nightliss's mother, Kaelissa, who resembled both her daughters, but favored Daelissa in more ways than one. This sera bore a striking resemblance to Nightliss, her dark hair, olive skin, right down to the perky nose. But she was taller and stouter than my late friend.

Elyssa groaned and pushed upright, blinking groggily at the scene before her. "Huh?" She leaned against a tree and shook her head. "God, I'm such a loser. Did I sleep through everything?"

"I've got it under control," I said, and turned my attention back to the sera at my feet. "Are you related to Kaelissa?"

"I do not know that name," the sera said.

"Do you know Nightliss—Naelissa?" I threw in her original name just in case.

She blinked. "How do you know my mother?"

Chapter 3

It felt like someone punched me in the stomach. *A kid?*

The question erupted from Elyssa in a tone of disbelief. "Nightliss had a child?"

"How old are you?" I asked.

"Very old." She struggled against her bonds.

"Release her," a tall burly seraph said. "We have done as you asked, now spare her."

"I will have your word that none of you will plot or commit harm to me, Elyssa, or any of our companions." I glared at them for emphasis, then knelt next to the sera. "I knew your mother. She was one of my dearest friends."

She narrowed her eyes with suspicion. "My mother died in a war thousands of years ago. How would you know her?"

"She didn't die—" I choked up and took a breath to soothe the knot before finishing. "At least, not in the first war. She died only months ago."

"That's not possible," the sera said, tears glistening in her eyes. "Why did she not tell me she survived the war? Why didn't she find me?"

I felt awful and a little angry with Nightliss. She'd never once mentioned having a daughter. Then again, she had plenty of good reasons not to. "If I release you, do you promise not to attack?"

She nodded.

I released the binding and backed up. "What's your name?"

The sera brushed dirt off her dark clothing and stood. "Issana."

I'd never heard the name spoken even once by Nightliss, but they had to be related if appearances were anything to go by.

"Why did you attack us?" Elyssa asked. "What's wrong with you people? We're trying to help Pjurna, but you act as if we're here to destroy it."

"They already answered that while you were asleep," I said. "They want me to agree to Arturo's peace terms." I said the last part with contempt.

Elyssa huffed. "What else did I miss?"

"My magnificent fighting, for one thing." I flashed a grin then turned back to Issana. "At the end of the first war, your mother was caught in the magical blast when the Grand Nexus was disabled. Most Seraphim caught in the blast were turned into dark husks for thousands of years until we found out how to restore them. Nightliss was saved at the last minute." I really hated to fill in the next blanks, but it was the truth. "Unfortunately, she lost most of her memories, including those of you."

Issana's eyes glistened. "Since I know almost nothing of her since she vanished, I will have to take your word for it."

"How long have you been with this legion?" Elyssa asked.

"Nearly seven months," she replied.

"I told you this was a terrible idea," the burly seraph said. "Now we'll be reported to Kohval and prosecuted."

Issana ignored him and directed another question my way. "Why do you not want peace?"

A sarcastic laugh burst from my mouth. "Peace is all I've ever wanted." I waved a hand at the forest around us. Blue leaves rustled in the wind, birds chirped in the distance, and something that looked like a squirrel danced onto a branch and chattered curiously. "Don't you think if I could, I'd stop and just enjoy life instead of rushing off to fight another damned war?" I threw up my hands. "I'm twenty years old. I'd rather sit at home and browse the internet all day instead of fixing the woes of the world."

"You're only twenty?" Issana said. Gasps rose from the group behind her. "Who would place such a burden on the shoulders of children?"

"Whoa, now," Elyssa held up her hands defensively. "We may be young, but we're not stupid."

"Let me get back on track," I said. "Nightliss wanted equal rights for all Seraphim regardless of affinity to Murk or Brilliance, and one nation united under those ideals. I believe in her vision and I want to fight for it. Just because Arturo is offering a non-aggression pact now doesn't mean it will last."

"My mother's vision was lofty," Issana said, "but I would rather take peace now than spit in the face of those offering it."

I couldn't argue with her logic, but I also agreed with Thomas's assessment that something else drove Arturo's offer. "You may be right, but we don't know all the facts. Now, if you'll kindly not kidnap us again and let us think this through, I think we can come to a compromise."

"Agreed," the big seraph said. "He's wise for a boy."

"I did not ask your opinion, Yolo." Issana swatted at the air. "We will discuss matters."

I snorted, barely holding back a laugh at the seraph's name. "Like adults." I focused my gaze on Yolo. "After all, you only live once."

Elyssa giggled, and I lost it while our former kidnappers watched in confusion. Yolo scratched his head and it only made me laugh harder.

At least we're mature most of the time.

I motioned for Issana to get a move on. "Why don't you lead the way?"

She seemed lost in thought and didn't respond at once. Yolo nudged her and she spun, hands up defensively. "What have I told you about touching me?"

He backed off, hands up in surrender. "Slade asked you a question."

"I heard it." Issana marched forward and her troop followed.

Despite the canopy of blue and red trees, the huge moon provided ample light to see our way. Issana slowed and paced alongside me. "Tell me about my mother."

I navigated around a green mushroom the size of a kitchen table and rejoined her on the other side. "I only knew her for a brief time in the grand scheme of things. When I found her, she was in cat form. I saved her from a dog and she later revealed herself as a Darkling. She was kind, generous, and willing to do whatever it took to protect her friends."

"She was strong," Issana said certainly. "A warrior."

"Yeah, that too." I plucked a blue leaf from a low-hanging branch and twirled it in my fingers. "How old were you when she left to go to Eden?"

She tapped a finger on her chin. "Perhaps fifteen. It was so long ago I find it hard to recall specifics."

"Why didn't you go with her?" Elyssa asked.

Issana flicked an annoyed gaze at Elyssa. "I stayed with my father."

I perked up, curious to hear who Nightliss hooked up with back in the day. "Who is your father?"

"Gussor, of direct lineage from Ussor himself," she said proudly. "He died long ago."

Flava had given me a crash course in Seraphim naming conventions, and why they only had first names. Back in the day, children took the last parts of the matriarch or patriarch's name and combined it with the first part of their name. Issa was the matriarch of the line of Kaelissa, Daelissa, and so forth, which meant after a while, all the names in a family started to sound the same. These days, Seraphim parents named their children whatever they wanted which made me wonder what happened when more than one child had the same name.

"What have you been doing all these millennia?" I asked.

"Traveled the world," Issana said.

I waited for exposition, but she didn't offer anything else. "That's a long time to be travelling."

"I stayed in some places for many years and moved on."

Elyssa quirked an eyebrow. "I'm curious to hear about the other parts of Seraphina. What kinds of wild animals are there here?"

Mild confusion flashed through Issana's eyes. She blinked and stopped walking, standing and staring.

"She does this sometimes," Yolo said. "She suffered a bad head injury."

I grimaced. "Healers couldn't patch her up?"

"It was before she joined our legion," he said.

Issana snapped out of her state and continued walking as if nothing had happened. "There are many exotic animals in Ijolica. It is a wild place with few people." She went silent, stepping around bushes and running her hands along the rough bark of trees each time she passed one, as if the tactile sensation were new to her.

Elyssa gave me a look, so I slowed down and let the others get a little ahead of us.

"She looks a lot like her mother, but she needs an attitude adjustment," Elyssa said in English.

I bit my lip and watched Issana for a moment. "I think she's got some serious issues. If she really has a head injury that makes her catatonic sometimes, then how in the hell did they let her join the legion? What if she goes braindead in the middle of a fight?"

"Maybe it's just because she led the operation to kidnap us, but I don't trust her." Elyssa stopped to sniff a glowing yellow flower as we passed through a small glade. "We need to be very careful trusting anyone here."

"Not a good way to start things off." I spotted the village just beyond the edge of the forest and slowed. "Maybe we should just forget dealing with any of this crap and find out what passes for cows around here so I can have a burger."

Elyssa snorted. "Thinking with your stomach as usual."

"Guilty as charged." I let my smile fade. "I still don't know what to tell Arturo tomorrow even if we get good intel tonight."

"Let my father worry about the answer," Elyssa said. "He knows what he's doing and we don't."

"Gladly." I wiped my hands and spread them palms out as if washing them clean.

Issana waited alone at the edge of the forest. "Did my mother trust you, Slade?"

"Call me Justin," I said. "That's an order."

24

She bristled with a frown and seemed to fight the urge to countermand me. When she spoke it was through clenched teeth. "Did she trust you, Justin?"

"With her life," I said. "She died saving me and thousands of others."

"I hope she was not mistaken." Issana studied me through narrowed eyes. "Anyone who chooses war over peace is not to be trusted." She frowned and walked away.

I turned to Elyssa. "Is it my imagination, or did she just verbally bitch-slap me?"

"She just backhanded you across the room." Elyssa's lip curled into a snarl. "Speaking of those who are not to be trusted, how about the ones who kidnap you?"

"I really hate to say this, but"—I shivered—"I really don't like Nightliss's daughter."

A part of me yearned to go after her and dig into her past. There was something highly suspicious about her head injury story. It sounded like a good excuse to keep secrets. For now, it would have to wait.

"Me either." Elyssa rubbed her arms to ward off the goosebumps from the cold. "Let's go inside. We need to gear up for the operation tonight."

We approached our dwelling and I charged the gem so we could enter. Though we were still a bit woozy from the knockout magic used to kidnap us, we shook it off and put black strips of cloth around our waists. A pinch at the hem sent the cloth flowing up our torsos and down our legs until we were covered from the neck down in Nightingale armor.

"Templar condom ready!" I ran a hand down the smooth black cloth and mimicked a karate stance. "I'm ready to thrust myself into danger."

Elyssa giggled and grabbed her broom. "You keep joking about the armor and one day the armory officer might actually switch it with a rubber suit."

I picked up my broom. "Hey, as long as it has breathing holes."

We opened the doorway and peered outside. The way was clear
for us to sneak around the back of the domicile. I hopped in the
broom's saddle and fit my feet in the metal stirrups. It felt so much
like riding a flying horse I thought about taking the head from a stick
horse and putting it on the end of my broom. I put that idea in my
Great Ideas box. It'd be hilarious to fly up and down the lines of
super-serious Templars on my flying stick horse.

A flash of shadow tore me from my thoughts. Elyssa leapt from
her broom and blurred forward to intercept the silhouette. Two figures
fought by moonlight, limbs kicking, punching and twisting. There
was a loud grunt and one of the figures went down.

Elyssa pinned the other person to the ground and pulled off a
mask. "Issana," she hissed. "What are you doing?"

"Watching you," the sera hissed back. "I knew you could not be
trusted."

"We're just going on a midnight ride." I got off my broom and
knelt next to her. "Are you stalking us?"

"Do not lie to me." Issana struggled, but Elyssa had her in a ninja
grip I'd experienced a few times myself. "Where are you going?"

I didn't have time to deal with this. "Look, if you must know,
we're going to spy on the Brightlings. We need to know more before
we commit to a treaty."

Issana narrowed her eyes. "If this is true, then you will not mind
me coming along."

"We don't have another broom," Elyssa said.

"I am skilled at flying," Issana said. "Let me come or I will report
you to Kohval." She flashed a sarcastic smile. "Besides, you will
never get past the sentinel towers undetected without me."

Elyssa and I had counted on the guards just letting us through the
shield. Then again, they'd probably report it to Kohval immediately
and he would think we were traitors or at the very least use it as an
excuse to lock us away.

"Undetected, huh?" Elyssa shrugged and looked at me. "Might be
worth it."

"Promise you're not going to run off and report us the minute
Elyssa lets you go?" I pressed a hand to her shoulder and squeezed

26

hard enough to make her wince. "Because if you do, I promise I'll make you regret it."

Issana's eyes glinted in the moonlight. "I promise, Slade."

Elyssa released her. I reached out a hand, but Issana slapped it away.

"You're nothing like your mother," I said as I stood. "You're grouchy, unpleasant, and you seem to see only the worst in people."

"Those are my strengths," Issana said without a hint of humor in her voice. She brushed dirt and leaves off her dark uniform and turned her back to us. "Are the gems on my shoulders clean?"

Elyssa dusted off the two aether gems embedded in Issana's uniform. "They look fine. What are they for?"

"The help me fly faster," she said.

"I hope you can keep up." I hopped back on my broom and Elyssa got on hers. I pointed up. "Lead the way."

Ultraviolet wings blazed to life on Issana's back before dimming to a spectrum of black light nearly invisible in the darkness. She launched upward in a flash, wind whistling past her wings. Elyssa and I took off after her and caught up. She was definitely moving fast, maybe even a little faster than Arturo's archangels. Our brooms could have gone faster, but there was no need.

"Are you the only one with this flying suit?" I asked Issana.

She glanced back at me, eyes narrowed then faced forward without answering. I decided to let the question lie for now.

We followed Issana's lead into the Northern Pass. Hugging the cliff walls, we stayed out of sight of Darkling patrols, sometimes stopping to hide behind rock outcroppings while soldiers on cloudlets floated past.

The shadows of the sentinel towers loomed ahead, their silhouettes like cardboard cutouts against the brilliant light projected from the aether gems on their northern faces. For two hundred yards past the towers, everything from the ground all the way to the top of the pass was clearly illuminated. Between the towers hung a curtain of ultraviolet—the shield I'd had to go through earlier.

It was a formidable obstacle—one that could easily stop an enemy legion from forcing its way through the pass. I wondered how Issana planned to get us past it.

Our guide dove a hundred feet lower and landed on a small ledge. She sent a charge of Murk into a normal-looking stone on the face and entered a small crack that appeared. I landed on the ledge and walked after her. When Elyssa was inside, Issana sent another charge of Murk into another stone, and the wall reappeared.

"Neat trick," I said.

We walked through a narrow passage for several hundred yards and arrived at a dead end. Issana opened the wall the same way she'd opened the first. We emerged on a small ledge on the northern face of the mountain on the eastern side of the pass.

Issana gave us a sarcastic smile. "Welcome to Brightling territory."

Chapter 4

"How did you know about that secret passage?" Elyssa gave Issana a suspicious look as we glided north across the clear moonlit sky.

Issana's brow furrowed in concentration. "I do not wish to say."

"Why not?" I said.

"It is private." She seemed genuinely embarrassed. "I assure you there is nothing sinister about it."

I didn't like such a vague excuse. Then again, I didn't particularly like Issana. A part of me desperately wanted to prove this sera couldn't possibly be related to my dearly departed friend. Issana's personality meshed more with Nightliss's evil twin sister, Daelissa, than it did her mother. For now, I had to hope she was really on our side.

"What is the objective of this operation?" Issana asked as we neared the coast.

"To spy on Arturo," I said. "Maybe look through his quarters."

The Brightling camp resembled a small coastal village. Hundreds of white capsule-shaped buildings dotted the grassy lands south of the beach. A domed crystal mini-palace towered in the center. One might have also expected to find a harbor there as well, but Seraphim didn't use water vessels, preferring airborne cloudlets and high-speed skyways to move their troops.

It didn't take a genius to figure out Arturo was staying in the palace since I highly doubted he'd house himself in one of the barracks. Issana landed atop a ledge with a good view. Her wings shimmered away like mist as she crouched and pointed out the silhouettes of patrols drifting about the perimeter of the camp on fluffy cloudlets.

"This is strange," Issana said. "Normally there are ten times the number of patrols, both in the air and on foot." She pointed to a swath of dark barracks. "There seems to be no power to those buildings, as if no one is using them."

Elyssa met my confused look as we both thought the same thing. *How would Issana know about the patrols here?* Again, we decided not to question the feisty sera.

I compared the number of lit barracks with dark ones and concluded that either they had a power issue—unlikely—or there were no longer troops inside the buildings.

Elyssa took pictures with her arcphone. "We should verify those barracks are empty."

"Spot check?" I asked.

She nodded.

"There is no other reason they would be dark," Issana said. "It would be a waste of time to check."

"I don't agree," Elyssa said. "Confirmation is always better than assumption."

Not to mention neither of us trusted her at the moment.

Issana frowned. "Well, it should be no problem to sneak in with so few patrols."

"Before we go another step," Elyssa said, "tell me how you know what their security normally looks like."

Issana looked down like a guilty child caught with her hand in the candy jar. It was so incongruent with her supposed age of thousands of years that I rocked back on my heels with surprise.

"I am a spy," Issana said after a long pause. "I've been here many times."

For a moment, she reminded me so much of Nightliss that my heart filled with pain. I swallowed a lump and said, "How many times have you been here?"

"Too many to count," she said.

"You're one of Kohval's spies?" Elyssa asked.

Issana didn't answer.

Elyssa frowned. "If you're a spy, why do you have to sneak through the perimeter? Who made that secret tunnel?"

Issana blinked rapidly, but remained silent.

Elyssa leaned closer. "Tell me now, or I'll knock you out and leave you behind."

Hands curling into fists, Issana rose, trembling. "I was told never to tell anyone."

I took a wild guess. "You're not working for Kohval, are you?"

Issana grimaced. "No."

Elyssa's eyes flashed. "Who then?"

The sera clenched her fists and stomped a foot like a child throwing a tantrum. "Is it not enough that I'm helping you? Now stop asking me questions."

I backed up a step, certain Elyssa was about to throw down on Issana, but my girlfriend ignored the outburst and asked again. "Who are you working for?"

I took a different approach. "Issana, we need to trust each other. Nightliss trusted me and so can you."

Her hands trembled and her shoulders slumped. "An old seraph who lives—or lived in Kohvalla." Issana looked down. "His name is Neemah."

That name sent a shard of ice into my chest.

Elyssa noticed my shock. "What is it, Justin?"

"Neemah was with the Ministry of Research." I remembered meeting the aged security director as if it were yesterday. "He was there when I rescued Nightliss from Pross and Cephus."

Issana's head jerked back. "You know Cephus?"

I tried not to let surprise show on my face. "Yes, I know Cephus. Do you?"

"Did he also send you to be his eyes and ears?" Issana looked at me hopefully.

My heart felt heavy as a terrible idea crossed my mind. Now wasn't the time to pursue this, nor was it the time to lie to Issana. "No, he didn't." I held up a hand to ward off further questions from Elyssa. "I think we should finish this operation and get back."

Issana looked at me for a moment, then nodded slowly. "Yes, that would be wise."

Elyssa gave me a questioning look, but I didn't want to talk about my suspicions in front of Issana, so I climbed back on my broom and nodded forward. "Let's go."

Issana flew down to the forest bordering the base of the cliff and we followed her through the darkness lit only by glowing mushrooms and dangling moss. I flicked on my demon night vision, casting everything in a bluish glow, and saw the violet glow in Elyssa's eyes, evidence of her dhampyric night vision.

It was obvious Issana hadn't been lying about her frequent visits because she seemed to know exactly where she was going. Issana held up her hand and we hid behind trees whenever squads of Brightlings patrolled past. She motioned us down when airborne guards flew overhead, and within an hour, we'd reached the darkened barracks at the outskirts of the camp.

Issana opened the nearest capsule-shaped building and we went inside. Beds lined both sides of the room, and empty shelves stood at the back. She took us inside several more as we made our way toward the center of the camp, and each one proved just as empty as the last.

Not once did Issana fail to regard Elyssa with a sarcastic smile as she proved she hadn't been mistaken.

The frequency of patrols increased as we neared the palace, and we had to duck and hide every few yards to avoid detection.

Issana opened the doorway on one of the lit barracks and motioned us inside. Elyssa gave me a worried look and I could practically read her mind—*Is this the part where she betrays us?*

If my theory about her was correct, I knew she wouldn't.

We followed her inside and found her removing clothing from the shelving at the back of the room. Issana held up a uniform to Elyssa. "You are thick, but I believe this will fit."

"Thick?" Elyssa hissed. "What's that supposed to mean?"

Issana handed me a uniform and then motioned us back outside. We retreated to one of the abandoned barracks where we slid the white Brightling uniforms over our skintight Nightingale armor. Issana turned her back to us and stripped naked since her uniform was

32

too bulky. A small white scar at the base of her neck and another near her spine glowed in my night vision.

Elyssa's hand tightened on mine. I turned to her and mouthed, *Cephus did something to her.*

A nod indicated she understood.

Seraphim didn't scar easily, so whatever had happened to Issana had been traumatic. Cephus had brainwashed Tarissan citizens and turned them into flying soldiers. It was possible he'd somehow captured Nightliss's daughter and done something terrible to her as well. I almost hated that Cephus was dead, because I wanted to beat the ever-loving snot out of him once a day for the next twenty years to let him know exactly how I felt.

Issana turned back around and nodded. "We should be able to walk freely now."

Even so, it took everything I had not to run and hide when we walked past the next squad. The soldiers looked tired and bored. Only a couple even spared us a glance.

The palace itself was surrounded by barracks on all sides, so there was only a circular path around the inner perimeter and nothing keeping us from slipping inside when the coast was clear.

We sneaked through the corridors, but there seemed to be few guards on the first floor. Issana held up a fist as we finished searching a hallway and reached a levitator alcove. "Wait here."

Before we could object, she stepped into the alcove and vanished upstairs. As with many other Seraphim buildings, there seemed to be no stairwells and no other way up. I was going to follow her, but Elyssa shook her head and pointed down the next hall where a wide doorway was the only opening in the wall.

We padded that way and looked inside. Stadium seating encircled a thin white pedestal rising from the center of the room. It looked similar to Kohval's war room, except it was in all white instead of red and purple. Brightlings weren't the most imaginative when it came to color.

Elyssa walked around the top of the room and entered a niche. I followed her inside and found a wall studded with square aether gems, each one perhaps a quarter of an inch wide.

"Crap," Elyssa said. "There are so many." She traced a finger down the wall, but there were no labels to help us narrow our search. "I count twenty-one."

I tugged on one of the gems and it popped from the slot on the wall. I rolled it between thumb and forefinger, then charged it with a shot of Brilliance. A holographic image appeared, showing some kind of major ceremony in a Brightling city. I deactivated the gem and popped it back in its slot.

Rather than remove the gems one-by-one, I charged the first one and watched a snippet of video explaining how to keep your armor clean and ready for battle. The next few were all very basic instructional holograms and I began to lose patience with the process. "What if they don't keep top-secret intel in here?"

I skipped ahead to the last gem. It showed Arturo and the archangels streaking through the sky, firing Brilliance from their lightning lances while below, crowds of Brightlings bowed and cried.

"Today we mourn the loss of our Empress, Daelissa," a deep voice intoned. "The barbaric mortals stole her life and her body from us, but we will rise again, and avenge her murder."

I deactivated the gem and scowled. "Doesn't sound like they want peace."

The patter of footsteps drew my attention. I peered around the corner of the niche and saw Issana hurrying our way. She didn't have a squad of soldiers with her, which proved that I was right about her allegiance. Cephus had probably done something to her. So long as we played along, she would be on our side.

Issana stepped inside. "I told you to wait on me."

Elyssa ignored the statement. "We found the war room, but we don't know if any of these gems have information on them."

"Of course they don't," Issana said. "There's a secure vault in the royal quarters on the top floor. I was told to check it frequently and report any information to Neemah." She showed us two blue gems. "If there is anything important, it will be on one of these."

Cephus had brainwashed this poor sera and sent her into danger time and time again. It followed his pattern of using and abusing others to achieve his own means. I felt awful for Issana, but I didn't dare let her know. Cephus might have built safeguards into her mind to keep others from helping her. I wished Flava wasn't so far away. She was the only healer gifted enough to help someone with such deep trauma.

"You took them that easily?" Elyssa's eyes narrowed.

"Perhaps if you'd infiltrated this place as many times as I have, it would be easy for you."

Elyssa paused a beat. "I guess so. Let's have a look at the gems."

Issana motioned toward the center of the war room. "They will only work in the pedestal."

"How were you able to sneak in when they still had a full contingent of soldiers here?" I scanned the war room to make sure no one had sneaked inside while we were talking. "Security around here can't be that awful."

"I have extensive training at subterfuge." Issana walked down the stairs toward the pedestal as casually as if she were in her own living room. "This building is exclusively for royalty and military leaders, which is why this war room is so small."

"Are you saying the Brightling leadership lives here?" I asked.

Issana pointed up. "The living quarters are on the third level. The top level is reserved for royalty and the vault."

Elyssa looked skeptical. "So Ambassador Arturo is on the third floor?"

"Why in the hell would they have so few guards here?" I said.

"Because there is nothing of import on this floor," Issana said. "The third and fourth floors each have a dozen soldiers guarding them. They very rarely change their routine which makes it a simple matter to sneak past."

Elyssa pursed her lips and nodded, obviously impressed. "Let's take a look at those gems." She took out her arcphone and began recording a video that we could show Thomas later.

Issana placed the first one on the pedestal. A series of Cyrinthian symbols filled the air. She quickly flicked her fingers, connecting several symbols together to spell the word *Power*.

The symbols vanished, replaced by Arturo. He sat in a room with an ornate crystal sculpture of Daelissa behind him, and nothing else.

35

"Legiaros Pagos, I will arrive in two days. By that time, I expect you to have moved out the first two-thirds of your troops to Cabala. I understand your concerns, but a temporary peace is for the best until we have procured what we need to defeat any who stand in our way. We have been commanded into Voltis, and there we will go." The video went blank.

Elyssa bit her lower lip. "I don't like the sound of that at all."

"This is not the first communication concerning Voltis," Issana said. "Two weeks ago, another Legiaros sent a gem to Pagos and asked why they were being sent to invade Voltis."

"Do you have that gem?" Elyssa asked.

Issana shook her head. "They destroy the information every week. That is why I must come here on a regular schedule."

"Let's look at the next one," I said.

Issana put it on the pedestal and used the same password as last time.

"They don't ever change the passcode?" I asked.

"I suppose it is easier to remember," Issana said. "People grow lax and lazy when they believe they have nothing to fear."

A holograph of Arturo once again played. "The Empress is pleased, Legiaros Pagos. Soon, nothing in this realm or the next will stop us."

"I get the feeling Arturo is gonna stab us in the back once they get whatever it is they want from Voltis." I heard footsteps and we dashed back up to the niche to hide until a patrol of four guards sauntered past without a worry in the world.

"What is Voltis?" Elyssa asked.

Issana squinted as if deep in thought. "I asked Neemah, but he said it was nothing I need worry about."

"We need to have a talk with Neemah when we get back," Elyssa said.

"That's impossible." Issana rolled the blue gems around in her palm. "Neemah disappeared after my last report."

"Probably because Cephus got his ass kicked," I muttered. "We need to get out of here. Issana, can you put those gems back in place?"

"Of course." She headed back out to the corridor and went back to the levitation alcove. "I will return shortly."

The wait felt like eternity, but she reappeared in the alcove about ten minutes later and we made our way back out to the perimeter barracks where she'd left her uniform. From there we continued stealthily back to the cliff.

The trip back was uneventful, thanks to the secret passage.

"Does anyone else know about this passage?" I asked when we arrived back at our guest quarters in Kohvalla.

Issana shook her head. "I do not know. There is another one in the Northwestern Pass as well."

Now that her secrets were out, she seemed a lot more mellow, though not entirely likeable. I wondered if removing Cephus's programming from her head might make her more like her mother.

"Now that Neemah is gone, you should be able to leave this place." I held her gaze. "We have a friend named Flava who could use your help."

"I thought you weren't working for Cephus."

"We're not, but since he's dead, you might as well help us." I shrugged. "I mean, unless you see a point to sneaking into the Brightling camp when it sounds like they're abandoning the place."

Issana's forehead pinched into a V. "I think you're right. I could probably help in some other way until the Brightlings return."

I smiled. "Exactly. Take the skyway into Tarissa tomorrow. You'll find Flava in the Ministry of Healing."

Issana held out a hand palm down, fingers splayed. "Take care, Justin Slade."

I returned the gesture. "Take care, Issana."

She turned to Elyssa and repeated the farewell, then channeled her wings and flew away.

"I hope we can trust Issana." Elyssa squeezed my hand. "For all we know, Cephus has more sleeper agents in the village."

"I hope so too." One thing was certain—neither of us would be sleeping soundly tonight.

John Corwin

Chapter 5

We met Thomas in the war room at the base headquarters the next morning. I closed the doorway so no one could intrude on our meeting.

"How'd it go?" Thomas asked.

By the time we finished our story about our kidnapping by Issana, and later, her help procuring the intel we needed, even the stony-faced commander looked a bit confused.

"You think she was brainwashed by Cephus and used to spy on Victrix Legion and the Brightling camp?" Thomas folded his arms and pressed his lips together. "Something tells me that is only part of Issana's story. For one thing, how did Cephus manage to locate the one child of Nightliss in all of Pjurna?"

"There are tons of holes in her story," Elyssa said, "but I think we need to put that aside and consider Voltis and find out why Arturo believes it'll give the Brightlings the edge they need to conquer the world."

He nodded. "Agreed. There's no certainty that this sera is even related to Nightliss. It could be an idea Cephus implanted in her brain for some unknown reason."

I shuddered. "Twisted. Pross held Nightliss captive long enough to probe her mind. Maybe that's how they found out about Issana."

Elyssa checked the time. "Arturo will be arriving at the rendezvous in two hours. What should Justin tell him?"

Thomas switched gears. "Tell him that we must forge a document that is agreeable to both sides. I want to slow the process so we can keep him busy here while we find out more about this Voltis."

"Do you think he'll go for that?" I asked.

"Doubtful, but it's worth a try." Thomas activated his arcphone to display a holographic map and zoomed out to show the continents of Azoris and Sazoris, similar to their geographical counterparts in Eden, North and South America. In this realm, they were both continents and nations, all part of the Brightling Empire, and the land masses were noticeably smaller. Where Florida jutted far south in Eden, it was only a nub here, maybe reaching only as far as Jacksonville. A mountain range occupied the approximate area where the Florida Keys islands dotted the ocean in our home realm.

The capitol city, Zbura, sat atop Mount Hein in this mountain range—an odd location given that it wasn't actually connected to any of the major land masses it ruled. Then again, there were billions of humans on Eden, and only thousands of Darklings and Brightlings total in all of Seraphina. Most of the land was uninhabited, and if the population hadn't grown much in thousands of years, I doubted it would change much over the next thousand.

Longevity tended to have an inverse effect on procreation.

Thomas scrolled to the western coast of Azoris where it appeared most of California and Baja had fallen into the ocean, leaving behind another mountain range and an inhospitable zone marked with aether vortexes. There were no fifty states, just territories and cities. One of the names stuck out to me—Cabala.

"That's where Arturo is moving the troops," I said.

Thomas highlighted the coastline red. "Pjurnan spies have also reported Brightling troops massing there."

Elyssa scrunched her forehead. "But there's nothing to the west but a thousand miles of ocean."

"Precisely." Thomas touched the map legend and dotted blue lines crisscrossed the blue expanse. "These are the trade routes used by the Mzodi, the sky fishers." He touched another part of the legend, and blue ship icons dotted the western coasts of Azoris and Sazoris. "These are their trading ports."

I examined the trading lanes and noticed they veered wide of a large area in the center of the ocean with no markings. "What's there?" I jabbed a finger in the blank space.

"That is the question," Thomas said. "I questioned the Mzodi about the ocean, but they say no one braves the turbulent vortexes at the center of the Castigean Ocean."

But it gets more interesting," Thomas said. "The Mzodi sent me an older map." He switched to another overlay and a new label appeared in the blank space. *Voltis.*

"This makes even less sense than before." I scratched my head. "Voltis is in the middle of the ocean. I don't see anything there but water."

Elyssa made a thoughtful sound. "That's roughly where the Hawaiian Islands are in Eden."

I strained my brain to equate Voltis with an English word, but the closest connection I made was the word "eye". I'd been through the Great Barrier Vortex with the sky fishers and it had been enough to scare me witless and beat me senseless. I couldn't imagine how violent the vortexes must be if even the Mzodi wouldn't venture there to harvest gems.

Thomas touched another part of the legend and black dots appeared at the fringes of the red zones around the Great Barrier Vortex off the eastern coast of Pjurna, and all along the trade routes where they intersected the Piscan Vortex off the western coast of Azoris. "These are dragon incursions as mapped by the Mzodi."

I counted at least a hundred. "In his message to Legiaros Pagos, Arturo said that once they had what they wanted, they wouldn't fear anything in this realm or the next. I wonder if they plan to recruit dragons to their cause."

"He looked awfully confident." Elyssa's nose wrinkled. "I can't imagine having to fight dragons."

"Cephus's experiments with the crimson arch likely caused the breaches between Seraphina and Draxadis." Thomas drew a circle around the areas where dragons had been spotted. The highest concentration seemed a few hundred miles south of Voltis. "The Mzodi probably only encountered a tiny percentage of dragons that were drawn through and trapped in Seraphina."

"In other words, that area of the ocean could be swarming with dragons." Elyssa stared at the map. "With dragons added to their legions, the Brightlings would be unstoppable."

It sounded scary and awesome, but something else nagged at me. "How could Cephus's arch experiments have caused a breach way out there?" I traced the route from Tarissa to the middle of the X. "That's over five thousand miles away."

"It's possible during his early experimentation he launched a crystoid into Draxadis by accident." Thomas shrugged. "Shelton and Adam found records indicating there were over eighty test launches before Cephus unleashed the one that destroyed the Tarissan Legion."

"How certain are you that dragons are the threat?" Elyssa asked.

"Thirty percent," Thomas replied. "Justin can move the needle to a hundred if he asks the right questions today."

"Talk about putting me on the spot." I crossed my arms and tried to look confident. "Do I ask Arturo directly or try for subtlety?"

Elyssa laughed. "Babe, you wouldn't know subtle if it bit you in the ass."

"Yeah, but I can try." I stroked my chin in an attempt to look thoughtful. "The dragons we encountered on Cora's ship, the *Evadora*, attacked us immediately. I'm curious how Arturo plans to bargain with creatures like that."

"No telling, but I doubt it'll be as easy as he thinks," Thomas said. "They likely want a non-aggression pact with us so they can fight and tame the dragons with worrying about an attack from the rear."

"There's no way we could get our army out there to fight them," Elyssa said. "Even if we did, the Brightling legions would squash us."

Thomas nodded. "Perhaps we should send our own emissaries instead."

I snapped my fingers. "We ally ourselves with the dragons before Arturo does."

"It's our only hope." Thomas removed the overlay with the current markings and replaced it with another that he, Elyssa, and the other Templar commanders had been working on—Operation Dark Day, the invasion of Zbura.

Pjurna was halfway around the world from Azoris, and Zbura was on the eastern coast of the enemy nation. Located approximately where Sydney, Australia sat in Eden, Tarissa seemed impossibly far from the enemy capitol. We'd have to ferry our troops all the way across the Castigean Ocean and through the Great Barrier Vortex, cross the island chains connecting Azoris and Sazoris, and then hook north to reach the destination.

On top of that, we didn't have the full backing of the Mzodi who took no sides in the quarrels between the Darkling and Brightling nations. They refused to give us passage on their flying ships if it was not for neutral purposes.

Since there were no skyways connecting Pjurna to the other continents, that left only travel via cloudlets. What might take a day in a flying Mzodi ship would take nearly three times as long on a slow-moving cloudlet.

"Why are we looking at the invasion plans?" Elyssa said. "I thought we didn't have the resources to pull it off without the Mzodi."

"If we recruited dragons, we'd have everything we need to succeed in such an invasion." Thomas sounded awfully confident, which usually meant he was right. "If we beat the Brightlings to Voltis and secure an alliance first, a united Seraphina might be just around the corner."

"The alternative is Arturo secures his secret weapon—dragons, dinosaurs, whatever he's after—sweeps in and controls Pjurna within months." Elyssa turned her worried gaze on me. "We've got no choice but to beat him to Voltis."

Thomas nodded. "In the meantime, I suggest we not sign any treaties so we can keep our military options open."

"Agreed," Elyssa said.

The doorway misted open to reveal Kohval on the other side. At his back stood a retinue of his elite Daskar soldiers in black crystalline armor, full-faced helmets staring at us with dead black eyes.

Kohval stepped inside. "The peace talks resume in an hour, Commander Borathen. What will be our response?"

Thomas eyed the soldiers, gaze calculating. "If we don't have the answer you want, what will happen next?"

"I will arrest you and my people will deliver an answer." Kohval stared right back at Thomas. "I am here to ensure we reach the correct agreement."

"That is not a road you wish to travel." Thomas's voice remained icy calm despite the thick wall of tension building brick-by-brick.

I stepped between them and faced the Legiaros. "I'm so damned tired of the bad attitudes around here, Kohval. We saved Tarissa, we're rebuilding the city, and we're trying to reestablish a government, but you act like we're invaders."

"You are invaders," he said. "We didn't ask for your help. In due time, we would have returned to Tarissa and defeated Cephus ourselves."

"Really?" I loaded the word with scorn. "You knew Tarissa was under siege months ago, but you did nothing?"

"The religious zealots doomed Tarissa when they left their posts and followed you to Eden," Kohval replied. "Had you never come to Seraphina, none of this would have happened."

His first sentence about zealots raised about a dozen red flags with flares and rockets going off. "Are you a follower of the Void?"

Kohval slashed a hand through the air. "Absolutely not. I simply don't believe any of that Progenitor garbage, and I've forbidden the religion anywhere near this military base."

I made a theatrical show of gasping as if coming to a realization. "Now I see. You didn't care to help Tarissa because in these parts, you're the ruler. With the government gone, you're free to do as you will."

He smirked. "I believe you have a grasp on the situation, Slade."

His confession made it obvious why he wanted peace. It meant he could cement his hold on this region without fear of the Brightlings interfering. The only unity Kohval wanted was a Darkling nation united under him.

"There's far more going on here than you realize," Thomas said. "No matter what we tell Arturo, we're only delaying war."

43

"Nonsense," Kohval barked. "I don't know why Arturo insists on bargaining with this boy, but I'm sure he'd accept an answer from my people."

"I wouldn't be so sure about that," I warned. "If anything, you might just piss him off."

Kohval worked his jaw back and forth as the gears spun. "What do you plan to tell him?"

"We will agree to a provisional treaty," Thomas said. "It will buy us time to investigate the real reason Arturo is so eager to sign."

Eyes narrowed suspiciously, Kohval stared at us. "Primarion Arturo is weary of war. What other reason could he have?"

"There's a threat in the Castigean Ocean," Thomas said.

Kohval glanced at the map and scoffed. "In the ocean? Does the water mean to attack the shore?" This drew scornful laughs from the soldiers, the helmets making them sound hollow and alien.

"We think Cephus's experiments opened a portal to Draxadis," Thomas said.

"Dragons?" Derision dripped from Kohval's exclamation. "The few that live on Seraphina keep well enough to themselves. Why should they want to attack Azoris?"

"Look, I'm giving Arturo the answer you want, Kohval." I squared my shoulders, trying to look bigger. I didn't like it when people called me a boy. "Do you have a problem with that?"

Kohval swatted the air as if I were nothing more than a pesky mosquito. "Make the peace and leave as soon as possible. I grow tired of your presence." He squared his shoulders. "Test me and you'll enjoy the hospitality of our prison." Kohval spun and marched toward the exit. His entourage did an about-face and followed him out.

For once, I saw alarm in Thomas's eyes. I felt a definite squirm in my stomach as well.

Elyssa voiced what we were thinking. "We're not just dealing with stubbornness here. If we don't glue this country back together, we're going to have a civil war on our hands."

"I suggest we leave." Thomas tapped the special communications gem given to him by the Mzodi. "I contacted the flagship *Uorion* and requested a rendezvous with the *Falcheen*. We'll use it as a base of operations until we determine our next steps."

The *Falcheen* was half the size of the other sky ships used by the Mzodi, but made up for the difference with speed and agility. Even then, it still stretched two hundred feet long and had three decks. After dropping us off at Kohvalla the ship had sailed onward to the northern vortexes with Harry Shelton and Adam Nosti still aboard since they wanted to see how gems were harvested.

"When and where are we meeting it?" I asked.

"We'll talk about it on the way," Thomas said. He gripped our arms. "Whatever happens, we need to make sure word gets back to Tarissa about our suspicions. I haven't been able to make contact with anyone that far south since yesterday."

"You think Kohval is blocking our transmissions?" Elyssa said.

"It's a distinct possibility," Thomas said. "Thankfully, the *Uorion* was within range."

"After I talk with Arturo, we'll head straight to Voltis." I grabbed Thomas's arcphone from the table, switched it off, and handed it to him. "I want to see what's going on with my own two eyes."

"Agreed," Thomas said, "but you'll have to slip through enemy lines to do it."

"The Mzodi have passage anywhere," Elyssa said. "They can smuggle us past."

Thomas's eyes went distant for a moment. "I suggest we split our efforts. You two rendezvous with the *Falcheen*. I'll make for the southern skyway and return to Tarissa."

"We should go with you," Elyssa said. "Make sure you get there."

Thomas shook his head. "I'll fly north with you to the rendezvous and circle around the town. That will give appearances we're doing as Kohval expects."

Thomas retrieved his flying carpet—he didn't care for broomsticks—and we left the room and headed for the levitator shafts.

The corridors bustled with Darkling soldiers clad in the standard black uniforms of the legion. Spun by focusing aether through gems, the cloth felt soft as silk and guarded against magic and physical attacks, but was nowhere near as robust as Templar Nightingale armor. Only Kohval's elite Daskar soldiers wore crystal armor.

I didn't know how it compared to the crystal armor worn by the city guards in Zbura. When Daelissa added them to her army, they'd nearly wiped us out because their armor absorbed magic and allowed them to fire it back at us with their crystal swords. I hoped I didn't have to find out how tough it was. If Kohval changed his mind, we'd have a time fighting our way free.

We threaded our way past soldiers and officers, some casting curious glances at us while others regarded us with open suspicion. A line of people waited at the levitator shafts, each one stepping into the lit alcove and dropping or rising out of sight. I heard the tromp of boots in the hallway and turned to face a squad of Daskar marching our way.

Elyssa grimaced. "Crap."

"Just act natural," I murmured, and plastered on a fake smile.

Halfway down the hall, the Daskar seemed to pick up the pace. The sullen gleam in the black eyes of the helmets made it impossible to tell if we were their target, or if they were just passing through. The last person in line stepped into the alcove and I practically shoved Thomas and Elyssa into the shaft the moment she dropped out of sight.

"Rooftop, pronto!" I said in Cyrinthian. We shot upward, leaving the squad behind.

"First time I've seen Daskar patrolling the halls," Elyssa said. The levitator reached the top and gently deposited us on the roof.

Ordinary soldiers stood sentinel in towers around the building. The closest made eye contact with me but didn't raise an alarm or act as if anything were out of the ordinary.

"Apparently, Kohval means to let us go," Thomas said.

Elyssa mounted her broom. "Considering he could've arrested us on the spot earlier, I don't know why we're being so jumpy."

"We were tensed and ready to fight in that small space," Thomas said. "Had I been in his shoes, I would have defused the tension and surprised the smaller group outside, preferably with non-lethal methods."

I thought back to the knockout burrs used by Issana and pals and felt the hairs stand on the back of my neck. "Uh, let's go while the going's good."

Thomas stepped onto his flying rug and nodded. "Don't take the normal route. Follow me." He headed west off the building and over the main grounds, flying between the guard towers. Elyssa and I followed. As we rose higher, I spotted squads of Daskar on the taller buildings flanking headquarters. The northern route out of the valley would have taken us right between those buildings and right into an ambush.

The thought of being knocked out that far from the ground dragged another ugly realization from the shadows. *Kohval wants us dead.*

Elyssa bared her teeth. "It was an ambush."

My stomach tightened like a drum. "What now?"

"We'll see how long it takes them to adjust to our unexpected move." Thomas folded his arms. "Act as if nothing is wrong. I don't want to spark an aerial chase."

"I don't think an aerial chase would be much to worry about," I said. "We can easily outrun them."

Thomas looked back toward Kohval's headquarters. "I'm not so certain about that."

Elyssa and I swiveled our heads like owls and watched as the Daskar effortlessly lifted off the roof of headquarters and flew in pursuit on shimmering wings of Murk. Unlike the trainees, they formed a neat formation and jetted forward.

Kohval's ambush hadn't worked, so now he meant to stop or kill us directly.

Chapter 6

We raced for the Northwestern Pass. From there we'd have to circle north to reach the meeting place. The Daskar were a few hundred yards behind, but closing the gap fast.

Thomas crouched on his knees to reduce wind resistance. "We have to reach the rendezvous point. I don't think the Daskar will risk engaging Arturo's soldiers." His carpet shot forward.

Elyssa and I opened up the throttles on our brooms and paced him. We could've gone faster, but neither of us were about to leave her father behind.

Our brooms swept into the pass, a tight canyon with steep rocky walls and hazardous outcrops of rock. We dodged back and forth, diving and climbing to clear obstructions, steadily aiming higher.

Snow swept into the crevice, pelting my face and making my nose run. The Daskar shot into the pass about a hundred yards behind us and gaining fast. Their bodies shifted side-to-side to avoid obstructions, their ethereal wings sparking where they touched the rocky walls. We burst through a blanket of snow at the lip of the canyon and emerged onto a steep slope on the other side of the mountain.

Elyssa's broom lurched and stopped. With a shriek, she plummeted twenty feet and fell out of sight into dense snow.

"Elyssa!" I whipped the broom around.

Thomas turned and came to my side, sword drawn. "Where did she go?"

I spotted the divot where she'd landed. "She's there. Something happened to her broom." We didn't have much time before the Daskar caught up so I dove to the ground and found Elyssa struggling to rise through seven feet of powder.

"My broom won't turn back on," she called.

I levitated lower and flung a strand of Murk at her. She caught it and I willed it to shorten, towing her up and out. The broom sagged lower, unable to support the extra weight.

"Put her on my carpet," Thomas said.

Elyssa shook her head. "That's a one-person carpet. It won't carry us both."

A blanket of white covered the steep slope, broken only by black rock jutting out like broken teeth. In the distance, I saw the grassy blue plateau atop Mount Ulladon where Arturo would soon be expecting me.

"Commander, get to the mountain." I channeled a flat barrier of Murk on the snow. "Elyssa, get on the sled."

Elyssa dropped from the magical rope and onto my magical platform. "This isn't a sled."

"It'll have to be." I landed the broom next to her and looked back up at Thomas. "Sir, go to the mountain. We'll be there soon."

"Take care of my daughter." Thomas sheathed his sword. "I'll tell Arturo to expect you." He spun the carpet around and set off down the slope.

Elyssa twisted the handle of her broom to fold the saddle and stirrups into compact form, then slung it over her shoulder. She took my broom and did the same. Folded up, neither broom was much larger than a broomstick.

The first Daskar exploded out of the canyon, the gems on the back of his armor shimmering with energy. Apparently, they had flight suits similar to the one Issana had used last night. He rolled around and spotted us. "Down there!"

Another dozen whisked into view. Blazing pinions spread wide to hold them aloft. The Daskar aimed their fists and orbs of ultraviolet energy gathered to strike.

"That is so badass," I murmured.

Elyssa wrapped her arms around my waist. "It's gonna be *our* asses if you don't go!"

I snapped from my stupor and adjusted the shape of the Murk shield into the approximate size of a snowboard. With a shove from my foot we hit loose powder and gravity took over from there. Energy blasted the snow behind us, throwing huge white billows into the air. I leaned left to avoid rocks, but with so many, it was nearly impossible. My knees buckled to absorb the shocks. Elyssa grunted as we flew off a mound of snow and nearly plowed into a boulder.

My concentration wavered as we gathered momentum. Holding a shield while moving this fast was a tremendous chore. Elyssa's grip on my waist tightened. Her feet shifted and we narrowly missed a jagged boulder. She guided the snowboard into a narrow gap between more rocks and we hit open air.

I screamed as we plummeted all of ten feet to the snow below. The snowboard shimmered away to mist as my concentration broke, leaving nothing to land on but snow. We tumbled through the powder and came to rest against a shelf of rocks hanging over a slope so steep it made my pounding heart miss a few beats.

"Keep your concentration, Justin!" Elyssa grabbed my arms and snapped her fingers in my face. "Let me drive, okay?"

I pushed to my feet. Took a deep breath. "I can do this." I channeled another board beneath my feet. She hopped on in front and I grabbed her waist.

Daskar appeared overhead and spotted our black uniforms against the white almost immediately. Elyssa shoved off and took us over the rocky shelf and into a long fall to a forty-five-degree decline.

I held back a cry of terror and concentrated on maintaining the snowboard. We hit the snow and hurtled down the slope so fast, my eyes watered. Deadly blasts of Murk hammered the mountain behind and around us. It took every ounce of concentration I had to keep channeling the shield while moving so fast.

Elyssa expertly guided the snowboard around rocks and over small cliffs, each time finding a line in the snow that would guide us into the forest far below. We hit a ramp and flew through the air before landing on a narrow cliff at the edge of a ravine.

"Holy mother!" Elyssa whipped the board right, leaning hard to dig the edge into the powder. We skimmed the ledge, the Murk throwing sparks against the rock. The dark gorge below gaped like an open maw, ready to consume a meager meal. Wind whistled in my ears. Snow and ice pelted my face. My butt cheeks clenched tight and I barely maintained the pattern of the snowboard. If I lost the weave now, we'd tumble to our doom.

Despite the armor, my hands were freezing and I felt snot forming icicles on my nose. I spotted another issue looming ahead. The ledge narrowed to only a few inches wide.

I tightened my grip on Elyssa's waist. "Uh, babe?"

"I see it." She jabbed a finger right where a crack in the cliff wall formed a narrow tunnel. "Duck!"

I bent my knees just in time to avoid decapitation. Wind howled through the tunnel, propelling us faster and faster. We shot from the other side and hit a wide open slope. The Daskar reappeared overhead shortly after and resumed their attacks. Snow exploded in front of us leaving us blind for an instant.

A deep rumble vibrated me all the way down to the bones. I wiped the powder from my eyes and looked back. A tsunami of snow cascaded down the slope after us. "Avalanche!" I shouted.

Elyssa looked back at the wall of doom rushing after us. "Can you shield us?"

"Maybe." I couldn't even begin to calculate the immense power my barrier would have to withstand. It was all I could do to keep the shield beneath our feet. "Can't we outrun it?"

"I don't think so." Elyssa looked at the great white plain before us and shook her head. "We've got another problem."

"Another problem?" I peered forward and saw what she meant. The slope vanished over a cliff. It might be a small drop off to another slope or it might be thousand feet to the ground.

"Please tell me you have an idea." Elyssa gripped my hands still tight around her waist. "We're running out of mountain."

We had only one chance but it would require some top-notch channeling on my part. I fortified my confidence with a deep breath. "Go with the flow, babe. I got you."

That was all I needed to tell her. She lowered her head against the biting wind and we barreled toward the Devil's mouth with Hell right on our heels. The Daskar circled overhead like vultures, eager to watch us die so they could pick at our bones and take them home to their master. Somehow, I had to make them believe we died, or else they'd swoop in and finish us off.

We reached the end of the line and leapt off the cliff. The only thing between us and the valley below was open air and the promise of death. I released the channel for the snowboard. It vanished in a puff of ultraviolet mist. Holding Elyssa by the waist, I adjusted our angle of descent. Gravity wrapped us in its merciless embrace and pulled us toward our doom. A storm of snow followed us over the cliff, blotting out the sky and the Daskar.

I closed my eyes and concentrated on my shoulder blades, imagining the itch that meant I was doing it right. My magical muscles were exhausted from the strain of channeling the snowboard through all the high-velocity maneuvers and for panicked instant, I didn't think I'd be able to manifest my wings.

"Uh, Justin?" Elyssa's voice sounded on the verge of panic. "Wings, please?"

Gritting my teeth, I dug deep and pulled on my reserves. First an itch, then knifing pain as flaming wings sliced through my skin. Blazing white energy shimmered on my right, and ultraviolet to my left. I quickly folded them against my body.

"Yes!" I would have pumped a fist, but I needed to hold onto Elyssa.

"Why aren't you spreading them?" Elyssa said as we continued to fall at terminal velocity.

"The Daskar need to think we're dead, and I don't want the snow to catch up with us." I let the edges of the wings catch just enough air to angle us to the right and the edge of the snowstorm on our heels. If I spread my wings all the way, we'd be buried in snow and forced to the ground.

The fringe of the avalanche reached us. Powder and ice stung my face. Wind whipped my hair and did its best to blind me with tears. The air thundered with cracking rock and the chafe and grind of tons of snow. A massive boulder streaked past, narrowly missing us. We were a thousand feet from the ground, and a few hundred yards from the edge of the storm. I risked a little more wing to sharpen our angle, but it was too much and the main body of the avalanche nearly engulfed us. I quickly retracted my wings, but we'd lost too much speed.

Elyssa looked up. "Watch out!"

Another boulder nearly took off my head. A crazy idea smacked me in the noggin and I risked it. Flinging out a strand of Murk, I caught the boulder and let its heavier mass pull us after it and out of the lighter snow. Back in relatively clear air, I released the boulder and angled once again for the edge of the avalanche.

A hundred yards. Fifty. Thirty. Ten. We cleared the fringe with a few hundred feet to spare before the ground claimed us. I spread my wings and held Elyssa tighter. My shoulders ached and Elyssa seemed to gain a hundred pounds as we fought gravity and glided in for a graceful landing on the ground.

By graceful, I meant we smacked into a giant sunflower and tumbled head over ass until we came to rest in a patch of scrubby grass. Thunder echoed through the valley as the avalanche crashed into the ground, sending up a bank of mist for hundreds of yards in all directions.

Now that we were out of the snow zone, the temperature climbed from frigid to balmy, but my limbs were still shaking, and my face felt numb.

I couldn't see the Daskar, which likely meant they couldn't see us. Groaning, I staggered to my feet and found Elyssa woozily shaking her head a few feet away beneath a sunflower nearly ten feet tall.

A forest of the giant flowers stretched in all directions, their heads catching the sun and beaming multicolored rays back into the sky. I touched one of the golden stalks and felt warmth emanating from it. "Brings a whole new meaning to the word sunflower."

"No time to sightsee." Elyssa grabbed my hand and pulled me along. "We need to reach Mount Ulladon."

"Where is it?" I turned in a circle.

"Over there." Elyssa grabbed my chin and angled my peepers right. About five miles away Mount Ulladon rose from the middle of the valley. She grimaced. "You have frozen snot all over your nose."

"Really?" I rubbed my nose with a finger and felt the crusty grossness. "Ugh!"

"Hold on." Elyssa reached into her ninja fanny pack, took out a wet wipe, and applied it to my icky spots. A moment later she grunted in satisfaction. "You're presentable now."

"Wouldn't want to negotiate peace with boogers hanging out of my nose."

She laughed. "It'd be funny though."

I massaged my temples. "God, my head hurts."

Elyssa checked the time on her arcphone. "We only have an hour. We need to run."

I unslung her broom from my back and tried to activate it, but it was dead as a doornail. "I don't get it. Your broom doesn't look damaged."

"It died like it ran out of charge." Elyssa pushed past a giant stalk. "We don't have time to figure it out."

"This model should have had plenty of aether left." I flipped open the broomstick and checked the aether battery, stumbling as I tried to walk through the scrubby underbrush without paying attention. I checked the magic meter. "The battery is still at eighty percent."

"Justin, you need to pay attention so we can run." Elyssa looked up. "The Daskar will see us the moment the snow clears."

The sunflowers hid us so long as we were careful to stay beneath their wide crowns, but running would quickly reveal us to anyone with sharp eyesight. It wasn't like we had much of a choice if we were to reach Mount Ulladon in time. I replaced the aether battery and slung the broom back over my back. "Let's go."

Elyssa started at a jog, dodging around the thick clumps of grass dotting the ground, then picked up speed as we gained knowledge of the terrain. She sprinted ahead and I followed—carefully. Our reflexes were supernatural, sure, but at top speed, even my ninja girlfriend had issues dodging giant sunflower stalks on uneven ground.

I looked back to check for pursuit and smacked into a sunflower, cracking the stalk and landing me on my butt. "Son of a—" I hopped back to my feet and spotted crystal armor glinting in the sunlight. The

Daskar circled over the debris from the avalanche and didn't seem to be looking our way.

I hurried to catch up with Elyssa and found her waiting impatiently a few yards ahead.

"They' haven't seen us," I told her.

"Good." She gazed up at Mount Ulladon. "Maybe we have a chance."

We ran onward and reached the mountain thirty minutes later, only to find the next challenge. A steep cliff loomed for a hundred feet before turning into a slope we could hike. I flung out a hand and tried to channel a strand of Murk to help us scale the cliff quickly, but my mental faculties were shot from too much strain.

Concern flickered in Elyssa's violet eyes. "Spider powers not working?"

I squeezed my eyes shut and clenched my fists, digging deeper, but trying to force aether through my exhausted system only gave me a headache. I tried another tactic, using Arcane spell casting instead. Taking a breath, I drew aether into my well. The moment I tried to cast a spell, fist of pain kicked me in my cerebellum. I staggered back.

"Gotta rest my brain." I rubbed my temples to sooth the ache.

Elyssa pressed a hand to my head. "You're burning up."

"You know how I've always had trouble holding a shield while moving?"

She nodded. "Yeah, you said you had to calculate movement speed or physics or something like that."

"Constantly channeling a solid object in a specific position while I'm moving at high speeds requires a ton of extra energy and brain power." I stared up at the cliff. "How are we supposed to get up there?"

Elyssa dug her hands into the thick clay earth and rubbed it on her hands. "The old-fashioned way."

"Rock climbing?" I looked straight up and felt dizzy from vertigo. "Uh, I've never done that before."

"Technically, it's called bouldering." Elyssa grabbed a clump of blue clay and mashed it into my hand. "Rub this on your hands. It'll help your grip."

I did as instructed. "Now what?"

She inspected the rock face. "I see the line we can take. Luckily, it hasn't been worn smooth."

I saw a few rocky outcrops and some cracks, but I didn't see how in the world I was supposed to reach all of them. "How about I use my broom and you climb?"

Elyssa nodded. "That's fine. Catch me if I fall?"

I grinned. "Always." I unslung my broom and activated it. Instead of levitating it dropped to the ground. "What's going on with our brooms?"

Elyssa frowned. "Did you break it during our crash landing?"

I ran my fingers up and down the polished wood, but found no cracks. I took out the aether battery and verified it still had most of its charge left. "It's doing the same thing yours did. Everything looks fine, but it doesn't work."

Elyssa checked the time. "We're down to twenty-five minutes."

"We'll never make it in time."

"Not if you try to fix the brooms." She grabbed a ledge and pulled herself up. Bracing a foot on an outcrop, she leapt five feet and gripped another ledge, holding on by her fingers. Hanging fifteen feet above me, she looked down and said, "Do as I do. It's only a hundred feet."

I gulped and put the brooms back over my shoulders. "I should've made you carry these."

"Want me to come back down and take them?"

I shook my head and girded my loins. "Nah, I got this." *Time to man up, you little wimp.* I gripped the first ledge and felt the rough stone bite into my fingers. My muscles were already warmed up, and my supernatural strength hadn't been affected by my magic strain, so I easily pulled myself into position.

Elyssa had already climbed another ten feet. I saw the path she'd taken and leapt up. I overshot the intended ledge and barely grasped a crag before falling back to earth. Holding on with both hands, I braced my feet on the rough surface and took a deep breath before resuming the climb.

56

I took a more conservative approach from then on, careful to gauge my jumps if needed, while Elyssa clambered onward like a monkey girl. She reached the top a good ten minutes ahead of me, breathing heavily, face flushed, and a big grin on her face.

"It's been too long." Elyssa set her hands on her hips and stared down at me. "Isn't this fun?"

Heart racing from the thought of the long fall, I looked at her like she was crazy. "It's terrifying!" I scrambled for the next grip and refused to look down. Elyssa grasped my hand and pulled me up and over the lip.

"Templar basic training involves base jumping, skydiving, and bouldering." She rubbed her hands in the blue grass to remove the clay. "It was my favorite part of boot camp."

I rolled onto my back, grateful to be back on solid ground. "I prefer having a broom between my legs."

She laughed and kissed my forehead. "Up and at-em, sunshine. We're running low on time."

"I know, I know." I got up and looked at the slope. The summit lay several hundred yards away, but Ulladon—thank the heavens— was small for a mountain. We set off at a jog and made good time, despite a couple of areas with loose soil and prickly bushes that forced us to circumnavigate their thorns.

Ten minutes overdue, red-faced and sweating, we crested the summit and found Arturo standing outside the white meeting tent. His forehead creased when he saw us, confusion and maybe a little worry drawing deep lines in his youthful face. I spotted Thomas's carpet on the ground nearby and strode over to Arturo as if everything was copasetic.

"Where's Commander Borathen?" I asked.

"He's inside explaining why you're late." Some of Arturo's imperious attitude crept into his demeanor. "You're filthy, and you were supposed to come alone."

I wasn't sure what Thomas had told him, so I kept it vague. "Circumstances forced me to do otherwise." I motioned toward the tent. "Shall we?"

Arturo considered Elyssa for a long moment and nodded. "Proceed."

I unslung the brooms and set them on the ground. When Elyssa and I walked toward the tent Arturo made no move to follow us, remaining instead with the squad of archangels standing at attention outside.

"You coming?" I asked.

His lips tightened into a line. "Only if the Empress wills it."

Cold chills ran from my nipples all the way down to my belly-button, forming an arctic triangle of heebie-jeebies. "Empress?" I hadn't expected him to bring their new ruler along.

"Yes. She decided to attend this matter personally." He jabbed a finger toward the opening. "She awaits you. Enter."

I pulled back the flap of the tent, and saw Thomas sitting at the table, eyes steely, his face set in stone. Across from him, her back to us, sat a sera with long golden tresses. Her white dress shimmered like gossamer threads and her hands and bare shoulders were white as porcelain.

My first thought nearly stopped my heart. *Daelissa?*

Thomas's concerned gaze found us. "They're here, Empress."

The sera turned and regarded Elyssa and me. "Welcome, boy. It has been too long."

Chapter 7

She wasn't Daelissa.

My dread enemy was still rotting in her grave, but seeing who now sat on the Brightling throne twisted my insides with uncertainty.

"Kaelissa." I offered her a slight bow. "How—"

"I am the mother of she who ruled the Brightlings," she said. "My blood is ancient, my powers formidable. Though my affinity is for Murk, I am powerful with Brilliance."

"They made you Empress just like that?" I snapped my fingers.

Kaelissa tilted her head slightly. "Do you mock me, boy?"

I waved my hands defensively. "Absolutely not Your, uh, Eminence. I just find it surprising the Brightlings would raise a Darkling to the throne."

"I am the mother of Daelissa." Kaelissa stood and hooked a fingernail under my chin, pulling me closer. "When last I saw you, I decided it was time to bring greatness back to this sad realm. I journeyed to Zbura and met with Arturo. It took only one look for him to realize I was the rightful Empress. Once I demonstrated my power, the others swore their loyalty and I took the throne."

I jerked up my chin and backed away. "Really? That easy?"

"Of course I am glossing over details, a few individuals who refused to acknowledge me." She pursed her lips. "It was a small matter to dispose of them." Her tone sounded so much like Daelissa's it made me shudder. Kaelissa had spoiled her blond daughter and disdained Nightliss. For millennia she'd done little but breed in an attempt to create another perfect daughter, but all had come into the world bearing the taint of the Desecration from the end of the First

Seraphim War. All would die of old age because Daelissa's defeat had cursed them.

Thomas spoke. "Kaelissa—"

"*Empress* Kaelissa." Her eyes went hard as stones.

Thomas didn't miss a beat. "Empress Kaelissa has expressed interest in uniting the nations under one rule," Thomas said. "She has modified the treaty Primarion Arturo discussed." He tapped a gem on the table and stood up. "Perhaps you should take a look."

I sat down on the crystal chair and charged the gem. Cyrinthian words projected into the air. The treaty was short, to the point, and about as one-sided as it gets. "You want the Darkling legions and our army to disarm and leave the borders."

Kaelissa sat back on her chair. "Of course. It shows that you are ready to unite under one government."

I barked a laugh. "No, it means that we're to roll over on our backs so you can scratch our bellies."

Kaelissa attempted an empathetic expression, but it came across as condescending instead. "I understand the plight of the Darklings. I do not wish them to suffer under the thumb of oppression. Once they have demonstrated obedience, I will grant them equal rights." She spread her hands as if preparing for a hug. "We will again be one people."

I didn't believe her for a second. "And if we don't?"

Her face hardened. "There will be war. I am the rightful ruler of all in this realm, and I will not accept defiance."

I wondered how Kohval would feel about this new peace treaty. Unless Kaelissa gave him assurances of power, he'd probably do an about-face on his stance. "You may have nearly three times the soldiers we have, but they still have to breach our defenses. Are you willing to sacrifice thousands?"

A confident smile spread across her lovely face. "I am willing to do whatever is necessary." Kaelissa stood. "There is little hope you could win a war. If you refuse, I will soon sing a song none can resist."

I held up my hands in mock terror. "Please don't karaoke us to death!" Kaelissa was too confident for my comfort. It was almost as if whatever she expected to get from Voltis was a sure thing. I wanted to straight-up ask her what it was, but then we'd lose an advantage. If her secret weapon was so guaranteed, maybe we could sneak in and steal it first.

Kaelissa's chin tilted imperiously. "We will meet here in two weeks. I expect you to have the documents signed by then."

I felt my eyebrows climb my forehead. "We don't even have a proper government in place. Who's supposed to sign it?"

Kaelissa pressed a cool hand to my cheek and gave me a motherly look. "I am certain either you or the commander is qualified."

"What if the legions don't agree to it?" I asked.

"Then we will see if your prediction of our losses is as dire as you believe." Kaelissa turned gracefully and strode from the tent. I stood and followed her, hoping to talk some sense to Arturo, but before I could get his attention, pinions of white fire burst from Kaelissa's back. "Two weeks," she told me and leapt off the cliff, soaring gracefully away.

Arturo and the archangels sprouted wings and followed her without so much as a goodbye, take care, or see you later, alligator.

"She can't be serious," Elyssa said. "Kaelissa is crazy!"

Thomas stared into the distance, eyes lost in thought for a moment. "It would seem whatever she expects to gain from Voltis is powerful indeed. Even without the peace treaty, she seems confident Pjurna won't be a threat."

"My thoughts exactly." I pinched the bridge of my nose as my headache intensified. "We can't let her have it. Somehow, we have to reach it first."

"Agreed," Elyssa said. "The only question is, how do we get there? Will the Mzodi help?"

"Perhaps," Thomas said. "I'll communicate with Xalara and see if she'll agree to providing transport." He looked us up and down. "I take it there was some difficulty shaking the Daskar?"

"Eh." I gave him an unconcerned shrug. "It wasn't so bad."

Elyssa snorted. "Yeah, piece of cake."

"Would've been easier if our brooms hadn't died," I said. "Both of them conked out on us."

Thomas took one of the brooms from Elyssa's back and unfolded it. He inspected the shaft and the saddle. "The more I thought about the broom malfunction, the more suspicious I became." He grunted and turned the broom to reveal a tiny gem hidden between the seat and the broomstick. "Someone sabotaged this broom."

I picked up the other broom and found an identical gem in the same spot. I hadn't even thought to check my broom for anything suspicious. "Why didn't mine stop working at the same time?"

"Perhaps it would have, but you turned it off first," Thomas said. He pried the gem loose and flicked it away. "Give it a try now." He held it out to me.

I placed my hand around the control runes and twisted it. The broom hovered in place. A growl rumbled in my throat. "I'm gonna break Kohval in half."

Thomas put a hand on my shoulder. "Later. For now, you need to rendezvous with the *Falcheen* and request they take you to Voltis. I'll circle wide around Kohvalla and connect with the skyway to Tarissa far to the south. It's imperative I notify McCloud and the other faction leaders about the tenuous situation here."

The capitol city of Pjurna was a long way south of Kohvalla, even by skyway. I blew out a sigh. "Yes, sir."

Thomas turned to his daughter and gave her a brief hug. He kissed her forehead. "Be careful. I'll see you soon."

"I'm worried about you trying to reach Tarissa alone," Elyssa said. "I thought the plan was for you to come on the ship."

He shook his head. "We don't have time for the *Falcheen* to detour to Tarissa." Thomas checked the time on his phone. "They'll meet you at the eastern mouth of the Acheron Canyon within the hour. You should leave now."

Elyssa gave him one last worried look and nodded. "See you soon."

Thomas strode back to his carpet and took off to the east so he could circle around Kohvalla. We hopped on our brooms and headed north toward the valley.

This part of the Vjartik Mountains was relatively easy to traverse, filled with low peaks and shallow valleys. We flew low in case the Daskar were still on the hunt, but I suspected it would take them days of searching snow and debris to realize we weren't dead and buried. Even so, I wanted to avoid any Brightling patrols that might be out this way. I hoped with their greatly reduced numbers, the chances of running into a patrol would be slim.

"Isn't this the place?" Elyssa slowed as we entered a wide canyon.

I checked the map on my arcphone, Nookli, and found the label for the Acheron Canyon. "It says we're here."

Insects hummed and a flock of golden doves exploded into the air when a herd of pink zebras galloped into a grove of trees. Except for the chilling heights of the mountains, it was much warmer here in northern Pjurna than in Tarissa far to the south. My stomach growled, reminding me I hadn't had a decent meal since breakfast.

Elyssa pointed down. "I think those are glurk trees."

I grimaced. Glurk was filling, but it was also the chicken of Seraphina—eaten for nearly every meal. My stomach gurgled to remind me that it was too empty to turn down a meal so I sighed and nodded. "Might as well eat while we wait."

We dropped down to the trees and harvested some of the tomato-like fruits then flew back up and perched on the lip of the canyon for a better view when the *Falcheen* showed. I peeled open the glurk to reveal the thick pasty insides. Lacking a utensil, I tried to channel enough magic to make a spork, but a spike of pain in my head warned me my body wasn't ready yet.

I found two thin pieces of hard clay and dusted them off for us to use as makeshift scoops.

Elyssa noticed my wince. "Magic still not cooperating?"

I swallowed a mouthful of glurk. "I'll be fine after a night of sleep."

"I hope so." She looked up into the cloudy sky. "Looks like it might rain."

Moments after her prophetic statement, the heavens dropped a load on us. Despite the warmer climate, the rain was freezing cold. I couldn't even channel an umbrella to keep us dry, so we huddled together for warmth and waited until it stopped. By the third hour, I prowled restlessly around, scanning the gray skies for any sign of the ship.

"Something must have happened to them." I looked at the map again and confirmed we were in the correct canyon on the eastern side. "Nookli, is our location accurate?"

"Justin, there is one Indian restaurant nearby," Nookli reported in its slightly robotic monotone. A blue blip highlighted the glurk tree.

Elyssa raised an eyebrow. "I swear to god, I think your phone likes to punk you."

I didn't know why Nookli had an obsession with incorrectly translating my queries into a desire to locate fine Indian cuisine, but it was comforting to know it cared. I repeated my question, and this time it confirmed that we were in the right spot.

"How far are the northern vortexes from here?" Elyssa asked. "Maybe the *Falcheen* is still out to sea."

I ran the query past Nookli and calculated a distance of a couple hundred miles. It didn't take the sky ships long to traverse such a distance, but if they'd encountered problems in the vortex, that could have slowed them considerably. As the sun began to reach for the horizon, I realized there wasn't much else we could do except wait.

Elyssa's comm gem beeped and Thomas's voice crackled. "Elyssa, are you reading me?"

She tapped the gem. "Yes, but there's a lot of static."

"I'll make it quick then," he said. "Xalara said she would consider the request about Voltis, but that was several hours ago. I'll let you know when that changes."

"Confirmed," Elyssa said. "The *Falcheen* still hasn't shown for our rendezvous."

"Hmm." Thomas went quiet. "Could be they're just running late. I'll check back within two hours, provided I can break through the interference. I'm nearly to the skyway."

"Be safe," Elyssa said.

"Same," Thomas replied, and the gem went quiet.

"I'm sick of waiting." I blew out a sigh. "What if they came already, didn't find us, and left?"

"Shelton would never let them leave without us," Elyssa said.

"The Mzodi don't always listen to us," I reminded her.

"True," she admitted, "but I'm sure Shelton would've left something behind to let us know."

The Mzodi were an interesting group of Seraphim, both Darklings and Brightlings who worked together to harvest aether gems from the intense magical pressures of the vortexes all over the realm. Unlike their land-dwelling brethren, they held no prejudice against Seraphim simply because of the kind of magic they channeled. In a sense, they were like a nation unto themselves, their homeland a secret place I'd never seen.

They were also driving me crazy with this long wait. I tapped on the Mzodi communication gem on my waist, a small silver stone, and waited for the chime that told me the flagship *Uorion* received my request. Like arcphones, the gems utilized aether to transmit communications, but beyond that, I didn't understand the mechanics. Shelton told me the gems were charmed to have an affinity to one another, meaning they all operated on the same frequency.

I hadn't used it yet because bugging the leader of the Mzodi was the last thing I wanted to do, especially since Thomas had already contacted them. Unfortunately, my patience had reached an end.

A faint chime emanated from the gem and the image of a sera with a sharp nose and hawkish eyes projected into the air before me.

"How may I assist you, Minister Slade?"

I had a different title for every group I dealt with—minister, commander, Kohvaniss, and so on. I'd reached the point where I just accepted it and moved on. "We're still waiting on the *Falcheen*. Any word on its arrival?"

"We sent the rendezvous request and received affirmative ping several hours ago." She looked at something to the side. "They are scheduled for the Acheron Canyon, correct?"

"That's right." I shifted impatiently. "Can I contact them directly?"

"Not without the proper gem," she said. "I will resend the request. Please hold."

The magical projection went blank but didn't disconnect. I gave Elyssa a disbelieving look. "They just put me on hold!"

She rubbed my arm. "At least they're more responsive than customer service at a cable company."

The wait stretched on a few minutes and the sera reappeared. "Apologies, Minister Slade, but I received no response."

Fingers of ice gripped my heart. "Meaning what?"

"Either interference from a vortex is blocking communications or"—her forehead creased with worry—"something happened to the ship."

I'd ridden through a vortex on a sky ship and thought the turbulence was going to kill me. The sky fishers did what sailors do, shouting and running around a lot, but had gotten us through the storm with our pants soiled, but our bodies unscathed. My mouth went dry and I struggled to swallow. "Is it possible they shipwrecked?"

"Despite our best precautions, it does happen." She looked to the side and nodded, probably to acknowledge someone standing near her then turned back to me. "Maintain your position and we will let you know the moment anything changes." Her holographic image flickered away.

Elyssa squeezed my hand. "I'm sure everything is okay, babe."

"Shelton and Adam are on that ship." I jumped to my feet and grabbed my broom. "We've got to go look for them."

"Not a good idea." Elyssa gently took the broom away. "Flying a broom into a vortex is only going to get you killed."

I threw up my hands. "We've got to do something."

The sad look in her eyes told me there really wasn't anything we could do. Without a sky ship, we couldn't investigate Voltis or launch a rescue mission. But that wasn't the worst part. What really drove a knife into my guts was that my best friends might be dead.

Chapter 8

We spent the night huddled behind the shelter of a boulder. Despite the hard ground and the gut-wrenching anxiety, we somehow fell asleep.

An insect tickled my ear, dragging me from slumber just enough to scratch myself. It landed on my nose. Irritated, I rubbed the spot. Next, it landed on my forehead. I slapped at it and smacked myself in the face.

The sound of two grown men giggling jerked me the rest of the way to wakefulness. I looked up and saw Shelton and Adam hovering over me, a feather in Shelton's hand and big grins on their face.

"You dirty bums." I jumped up and squeezed Shelton in a hug. "I thought you were dead!"

Shelton clapped me on the back. "We had a close call or two."

Adam's grin faded. "Gems aren't the only things inside the vortexes."

Elyssa stood near the rock, a smile on her face, and I realized she'd been awake while Shelton tickled my face with the feather. "You traitor."

She laughed and held up her hands in surrender. "Guilty as charged."

"Yeah, she wanted to wake you up, but we convinced her that our way was better." Shelton tucked the feather into the band on his wide-brimmed hat. "What the heck are you doing way out here, anyway? I thought we were gonna meet you back in Kohvalla."

"Turns out Kohval has his own plans," Elyssa said, and explained our wonderful experience with the Legiaros.

Adam's forehead pinched with confusion. "He tried to kill you?"

I kicked a stone off the ledge. "I don't think the Daskar were chasing us down to give us goodbye hugs."

Shelton snorted. "Sounds like it's story time."

I looked around but saw no sign of the *Falcheen*. "Where's the ship?"

Adam walked to the edge of the cliff and pointed down.

I looked over the edge and spotted the *Falcheen* hovering in the canyon. Its shape resembled a sword with a hand guard that curved forward into points. The ship's crystal hull shone like polished pearl with black crystal decking in between.

Large round aether gems called foils protruded from the lower hull in six places. Nearly six feet in circumference, each foil kept the ship afloat in the sky. Rubies the size of my head studded the upper hull. Each one was capable of firing magical death rays, provided someone channeled magic through them.

A long gash ran down the side of the outer hull, and the deck was splashed with dried blackened fluid.

"What happened to her?" I asked.

Adam opened his mouth to reply, but Shelton interrupted. "Man, this huge crystal"—he spread his arms wide like a kid trying to describe something big—"came outta nowhere and smacked into the side of the ship, knocking us off course and out of the vortex."

Adam jumped in. "Then this monster reptile dove in before we knew what had happened and started tearing into the Mzodi."

"I got my staff and blinded the dragon—" Shelton started.

"Then I used one of my disorientation spells," Adam said.

Shelton elbowed him aside. "Then the Mzodi came in and cleaned its clock."

"You two are great story tellers," Elyssa said dryly. "Maybe you could get lyres and lutes and become modern day bards."

"The stories would be better if Adam didn't interrupt all the time," Shelton grumbled.

Adam snickered. "Can you imagine Shelton singing?"

Elyssa cringed. "Maybe he should play the lute."

I steered the conversation wagon back on track. "They're still encountering dragons?"

"From what the crew said, they don't see nearly as many off the east coast anymore." Adam gazed down at the ship. "The north seems to be the hot spot now."

Shelton scratched his head. "Where's Commander Borathen?"

"Yeah, how'd the peace talks go?" Adam asked.

"Not so hot." Elyssa rubbed her stomach. "How about we discuss it over breakfast?"

Shelton's eyes lit up but his shoulders deflated. "Breakfast here is miserable." His eyes misted over. "I miss bacon so much."

"They have really good bacon and pizza in Kohvalla," I said.

His mouth fell open. "Are you for real, man? What are we waiting for? I want bacon pizza right now!"

Adam dared look hopeful for a moment but saw my grin and groaned. "Don't play with our emotions like that, Justin."

"So cruel!" Elyssa giggled. "Unfortunately, they have the same crap in Kohvalla as anywhere else."

Shelton glared at me. "Just the thought of bacon almost made me feel human again."

I threw up my hands. "Payback's a bitch."

"For the feather tickling?" Shelton rolled his eyes. "You toyed with a man's emotions—his soul."

"I think you mean his stomach," Elyssa said. She pointed at the ship. "Breakfast please? I don't want to have to eat one of you."

Shelton took out his wand and launched a flare into the canyon. A moment later, the ship rose on glowing levitation foils and extended a gangway to shore. I strode onboard and snapped a smart salute to the tall broad-shouldered captain, Illaena. She'd served as first mate on the *Evadora*, but Captain Cora had rammed her ship into Cephus's crimson arch to destroy it before the Beast escaped the Void.

Illaena stared back at me. Mzodi didn't salute their captains, they simply obeyed them. Even the head honcho of the sky fishers, the Muhala Kajeen, didn't get any bows or major signs of deference, which was kind of strange. I wondered if it was like that back in their homeland, wherever that was.

"Are you ready to return to Tarissa?" Illaena said.

"Actually, we have other plans." I took out my arcphone and displayed the Castigean Ocean on the screen instead of projecting it. "Can you take us here?" I touched Voltis.

Illaena's eyes flashed wide. "The Voltis Maelstrom? Have you lost your mind?" Her eyes narrowed. "Why would you want to go there at all?"

"Can we discuss over breakfast?" Elyssa said.

"Of course." Illaena led us below to the galley where a long table bore crystal dishes filled with a variety of food—all of it fruits and veggies since Seraphim didn't believe in killing for meat.

Elyssa grabbed some panari, a bread-like substance, and I helped myself to a bowl of nuts and grains since I was sick of glurk. Then we sat around a table.

I set my phone in the center and projected the map again. "The Brightling Empire is massing soldiers in Cabala."

"Yes, I know that," Illaena said. "Our ships visit nearly every coast in the realm."

"The Brightlings want a peace treaty, but refused our conditions for uniting or granting equal rights to Darklings." I ate a spoonful of muesli and let that sink in.

"The land dwellers have always been backward in their beliefs," Illaena said. "Why should they change now?"

Her point was hard to argue against, so I plowed forward. "I met Primarion Arturo for the first meeting."

"Whoa, whoa, whoa!" Shelton slapped a palm on the table. "That bastard is still alive?"

"Alive and kicking," Elyssa said grimly. "You're never going to believe who showed up the next day."

Before I got into that, I told them about our espionage in the Brightling camp, but didn't get into the story of Issana yet since that was another can of worms. "From what we can tell, Arturo believes there's some sort of powerful weapon in Voltis."

"Man, sounds like whatever it is would put them on Easy Street," Shelton said. "So who's the new emperor?"

Elyssa let the tension simmer a moment before answering. "Kaelissa is the new empress."

"What?" Shelton nearly choked on a quinto. "Who put that crazy bitch in charge?"

"Arturo, apparently." Elyssa shook her head slowly. "Since Daelissa was her daughter, she apparently didn't have any problems taking over."

"The politics of the land dwellers are of no concern to us," Illaena said. "What does this have to do with Voltis?"

"The intel we stole proves the Brightlings are moving on Voltis to secure a powerful weapon that'll allow them to take over the world." I went for a touch of the melodramatic just for emphasis.

Illaena didn't buy it. "Impossible. Voltis is an uninhabitable region with volcanoes, aether storms, and nothing resembling a weapon."

"What if Cephus's crimson arch made a new ally or enemy available?" I said. "What if there are dragons inside Voltis?"

Illaena looked at me blankly for a moment. "The dragons have proven themselves capable of surviving the vortexes. It is possible they could survive Voltis as well." She shook her head. "Even so, they are unintelligent beasts, incapable of allying themselves with any faction."

"There are ancient, incredibly intelligent dragons in Eden," Elyssa said. "Thankfully, they prefer to remain hidden deep in the earth."

"What sort of dragon lives beneath the ground?" Illaena said.

"Earth dragons." I displayed an image of Altash, his massive red form coiled up in the caves beneath El Dorado, Colombia.

Illaena's jaw dropped. "Monstrous."

"They ain't so bad," Shelton said. "They helped us revive Seraphim that were husked when the Grand Nexus exploded."

Illaena turned to me. "They are your allies?"

"Not exactly." Her question sparked an old memory of mine back to life. "Altash and Lulu refused to help in the war against Daelissa because they claimed it would bring an ancient nemesis into the fray."

"The problem is, they never explained any of that crap." Shelton leaned back in his chair. "Are you sure there's something in Voltis? Maybe the Brightlings are massing for an attack on Pjurna."

Elyssa shrugged. "Whatever the case, I think their peace offering is meant to lower our defenses. We need to go to Voltis and see what's there. If the dragons are really a threat, they'll affect everyone in Seraphina."

"I will not risk my new ship in the maelstrom." Illaena stood. "Unless you discover proof a threat exists in Voltis, I will not venture inside."

"Can you at least take us near it?" I asked.

She pursed her lips. "No. I will return you to Tarissa. If the Muhala Kajeen sees fit to grant you another ship and crew, that is her decision. I have already lost one captain and the finest ship our fleet has ever known. I will not lose the *Falcheen*."

"Cora made a decision that saved the entire realm," Elyssa said. "You didn't lose her. Please, Illaena, taking us to Voltis will help everyone."

"You have no proof." Illaena stood. "You merely wish to involve the Mzodi in a conflict between kingdoms. We take no sides with the land dwellers."

"How are we supposed to get proof if you don't take us?" I asked.

She shook her head and headed for the door. "We have business to attend to tomorrow. After that, I will return you to Tarissa."

"Illaena, please." Elyssa clasped her hands together imploringly. "This weapon could threaten the entire realm."

Shelton piled on. "What would Cora do?"

"I am not Cora," Illaena said. "I knew it was a mistake to continue such an intimate association with land dwellers. I will ask the Muhala Kajeen to discontinue this relationship at once." She stormed away before anyone could say another word.

"She has a point," Adam said. "All we have is some video of Arturo acting cocky."

"My father agreed with our assessment," Elyssa shot back. "Do you really think he'd send us out to check if he thought there was nothing to it?"

"We need a contingency plan." I racked my brain for alternatives, but came up empty.

"The problem is the Mzodi are the only ones with sky ships." Shelton exchanged a look with Adam. "Maybe we could build our own."

"That might take months," Elyssa said. "And where would we get a seasoned crew?"

"I've been studying this ship inside out ever since we boarded it." Adam tapped his phone. "I've made schematics and studied the propulsion gems. We could probably recreate this ship, but training a crew is the show-stopper."

"We have two weeks to do something," I said. "That's how long it'll take Arturo and Kaelissa to get back to Cabala and leave for Voltis."

"Unless they have faster transportation," Elyssa said. "How do they plan to get to Voltis without a sky ship?"

"I'm sure Kaelissa has a way," I said. "She has the Brightling Empire behind her now."

"Well, ain't that peachy?" Shelton rolled a quinto between his fingers, a grimace on his face. "Maybe it's time to call the Muhala Kajeen direct. If anyone can get you a ship, she can."

"Thomas already asked her." I shook my head slowly. "Apparently, she hasn't acted on his request."

"Then we're up the creek without a paddle." Shelton tossed the uneaten quinto back on his plate. "From what you've said, it sounds like Kohval wants to start his own little kingdom, and Kaelissa wants to pick up where her insane daughter left off."

Adam slapped a hand on the table. "I'm about ready to just find a nice quiet place to settle down and let the idiots kill each other."

Shelton pointed a finger at him. "I'm with you."

"Tempting," I said. "Maybe we could join the Mzodi and get the hell out of Dodge."

"What about all our other people?" Elyssa said. "Lycans, felycans, Arcanes—"

"Vampires," Shelton finished with a scowl.

"Hey, they fought too," she said in a pointed tone. "We can't just abandon our ideals because some rotten apples want to spoil it."

"How, pray tell, are we supposed to reach Voltis and take a peek?" Shelton said. "How are we supposed to fight Kaelissa's big-ass army if Kohval doesn't want to?" His forehead creased. "Did it ever occur to you that Kohval might strike a deal with her so he can keep his little fiefdom?"

Elyssa quirked a disdainful eyebrow. "Yes, as a matter of fact, it has."

"Seems there's only one way to solve our current problem," Adam said in a quiet voice.

Shelton shifted toward him. "We swim?"

Adam shook his head. "Mutiny."

The word summoned images of sword fights and wooden decks covered in blood. I'd seen plenty of pirate movies. I knew what mutiny meant, but the thought of actually committing it made me feel dirty and evil. On the other hand, how else were we to reach Voltis? We needed a ship and crew.

Shelton laughed uneasily. Elyssa frowned and looked at me.

I shook my head. "We couldn't pull it off."

"Sure we could," Adam said. "All it requires is a bit of trickery and deception."

"Hang on a minute." Shelton bolted upright in his chair. "You're serious about this."

Adam waggled a hand in a so-so motion. "Partially. If Thomas Borathen thinks Arturo might get his hands on a super weapon, then we should find a way to check it out. Seems like we can't do it without a sky ship."

"Mutiny is too much," Elyssa said. "There must be an alternative."

The ship lurched upward as it began to get underway. "I gotta go up top for a minute," Shelton said. "The takeoffs get me airsick if I don't get some air."

Adam chuckled. "You need air for airsickness."

"Shut it, Nosti." Shelton got up and the rest of us followed him up to the top deck.

Illaena stood near the bow giving orders in a conversational tone while her first mate shouted them to the rest of the crew. The *Falcheen* rose higher and higher until it reached cruising altitude of a few thousand feet. Even at that height, it was still far below the peaks of the barrier mountains to the south.

The ship rotated east and sailed toward the ocean and presumably the rendezvous with the *Xanda*. Illaena left her post and approached us, eyes hard as stones. "The Muhala Kajeen agrees with me that it is time to end our association with you and your people. We will continue to trade, but we will not take sides in your conflict."

Anxiety knotted my intestines tight as a trampoline and anger hopped up and down on it. "What if we just ask for rides?"

"We assisted you against Cephus because he posed a risk to the realm," Illaena replied. "War is never good, but it will not disrupt trade."

"What do you even trade for?" Shelton blurted. "Nobody uses money here."

"Goods, services, food," she said. "Not that it is any of your concern."

"Can you at least put us on a ship headed to Azoris?" I asked.

"So you can spy on their army?" Illaena's eyes flared. "Granting you passage would be assistance."

"Technically, we're not citizens of Pjurna," Elyssa said. "We're a third party."

"No matter your allegiance, you are not Mzodi." Illaena crossed her arms. "There will be no more rides after I return you to Tarissa." She snapped her fingers and a group of soldiers marched up behind us. "Confine them to quarters."

My knuckles cracked and my inner demon rammed against my consciousness. *Fight! Destroy!* He was a jackass, but in this instance, I felt the same way. Unfortunately, my magical side still felt puny and a direct confrontation might get us killed. There were only four of us versus ten soldiers and the rest of the crew. I also didn't want to hurt any of them, because then we could forget ever getting their help again.

Elyssa's hand tightened on my arm. "Let's do as she says."

The soldiers marched us down to the lowest deck and put us in a large room with several bunk beds. Using the gem outside the room, they phased the wall back into place, leaving us trapped inside.

Shelton used his wand to charge the gem on a bed, and a cloud mattress billowed into place. He pushed down on it with his hand. "Well, at least we get to sleep in style."

"I'm not tired," I said.

Shelton vanished into a small room in the back and hollered, "Thank god the bathroom works!"

Adam groaned. "Is that really at the top of your priorities right now?"

Shelton stuck his head out the door. "Hey, all this conflict upsets my stomach." He patted his belly. "Plus, I ain't gonna lie, these magical angel bathrooms make my man bits tingle."

Elyssa gagged. "Christ, Shelton, why don't you just lock yourself inside the bathroom and shut up then?"

Adam burst into laughter but quickly clamped his mouth shut when he saw the rest of us weren't as amused.

I glared at the wall, anger boiling my insides like rock lobsters and maybe even potatoes. I turned to Adam. "You said we needed trickery and deception to get what we want. What did you have in mind?"

He looked up at me, confusion arching his eyebrows. "Huh—oh, you mean for my earlier idea?"

"Yeah," I said in a gravelly voice. "It's time to plan a mutiny."

Chapter 9

Shelton groaned. "There are thirty-one Mzodi on this ship. How in the hell are we gonna convince them to help us steer the thing?"

I leaned against the wall and turned to our resident genius. "Adam, do you know how to control the ship?"

He waggled his hand. "More or less. This ship has control stations for six navigators—those are the crew who control the levitation foils." Adam put his phone on one of the beds and projected a diagram of the *Falcheen*, displaying a skeletal outline of all the cabins, the huge levitation gems on the hull, and stations from stem to stern.

"Wow, how did you get it so detailed?" Elyssa asked.

"Shelton and I came up with an advanced scan spell." Adam traced a finger along the holographic hull. "All we had to do was walk back and forth on all the decks a few times until it filled in all the blanks."

"It ain't as easy as it sounds when you got nosy soldiers asking what you're doing," Shelton said.

Adam displayed one of the navigator control stations. A stool with a strap held the navigator in place while a crystal rod that resembled a flight stick extended from a hole in the deck. "The navigator channels aether through the rod and into the corresponding levitation foil on the bottom of the hull." He zoomed out to display the six large levitation gems. "There's one navigator for every foil, and each one is controlled independently."

Adam overlaid an image that looked like water flowing beneath the hull. "Once the ship reaches an aether current—think of it as a river of aether in the air—it's much easier to maintain power and propel the ship forward."

"Aether streams are the magical equivalent of airstreams," Shelton said. "Without those, it would be hard to power one of these ships with just six crew."

"I didn't realize that," Elyssa said. "I thought the gems kept the ships afloat."

"Yeah, well it took a lot of detective work to find that out," Shelton said. "You ever hear of a scramjet?"

I nodded. "I remember NASA testing one. Once they hit a certain speed, the air itself fuels and propels the aircraft."

Adam traced a finger along the flowing lines. "That sums up how these ships operate. They need assistance to reach the nearest aether stream, but once they get there, all the crew has to do is steer."

"There's still a lot we don't know about the aether streams," Shelton said. "The Mzodi have charts with all the streams on them, but they nearly took off my head when I asked to see one."

"Top secret," Adam said. "Even though concentrations of aether are high enough to reach the visible spectrum in the vortexes, most of the aether streams are invisible."

"This just got a lot more complicated," Elyssa said. "We don't know how to pilot the ship, and we don't know how to find the aether streams."

"Not true." I tapped my temple. "Remember my incubus vision can see invisible aether. I can keep us on the road."

"Hell yeah!" Shelton clapped his hands. "Since the ship is already in an aether stream we don't need six navigators to power the ship into position. We just gotta figure out how to steer it."

"Sounds like we might be able to handle that." Elyssa pursed her lips and nodded with satisfaction. "Aside from taking the ship from thirty angry Mzodi, I'd say we've got this covered."

Shelton snorted. "Totally."

"Why don't they centralize the steering?" I said. "Seems like it'd be much easier to consolidate six navigators into one big steering wheel."

"I don't disagree," Adam said, "but it's likely the Mzodi have their reasons."

"Doubtful," Shelton said. "If you look at the layout, I'd be willing to bet this entire design came from water-borne ships." He pointed to the control rods. "Those look like the ends of oars. I'll bet the Mzodi started with water ships with oars and adopted the same design once they figured out how to fly their ships."

Adam pinched his chin between thumb and forefinger and looked at the diagram. "You have a point. It may simply be the Mzodi adopted the design from regular ships and never changed the way they do things."

"Four of us steering with six stations is a problem," Elyssa said, "but first we should worry about the thirty Mzodi we have to get past."

Adam flashed a grin. "That's where deception comes in." He flicked his hand across the diagram of the ship and red blips appeared on the screen, thirteen on the top deck, ten more scattered around the ship, and the remaining eight concentrated in a room on the lower deck. Adam pointed at the last group. "These are the gem sorters. Since we just pulled in a big haul, they're busy evaluating the catch."

Shelton pointed his wand at the top deck. "That's the captain, the first mate, six navigators, lookouts, and soldiers."

"The ones on the lower decks are soldiers," Adam said. "I don't think they usually patrol the ship, but since we came onboard, they followed us around and guarded the captain's quarters."

Shelton blew out a breath. "Yeah, after we asked about the aether stream charts, they got real suspicious."

"These aren't current personnel positions, just approximations?" Elyssa asked.

"The gem sorters are definitely in the hold except when they eat." Adam pointed to the top deck. "The deck crew is always in position in case of bad weather or dragon attacks."

"Should we attack when they're asleep?" I asked.

Adam shook his head. "No, because they almost always land the ship at night unless it's during an ocean voyage. Then they sleep in shifts while the ship floats in the aether stream."

"These ships are fast." Shelton zipped his hand through the air as if to illustrate. "They ain't as fast as a jet airplane, but it doesn't take them more than a few days to cross from here all the way to Ijolica, according to the crew I asked."

Elyssa held up a hand. "How, exactly, are we deceiving them?"

"The soldiers always eat together," Adam said. "They have a toast with wine at every meal."

"Even breakfast?" I asked.

"Every meal," Shelton reiterated. "Some kind of custom that brings good luck."

"In my bags, I brought along some potions that Meghan made to help me sleep." Adam grinned. "All we have to do is slip some in the wine."

"Knock out the soldiers, lock them up," Elyssa finished. "The gem sorters are already in the hold, so we just have to lock them inside."

Shelton held up a finger. "And that's where I come in."

"Remember how we said Seraphim magic can't be hacked?" Adam said.

"Yeah," I said, dragging out the word. "It's because they channel magic without using spells."

"Right." Adam mimicked my drawl. "Well, it turns out gems are actually charmed."

"Attenuated is the right word," Shelton said. "You can lock out a gem's magical functions by encoding it with Cyrinthian symbols. Regardless of if the aether gem is enchanted to open doors or wipe your ass, it won't do it without the magic word."

Elyssa wrinkled her nose. "Ass-wiping? Really?"

Adam chuckled and continued. "In other words, we need to hack the code."

"Once we escape, we can encode the gem in the hold, locking the gem sorters inside." Shelton flashed a grin. "One problem down."

"We can lock away the soldiers the same way." Adam chopped a hand into his palm. "That's over half the crew taken care of without hurting anyone."

Elyssa looked impressed. "That leaves us with thirteen people on the top deck."

"Tricky, but not impossible," Shelton said. "The Mzodi soldiers are great when it comes to fighting dragons, but the crew usually stays out of the way."

I nodded in approval. "Well, it appears our plan is ready to put into motion."

"Yeah, we want to do this before reaching the *Tozarian*, or we're screwed." Shelton walked over to the gem on the wall and zapped it with his wand. As predicted, a doorway didn't appear. He dragged a table beneath the gem and set his arcphone on it, then activated one of his spell hacking programs. A tiny laser shot from the phone and into the gem, and a stream of symbols filled the air next to it.

Shelton brushed his hands together and turned around. "It'll take a while for the program to hack the gem."

"How do we encode a lock into a gem?" I asked.

"Gems are made of highly compressed aether," Adam said in his nerdy lecturing voice.

"Think aether diamonds," Shelton added.

"Right," Elyssa said. "How do we lock them?"

"The sorters code each gem with a set of basic symbols before overlaying more complicated spells." Adam pulled up a string of Cyrinthian symbols beneath the picture of a red gem. "The new owners are given the unique combination which allows them to add their own enchantments to it." His forefinger touched the bridge of his nose, as if pushing up the thick-rimmed glasses he used to wear. Adam didn't even seem aware of his nervous habit.

"We gotta hack the basic code," Shelton said. "Once we know it, we can lock or unlock any gem."

Adam grinned. "That's the flaw in their system. Even if the door is locked with a complex code, it's really only overlaying the root code."

"And you only need the root to hack the entire thing." I snapped my fingers. "Brilliant! I'm surprised the gem charmers don't know about this flaw."

"That's because they don't have magic technology here." Shelton looked adoringly at his arcphone. "I'll bet they never even heard of hackers in this sorry-assed realm."

Elyssa looked from the ship diagram to Shelton's arcphone as it worked to decode the aether gem's root enchantment. When her eyes met mine, I saw the uncertainty lurking inside.

"What if we fail?" Elyssa said.

I shrugged. "Illaena made it clear we're not welcome on their ships anymore. I don't see how we could make it any worse."

"They could dump us in the ocean," Elyssa said. "Execute us."

"We still have our brooms." I shifted to Adam. "Did you and Shelton bring brooms or flying carpets?"

"Brooms," Adam said.

"If things go south we can make like Mary and get the flock out of here," Shelton said.

"You realize this ship is a lot faster than our brooms, right?" Elyssa said.

"But not as maneuverable." I leaned forward. "Look, we've been forced into this situation. We don't have a choice."

"I wouldn't go that far." Adam swallowed hard and looked around nervously. "Mutiny is kind of a big deal."

"Is it even mutiny if you're not part of the crew?" Shelton said. "It's more like a hijacking if you ask me."

"All I know is that if we don't beat Kaelissa and Arturo to whatever they're looking for in Voltis, this entire realm could fall to them." I let that sink in. "I don't know what it is they're after, but I do know that Arturo is no slouch when it comes to strategy. If he thinks that this secret weapon can make taking over Pjurna a breeze, then I believe him."

"How about we just knock out the Mzodi soldiers and play it from there," Shelton said. "If we get cold feet, we'll just come back here, lock ourselves in, and pretend we're innocent."

The others looked at me and I felt the weight of the decision settling on my shoulders.

The thought of mutiny made me queasy. I had nothing against Illaena, but the way she'd locked us up like criminals pissed me off.

Not only that, but if the Muhala Kajeen was really banning us from all the ships, then Pjurna would lose a huge asset in the war. Even if they didn't fight with us, their intelligence gathering ability was phenomenal.

I also felt absolutely certain that we had to reach Voltis before Kaelissa got what she wanted.

"Let's do it," I said grimly. "And pray we don't fail."

Shelton's phone whizzed through code for nearly thirty minutes before displaying a string of symbols. When it chimed success, he pumped his fist. "Got it!"

"All we have to do now is send this root code to the gem and then overwrite the lock enchantment with our own," Adam said.

"I just think the code?" I asked.

"Yup," Shelton said. "Visualization and willpower—same as anything else in magic."

I regarded the seemingly random string of symbols representing the root enchantment of the gem. Though Cyrinthian was a language, its letters also served as powerful runes for designing enchantments. During my brief tenure at Arcane University, I'd read theories on why Cyrinthian symbols were more magical than others, but none of them answered the basic question: How were symbols intrinsically magical in the first place?

Their answer: "This is one of those things you just have to accept and move on."

I took the answer Shelton and Adam's hacking program gave me and imagined the symbols in my mind while zapping the gem with aether. The current lock code flashed in my head.

"Got it?" Shelton asked.

I sent the lock code to the gem and the wall misted away, revealing the corridor outside. I looked at Shelton and wrinkled my forehead. "No, what am I supposed to do again?"

He punched me on the shoulder. "Jackass."

Charging the gem hadn't given me a headache, which meant I was mostly recovered from yesterday's snowboard escape. I hoped I had enough juice to take on anyone who got in our way.

"We've got forty-five minutes before the next meal," Elyssa said. "I suggest we hack the lock on the sorting room where the gem sorters are so we can lock them in when we're ready."

"Good idea." Adam's finger pushed up where his glasses used to be. This time he frowned at his finger, then shook his head and continued. "Shelton and I can take care of that while you and Justin spike the wine."

Elyssa pointed to the floor. "Meet back here so we can decide if we're moving forward."

"I need to get the potions and brooms from our room," Adam said and motioned us to follow him. He led us down the organic curves of the corridor to a green gem and jolted it with aether from his wand. The wall puffed away and he went inside, returning a moment later with two glass vials and brooms.

Shelton took his broom and tucked it under an arm. "Maybe we should stow the brooms somewhere for our escape if things go to crap."

"It'd be more convenient than hauling them around." Elyssa bit her lower lip. "I'll stick them in our prison room so all the brooms are together."

Adam and Shelton handed us their brooms and checked a diagram of the ship. The entrance to the sorting room was on the port side near the stern while the galley was up on deck two midship.

Adam saluted. "Good luck."

Shelton gripped my hand. "Take care, bro."

"You too." I watched them disappear around the curve in the corridor then turned to Elyssa. "You ready for this?"

She eyed the vials in my hand. "I have really mixed feelings about hijacking the ship, but without it, we're dead in the water."

"Yeah." I handed her one of the vials. "I forgot to ask Adam how long this stuff takes to kick in."

Elyssa smiled wanly. "Knowing Meghan, I'm sure they're quick and efficient." Adam's girlfriend didn't play around when it came to healing or potion-making.

I checked the time. "We have to spike the wine now or it'll be too late."

Elyssa consulted the diagram of the ship Adam had given us and we took off at a jog toward the bow. Following the winding ramps up to the second deck, we stopped and listened for sounds of patrols, but the corridors remained empty except for an occasional lone Mzodi hurrying down the hall.

"No patrols," I said. "They must figure we're safely locked up."

"Good thing for us." Elyssa peeked around the curve at the top of the ramp and declared the coast clear with efficient Templar sign language.

We crept down the corridor, hugging the inner curve of the wall. The midship area bulged wider than the bow, and we made the most of the little extra concealment. The galley was empty, the table laden with fresh fruits and veggies.

I held up my hand. "Watch the door."

Elyssa nodded and gave me the other vial. I dashed to the crystal decanter at the end of the table and dumped both vials into the dark blue liquid that passed for wine in Seraphina. On a whim, I grabbed some panari and met Elyssa in the hall.

"The trap is set," I said grimly, and took a bite of the sweet bread.

"That would sound so much more ominous if you didn't have crumbs on your face." Elyssa wiped my lip with her thumb.

I wiped my face with the back of my hand and tried again, setting my jaw in a tight line. "The trap, is set. The game is now afoot."

Elyssa rolled her eyes. "Let's find someplace to hide before the soldiers come."

The stomp of boots and murmur of voices echoed down the hall. A quick check of the time told me the soldiers had decided to take lunch early today.

Chapter 10

"Quick, find somewhere to hide!" Elyssa dragged me into one of the nearby door niches lining the hallway. "Try to open the door."

I tested the door gem, but it was locked. Boots tromped closer and closer, instilling me with mild panic. "The soldiers are almost here."

"Try more doors," Elyssa whispered. "Hurry!"

I checked two more gems, but neither responded. The footsteps and murmurs of conversation grew louder until the soldiers sounded as if they were right around the curve from us. I grabbed Elyssa's hand and pulled her into an alcove three doors down from the galley. We pressed our backs to the wall and held our breaths.

"I do not like it," one of the soldiers said. "The first haul of a new ship always goes before the Muhala Kajeen. Now Illaena wishes us to go on another expedition without following tradition."

"It's unheard of," a female said.

"Bad luck," grumbled another.

The footsteps echoed in the galley followed shortly by the clinking of crystal. "May the waning hours of the day bring us fortune," someone said.

"To fortune," the others intoned. Crystal clinked and the conversation went quiet for a moment."

"So, tomorrow we sail for Guinesea again?" asked a woman with a deep voice.

"We should sail for the Golden Skylets as custom demands," a soldier said. "We already suffered enough bad luck in the north."

"Illaena has acted strangely ever since we left Guinesea. I think she is too friendly with the land dwellers."

"Careful, Sholea," said a male voice. "Do not make accusations against one of our own."

"I never accused her of anything," Sholea replied. "But her orders have been strange of late, have they not? We aren't even allowed near the gem sorters for the rest of the trip."

"Does the wine taste a bit sour today?" The deep-voiced sera asked.

"What do you expect?" the male said. "We traded for it on Guinesea. Brightling soldiers have no taste for good wine."

"It tasted fine this morning," Sholea said. "I wonder if it spoiled."

Elyssa gave me a concerned look. "I hope it kicks in before they realize it's spiked," she whispered.

That definitely concerned me, but Sholea's mention of a Illaena's strange behavior threw up a red flag. Had something happened in Guinesea? My stomach clenched. What if Illaena met with Kaelissa while she was there and decided to throw in with the Brightlings?

A thud sounded from the galley followed by cries of surprise.

Crystal shattered. "Why did you knock away my wine?" Sholea asked.

"It has been tainted!" the male shouted.

"Petyris is right," the deep-voiced female said. "We have been betrayed."

"Can't keep my eyes open," another soldier said in a groggy voice.

"Is he dead?" Sholea asked.

There was a pause before Petyris answered. "No, he's asleep." His word grew heavier.

"Can't—" Whatever Sholea meant to say cut off in mid-sentence.

Elyssa and I waited for another full minute before risking a peek into the galley. Soldiers lay slumped over a table where they sat, though some had toppled to the floor. One seraph lay face-down with his butt poking into the air.

Elyssa blew out a breath of relief. "It worked." She bit her lower lip and looked around. "We still need a place to put them."

I did a quick headcount and came up with eleven soldiers. Before I could tell Elyssa we were missing someone, a female with a book tucked under one arm entered the galley.

"I nearly forgot—" she stopped, staring at us wide-eyed for a brief instant before turning to run.

Elyssa dove and tackled her. I blurred over and clamped a hand over the sera's mouth before she could scream a warning to others. A quick chop to the base of her neck stopped her struggling. I felt her pulse to make sure I hadn't hit her too hard and nodded when I felt it beating.

"That was close," I said.

"We were sloppy and unprepared." Elyssa hit her thigh with the bottom of a fist. "Stupid!"

"Hey, we're making this up as we go along," I said. "Unfortunately, this means there's no going back since that soldier saw our faces."

Elyssa grimaced. "Maybe. There's always another option."

"I won't kill her in cold blood," I said. "These soldiers are just following orders."

"Soon those orders might be to execute us for hijacking," Elyssa said. "I don't condone killing her either, but we may have no choice."

"We'll burn that bridge when we come to it," I said.

"You mean cross it?"

I shook my head. "You know I like doing things the hard way." I jabbed a thumb at the corridor. "I'll find a room to stow our sleepyheads while you separate them from their weapons and communication gems."

Elyssa got to work removing swords and armor from the unconscious soldiers. I went into the corridor and tested the gems in the door alcoves until I found one that responded to my request. The wall misted away to reveal an empty cabin that would serve as our makeshift prison.

I returned to the galley and tucked a Seraphim under each arm, deposited them in the room, and repeated until all the soldiers snoozed comfortably on the floor in the room. Elyssa dribbled wine into the mouth of the sera we'd knocked out so she'd stay asleep as long as her comrades.

After making sure our guests were tucked away, I found another open room and we dumped their armor and weapons inside. The only thing left was meeting Shelton and Adam so we could lock the room with the soldiers.

"Shouldn't they be here by now?" Elyssa asked.

I looked down the corridor, but the curve of the hull made it impossible to see very far. "They might be in trouble."

"They *are* trouble." Elyssa sighed. "Let's go find them."

We set off at a fast but stealthy jog until we reached the aft ramp and headed down. We literally ran into Shelton just around the first curve and sent him tumbling with a yelp back into Adam. The pair backward-somersaulted into the wall and came to rest with Shelton's face on Adam's backside.

Elyssa covered her mouth, shoulders shaking and face red as she tried not to burst into laughter. A snort escaped me before I put a lid on it. Restraining the laughter brought tears to my eyes.

Our friends disentangled themselves with as much dignity as they could muster, Shelton casting murderous looks at us while Adam shook with silent laughter.

"We're in the middle of a deadly mission and you think this is funny?" Shelton hissed.

"Did Adam make your man parts tingle?" Elyssa said through barely repressed giggles.

I wiped tears from my eyes and nodded. "Even pirates have to laugh sometimes."

A growl rumbled in his throat. "In case you care, the gem sorters are locked in the sorting room."

"Good." Elyssa's voice trembled with mirth. "I hate to ask, Shelton, but how did you like Adam's pirate booty?"

That brought a fresh round of snorts from everyone except Shelton who released a sigh of the long-suffering.

Adam slapped him on the back. "C'mon, dude, admit it was funny."

"Hee-larious," Shelton said with a scowl.

Elyssa took a deep breath and straightened her mouth into a semblance of seriousness. "The soldiers are in a room but need to be locked up."

"Yeah, we would've been done sooner," Adam said, "but there's something strange going on in the sorting room."

That perked my eyebrows. "Strange? Are they practicing acapella pop music while they work?"

"Nah, more like arguing and yelling," Shelton said. "I heard someone threatening them."

"Maybe that's how they work." Elyssa frowned uncertainly. "The deck crew certainly yells a lot."

"I could've sworn someone threatened to cut off a sorter's hand if they didn't keep working." Adam looked at Shelton. "That sound about right?"

"Sounds exactly right," Shelton said.

Elyssa's forehead pinched as she turned to me. "Didn't one of the soldiers complain about not being allowed near the gem sorters for the rest of the trip?"

My forehead mimicked hers. "Yeah, but what does that have to do with what Adam said?"

"Illaena handing out strange orders, forbidding the crew from seeing the gem sorters, not taking the first haul to the Mujaha Kajeen—" Elyssa laced her fingers together. "Put that together with what Adam and Shelton overheard and it sounds like there's a conspiracy on this ship."

"Forgive me if I'm wrong," Shelton said, "but ain't we the conspirators here?"

"We need to hack the door gem where you're keeping the soldiers so we can lock them in," Adam said. "I optimized the code so it takes about twenty minutes instead of thirty, but we don't have any time to spare."

"What's the code for the gem to the sorting room?" Elyssa asked.

Adam looked from her to me, then flicked on his phone and showed us the symbols. "Don't tell me you plan to unlock that doorway."

"She's got that look in her eyes," Shelton said. "What did you overhear the soldiers saying?"

Elyssa repeated what we'd heard and drew frowns from Adam and Shelton.

"I think you're right," Shelton said. "There's something fishy going on here."

"Still need to lock up the soldiers," Adam said. "Can you show us the door?"

I put a hand on Elyssa's shoulder. "You show him the door; I'll take a look inside the sorting room."

"There are three ways into the room," Shelton said. "Use the aft door. The voices sounded farther away from there, so you might have a chance of sneaking in undetected."

Elyssa gave me a stern stare. "Don't go in too far. I'll be right back, okay?"

"I'll be careful." I pecked a kiss on her forehead.

Shelton looked at me expectantly. "Do I get a kiss too?"

Adam clapped him on the shoulder. "Haven't you already gotten enough booty today?"

"Thanks for reminding me," Shelton grumbled.

Elyssa led them up the ramp and I headed down. The door alcove Shelton told me about was a few paces to my right when I emerged from the ramp well. I pressed an ear to it and made out the faint sound of footsteps and murmuring voices. Since even my enhanced hearing couldn't make out the words, I assumed the speakers had to be on the opposite side of the room.

I charged the door gem and pictured the runes Adam had shown me. The doorway misted away to reveal translucent crystal chests filled with gems of all colors and sizes ranging from the size of a fingernail up to the dimensions of a fist. The containers, cylindrical casks with no locks or openings, didn't even remotely resemble the sort of treasure chests I'd seen in pirate movies.

The stacked containers stood tall enough to conceal me and the door and formed narrow aisles leading deeper into the room. Rather than take the first path, I chose to creep closer to the curved hull where the containers offered better concealment. The voices grew louder as I made my way along the hull until I was finally able to make sense of what they were saying.

"—that's no volgen, it's a volken!"

A male and female burst into laughter.

Heavy footsteps stomped and an angry female hissed, "Perhaps we should run around the ship announcing our presence, you fools."

The laughter cut off abruptly.

"Sorry, Racha," several voices said at once.

"You, what is the count?" Racha said.

Someone replied in the proud tone of a person who didn't like her attitude. "We found one."

"I have been graceful in my lenience," Racha said, her words grating with fury, "but your intentional delays leave me no choice."

I sneaked to the corner of the nearest stack and peered down the aisle. Shimmering nets bulging with gems hung from the ceiling near tables studded with more stones. Sorters sat at each of the tables, and around them stood people dressed in white uniforms with the white sphere of Brilliance emblazoned on the chest. One of the sorters held her palm to the larger gem in the front of the table and beams of energy flowed from the other gems and into the one I assumed she was evaluating in the center.

I identified Racha before she even opened her mouth by the imperious look she cast at the gem sorters as she drew a white crystal sword from the sheath at her side. "I warned you that if you had not found three gems, one of you would lose a hand."

One of her companions, a tall seraph in white robes spoke in a nerdy, lecturing tone. "Technically, you gave them fifteen more minutes, and it's only been ten."

Racha glared at him, and the man visibly withered.

"The gems you seek are incredibly rare," the sorter who'd spoken earlier said, his voice unafraid. He ran a hand over his bald head. "I warned you we would likely need another expedition to the core." He was a short, thin seraph, but his gaze was hard and unflinching despite the armed soldiers around him.

Racha bared her teeth. "I've heard enough excuses."

The sorter slid up the sleeve of his robe and laid his bare arm on the table. "Then take my hand and be quiet, for I am weary of your constant complaints."

Damn, that dude is a badass.

At this point even my slow wits had put the pieces together in this scenario. The Seraphim in white were bad guys, forcing the sorters to do their bidding. Were they Kaelissa's people, or was Illaena in cahoots with the Brightlings?

"If you take his hand, we will refuse to work," another gem sorter said. "Without us, you'll never find the gems you need."

The tall seraph in white dared speak again. "Maybe you should just let them work, Racha."

Racha gripped her sword with both hands and swung it in a chopping motion toward the gem sorter's hand. I acted on impulse and projected a shield over the seraph's wrist. The sword rang hard against the barrier. Racha cried out and dropped the weapon.

The time for stealth was over. It was time to fight.

Chapter 11

Before anyone could recover, I blurred in and smashed the tall seraph in the face with my fist. I dodged a thrusting sword and swept the legs from beneath the wielder. Using techniques television wrestling taught me, I gripped a fist with the other hand, and drove my elbow into the soldier's solar plexus. A cry of pain exploded from his mouth.

I channeled a block of Murk around my fist and sent him to La-La Land with a brutal face smash.

Racha picked up her sword and came at me with her remaining two soldiers. Orbs of Brilliance formed in their palms and they took aim at me. I tried to channel a Murk shield, but daggers stabbed my brain and my concentration vanished. Apparently, my mind hadn't fully recovered.

If you can't win fair and square, fight dirty.

I snatched a glowing net of gems from the ceiling and flung it at the soldiers just as they fired beams of destruction. The magic refracted through the stones in a kaleidoscope of raw energy. Sorters and soldiers shouted and took cover as white energy zapped through the gems in a feedback loop, crackling and sizzling like lightning. One of the bolts caught a sorter in the back. She screamed and face-planted on the floor.

The gems took on lives of their own, circling in the air through some form of magnetic cohesion caused by the surges of magical energy. I grabbed the sword from one of the fallen soldiers and threw it at the gems. It smashed them apart, flipped, and caught Racha in the chest with the hilt. She grunted and smacked into a table behind her.

The soldier on her left bent down to help her up. I snatched a big gem, wound up, and pitched a zinger at his head. My aim was off and the rock caught him in the side of the neck. Another hail of gems rained on the soldiers as the sorters jumped into the fray. They quickly overwhelmed Racha and the two soldiers.

"There are three more," said the gem sorter Racha had threatened.

Elyssa appeared, dragging two unconscious soldiers by the feet. "Not anymore." She dropped her load and jabbed a thumb over her shoulder. "The last one is lying back there."

"Who are you?" asked the bald seraph.

"I'm Justin and this is Elyssa." I knelt next to the sorter who'd been struck in the back and turned her over. "This sera needs help."

"I am Eor." The seraph put a hand over the stricken sera's mouth. "Her breath is strong and steady. She will survive." He turned to the others. "Don't just stand there like frightened children. Secure the prisoners."

The sorters immediately set to work without another word, binding the soldiers in the shimmering nets they used to capture gems.

"Who are these soldiers?" Elyssa asked.

Eor scowled. "Land dwellers. Pirates." He stood over Racha, fists clenching and unclenching. "They sneaked aboard while we were trading in Guinesea and forced us to sort the gems for a very special kind they desired."

I looked at the single gem they'd found. It was rough and uncut, about the size of a baseball and crimson in hue. I picked it up and held it to the light. Thick liquid bubbled inside. "What's so special about this stone?"

Eor plucked the gem from my hand and set it on the table. "We call them bloodstones because they are red and filled with liquid aether." His voice took on the tone of someone lecturing a particularly slow-witted child.

Elyssa peered at the gem but didn't touch it. "Aether can be liquid?"

"Aether can take many forms," Eor said with a sigh.

While I appreciated Eor's bravery in the face of adversity, I didn't appreciate his curt tone. "What are bloodstones used for?"

He covered the red stone with cloth. "Nothing good, I can assure you. We are forbidden from keeping those we find and cast them into the sea." Eor set his arms akimbo. "Now, I suggest you explain why you're down here. I assume you're the companions of that nosy pair of land dwellers who've been on board for the past week."

Apparently, Illaena hadn't told him who we were.

The other gem sorters gathered around him, some regarding us with uncertainty, others with the same naked suspicion in Eor's glare.

"Yes, the nosy pair are our friends, Adam and Shelton, and we just saved you from pirates." I squared my shoulders and stepped into Eor's personal space. "How about you show a little appreciation?"

"I have little appreciation for land dwellers of any kind." Eor turned and looked at the bound forms of Racha and her comrades. "I also have no patience for a captain who allows such crimes to go on right under her nose."

"Illaena knew about the pirates," Elyssa said. "She forbid the other crew from entering the main hold."

Eor faced us again. "Then I believe a conversation with our captain is in order." He turned to the other sorters. "Take these prisoners to the vault and lock them inside. Once you've finished, eat and relax for the rest of the evening. I want you fresh and ready for sorting first thing in the morning."

His underlings nodded and obeyed with murmurs of obeisance, eyes to the floor like a bunch of whipped dogs. I felt sorry for anyone who had to work for this guy.

"Uh, don't drink the wine," Elyssa said. "There's something wrong with it."

The sorters looked from Elyssa to Eor as if asking permission to believe her.

Eor's eyes narrowed. "What's wrong with the wine?"

I scrambled for a reason. "It came from Guinesea. We think the land dwellers there put something in it."

He scowled. "Very well. Replace the wine in the decanter with the stores we brought from home." Eor huffed and spun on his heel. "I will speak with Illaena and get to the bottom of this."

Elyssa and I traded concerned looks.

"Well?" Eor stamped his foot impatiently. "Are you coming or not?"

"Y-yes, of course," I said and hurried to catch up.

The moment we stepped into the corridor outside the main hold, Adam and Shelton rounded the corner from the ramps, running at full speed. They skidded to a stop when they saw us following Eor and brought their staffs to bear.

I stood behind Eor and held up my hands, motioning desperately for my friends to put down their staffs before the gem sorter grew suspicious. "We stopped the pirates and saved the sorters," I said, clueing them into the new reality that we'd just saved the ship instead of hijacking it.

"Oh, great." Shelton quickly holstered his staff and slapped Adam on the wrist so he'd do the same. "What now?"

"We're going to speak with Illaena." I cleared my throat. "This is Eor."

"The nosy pair." Eor huffed again. "I suppose you'll be bothering everyone with your ceaseless questions again."

"Are we really that bad?" Adam asked.

"We sorters prefer keep to ourselves," Eor replied tartly. "Now, come." He went up the spiraling ramp and we followed.

"That dude's got a stick up his ass," Shelton said in English. "What happened in there?"

I explained quietly in our mother tongue. Eor frowned and looked back at us but didn't ask for a translation. Maybe he figured we spoke some strange land-lubber language. When we reached the top deck, I expected the crew to shout and charge the moment they saw us, but Illaena faced away from us at the rear of the ship, staring at the sea of clouds, while the rest of the crew steered the ship.

She stiffened as our footsteps approached and turned to see Eor and the rest of us. Much to my surprise, relief flooded her eyes. "You escaped the enemy?"

"If by enemy, you mean the land dwellers who held us hostage," Eor said. "This boy intervened and rescued us, then explained that you forbid anyone from coming into the sorting room." He narrowed his eyes and put his hands on his hips. "An explanation is in order, captain."

Illaena stiffened and once again assumed her reserved rigid exterior. "After you were taken hostage, one of the enemy soldiers informed me that if I refused to do as told, they would kill you. I saw no way to free you without great loss of life."

"Those are Brightling Empire soldiers," Elyssa said. "How did they sneak onboard without anyone noticing?"

"I suspect they were part of the group delivering supplies into the hold," Illaena said. "It's also possible they were inside some of the crates."

"However they did it, they took me and my people unaware." Eor's face darkened. "They forced us to look for bloodstones."

I hoped for a revelation about bloodstones from Illaena, but she left me hanging and maintained a stony expression.

"Is this why you refused to take us to Voltis?" Elyssa asked.

"No, but it is why I confined you to quarters." Illaena pursed her lips. "How did you escape?"

"That's not important," I said quickly. "What I'd like to know is what use bloodstones are to the Brightlings."

"I cannot say," Illaena replied. "We are instructed to discard any that we come across and forbidden from inquiring about them."

"Who would know?" I asked.

"Perhaps the Muhala Kajeen." She shifted to Eor. "Where are the enemy land dwellers now?"

"Locked in the vault," he said. "What will we do with them?"

"Interrogate them," Illaena said.

"I have some good spells for that," Adam said. "If you'd like, we can find out what they were up to."

Elyssa glared at the captain. "Or do you plan to lock us back in a room again?"

Illaena scowled. "I have not decided what to do with you." She touched the gem on her collar and waited for a response. When none came, she tapped it again. "Why are my fighters not responding?"

"Uh, they're kind of asleep," Elyssa said. "There was something in the wine that you got from Guinesea."

98

Illaena's eyes flashed with alarm. "Are they dead?"

"No, just snoozing," I said. "When we escaped our room we went to the galley for food and heard them talking about something being in the wine."

"We heard them passing out and ran inside to see if they were alive," Elyssa said. "One of your other fighters saw us doing that, and we had to knock her out because we didn't want you knowing we'd escaped."

Illaena scowled, but appeared to buy our story. "You escaped, found my fighters unconscious, but what pointed you to the sorting room?"

"Your fighters talked about how you forbid anyone from going to the sorting room and questioned why the ship wasn't headed for the Muhala Kajeen for the blessing of the first haul." I gave her a moment to absorb the information and continued. "That was when we went below to investigate."

"What an interesting maiden voyage this has been," Eor said wryly. "A breached hull, a dragon attack, a platoon of pirates, and a gallant rescue by prisoners."

"Agreed," Illaena said. "What troubles me the most is that the intruders are soldiers of the Brightling Empire."

"Kaelissa has broken the neutrality accord with the Mzodi," I said. "You should notify the Muahala Kajeen so she can warn other vessels passing through Brightling territories."

"Did you really speak with Xalara about us?" Elyssa asked, using the Muhala Kajeen's name.

Illaena shook her head. "No. The Muhala Kajeen is grateful for your assistance defeating Cephus and ending the dragon incursions. While she would never ally the Mzodi with either of the land dweller empires, she would not ban you from our ships."

"Does that mean we can go to Voltis?" I asked.

Eor's eyes flashed with excitement. "Voltis? We have finally won approval to explore the great unknown?"

Illaena's jaw tightened. "I think it a fool's errand, but I will speak with Xalara."

"Like, right now?" I said, pointing down at the deck to indicate I wanted to hear the conversation with my own ears.

"I will confer with her in my cabin." She pointed at me and Elyssa. "You two may accompany me inside."

"What about us?" Shelton said. "I promise we won't look at your aether charts."

"Wait here with Eor," Illaena said. "We will return shortly."

"I pray for good news." Eor rubbed his hands together vigorously. "Can you imagine the gems inside the Voltis Maelstrom? It is a gem sorter's dream come true!"

Elyssa and I followed Illaena down a level and into a large cabin. A wide crystal table occupied the center and a cloud bed nestled against the hull in the back where crystal windows provided a breathtaking view of the sky. A shelf held an assortment of devices, most of them embedded with aether stones.

Staring out the back window, I switched to incubus vision. Invisible aether phased into view, small clouds of it floating past, and tiny lines threading through the crystal structure of the ship. But what I really wanted to see flowed behind and around us, carrying us in its current—a river of brilliant aether.

I switched back to normal vision and looked expectantly at Illaena. "Well?"

The captain tapped the communication gem on her collar. A chime responded. "This is Illaena. I would speak with Xalara."

"One moment, please," said a cheery female voice.

Seconds later, Illaena's gem projected the image of a tall woman with long brown hair woven in tight braids. A strong Italian-styled nose hung over a wide mouth with lips a shade too thin, and between cheeks a little too high for my tastes. Xalara resembled my inner vision of an Amazon warrior, though her dark eyes softened her harder features.

The Muhala Kajeen smiled warmly. "How goes the maiden voyage, Illaena?"

"Not well," the captain replied. "We suffered a breached hull deep in the northern vortexes and fought off a dragon."

Xalara's smiled faded. "A usual affair these days."

"My story grows worse," Illaena said. "We stopped in Guinesea for repairs but unbeknownst to me, were boarded by land dwellers of the Brightling Empire. After we set off to rendezvous with Justin Slade and his companions, a soldier named Racha came to me in the night and told me our gem sorters would be executed if we did not do as they said."

Xalara's eyes flashed and the kind leader was gone, replaced by a warrior princess. "How dare they! What were their demands?"

"Bloodstones," Illaena said.

Xalara's jaw worked back and forth. "How could they possibly know to seek bloodstones?"

"Do you know what they are?" I asked.

She blinked as if noticing me for the first time. "Greetings, Justin Slade. Illaena did not reveal your presence to me until now."

"Apologies, Xalara." Illaena bowed. "I meant to tell you at once, but the story of this voyage tainted my manners."

"All is forgiven," Xalara said and nodded at me. "To answer your question, bloodstones were once used for their healing properties, but another use for them was discovered during the reign of King Thussor, great grandson of Ussor."

The name conjured images of the ancient Seraphim I knew as Fjoeruss. Kaelissa had hinted he might actually be one of the original Seraphim, Ussor, and that he might also be my mega-great grand-pappy.

"And that is?" I asked.

"When channeled a certain way, the bloodstone links the conscious minds of one individual to another." Xalara shivered. "The initiator can then force the subject to obey her will."

Elyssa gasped. "Mind control?"

"Insidious," Illaena said.

Xalara shook her head sadly. "The Fallen, Gallifer, Sithain, and Purah, discovered this perverted use of bloodstones. They stole Thussor's mind and nearly destroyed the empire."

I probably shouldn't have changed subjects but my nerd side kicked in. "You mean to tell me there are fallen angels?"

"The Fallen were the children of the original bloodlines who forsook their lineage and took their own names," Xalara said. "Shunned by society, they left Azoris and vanished for centuries, only to reappear with their plot to destroy the empire."

"Are they still alive?" I asked.

"Perhaps." Xalara shook her head. "In the early days of the Mzodi, the first Muhala Kajeen forbade the harvesting of bloodstones and required their immediate disposal should they be found."

"Kaelissa must be behind the kidnapping of your sorters," I said.

Illaena and Xalara frowned.

"Why would Kaelissa have anything to do with this?" Illaena asked. "We have traded fairly with her for years, taking her unwanted daughters in exchange for gems."

"Because she's the new Brightling Empress," Elyssa said. "She was probably alive during Thussor's reign, and I'll bet she knows what the bloodstones can do."

"Hot damn," I murmured. "Kaelissa is out to take over the world with mind control." I suddenly knew why she was going to Voltis.

Chapter 12

Elyssa's eyes widened with realization. "You think—"

"Yeah." Things suddenly made a lot more sense. "Eor seems to think Voltis is a great place to fish for gems."

"It is the largest, most intense maelstrom in the realm," Xalara said.

"Which means more bloodstones for the harvesting," Elyssa said. "Kaelissa's secret weapon is mind control!"

"And it'll give her all the edge she needs to take over this realm and the next." I blew out a long breath. "This is even worse than I thought."

"Maybe that's how she became Empress so fast," Elyssa said. "Maybe Arturo is already brainwashed."

"Maybe, maybe not." I shifted to Xalara. "How many bloodstones typically turn up in a haul?"

"None," Illaena answered. "That is because you can only find them in the core of the most violent maelstroms. On the rare occasion we discover a bloodstone in our normal haul, it is because it was ejected from the core."

Xalara's eyes narrowed. "You mean to say those soldiers forced you to fish the core?"

Illaena nodded. "I only took them to the fringes."

"And your people netted one bloodstone," I said. "Racha wanted three."

"Why does she want three?" Elyssa said. "If they plan to fish more from Voltis, why not go straight there instead?"

As usual, Elyssa had a point. I took a figurative step back and wondered what Racha would do if she had three bloodstones. That was when it occurred to me she was just a thug. "Kaelissa wants three. That number is too specific to be some number she plucked at random."

"Obviously she wishes to control the minds of three people," Illaena said.

Xalara tapped a finger on her chin. "She already controls the Brightling throne. Who else must she tether to her will?"

"Maybe she wants to control the new leaders of the Darkling government once they elect another Trivectus." Elyssa's gaze seemed to turn inward for a moment. "Three bloodstones for three leaders."

I took another step back. "Are bloodstones a stepping stone, or her end game? The Brightlings have no way to fish Voltis without Mzodi ships, right?"

"That is correct," Xalara said. "They have no ships of their own."

"If Bloodstones are her endgame, I think she would've taken the *Falcheen* straight to Voltis instead of fishing the northern vortexes." I tapped a finger on my chin. "If bloodstones are a means to reach her endgame, then there's something else we're missing."

"In other words, there's something else in Voltis she's after," Elyssa said.

I nodded.

"Regardless of her intentions," Xalara said, "I will not stand idly by and let this breach of neutrality go unchallenged."

Illaena's eyes sparked with worry. "What are you saying, Muhala Kajeen?"

"The *Xanda* is in port in Zbura," Xalara said. "I will ask Captain Nin to speak with our official contacts there and lodge a complaint."

"Do you really think a complaint will do any good?" Elyssa said.

"Sadly, no." Worry clouded Xalara's face. "But I must exhaust all diplomatic means at our disposal before discontinuing trade with the Brightling Empire."

I'd really hoped she might go a step further and ally with us, but this was at least a step in the right direction for our cause. "Xalara, I believe answers to Kaelissa's plan lie within Voltis."

Xalara's eyes snapped to me. "Our ancestors journeyed into Voltis thousands of years ago. The great exploration ship, *Zhnosh*, sought to map every corner of the realm. When they returned from within Voltis, more than half the crew lost, the first Muhala Kajeen declared it a forbidden zone."

"What was inside?" I asked.

Xalara shook her head. "They never reached the core before they turned back."

My heart sank. Kaelissa had to know something we didn't. There might be more to Voltis than bloodstones. "What if the king of all bloodstones is in the core and allows Kaelissa to mind control everyone at once?"

"I pray to god that's a figment over your overactive imagination," Elyssa said.

All I knew was that we had to convince Xalara that passage to Voltis was a matter of life and death for the entire realm. "Elyssa, show her the map."

Elyssa set her phone on the table and projected the map with the Brightling troop concentrations in southern Cabala. In Eden it would be about a hundred miles east of Los Angeles, but in Seraphina, it was right on the coast since the land mass was smaller. Elyssa had drawn dashed lines to indicate possible troop movements, some leading into Voltis, others dipping southwest to head straight for Tarissa.

"Commander Borathen believes the Brightlings are gathering troops to invade Voltis." I traced a finger along the red line. "Elyssa and I found messages from Primarion Arturo, leader of the Brightling archangels, that indicate there is something in Voltis that will allow the Brightlings to control this realm."

Elyssa switched to the video she'd recorded of the messages.

"Inside Voltis," Xalara murmured. "What could possibly exist at the core?"

"Perhaps Kaelissa is simply mad," Illaena said. "There is nothing in Voltis but death. I have read the history and know it to be true. Let the insane Brightlings dash their army upon the fire and ice that awaits."

"This might be a stupid question," Elyssa said, "but why haven't the land dwellers built ships like yours?"

"They have tried," Illaena said proudly, "but they lack the proper gems and techniques to make them work."

"And if they ever tried to capture one of our ships, we can remotely destroy them," Xalara said.

"So you could preserve your monopoly on gem harvesting." I brushed an index finger across the top the other. "Shame on you."

"It would seem there is more to Voltis than what we know," Xalara said. "Kaelissa is one of the oldest Seraphim alive. Perhaps she knows the secrets hidden in the core. What she seeks may pose a threat to us all." She turned to Illaena. "I authorize an expedition inside the maelstrom."

The captain's eyes went wide. "We will be destroyed!"

Xalara shook her head. "The crew of the original expedition made a map."

Illaena blinked. "Why is there no mention of this in the history?"

"Because Voltis is a forbidden zone," Xalara said. "Why would we make public a map that might encourage rogues?"

Illaena didn't have a reply for that.

"The map, of course, does not go all the way to the center since the *Znosh* turned back." Xalara pursed her lips. "I know the loss of your first command weighs heavily, Illaena. If this is too much, I will find another captain."

"No." Illaena stiffened and her chin tilted up. "This time I will not fail."

Elyssa's troubled gaze met mine.

"You used to be a captain of another ship?" I asked.

"That is none of your concern, Minister Slade." Xalara smiled as if to soften her words. "Now, leave us so I may confer with my captain."

I nodded. "Of course. Thank you, Xalara."

"Do not thank me for a suicide mission," she replied. "May the streams carry you swift and safe to the heart of the storm."

I wasn't sure what to say to that, so I muttered a diplomatic, "Uh, thanks."

Elyssa gathered her arcphone and we left the cabin. Shelton, Adam, and Eor practically ran up to us, eyes eager.

"Will I finally see Voltis?" Eor asked. "If I could harvest but one gem from her stormy heart, I would die a happy seraph."

"Voltis, here we come," I said.

And lo, there was much rejoicing that day. Eor pranced and capered like a lunatic in celebration while the rest of us wondered if we should call a medic or an insane asylum.

Eager though I was to get to the bottom of the mystery, I hoped Illaena's captaining skills were up to the task. Knowing that she'd lost a ship before didn't exactly inspire confidence.

Adam tore his eyes from Eor's cavorting form. "What convinced Xalara?" Adam asked us.

I repeated the conversation, including my ultimate theory that a massive bloodstone capable of mind-controlling the entire world was at the core.

Adam's forehead wrinkled. "Man, I don't know what to think of all this. Why force this crew to fish for bloodstones if they're plentiful in Voltis? Something tells me Kaelissa is after something else."

I couldn't disagree.

"What's the plan?" Shelton said. "Are we plowing straight into the storm or checking out Kaelissa's troops in Cabala first? Maybe they know something we don't."

"I'll have to ask Illaena." It might make sense to look around before plunging headfirst into danger.

The captain emerged from her cabin after an extended period of time, her face a bit paler than normal. "Once we finish repairs and awaken the crew, we are ready for launch."

I decided to voice my concerns to her right away. "We should sweep the ocean between Voltis and Azoris to see how Kaelissa plans to get inside Voltis."

"That will not be necessary," Illaena said. "Xalara spoke with the captains of the *Xanda*, *Ptarn*, *Akata*, and *Dtirn*, all of which have recently passed through Brightling territory. They will be our eyes and ears."

I dared feel optimistic about our chances. "That's great."

Illaena scowled. "I do not like taking sides."

"Yeah, did you like it when Racha and her buddies took hostages on your own ship?" I gave her a hard stare. "The Brightlings broke neutrality first, Illaena. You have nothing to feel bad about."

Her eyes got a faraway look in them. "I nearly lost another crew to Brightling land dwellers. Now I fear to lose them to Voltis."

I didn't know what to say to that, but I sure hoped she was wrong about Voltis killing us all. "Where's the secret entrance to the maelstrom?"

Illaena swallowed hard. "The Voltis Maelstrom is a convergence of violent elements—volcanic eruptions, wind storms, lightning, ice, and massive water spouts, all made even more deadly by the aether vortexes. We will have to spiral inside the maelstrom to reach the end of the trail left by the *Znosh*."

"Spiral inside it?" I asked.

"There is no path straight through," she said. "We must enter on the southeastern side and weave our way through danger."

"Holy farting fairies," Shelton muttered. "I don't like the sound of that."

"It doesn't matter," Adam said. "This is a race."

I nodded. "And we have to win it."

"We will fish the five elements," Eor said excitedly. "The greatest gems in the realm will be ours!"

Illaena glared at him. "At least some of us are looking forward to the journey." She turned to her first mate. "Tahlee, set us down for repairs, and check on the well-being of our soldiers."

I gave a knowing look to Shelton and Adam who hurriedly excused themselves so they could unlock the room with the slumbering fighters inside.

Tahlee cried out orders to the deck crew and the ship shifted toward a bare stretch of valley.

"Justin, once we make land, you will make sure our unwelcome guests are off the ship before we leave tomorrow morning." Illaena patted a dagger at her hip. "I would gladly execute them, but we have no time for trials or tribulations."

"I'll start their interrogations right away," I said.

"Eor." Illaena snapped her fingers to summon the seraph back from fantasy land. "Continue the sorting. Bring any bloodstones you find directly to me."

His eyes went wide. "To you? But we are instructed to discard them in deep ocean water at once!"

"Xalara wishes to set aside that rule for now," she said.

"I will have to hear it from her mouth," Eor said.

"Then contact her directly." Illaena thumped his chest with the back of her hand. "Do it now before I throw you off the ship for insubordination."

"Well, I never," Eor grumbled. "Just because you're captain doesn't mean you can toss me overboard like so much rubbish."

Illaena bared her teeth in a feral grin. "Actually, it does, gem sorter." She held his stubborn gaze for a long moment before he frowned and turned away.

Illaena stared at his back and said to me, "I will be in my cabin." With that, she vanished back inside.

Eor tapped his gem and waited for the chime. "This is Eor. I would speak with the Muhala Kajeen about an urgent matter."

"At once," the cheery voice replied.

Xalara's weary voice sounded from the gem. "I assume you have contacted me about the bloodstones, Eor."

"Yes, Muhala—"

"They are not to be discarded," she said. "Do I make myself clear?"

"Of course," Eor said uncertainly. "But—"

"There are no buts, Eor. Do as you're told." The gem chimed as Xalara cut the connection.

He harrumphed and planted his hands on his hips. "Rude!"

I led Elyssa away toward the aft ramp below decks as the *Falcheen* glided in for a landing. "We need to find out more about these bloodstones. I don't like the idea of someone being able to control my mind."

"It's terrifying," Elyssa said. "What do you think Kaelissa wants with them?"

"I don't know." We reached the bottom deck and headed for the main hold. "We need to check in with your father and make sure he's okay."

"I've been trying," Elyssa said. "I can't get through to him or Tarissa."

"I hope he made it." I went inside the hold and heard Racha shouting curses at the top of her lungs.

Elyssa grimaced. "This is going to be so much fun."

"Tell me about it." I steeled my nerves and headed for the five Brightling prisoners.

The sorters had wrapped each soldier in an individual net, binding their limbs tight and rendering them completely immobile from the neck down.

"You!" Racha's dark eyes locked onto me like homing missiles. "You will release me and my people at once, or I promise there will be blood."

I sat down on a stool and put on an easy smile. "You know, I almost regret not letting you cut off Eor's hand."

"It appears our Empress was right about the scum they allow on these *ships*." Racha sunk her teeth into the last word. "You are the boy who cheated our beloved Daelissa from her true destiny."

It seemed I wouldn't have to press her too hard for answers since she'd already confirmed who gave her the orders to seize the gem sorters on the ship. "Tell me, Racha, were you in Eden for the war?"

Her lips trembled with anger. "No, but my beloved husband was in the Zburan Legion. Your cowardly troops lured them into an ambush and murdered them."

I almost countered her accusation with logic, but saw the rabid loyalty burning in her eyes. Racha was the sort of person who didn't need a bloodstone used on them. Kaelissa owned this sera, lock, stock, and barrel.

Using a technique I'd learned from Elyssa's brother, Michael, I disrupted her thoughts with a sudden change in subject. "What's in Voltis?"

Racha flinched. "How do—" she clamped her mouth shut and shook her head. "I don't know what you're talking about, boy."

110

I shifted again. "Why does Kaelissa need three bloodstones?"

The soldier frowned and blinked as if confused, then stiffened and glared at me. "That is the business of the Empress."

I channeled a ball of Murk in my left hand and was immediately punished with stabbing sensations in my head. I repressed a wince and slapped an opaque barrier over Racha's face and ears, covering everything but her nose so she couldn't speak or listen. A scream grated in her throat and she flailed against the netting holding her in place.

"I'm going to give the rest of you a chance to answer." I offered the other soldiers a reassuring smile.

"Never," growled a short, beefy seraph with more hair than a big brown bear.

I encased his head with Murk and repeated myself to the others: "Why does Kaelissa need three bloodstones?"

The tall nerdy one who'd gotten on Racha's case earlier cleared his throat. "We were only told what to do, not why. We weren't even told that the gems we seek are called bloodstones."

"It's true," said the next soldier when I turned my gaze on her.

I stifled a groan. I'd hoped to learn something about Kaelissa's mind-control plans, but it appeared our prisoners were as ignorant as the rest of us.

Chapter 13

"What's your name?" I asked the nerdy seraph.

"Lazan," he replied.

I stepped closer to him. "Lazan, why are Brightling troops gathering in Cabala?"

"Most of the legions on or near Pjurna were recalled to Azoris," he said. "We don't know why."

"Is there something to fight in the Voltis Maelstrom?"

The three soldiers looked at each other with wrinkled foreheads. Lazan turned his head back to me. "I haven't heard any rumors about Voltis."

One of the others growled. "Don't answer their questions."

Lazan looked back at him. "What do you suggest we do, Tator?"

I slapped another opaque barrier around Tator's face so he wouldn't interfere and Elyssa continued the questioning. "How many troops remain in Pjurna?"

Lazan looked uneasy. "I'm no traitor. I can't give you that information."

I covered his head in Murk, leaving holes for his nose, and did the same for the other soldier. Pinching the bridge of my nose, I gave myself a moment to recover from the knife stabs in my skull.

Elyssa wrapped an arm around my shoulder. "Are you okay?"

I nodded. "Yeah. I really need to feed off a human. My magic side is recovering more slowly than I thought."

"You can feed off me," she said.

I squeezed her hand and kissed her cheek. "I know, but I'm worried if I feed too much it could have adverse side effects."

"Just take a little." She held a finger slightly apart from her thumb. "I'm sure that'll be okay."

Seraphim didn't need to feed as they naturally drew on the aether in the air around them, but Daelissa had discovered that sucking human soul essence supercharged her powers. I could probably get by without leeching from Elyssa, but it might delay my recovery. I also needed her so I could refuel my demon powers and feeding both sides of my dual nature from her might be too much for her to handle.

"It might be better to feed on Adam on Shelton since"—I shrugged—"I kinda need you to keep my incubus happy."

She pursed her lips. "Can't you feed on Seraphim?"

I noticed the gem sorters looking at us curiously as we spoke in English and wondered if any would volunteer to feed my inner demon. Humans didn't usually notice if I latched onto them, but Seraphim had a sixth sense about it, even if they'd never seen a Daemos in their life.

"Possibly." My head felt a little better, so I dissolved the Murk around Lazan's head.

He blinked and sucked in a deep breath through his mouth.

"None of your companions can see or hear our conversation," I said. "Tell me how many troops are left in Pjurna."

"As I said, I'm no traitor." Lazan's chin tilted up defiantly.

It was obvious we weren't going to get much else from him, so I let him be. Adam and Shelton walked in moments later, faces flush.

"We unlocked the door to the room holding the soldiers," Shelton told me. "Hopefully, Illaena bought your story about the spiked wine."

Adam looked at the covered faces of the prisoners. "New interrogation technique?"

I shrugged. "Racha and her buddy"—I pointed to the individuals in question—"won't answer any questions." I nodded toward Lazan. "He's been moderately helpful."

"I have a couple of spells that might loosen tongues," Adam said. "Want me to give them a try?"

I shrugged. "As long as they don't violate the Geneva Conventions or anything."

"Hell, we don't even know if they'll work on Seraphim," Shelton said. He stared at the prisoners. "But we'll give it a shot."

Lazan's worried eyes flicked back and forth among us. Even though he didn't understand English, he knew we were talking about him. I hoped he had something useful to tell us.

We finished the interrogations three hours later, not much more informed than before. Adam's spell didn't work quite as planned, making the prisoners behave like drunks. None of them knew how many troops were left on Pjurnan soil, but believed most of the skeleton force remaining had relocated to a fortress on Guinesea.

If I'd learned anything, it was that Racha was a depressed drunk. Much to the surprise of her underlings, she spent most of her interrogation raging about her dead mate and crying.

Elyssa, Shelton, Adam, and I gladly left the main hold and went upstairs for food and more importantly, wine.

Elyssa held up her crystal glass and looked at the blue liquid inside. "Now I understand why my mother always had a glass of wine in her hand when my brothers and I were rug rats."

"Smart lady," Shelton said with a grin. "Kids are hell."

Adam grinned. "You'll get to find out firsthand, buddy."

Shelton paled and gulped. "Shut your mouth before I faint."

We burst into laughter and I held up my glass for a toast. "To a bunch of little Sheltons."

"To little Sheltons," Adam and Elyssa said.

"Not anytime soon." Shelton gulped half his glass and glared at us. "You're a bunch of jackasses."

Adam winked. "Pot, meet kettle."

The gem on Elyssa's Templar armor chimed. Her eyes flashed wide with hope as she touched it. "Hello?"

"I'm in Tarissa," Thomas said calmly, as if he'd just taken a walk around the block. "Did you make it to the *Falcheen*?"

Elyssa wiped a tear from her eye and nodded. "Yes. Why can't I see you?"

The link crackled with static. "…kind of interference. The communication gems on Mzodi ships work better. We believe Kohval is trying to cut off communications to and from Tarissa."

"Why would he do that?" Elyssa asked.

"Mzodi ships spotted Gallix Legion leaving their positions in the west," Thomas replied grimly. He said something else, but static consumed it.

"Please repeat," Elyssa said.

"Scouts report Victrix Legion is moving units south toward the capital." Thomas paused as if to let that sink in. "I think they both want to take control of the city while it's weak."

"The Brightlings have withdrawn most of their Pjurnan troops to Guinesea and beyond," Elyssa said. "Kohval and Meera must realize that without the Brightling threat, they're free to move their own troops."

With no defined leaders at the helm, it appeared Meera and Kohval had set their sights on a larger prize than the territories they'd guarded for so long. It seemed they wanted the whole enchilada. "Are we looking at civil war?" I asked.

"It looks likely," Thomas said. "Flava is recruiting citizens to reform the Tarissan Legion, but the friction between them and some of the factions from Eden are causing problems."

Hints of trouble between our people and the natives had surfaced even before we left. "Let me guess—the vampires."

"Yes, but also the lycans and felycans," Thomas said. "They insist on hunting animals for food which is something the locals despise."

Elyssa grimaced. "How bad is the friction?"

"Even though the hunting has been done outside of the city, there have been protests." Thomas grunted. "If they can't get past these differences, we may have to abandon the city."

"Abandon it?" My jaw went slack. "Why?"

"I won't place our army between Meera and Kohval," he said sternly. "Our obligation to unify Seraphina hinges on Darkling unity. So far they've done the exact opposite."

"In other words," I said, "we liberated Pjurna from one dictator only to open it up to two wannabes."

"I want to go back to Eden," Elyssa said. "It wasn't supposed to be like this."

"Even if the Alabaster Arch on Kdosh worked, I think leaving Seraphina in this state would be a bad idea," Thomas said. "Kaelissa's power play is the most dangerous right now. Meanwhile, we may have to let Meera and Kohval fight over who controls Pjurna. If you don't stop Kaelissa from reaching Voltis, she'll be able to march over the bodies left from the Darkling civil war and wrest control from the weakened victor."

"We'll have a unified Seraphina, but under the wrong ruler," Elyssa said. "Kaelissa will pick up where her daughter left off and, once she figures out how to repair the arches, invade Eden."

"Precisely." The static in the background grew louder, drowning out whatever Thomas said next and then the comm link went quiet.

"Dad?" Elyssa let a few beats pass and shook her head. "I guess we lost him."

"I'm here." Thomas's calm but unexpected reply made me flinch in surprise. "The Mzodi allowed me to use one of their amplification gems. Before I lose you again, debrief me on what happened after I left you."

Elyssa quickly and efficiently summed up our recent experiences.

"Bloodstones," Thomas murmured. "This doesn't bode well."

"I have a feeling if we don't stop Kaelissa, Kohval, and Meera, we'd better find a nice remote part of Seraphina to settle in." I blew out a breath. "This is not how I envisioned things at all."

"I'm scheduled to meet with Xalara tomorrow morning," Thomas said. "I suspect she'll tell me if the *Yalaran* was successful in its diplomatic mission with the Brightlings."

"Why do you think Kaelissa wants three bloodstones?" I asked.

Thomas remained quiet for a moment before answering. "Your guess about controlling a new Trivectus is a good theory, but it's also just as likely she has bigger fish in mind."

I struggled to think of anyone. "Like whom?"

"You, for example," he said grimly. "If she wants a weapon to help her take power, you'd be a good target. She might also consider me since I control the Eden Legion."

The thought of losing my mind like that sent spiders crawling down my spine. "I need to know more about how bloodstones work and if the effects can be reversed."

"I'll also put a contingency plan in place in case I'm compromised," Thomas said. "If you're compromised, then we're all in trouble."

Elyssa's worried eyes met mine. "Should we abort the mission to Voltis and come back to Tarissa?"

"No." Thomas's voice was resolute. "Kaelissa is the biggest threat and we need to know what she's after. I had the skyways leading into Tarissa deactivated so it'll take Meera and Kohval at least a week to reach the city using cloudlets."

Elyssa smiled proudly. "Good thinking. That'll buy us the time we need."

"Find out what Kaelissa wants in Voltis and return to Tarissa," Thomas said. "Keep me apprised if possible, though I suspect the communications interference will get worse as you travel northeast into the ocean."

Elyssa stiffened and almost reflexively saluted. "Yes, sir."

"And Elyssa?" Thomas's voice grew softer. "Be careful. Borathen out." The link chimed off."

"Holy fartburgers," Shelton said. "How in the hell are we supposed to stop Kaelissa and a civil war?"

"If she takes Pjurna, she'll have no problem wiping out the army we brought from Eden," Adam said. "Once she figures out how to reopen the Alabaster Arch, our realm is toast."

"It's time we stopped thinking these defeatist thoughts and figured out how to stop Kaelissa." Elyssa set her arms akimbo and stared down Shelton and Adam. "If all else fails, we have a bloodstone to use on her."

"We don't even know how to use it," Shelton said.

"Then we'll just have to figure it out." I slapped him on the back. "After all, that's what I have you two for, right?"

117

Shelton looked at me dubiously. "Well, we could run our analyzer spells on it. Maybe that'll turn up some answers."

"We should get started right away," Adam said.

I tapped my gem and thought of the person I wanted to contact. "Maybe my mom has some answers."

The link chimed open, but the connection was even worse than the one with Thomas. "Justin?" Mom's worried voice emanated from the gem.

"Hey, Mom—"

"Thomas just contacted me told me where you're headed," she said, voice trembling with worry. "The Voltis Maelstrom?"

"Yes, but—"

"Are you insane?" Mom's voice crackled with disbelief. "I know you've fought against the odds and won before, but Voltis is the most dangerous place in this realm. There's a reason no one dares venture inside."

"The Mzodi have a way in," I said. "We'll be fine."

Mom sniffled. "I'm sorry. I know you can take care of yourself, but—"

"It's because of Ivy, isn't it?" My sister was trapped all alone in Eden while the rest of her family was here.

"Nothing has gone right since we've been here, Justin." Mom sighed. "It's like we weren't meant to interfere with Seraphina."

"I know, but we have to keep pushing and do our best." I caught a sad look from Elyssa. "The reason I contacted you is because I need to know about bloodstones."

Mom gasped. "Bloodstones?"

"You've heard of them?"

"They were banned long ago and for good reason, Justin." Mom sounded like she was scolding me for riding a bike with no helmet. "I hope you aren't planning to use one."

Technically, I had thought of it, but didn't want to disappoint my mother. "No, of course not, but it seems Kaelissa has plans to use them. I need to know how they work and if they can be countered."

"Daelissa once sought bloodstones," Mom said, "but the Mzodi refused. I only know a little about them because I studied the ancient legends. The Fallen subverted the will of King Thussor and caused the civil war that split the Darklings and Brightlings apart."

That part really got my attention. "Hang on—you're saying the two factions were getting along until then?"

"The population of Seraphina had increased greatly by the third generation—the first generation to realize that they were no longer equally powerful in both Brilliance and Murk, but had an affinity for one or the other." Mom had switched to the story time voice that used to lull me to sleep. "In those days, a king ruled, though his decisions could be reviewed and overturned by the Quinvectus, a body of five representatives."

"Kind of like a Caesar and senate?" Elyssa asked.

"Precisely." Mom's holographic image flickered on in front of us and she flinched. "Oh, I guess the signal strength improved enough to allow visuals."

I grinned. "It's good to see you, Mom."

She held out a hand as if wanting to touch me and a look of regret crossed her face. "It's wonderful to see you too, son." Mom took a deep breath as if steeling herself. "I'm sorry if I sound emotional, but I can't stop thinking about Ivy."

Neither could I, but unless our people found a way to reopen the Alabaster Arch, there wasn't a damned thing we could do about it. "Me too, Mom."

Mom looked down. "Three Darklings and two Brightlings comprised the Quinvectus. When Sithain, Gallifer, and Purah took over King Thussor's mind, they did everything they could to undermine the Darklings."

"Did they hate Darklings?" Elyssa asked.

Mom shrugged. "I don't think so. I believe they saw a difference to exploit and only wished to divide the empire and make it easier to take power."

"While I think this is really interesting, what I really want to know is how to use and counter a bloodstone." I tapped a finger on my temple. "Can I protect myself against a takeover?"

"A bloodstone links the souls of the user and target," she said. "I don't know how to protect against it. I believe it requires channeling through the stone and into the subject, but couldn't tell you the specifics."

"How do you rescue someone who's under the control of a bloodstone?" Elyssa asked.

"You must destroy the stone," Mom said. "Unfortunately, aether stones are extremely durable. I don't know how to destroy one."

"I assume the bloodstone controlling Thussor was destroyed?" I asked.

"Yes, a Mzodi was able to do it." Mom sighed . "Unfortunately, he'd been under the influence for too long and his mind never recovered." Her forehead wrinkled with worry. "The best advice I can give you is that if you ever find a bloodstone, throw it into the deepest part of the ocean."

In other words, we had nothing to counter a bloodstone and still no idea how to use them. The best thing we could hope for was that Kaelissa never found another one.

Chapter 14

After ending the call with Mom I gave the others a hopeless look. "Looks like we're on our own with this one."

Shelton, as usual, had something to say about it. "A bloodstone enters a bar. There was no counter."

That earned him a groan from the rest of us.

"You need to go back to joke school," Adam said. "That was indescribably awful."

Shelton thrust out his chin. "It was a classic and you know it."

"Maybe you and Adam should start analyzing the bloodstone," I said, "while Elyssa and I offer prayers and incense to the gods in the hopes that we can find a way to prevent these things from latching onto our minds."

"We'll do what we can," Adam said.

Elyssa and I returned to the top deck and looked over the side where the ship had been damaged. The hull looked good as new aside from a few scratches that the crew polished by channeling magic through various gems.

"How do they figure out what gems work best for certain purposes?" I wondered aloud.

Elyssa tapped a finger on the railing. "Probably the same kind of people who decided boiled okra was edible and not a little green pod full of barfy slime."

I cast a curious look at her. "I never knew you were so passionate about okra."

"*Boiled* okra," she said. "I'd rather eat raw snails."

I gagged at the thought. "I'll remember that."

121

Eor thrust himself between us and looked down. "Thank goodness they're almost finished. I can hardly wait to embark on this epic voyage."

After I recovered from the mini-heart attack of his sudden appearance I decided to ask him a few pointed questions about gems. "Can you explain to me how gems are sorted and how you know their purpose?"

"Absolutely not," he said. "It takes years to learn all the types and how to properly enchant them. I would never reveal ancient Mzodi secrets to a land dweller."

I resisted the impulse to punch him and fell back on a pleasant smile. "I'm not looking for trade secrets, just a general understanding."

Eor narrowed his eyes and pursed his lips so tight, they turned white. "Very well, I suppose I can indulge you." He removed a light green stone from within his robes. "First, you must understand that color doesn't matter. Aether is neither limited to the ultraviolet of Murk nor the white of Brilliance, but spans an infinite rainbow. What land dwellers refer to as gems are technically called aetherium. True gems are geological formations—stone. Unfortunately, the ignorant masses think aethids resemble gems, so that's what they call them."

I tried to get a handle on what he was saying. "So an aetherium gem is called an aethid?"

"Precisely," he said. "Just as you have diamonds, rubies, garnets, and names for all the various precious stones, so do we have names for different sorts of aethids. As for sorting, we channel into an aethid to discover its inner structure. This helps determine what enchantments would be most fitting."

Eor held up the gem and channeled a small shaft of white energy inside. "Aethids either resist energy or amplify it, depending on the way they crystalized. Some are more multi-purpose, while others are fit for specific tasks."

"How do the ones that make cloth work?" Elyssa asked.

"Those aethids soften energy while also breaking a single channel into tiny threads which can be woven together in different configurations." He produced an opaque brown gem from his fanny

122

pack and held it up. "If you want tougher material, this type of crystal hardens aether and produces coarse threads."

It made sense, though I wasn't particularly interested in digging much deeper. "What makes a bloodstone operate the way it does?"

Eor's gaze darkened. "That is not for you to know."

"I need to know if I can protect myself from one," I said imploringly. "Believe me, I'm a prime target for mind control."

"I find that hard to believe," Eor said disdainfully. "You're but a boy."

"A *boy* who saved you from Brightling soldiers," I reminded him. "A boy Xalara spoke with in private."

He squinted and looked back and forth between me and Elyssa as if that might help him see what was so special about us.

I tried a little ego stroking to see how far it got me. "I've heard you're the best gem sorter in the entire fleet. If anyone knows about bloodstones, that would be you."

Eor quirked an eyebrow. "Did Xalara tell you that?"

"What do you think?" I waggled my eyebrows.

"Well, I have long suspected my superior sorting and management skills earned me the most coveted position on the newest ship in the fleet." He ran a hand through his short brown hair. "Xalara is correct, of course. Whenever there's an aethid that cannot be identified, it is brought to me, no matter what that fool Hudor tells people."

"Is Hudor also a sorter?" Elyssa asked.

"He likes to think he's the best because he's stationed on the *Uorion*." Eor wiggled a finger side to side and scowled. "As anyone knows, the flagship rarely fishes the maelstroms. The real sorters are out here on the frontiers." He jabbed a finger north. "The real sorters strike forth into the very heart of danger. Once we've cast our nets in Voltis, I am certain I'll discover gems the likes of which none have ever seen!" Eor struck a grand pose, arms akimbo, nose and chin tilted skyward.

Elyssa looked at me and rolled her eyes. "I'll bet that means you know a lot about bloodstones."

"Indeed," he said. "I took the time to study several before disposal."

"What can you tell me about them?" I asked.

Eor lowered his gaze back to us mere mortals and frowned. "Though I don't believe you're as important as you think you are, I can certainly ease your mind." He folded his arms and assumed a lecturing tone. "Bloodstones must be used in very close proximity, about ten feet or less, to be effective. I can't be certain how long it would take for one to finish the soul-linking process, but I would guess several minutes."

I wasn't sure if I should prod him for specifics, so I let him continue at his own pace.

"Therefore, the best counter to a bloodstone is to stay out of range." Eor might have looked down on us just then if we weren't taller.

"Let's say I'm captured and they start using the stone on me," I said. "What then?"

Eor sneezed and rubbed his nose vigorously for a moment. "I would say you have little chance of retaining your mind."

Elyssa's eyes flashed with alarm. "How do you destroy a bloodstone?"

"That, you see, is a rather complicated question," Eor said. "Aetherium is not easily destroyed by magical means since it is a solid, compressed form of magical energy." He tapped the brown rock against the railing. "Formed by intense pressure, they are also difficult to destroy by physical means."

"Like diamonds," Elyssa said.

Eor nodded. "Yes, much like diamonds. The only way to truly destroy aetherium is through normal usage." He channeled a beam of Murk into the brown stone. It was like running dough through a pasta machine, resulting in hundreds of aetherial noodles on the other side of the stone. "Channeling through a stone gradually wears away the concentrated aether and reduces the force holding it together. After a year of normal use, this particular gem will lose cohesion and revert to aetherial state."

That certainly brought the supply and demand side of the gem industry into focus. Since they didn't last forever, there was a constant demand for them. Unfortunately, it also made clear that I couldn't simply zap a bloodstone and blow it up.

Eor steepled his fingers and pursed his lips. "It's possible I could create an aethid that would allow me to destroy other aethids through amplified usage." He dug through his fanny pack and pulled out a clear gem. "Yes, it might be doable."

"If anyone can come up with a way, it'd be you," Elyssa said in an admiring tone. "You'd be the hero of the fleet and show Hudor who's the best once and for all."

Eor's eyes lost focus on the outside world, most likely turning inward so he could envision scores of Mzodi cheering him on while Hudor huddled in a corner and cried.

One of the crew repairing the ship shouted up at another person who relayed a message to the first mate, Tahlee that repairs were complete.

Eor offered a condescending smile and pat on my back. "I believe you have very little to fear since you certainly aren't valuable enough to squander a bloodstone on, but rest your mind, child, and I'll see what I can do."

I was about to show Eor how valuable his teeth were by breaking a few of them, but Elyssa grabbed my hand and squeezed it. "Thank you, Eor."

"You're quite welcome, children." Eor pocketed the brown stone and headed toward the aft ramp to below decks.

"*Children*," I muttered. "That guy gets on my last nerve."

Elyssa quirked her lips and nodded. "I think he does that to everyone."

Shouts echoed from the aft ramp as Mzodi soldiers led a struggling Racha to the top deck. The Brightling soldier wore a simple white tunic and no shoes. Her eyes shone with anger and fear.

"I demand you take us to Guinesea!" Racha shouted.

Illaena stepped from the deck cabin and motioned toward the railing. The soldiers dragged Racha there and bent her over the side.

"I am a soldier of the Brightling Empire!" Racha screamed. "Harm me and there will be retribution."

Illaena stood to her side and spoke calmly. "You held my crew and ship for ransom, and nearly killed one of my sorters. Why should I not demand blood for blood, soldier?"

"You refused a lawful order from the empire." Spittle flecked around Racha's lips. "You left us no choice but to enforce the order."

"The Mzodi are not subject to the whims of the Brightling Empire." Illaena nodded at her soldiers and they dumped Racha over the side.

Elyssa and I gasped. It was nearly a five-story fall to the ground below. Racha's scream cut short as the Mzodi soldiers caught her feet and let her dangle.

"You are fortunate the Muhala Kajeen asked me to spare your life, *land dweller*." Illaena flicked her hand and the soldiers roughly jerked Racha back onto the deck. "That does not mean you'll escape punishment."

Tahlee stepped forward and ripped away the tunic, leaving Racha nude. The Brightling soldier wrapped her arms protectively over her chest, but the soldiers gripped her arms and held her spread-eagle.

Elyssa gripped my hand and we backed up a step as Illaena channeled a thin strand of Brilliance. She touched the white-hot energy to Racha's right shoulder blade. Flesh sizzled and the soldier screamed in agony over and over until her throat went raw. Illaena dragged the sparking beam across Racha's back, drawing several neat Cyrinthian symbols. When she finished, Tahlee channeled Murk around her hand and pressed it to the burnt flesh.

Racha slumped forward, sobbing as the Murk cooled the wound but left behind the scar that spelled "Criminal" in her skin.

"Remind me to never ever commit a crime on this ship," I murmured.

Elyssa gave me a worried look and whispered, "Let's hope they don't find out about our attempted hijacking."

Illaena shook her head at the soldiers and they dropped the weeping Racha on the deck. The captain stood over her and snarled, "You and your people will remain on this ship until we discover what reception our other ships receive in Guinesea. If it pleases the Muhala Kajeen, you will be dropped near the island."

Racha wiped tears and snot from her face and glared defiantly up at Illaena. "You have made a terrible mistake harming me, Mzodi filth." She cast a disdainful glare at Tahlee. "You are abominations, all of you—Darklings and Brightlings mingling with one another."

"Perhaps I should have your eyes put out so you do not have to watch," Illaena said. She backhanded Racha hard enough to send the other sera skidding a few feet along the deck. "All were created equal in the eyes of the universe. Only fools believe they were made better than others, you tiny insignificant speck." She turned her back to Racha. "Take her back to the holding cell."

"At once," one of the soldiers said.

The Mzodi yanked Racha unceremoniously off the ground by her arms and legs and hauled her below decks.

"Secure the deck," Illaena said.

Tahlee turned toward the other deck crew. "Secure deck! Prepare for departure!"

The navigators raced to their positions and gripped the channeling rods that fed into the levitation foils. Elyssa and I leaned over the railing and looked down.

Speaking in a conversational tone, Illaena gave Tahlee another order. The first mate shouted it to the rest of the crew: "Cast off!"

The ship shuddered and surged upward fast enough to buckle my knees. Wind rushed against the crown of my head as we floated higher and higher. I shifted to incubus sight and spotted an aether stream flowing north by northeast far overhead.

I knew it probably wasn't a great time to talk to Illaena, but something about our earlier conversation regarding aether streams had me curious about which route we planned to take to reach Voltis. Illaena regarded my approach with a disdainful raise of her left eyebrow.

I spoke before she could tell me to go away. "Since there are no aether streams from here to Voltis, do we have to sail to Sazoris first, or is there another northern route?"

"I never said there were no aether streams to Voltis," Illaena replied. "Merely that there are none known to the land dwellers." She turned to Tahlee and spoke another command.

"Ahead to Voltis!" The fiery-eyed redhead relayed the commands in a deafening shout. "May the skies treat us with mercy!"

We reached the aether stream and the foils caught the current, propelling us forward like a stone from a slingshot. Illaena and the others watched with amusement as Elyssa and I staggered against each other in an attempt to remain standing. Elyssa planted her athletic legs and snagged my arm to keep me from sprawling in a heap.

"It is good you have a strong sera to guide you," Illaena said. "Most land dwellers are soft, but your Elyssa is fierce and hearty."

Elyssa blushed, but keeping a straight face looked at me and said, "Most men would die without a strong woman to keep them safe."

I rolled my eyes though I honestly couldn't dispute her assertion. "Elyssa has saved my life more times than I can count."

Tahlee looked at me and blinked. "Are you not Justin Slade, the great hero of Eden?"

I wasn't sure if she was messing with me or it had taken her this long to figure out who I was. Up until this moment she'd never actually spoken to me. "I don't know about being the great hero, but I've done my fair share of fighting."

"You do not look like much," she said. "Is it true the men of Eden claim the glory though it is their females who win the day?"

Elyssa snorted and quickly covered her mouth.

"Are all Mzodi men—seraphs—weak and incapable?" I asked.

"They are strong and superior to land dweller males," Tahlee said. "But there are few who match Mzodi seras for wits and skill."

"Nice to see the Mzodi run an equal opportunity operation here," I said. "I wouldn't want to file a sexual harassment complaint or anything."

Unfortunately, the Cyrinthian version of sexual harassment translated into something that meant sexual battle, sending Illaena and Tahlee's eyelids fluttering with blinks of pure confusion.

I took the opportunity to change the subject. "Are we headed straight for Voltis, or will we drop off Racha and her people in Guinesea first?"

"If I have heard no word from the *Xanda* by the time we pass the eastern coast of Guinesea, we will continue on to Voltis and keep the prisoners until our return." Illaena turned her gaze to the sky ahead. "Since time is of the essence, we will sail through the night. I suggest you return below decks and rest."

The sun touched the mountains to the west, tinging the sky with red. Thousands of miles ahead in the growing twilight the Voltis Maelstrom waited with its secrets. We were finally underway to either answers or a violent death.

Well, that's nothing new.

Elyssa and I took Illaena's advice, retiring to a cabin after telling Adam and Shelton what was going on. Before going to sleep, we joined the mile-high club on the cloud bed and shared some laughs about Tahlee's comments.

Even though being with my one true love was all I ever wanted, a hollow space in my chest seemed to expand every day we were trapped here in Seraphina. Cradling Elyssa in my arms, I stroked dark locks of her hair from her cheek and said, "Do you ever feel disconnected in this realm?"

She nodded. "All the time. It's like we're stranded on an alien planet and have to survive until we can return to Earth."

"That sounds like something I'd say."

Elyssa pecked a kiss on my nose. "Guess I'm a geek then."

"I wonder what's happening back in Eden with Victus and Serena." Heat flushed my face at the thought of all the lives lost from their betrayal. "I don't know if there's anyone left in the Overworld to stop them from doing whatever they want."

"Even though we're not there, people of good conscience will defend the Overworld." Elyssa's gaze grew distant. "They'd better hope Ivy doesn't figure out what's going on or she'll blast every last one of them."

I managed a wry chuckle. "She comes from the Daelissa School of Kill Everyone. I just hope she's safe."

129

Elyssa pressed a hand to my cheek. "I know she is, Justin."

I closed my eyes and savored the quiet moment with the woman I loved. Ivy was young but powerful. She could take care of herself. *I hope I'm right.*

In the meantime, we had to get to the bottom of this current crisis and stop it so we could divert all our attention to getting back to Eden. Knowing we'd cleared a major hurdle and now had a ride to Voltis allowed me to feel a little less stressed out.

I just hope the journey doesn't kill us.

Chapter 15

A great shudder jerked me awake and sent me and Elyssa rolling off the bed. My reflexes responded at once and I nimbly caught myself on my feet while Elyssa rolled gracefully to hers.

The floor lurched upward and sent us flying into the air. I channeled sticky strands of Murk and tethered us to the floor.

"How's your head?" Elyssa asked as we rode out another bout of violent turbulence. "Is channeling magic still painful?"

"I hadn't even thought about it until you mentioned it." I tapped my left temple. "No headaches." I channeled a ball of Brilliance in my right hand and waited for a stabbing sensation that never materialized. "Maybe I'm back to normal."

The ship righted and smoothed out. A thump and solid thud reverberating through the hull gave me the impression that we'd reached solid land.

"Let's see what's up," Elyssa said.

I stripped and went into the Seraphim equivalent of a bathroom for a quick cleaning. Charging the gem on the wall, I sent it the Cyrinthian command for wash. Ultraviolet mist sprayed from the gem and brushed against my skin, leaving a cool minty sensation in my lungs every time I drew breath.

Elyssa hopped in with me and held her arms out slightly. "Make sure it gets your armpits, babe. I love you, but your armpits stink when you don't let the mist reach them."

I stuck out my tongue and made sure to hold up my arms.

"Are you cleaning your tongue too?" she said with a wink.

"It's better than brushing your teeth the normal way," I shot back—which was true. The cleansing fog definitely made personal hygiene a breeze.

The mist evaporated, leaving me sparkly clean and slightly damp. I charged the gem and sent another command. Warm air blew against us, leaving us dry and ready to face the day—well, once we put on some clothes.

The ship sat on a blackened chunk of rock that barely passed for an island. Small blue waves lapped at the shore and a few seagulls circled overhead.

Mzodi bustled about the top deck. Near the bow, Tahlee checked the rising sun by peering through a short tube with gems affixed to the ends. It resembled a spyglass, but was likely something much different since she would've burned out her retinas staring at the sun like that. Illaena stood behind her, a hand on the other sera's shoulder.

A low rumble jerked my gaze north where I caught my first glimpse of the Voltis Maelstrom. We were still miles away, but the border of the massive storm looked like a wall of gray clouds with the constant flash of multi-colored lightning. A distant boom thundered and the clouds turned brilliant red before returning to gray.

"We're sailing into *that*?" Even Elyssa sounded concerned.

"Holy butt muffins!" Shelton leaned against the railing to my left. "I hope someone brought umbrellas."

Adam held out his phone to record the massive storm in the distance. "I think that was a volcanic eruption."

Shelton gazed uneasily at the captain and first mate. "Here's hoping Illaena knows how to steer this ship through it."

A gout of water sprayed fifty feet into the air just off the northern side of the island, and a monstrous whale nearly the size of the *Falcheen* broke the surface of the water and regarded us from less than a hundred yards away.

"I hope it doesn't try to mate with the ship," Adam said in a worried voice.

"Look at its eyes," Elyssa said. "They're so big and round."

The pupil in the whale's huge green eye narrowed to a slit. The creature dove beneath the water, leaving behind a massive wake that splashed against the tiny island. One of the crew shouted at Tahlee who tucked away the spyglass and consulted with Illaena. The captain twirled a finger in the air and the deck crew raced into position.

"I think they're worried," Shelton said. He leaned over the railing and looked out into the water. "I see something."

Adam joined him. "Is it coming toward us?"

Though the creature had dived deep, the water was so clear and the sun so bright I could see a massive shadow beneath the surface growing closer and closer. "It's definitely coming at us!"

The ship shuddered and lifted off. The four of us grabbed hold of the railing as the vessel abruptly shot forward to the east. The water exploded and the whale leapt onto shore where we'd been, its massive maw gaping wide. What I'd mistaken for a whale more closely resembled a shark, but without the trademark dorsal fin to give it away.

"Jumping Jehoshaphat!" Shelton shouted. "Get us out of here!"

The monster slid back into the ocean and veered toward us. The *Falcheen* shot upward just as the massive predator exploded from the ocean, tooth-lined maw gaping wide, a torrent of foaming salt water rushing down its sides. The jaws thundered shut on empty air and the creature belly-flopped in the water with a mighty roar.

I leaned heavily on the railing, heart thudding in my chest. "What was that thing?"

Illaena appeared at my side and looked over the railing. "A tartha."

"How odd that one should be so close to the surface," Tahlee said. "It is not mating season."

My gaze wandered to a fountain of seawater blown from the spout of a tartha. Then I spotted another and another as far as the eye could see. "It must be party season," I said and pointed to the other spouts. "I count at least a dozen of those things."

Hot wind gusted across my face followed shortly by an icy breeze. An explosion in the distant maelstrom threw volcanic ash high into the air.

"The tartha will make the entry into Voltis more difficult," Tahlee said.

Shelton's eyebrows arched. "Can't we just fly over them?"

Illaena sighed. "Set course and prepare for entry."

Tahlee relayed the orders with deafening shouts that could probably be heard all the way inside Voltis, and the *Falcheen* shot forward.

"You didn't answer my question," Shelton said.

Illaena huffed impatiently. "We have to fly low during the approach to enter a mountain tunnel which will deliver us safely past the outer layer of storms."

Shelton jabbed a finger at the red flames licking the gray outer barrier of Voltis. "Volcanic eruptions and earthquakes are constantly rocking that place. I ain't no geologist or volcanologist, or even an earthquakeologist, but how in the world could a mountain tunnel survive in that environment?"

"I think you mean seismologist," Adam said helpfully.

Shelton threw up his hands. "Whatever!"

Illaena and Tahlee exchanged a look of disdain.

"I do not know," Illaena said. "I can only trust the Muhala Kajeen would not mislead us with false instructions." She turned and went back toward the command pedestal in the middle of the deck.

Adam patted Shelton on the back. "Looking a little pale there, buddy. Want some Dramamine?"

Shelton looked at him hopefully. "You got any more of those sleeping potions? Something tells me I don't want to be awake for this next part."

I snorted. "I don't want to have to drag your unconscious body around during an emergency. Best you stay awake."

We walked to the bow and stared at the black clouds billowing on the horizon. The wind changed temperatures and directions, slicing to my bones with freezing cold one moment before roasting my eyebrows the next. Brimstone tickled my nose and bits of rocks and ice pelted us. A hundred feet below, the water foamed and rocked as tartha tried to pace the ship, though their massive bulk made it impossible to match the nimble vessel.

Another shout from Tahlee rang out and the *Falcheen* dipped lower toward the ocean. A tartha burst from the waters ahead, jaws gaping, and missed us by a mile. The next beast that tried to make a meal of us leapt toward our port side, but fell well short of its goal. Just ahead, I saw the water rippling as another sea monster came at us, timing its leap perfectly.

The gaping maw came right at us. Tahlee shouted and the ship lurched to starboard. Adam and Shelton shouted with surprise, feet flying out from beneath them. I flung tethers of Murk and strapped my friends to the railing as the scaly hide of the tartha roared past less than fifty yards from its intended meal, its huge eye glaring angrily at the missed opportunity. The foul stench of fish breath and the bucking and swaying of the ship made me feel green around the gills.

The ship leveled out and resumed a beeline for a pitch-black mole on the swirling gray face of Voltis. A tartha trumpeted in the distance and others of its kind picked up the call until it sounded like a pack of dinosaurs lamenting their missed meal.

Shelton shuddered. "That sound gives me the creeps."

"What a bizarre noise for such huge creatures." Adam held out his phone to record another tartha making a last-ditch effort to catch us.

I looked up at the unassailable wall of churning clouds, aether, volcanic ash, and ice stretching as far as the eye could see in all directions. "Looks like the surface of a gas giant."

"Like dark Jupiter." Shelton jabbed a finger toward a spinning ball of ice. "Look at that!"

Plumes of fire exploded from holes in the side of the ice, a comet streaking from the heavens. The object plunged into the ocean several hundred yards away and exploded in a geyser of steam. Huge waves rose in its wake. The *Falcheen* rose above the water and let the ripples subside before dropping back down on course.

Shelton gripped the rail with white-knuckled intensity. "Is that the tunnel?"

The black spot had grown into an uninviting maw. Salty mist whipped across the deck and the turbulence vibrated the deck beneath our feet until I thought the ship would fly apart. The temperature soared and dipped, making my nose run while the constant roar of the

Voltis Maelstrom thrummed my entire being like a guitar string. "I'm gonna catch a cold if this keeps up."

Almost there now, the navigators fought with the crystal rods, pushing, pulling, and rotating them to keep on course as elemental fury pummeled the *Falcheen* from all sides. A huge wave swelled ahead.

Tahlee shouted, "Hold fast!" and the ship held course.

"You've got to be kidding me!" Shelton gripped the railing.

I cast a shield spell over the four of us just as the huge wave crested twenty feet above the deck. The *Falcheen's* sharp bow pierced the wave and sliced through it. Water cascaded across my shield and ran across the deck like a small river. Some water froze into icy puddles, leaving treacherous footing for the members of the deck crew that ran from station to station assisting the navigators.

The tunnel grew larger and larger, its face rough basalt, dense and dark from eons of volcanic activity, its insides a mystery of dark pitch. The gaping maw swallowed us. The turbulence went still and the roar of the maelstrom dropped to a whisper.

I looked back and watched as the last shreds of daylight vanished from the hull of the ship before darkness devoured it. For a moment, I felt no rush of wind, no pull on my guts to tell me if we were moving or sitting still. *What if we're about to hit a wall?* I panicked and channeled a light globe, but it did nothing to penetrate the thick darkness.

Tahlee's shouts rang through the darkness and beams of light speared out from the weapon gems on the outer hull. Soon the dark surface of the tunnel became visible, though the way ahead was shrouded in pitch. We coasted slowly for hours, navigating narrow turns and sudden dips as the tunnel wound like a serpent through the bowels of the mountain. A river of lava flowed along the bottom of the next cavern, giving us a sweltering journey until we reached the cold darkness once again.

Ghostly wails echoed from ahead, making me wonder if the sound was a trick of the wind, or hints that something horrible lay in wait.

136

I shivered. "Reminds me of El Dorado." Icy fingers walked up my back at the thought of the light-draining creatures that tried to devour us in the depths of that cursed city.

"I keep waiting for a giant worm monster to eat us," Shelton said.

Adam grinned. "Let's tell each other ghost stories."

Shelton gave him a withering glare. "You start that and I'll throw you overboard." He sighed. "Man, I wish Bella was here."

"I have a teddy bear you can borrow," Adam said with a straight face.

Shelton balled up a fist. "Keep it up, wise guy."

The spooky wails grew louder, like hearing the echoes of distant conversations as the ship reached a sharp bend in the tunnel. The crew steered carefully, pivoting the back end to keep the middle of the ship from scraping the tunnel wall. It reminded me of trying to carry a long couch around the corner of a hallway, just on a much grander scale.

When we cleared the bend, the ship climbed a rise toward flashes of orange light.

"I think we're almost through," Shelton said hopefully.

Adam frowned. "I don't think that's sunlight."

"I hope it's not another lava cave," I said.

The truth was much worse. Plumes of fire jetted from pockmarked holes in the wall of the tunnel at seemingly random intervals. To make matters worse, the tunnel snaked around another bend just ahead.

Tahlee cried a command and the ship glided for a landing on the tunnel floor. The crew slumped, many lying on the deck next to their stations.

"Must be break time," Shelton said.

"Man, I feel kind of guilty." Adam leaned against the railing. "I can't imagine having to keep this ship aloft through the kind of weather we went through out there."

Illaena and Tahlee joined us at the prow and looked at the next challenge. I carefully watched their faces to see if they looked worried, but neither sera betrayed any emotion, conversing with one another in a businesslike tone.

"Would it be wrong of me to ask how much further?" Shelton asked.

Elyssa rolled her eyes. "Really?"

"Well," he said, "aren't you a little curious?"

Illaena projected a holographic map from a gem, displaying a tunnel that snaked through the mountain before emerging in a blank gray area. "This is the halfway point of the tunnel. From here until the end, things will be much more challenging."

Shelton grimaced. "More fire spouts?"

"Fire, ice, and water," she said, "and the tunnel is only the first third of the trip."

"The first third?" Adam's mouth dropped open.

Illaena nodded grimly and looked at me. "Let us hope this journey is worth it, for the way ahead is fraught with danger."

Chapter 16

I didn't exactly find Illaena's words encouraging, and the thought of facing a gauntlet of elements didn't sound appealing. On the other hand, we had no choice. We had stop Kaelissa from obtaining her secret weapon.

My imagination ran wild with possibilities. An army of dragons? A herd of unicorns from another realm? The Tooth Fairy?

"Probably the Easter Bunny," Shelton suggested as we sat down for lunch a few minutes later. "Probably keeps his harem of egg-laying bunnies in there too."

Adam studied the recordings of the maelstrom he'd made as we approached it. "Even magic has to follow rules."

"What's that supposed to mean?" Shelton said. "You don't believe in the Easter Bunny?"

"No, I mean the actual storm itself." Adam enlarged the hologram and focused on the brilliant light show of fire and lightning. "It seems impossible to have hot wind one second and freezing cold the next. And how has such violent geological activity like volcanoes and earthquakes continued nonstop for eons?"

"You're saying magic doesn't explain this?" I asked.

He shrugged. "Maybe I'm wrong. After all, Seraphina is so full of aether, maybe it acts as a catalyst to keep the maelstrom churning for eternity."

"That'd be my guess," Shelton said. "The only other thing that could be causing it is whatever is at the center."

"That worries me," Elyssa said. "What if this is a Glimmer effect?"

That raised a few confused eyebrows.

I frowned. "Glimmer effect?"

"Yeah, like in Eden where our realm touches the Glimmer, we have pocket dimensions." Elyssa made a fist and circled a finger around it. "You know how the realms orbit around the moon in the Glimmer?"

"The Anchor Stone," I clarified. "What does that have to do with the maelstrom?"

"What if there's a big hole in the realm at the middle of Voltis?" She dug a finger into her glurk and hollowed it out. "What if there's a pocket dimension or a black hole in the middle?"

A crazed look flashed across Shelton's eyes. "Holy supermassive black holes—I never thought of that."

"But the Mzodi have been there before," Adam said. "How else do they have a route?"

"They didn't make it all the way through," Elyssa said. "Xalara seemed pretty clear on that. Maybe we should ask Illaena if she's withholding information from us."

"Yeah," Shelton said dryly, "because she's been so forthcoming with us already."

"Probably not a good time right now since they're all asleep." Adam poured himself another glass of blue wine and took a long drink. "I think Elyssa might have a point about a pocket dimension in the center. If all the realms touch the Glimmer, it stands to reason they each interact with it in a different way."

"Eden touches the Glimmer in at least a dozen different places all over the world," I said. "If that's true with Seraphina, why is there only one Voltis Maelstrom?"

"It's possible the massive aether vortexes all over the planet are areas where Seraphina touches the Glimmer." Adam swished the liquid in his glass into a miniature whirlpool. "Even vast quantities of aether don't naturally create vortexes unless there's a catalyst."

That got me to thinking about the field trip Elyssa and I had taken to the Glimmer. "If you're right, maybe there's a way to enter the Glimmer through one of these juxtapositions."

Elyssa's eyes brightened. "If we can get to the Glimmer, we might be able to get home!"

"Yeah, but don't you need a green rock like Cora had?" Shelton said. "I thought you had to go through the reflected world and all that stuff too."

"Maybe." The Rift—a void of stars—separated the Glimmer from Eden, and inside the Rift were guardians. Using the green pebble Cora had given us, Elyssa and I had jumped into water and entered the reflected world—the mirror version of the real world. The guardians weren't present in that reality, making it easier for us to scoot through the Rift. On the other hand, if you tarried in the reflected world too long, your own reflections would catch you and steal your soul.

Adam rubbed his hands together. "Man, this is exciting! Maybe we can back door our way to Eden and give Victus and Serena the ass-whooping they so richly deserve."

"Amen, brother!" Shelton held up a hand and Adam smacked it with his.

The sharp tug of gravity woke us early the next morning. Elyssa and I headed to the top deck and held our collective breath as the crew deftly navigated us past the fire spouts and around narrow bends. Sweat dripped down my face as the temperature rose until it felt like an oven.

Other crew kept the navigators supplied with water, swapping positions when someone became too tired to continue. Hours later, we reached the end of the fire tunnel and entered a white cavern. It was like being tossed from the furnace into a freezer. Sweat crystallized on my skin and before long, we were all shivering and rubbing our arms for warmth. Illaena and Tahlee studied the tunnel map and consulted. I overheard them arguing about heading forward or backing up for more heat and resting.

"Sounds like there's a little friction," Elyssa commented, her enhanced hearing picking up the conversation as well.

Tahlee motioned over one of the navigators and spoke with her for a moment then folded her arms and stared at Illaena with an *I told you so* look plain on her face.

Illaena frowned and slashed a hand forward. The crew took their positions and we launched forward through the ice cavern at high speed. Within seconds, the wind had frozen all the sweat on my body, and my shivering was uncontrollable. Though the navigators wore determined looks on their faces, shivering, chattering teeth, and freezing tears on their cheeks showed their suffering.

The navigator controlling the first control rod on the port side slumped at her post and the ship lurched hard left. Tahlee shouted a command, but all of the backup crew were already in use and the other navigators were huddled and resting around a glowing gem for warmth.

"All stop," Illaena commanded.

"We can't stop!" Tahlee shouted to Illaena. "There's no safe place to land."

Seeing no alternative, I raced to the unmanned control rod as the other navigators fought to keep the ship straight. "What do I do?"

Tahlee bared her teeth. "Channel into it!"

A sphere of Brilliance gathered on my right fist and I focused it into the rod. At once, the *Falcheen* leveled off and straightened.

Tahlee frowned and stared at me. "How are you channeling so much power?"

I stifled a grin and shrugged. "I slept well." The other crew stared at me as well, but the freezing wind was really wearing on me and I just wanted to get the hell out of this cavern. "What now?"

"Push the rod in different directions to control direction and altitude." Tahlee jogged over to my position and indicated the arrows at the base. "Right now you are holding the rod in neutral which provides only levitation. Push forward, pull back, or shift to the side for lateral movement, and pull up or push down on the rod for altitude."

It didn't sound hard, but considering I had to synchronize with five other navigators, it sounded like a lot. "I'll do my best."

She nodded curtly. "Listen to my orders and you will be fine." Tahlee resumed her position next to Illaena on the control pedestal and shouted an order. "Fast forward, ninety degrees."

142

The ship shot forward, but my side began to vibrate wildly, as if something was dragging against a rough surface. Since I was at the front control rod, I glanced at the navigator behind me and saw her pushing her rod forward while pulling up. I mimicked her and the movement of the *Falcheen* smoothed out.

I caught an acknowledging nod from Tahlee and suppressed the urge to pump my fist and whoop it up. Elyssa came up beside me with a glowing red gem and held it next to me. The warmth melted the ice in my bones, though freezing wind still buffeted my skin.

"Your hair is frozen on end," Elyssa commented. "Guess you won't need any styling gel."

"S-s-shush," I said through chattering teeth. "Why isn't the Templar armor keeping me warmer?"

"We wore out the charms." She huddled behind me to keep the wind at bay. "We have a knack for wearing out armor."

"T-t-tell me about it." I nearly channeled a shield in front of me to cut the wind, but I didn't want to overdo it like I had last time.

Lightning flashed ahead, highlighting a jagged crack silhouetted against boiling gray. More flashes of alternating colors struck the lip of the tunnel exit again and again, guiding us toward it while also warning us away.

"How are we supposed to get through that?" Elyssa said. "The lightning strikes are too fast."

Tahlee ordered a course correction as the gusting wind drove us a few degrees off course. I followed the example of a nearby navigator and we continued heading straight for the storm. Electricity arced back and forth across the exit, like a short-circuited bug zapper.

Illaena consulted her map and pointed out something to Tahlee.

"Thirty degrees starboard, ten degrees incline," the first mate commanded.

I followed the adjustments of the navigator behind me and the ship tilted up and right. The *Falcheen* looked right on course to cut through the center of the big hole—the exact place we needed to avoid since it was subject to a constant barrage of lightning. Stomping feet drew my attention aft. Mzodi soldiers ran toward the bow with a contraption that looked like a giant crossbow.

143

"Looks like a ballista," Elyssa murmured. "Totally Medieval."

They sealed the base of the unit in place with gems, and channeled Murk into red stones on the sides. A thick strand of Murk formed between the prongs and the soldiers placed a head-sized aethid in a small pocket there. The chunk of aetherium looked rough and uncut, spiking out in all directions like a crystoid.

The nose of the ship closed to within fifty yards of the lightning barrier. Illaena cocked back her arm and a soldier aimed the crossbow at the storm. She flung forward her arm and the soldier channeled a burst of energy into a gem on the handle. The rock shot forward and into the storm.

"All speed ahead!" Tahlee shouted.

Every navigator punched it forward and the *Falcheen* sailed toward certain doom. Just yards ahead of us, the launched rock hit the lightning field. Blinding light flashed, leaving the afterimage of a dark blot against white. I shouted and tried not to panic as we hit the hole…and burst through unscathed.

Moments after the stern cleared the exit, a bolt of magical energy struck the edges of the hole and arcs snaked back and forth across the hole once again.

"All stop," Tahlee cried. "Prepare for landing."

The weary navigators groaned with weariness.

We set down on a narrow shelf of rock a hundred feet below the tunnel hole with our port side near the rock. A massive gray wall of clouds and aether roiled a hundred yards to starboard, electricity crackling along the surface like malevolent light serpents. An occasional bolt struck the basalt around us, but left it entirely undamaged.

Adam reached over the railing and rubbed a hand along the rock after he and Shelton emerged from hiding below decks. "No wonder that tunnel survives all the earthquakes," he said. "This rock is incredibly dense."

"Might even be some form of aetherium," Shelton said.

"I didn't know you knew the correct term for gems," I said, mimicking Eor's imperious tone.

Shelton snorted. "Eor kept peering over our shoulders when me and Adam were analyzing the bloodstone."

"Yeah, he doesn't like noobs," Adam said. "On the other hand, he did teach us some useful basics that might help our analysis of the bloodstone."

"That's a plus," Elyssa said. "Any luck discovering its secrets?"

Shelton shook his head. "Nothing yet. We're still working out the bugs in our analysis spell."

Adam peered over the railing at the ledge below. "There are loose stones down there. I want to go to the surface and collect some samples."

"Yeah, maybe we'll find something even Eor hasn't seen," Shelton said.

I pretended to inspect them. "Well, neither of you are wearing red shirts, so you should be safe."

Shelton snorted. "I'll be sure to redirect any alien life forms to Adam so they can probe him."

The pair headed below decks to gather their equipment.

My stomach grumbled and my head ached. "I want food and sleep."

"Sounds good to me." Elyssa took my hand. "Whatever my brave navigator wants."

"Ooh, whatever I want?" I flashed a wide grin.

Illaena intercepted me and Elyssa as we headed toward the aft ramp below decks. "You acquitted yourself well for a land dweller."

I almost played it off like it was nothing just to throw her snob attitude back in her face, but took a more diplomatic route instead. "I'm glad I was able to help."

"His control was rough at best," Tahlee said. "Still, he helped more than hindered."

Elyssa raised an eyebrow. "Without someone manning that control rod, the ship would've crashed."

"Perhaps, though I could have stepped in," Tahlee said.

I widened my eyes and opened my mouth in mock disbelief. "You mean I could've yelled commands at everyone instead of you?"

"Perhaps it would be wise to instruct you on the finer points of control," Illaena said. "The journey ahead will not be any easier."

I shrugged. "Sure, just let me know what to do."

"Come with me," Tahlee said.

I jabbed a thumb over my shoulder. "I'm gonna eat and rest first."

She looked down her nose at me. "Very well. Meet me up here when you're ready."

"You got it." I grabbed Elyssa's hand and made a beeline down the ramp and to the galley.

We stuffed our faces and then I snuggled up with my ninja princess. I really wanted some hanky panky, but I dozed off the second my head hit the cloud pillow.

After snoozing, I met Tahlee on the top deck and let her walk me through a crash course in flight control. The crystal rod connected to the levitation gem provided a full range of controls along the x, y, and z axis, though she explained to me in no uncertain terms, "There is never a reason to fly the ship upside down."

"Not even to do a cool barrel roll?" I asked.

Tahlee frowned because the word-for-word translation didn't work well in Cyrinthian. "In any case, you must remember that if the ship requires a tilt starboard, the port side pushes while the starboard pulls."

"I used to play space simulations," I told her. "I know how to use positive and negative thrust."

Her forehead pinched into a confused V.

I explained to her what a thruster was and how it worked on space ships, then using my hand as a pretend star fighter, tilted it back and forth. "If the port thruster on the nose of the ship and the aft starboard thruster fire at the same time, the ship will spin on its axis."

Tahlee's gaze grew distant as she considered this new concept. "We have never had a reason to spin the ship around in such a way. We typically steer it into a normal turn."

"Well, you have more weapon gems on the sides of the ship than the front or back, so you could spin the *Falcheen* sideways and fire all cannons at an enemy." I wiggled my fingers and pretended my hand spaceship was firing weapons. "Pew, pew, pew."

"That could be useful." Tahlee leaned over the railing and looked at the weaponized gems in the hull. "Perhaps such a tactic would be useful against dragons."

"Why didn't we use the weapons against the tartha?" I asked.

She raised an eyebrow. "Why would we injure a tartha?"

"I dunno, because they tried to eat us?"

"They are easily avoided," she said, "unlike dragons."

I hadn't thought they were that easy to avoid, but then again, I was a noob sailor. Considering what probably lay ahead, they'd better pray I never had to help fly this ship again.

Chapter 17

After we were done with lessons, I found Adam and Shelton freshly returned from their visit to the surface of the mountain with Eor tagging along behind them.

"How'd it go?" I asked.

The gem sorter was beside himself with excitement, lugging a sparkly net full of black rocks behind him. "I will be below inspecting these," he informed the others and vanished down the ramp.

"Finally!" Shelton wiped sweat from his forehead and sighed. "Remind me to never take Eor anywhere with us again."

"Got that right," Adam grumbled. He held up a shiny black crystal. "I'm curious to see if this is just rock, or aetherium."

Tahlee's voice rang out from the middle of the bridge. The navigators took their positions and prepared for takeoff.

"Hope they got enough rest," Shelton said. "I wasn't sure we'd make it through that lightning field earlier."

"I'm gonna tie myself down somewhere," Adam said. "My body is black and blue from being tossed around."

Elyssa appeared on deck, fair skin flushed.

"What have you been up to?" I asked.

"While you were napping, I met with the Mzodi soldiers and asked if I could train with them in case of another dragon attack." She shrugged. "You know how I hate feeling left out."

"How'd that go?" I asked.

Elyssa grinned. "Let's just say I taught them a few Templar moves that will make their lives easier."

The *Falcheen* eased into the narrow alley between the mountain and the wall of roiling aether to starboard. Wind gusted across the deck, blowing my hair straight back and tearing Shelton's wide-brimmed hat off his head. The leather strap around his neck was the only thing that kept it from flying away.

The navigators eased the control rods forward and we began the next phase of the perilous journey. It took only moments to leave the relative calm of the landing zone and enter the next level of hell.

The aether storm roiled and roared to starboard while the outer layer of volcanic fire and arctic ice churned to port. The *Falcheen* bucked and shuddered through the resulting turbulence while the navigators fought with the control rods to keep us from veering too far left or right where the elemental forces would tear us apart.

Eor appeared on deck and began arguing with Illaena about something. After a time, she shook her head vehemently and stabbed a finger back toward the ramp. Face red and scrunched up with anger, Eor spun on his heel and stormed away.

"I can guess what that was about," Adam said.

"Crazy fool." Shelton clamped his hat back on his head but had to hold it down because of the wind. "He kept going on about how he wants to descend to ocean level and cast a net inside the storm."

I stared at the beautiful but deadly display the massive storm and shook my head. "Even the most violent vortexes are nothing compared to that."

"This ship could probably withstand a small hurricane," Adam said, "but that aether storm looks like it eats hurricanes for breakfast."

The climate grew more humid as we sailed until it felt like I was breathing more moisture than air. Even without the oppressive heat, it was enough to make everyone miserably sweaty. A cool rush of air granted everyone a moment of relief and then it started to rain.

Elyssa bound her long soaked hair into a ponytail and smoothed the sodden locks from my face. I leaned down and kissed her as the torrential downpour continued unabated.

She nuzzled her nose against mine. "I like kissing in the rain."

I pecked kisses up her cheeks. "I like kissing you, period."

Shelton groaned and tilted his hat to ward off rain in his face. "I'm going back to my room."

Adam shielded his hand with his face and looked into the gray gloom ahead. "Think I'll join you so we can analyze these rocks." He turned to me. "Just let us know if we're about to die, okay?"

I chuckled. "You got it."

The pair headed back to the aft ramp well, wobbling side-to-side as the swaying ship made for unsteady footing. Not long after they'd gone, the rain turned colder and then sleet slapped us in the face. I wrapped my arms around Elyssa and shivered.

"Maybe we should go below too."

She shook her head. "We need to be here in case they need help."

I wanted to argue with her but considering how quickly things had taken a turn for the worse in the lightning tunnel, she was probably right.

A chunk of hail smacked into my chest and surprised me more than it hurt. "That's not good."

And it wasn't. The hail grew larger until fist-sized chunks crashed against the deck. The Mzodi soldiers raced from below and held crystal shields above the navigators to protect them from the deadly storm. Illaena channeled a shield over her and Tahlee while the backup navigators huddled beneath crystal shields like those the soldiers used.

I threw up a shield of my own, using the ship as an anchor to make it easier to maintain the channel while moving. "I wonder why the backup crew aren't channeling shields."

"Too much energy," Elyssa said. "They probably need everything they can get just to keep the ship flying without a stable aether stream."

The hail stopped as abruptly as it had come, this time replaced by snow. The flurry turned into an all-out blizzard within seconds, blinding us to whatever lay ahead. Somehow, Illaena knew how to keep the ship on track and continued relaying commands through Tahlee. I released my shield and channeled a ball of Brilliance to keep me and Elyssa warm.

We sailed on through the endless blizzard, Tahlee's shouts ringing out every few seconds.

"I don't see how she yells so much without losing her voice." Elyssa held up a hand to shield her eyes from the snow.

I was about to reply when a shadow came out of nowhere and plowed right into me. At first I thought it was an accident, but the dagger aimed for my chest told me otherwise. I twisted out of the way and karate-chopped the wrist of the wielder. There was a cry of pain and the face of the figure became clear.

It was one of Racha's soldiers—the seraph named Tator. I heard shouts and the clash of weapons, but couldn't make out anything except shadows and flashes of magic in the snowy gloom.

Tator roared and lunged at me. Elyssa's foot intersected his face and sent him skidding away into the darkness. Brilliant sparks lit up the storm and the ship shuddered and bucked. Shouts and cries echoed and I just knew we were about to die.

The snowstorm abruptly abated and we hit clear air. The ship lurched, tossing everyone on deck into the air like rag dolls. Elyssa landed on her feet like a cat. I twisted and caught myself, stumbled, and skidded on my knees.

I immediately saw why the ship was bucking like a bronco. The starboard wing grazed the wall of the maelstrom and drifted closer and closer as Racha's soldiers fought with the crew. Several Mzodi soldiers lay dead. Tahlee lay prone on the deck, a bloody gash across her forehead. Illaena woozily pushed up off the deck, crimson trickling down her face.

I charged across the deck and immediately busted my ass when the *Falcheen* lurched drunkenly to port as the navigators on that side tried to compensate. The fighters stumbled and went down as well, sending weapons clattering across the deck.

I spotted Racha driving a dagger into the chest of a navigator and screaming, "Glory to the Empire!"

"You stupid bitch!" I shouted above the roar of the storm. Ropes of Murk shot from my hands and I pulled myself across the deck to her. Tator leapt in front of me, a short sword in hand.

151

Keeping myself tethered to the deck by the waist, I channeled a sword of Brilliance and held it in a defensive position. "Hello, my name is Justin Slade. You attacked my ship. Prepare to die."

If Tator had seen *The Princess Bride*, he might have at least chuckled before trying to impale me on his sword. Instead, he yelled, "You will be the one dying today!" and charged me. Using the firm footing granted by the magical tether, I easily dodged his clumsy attempts to run while the deck shifted beneath his feet, and drove my sword of destructive energy through his back.

Flesh sizzled and smoked, and Tator screamed his last as white heat cauterized his heart into a lump of ash. I released the channel on the sword and headed straight for Racha. The bodies of navigators and soldiers slid through crimson pools as the *Falcheen* listed hard to starboard. Even my tether wasn't enough to counter the sharp tilt when my feet were in slick blood. The port navigators did their best, tilting the ship back the other way and bodies crashed into me. One of them shrieked and bared her bloody teeth.

Except it wasn't a body, it was Racha.

Her sword chopped down on my arm and I screamed in pain. Thankfully, some of the protective charms in the armor still worked enough to keep her from amputating my limb. I rolled to the side and found my footing on a dry section of deck. Holding up my arm, I wiggled my fingers and tested my wrist to make sure she hadn't broken any bones.

A huge green gem hurtled from the maelstrom collided with the starboard wing. With a loud crack the crystal pinion shattered and the ship shuddered violently, launching me through the air and into the pool of blood coating the deck like some macabre impressionist painting. Another lurch to the right slammed me into the railing. I heard a loud scream and scooted out of the way just as Racha smashed into the place where I'd been.

She pushed to her feet, covered in blood from head to toe and baring her teeth in a bloody smile. "I will die this day, but so will you, boy!" Racha wrapped her arms around me and flung us over the railing.

It must have been sheer reflex, but I cast a strand of Murk at the railing and hung on for dear life while the madwoman clinging to my back tried to drag me into oblivion with her. I wriggled and elbowed the crazy bitch in the stomach. Racha slid down my torso and to my legs. Her feet grazed the outer edge of the maelstrom and a terrible scream tore from her throat.

I tried to think of a witty one-liner to impart before she went to the afterlife, but I was far too concerned with the fact that despite the maelstrom eating her alive, she wasn't letting go of me. The terrible pull of the mad energy jerked us sideways and the roaring storm ate the remains of the port wing and Racha along with it. I flailed like a caught fish but couldn't shake her free. Just as the gray clouds reached her waist, Racha fell silent and her grip went limp. Her remains fell silently away and vanished into the storm.

I fought the wind and suction of the maelstrom, willing the Murk strand to shorten enough so I could grab the railing. Elyssa's face appeared over the side and she pulled me up and over.

Illaena was back on her feet shouting commands to the remaining navigators, but from what I saw there weren't enough of them left standing to fly the ship. Two navigators remained port while one of them had rushed to the center control rod on the starboard side to keep the ship as level as possible.

Instead of taking the proper time to thank my girlfriend for saving me, I skidded through blood and reached the starboard bow control rod. Putting my lessons to good use, I helped the others wrench the ruins of the starboard wing out of the maelstrom and back into the clear.

"Rise forty," Illaena shouted.

Groaning with strain, the other navigators and I followed her instructions, though I didn't know why she wanted to gain altitude. Then again, the volcanic mountains to port were covered in clouds of ice and ash and there was probably nowhere safe to land.

"How are we supposed to keep this thing in the air?" I asked through clenched teeth.

The weight of the ship seemed to bear down on me and I could only imagine what the other navigators felt, having somehow maintained control during the fighting. An instant later, my body felt light as air, as if a load of bricks I'd carried on my shoulders all day was gone.

"All stop!" Illaena's shoulders slumped.

The *Falcheen* glided to a halt in a section of calm air, a glimpse of serenity surrounded by chaos and death. I didn't have to switch to incubus vision to know why the ship could suddenly hold itself up. We'd reached an aether stream.

The other navigators slumped with weariness, but rather than curl into balls and cry, they rushed to the bodies strewn about the deck and checked for signs of life.

I staggered over to Illaena where she knelt next to Tahlee's body.

Elyssa pressed her fingers to the redhead's neck and sighed with relief. "Her pulse is strong, Illaena. She'll be okay."

"My crew," the captain whispered in a haunted voice. "*My family.*" A tear trickled down her face.

My throat knotted with grief. I didn't know what to say, but I knew what we had to do.

Elyssa and I helped the others check each body for vitals. We found four surviving soldiers, and one navigator that had been knocked unconscious but was otherwise unharmed. Of the twelve deck crew, only five navigators, the captain, and first mate remained. Of the soldiers, nearly half were dead.

All of Racha's people were dead but by the time we sorted them out, we realized there was one Brightling soldier none of us had previously seen.

"There must have been another soldier we didn't know about," I said. "He must have hidden after we captured Racha." My heart froze with fear when I thought about what might have happened. "We need to check on the others."

Elyssa's face wrinkled with worry. "Oh, god. I hope Adam and Shelton are okay."

We treaded carefully aft across the blood-slicked deck and sprinted down the ramp to the lower decks. A lone Mzodi soldier lay dead at the end of the hall where his body had slid during the fight. Judging from the cauterized wound in his chest, he'd been stabbed with Brilliance. The doorway to the cell holding Racha and friends was open.

"That other Brightling soldier must have forced the Mzodi to open the door," Elyssa said. "I'll bet when the other soldiers went to the top deck to help the navigators with the hail, they only left one guard here."

I checked inside the cell and made sure it was empty then ran into the sorting room. Some of the sparkly nets had broken and spilled gems covered the floor. Several sorters nursed bruised body parts while others tended to them, but otherwise they all seemed clueless about what had happened on the top deck.

"What are we going to do about this mess?" Eor wailed as he waded through a pile of stones.

I gripped his arm. "We've got bigger problems." I told him what had happened.

"No!" He shouted. "That can't be true."

"Sweet Rana can't be dead," another gem sorter cried. "She was like a sister to me."

I imagined it was like Illaena had said. These people were more than crew—they were family. Spending months or years aboard a ship together probably brought the crew together emotionally unless they were jackasses like Eor. Even though the *Falcheen* was a new ship, many of the crew had probably served together on other ships.

Elyssa and I left the gem sorters and raced to Shelton's cabin where we found him and Adam lashed to the bed. I let a humorous observation die in my lips since nothing seemed funny right now.

"Mother of pearl, what in the hell is going on up there?" Shelton said when we walked inside. "We had to tie ourselves down before the ship beat us to death."

Adam massaged his temples. "Man, I have a headache. I need to find my potion pouch."

I leaned against the wall and squeezed my eyes shut. "Racha and her soldiers escaped. They killed a lot of people and nearly dragged the ship into the maelstrom."

Shelton's jaw fell open. "How many crew are left?"

"Hardly enough to fly the ship," Elyssa said. "There aren't any backup navigators."

Worry filled Adam's eyes. "How are we supposed to go on without backup crew? It was hard enough flying with a full complement."

I couldn't answer his question, but we were stuck in the middle of crap creek without a paddle.

Chapter 18

"There must be a better solution," Eor complained. "We can't simply leave Voltis without fishing it!"

Illaena folded her arms and stared daggers at the sorter. After the remaining crew pitched in to clean the top deck and arrange the fallen, she'd gathered everyone in the galley. "I will hear no more of fishing the maelstrom." She sighed. "It is my decision that we will turn back while we can."

The remaining navigators looked down, some of them with tears in their eyes.

"Why turn back?" I asked. "We're nearly halfway there. Going back is probably as dangerous as pushing on."

"Yes, but how shall we leave if we even make it to the center?" Illaena said. "The odds are slim enough that we will last another day."

Tahlee ran a hand over the healing gash in her forehead and cast a worried glance at Illaena. "You will not lose the *Falcheen*. I swear it."

Some of the navigators murmured in agreement.

"We will see her safely home," one of them said.

Illaena swallowed hard. "I'm sure you will."

This was the moment where I should have stood and argued with her that turning around was wrong, but really, it was the right decision. If a skilled Mzodi crew hadn't been able to make it to see the secret of Voltis, then how would Kaelissa manage it? Unless she knew something we didn't, there was no way to make it without the route Xalara had provided, and even then, it was exceedingly perilous.

If we turned around now and survived the return trip, maybe we could still stop a civil war from engulfing Pjurna and fortify our defenses against possible Brightling attacks.

And pray Kaelissa can't get any further into Voltis than we did.

It was depressing to think about but what else could we do?

One of the navigators, a short but sturdy looking seraph, stood and gazed at his captain. "I lost my best friend and lover. Nara died in my arms, and I will mourn her for with every passing day. But captain, I do not wish to turn back. I would rather die pushing forth into the heart of darkness than let the cowards who killed my love win."

"Aye!" another navigator shouted. "None sail the skies like the Mzodi! No land dwellers can win a race against us!"

Another spoke. "There is no sea, no storm, no force of nature that will stay our course." Other navigators joined her, chanting along as if this were some pledge they all knew by heart. "No enemy shall tear us from our ship, our home, our lives. By the captain's will, we go forward and never waver."

A cheer went up from the other Mzodi—all but Illaena who looked with trembling lips at her crew.

Tahlee put a hand on her captain's shoulder and squeezed it. "I know you fear the loss of the *Falcheen* more than death itself, Illaena, but we will see her through to the journey's end one way or the other."

Illaena remained quiet for a long moment, as if fighting the inner demons of doubt I knew all too well. She had lost a ship and crew before. Risking everything in this hellish place was probably her worst nightmare. Her shoulders stiffened and a curt nod signaled her decision.

"You are a brave crew," Illaena said in a quiet voice. "I could not have asked for better." She raised a fist. "Together we push on. Together we conquer nature's might. *Nothing* will stop us but death itself."

Cheers roared through the tiny room and I found myself unable to resist shouting along with them. *Man, nothing beats a good inspirational speech.*

I just hoped it was enough to see us through.

After a much-needed rest for the crew, it was training day for soldiers and sorters alike. I thought that most of the Mzodi were capable of filling in for navigators. After all, they'd spent most of their lives aboard flying ships, learning whatever role they wanted.

I was wrong.

Just like Arcanes, not all Seraphim were created equal when it came to magical power, physical abilities, or mental attributes, and it quickly became apparent to me why sorters were poorly suited to take over as navigators. Most of them didn't pump out the same kind of magical wattage as soldiers or navigators, but they were typically much smarter and more precise with their skills.

In other words, the sorters were the nerds of the Mzodi.

Tahlee identified two soldiers with enough raw power to charge the levitation foils and put them through an aviation crash course similar to what I'd endured. One of the sorters qualified as a backup soldier in case it came down to fighting, though Eor fought the reassignment of his people.

"We have a tremendous backlog of aethids to sort already," Eor whined. "I can't afford to lose anyone."

Tahlee stared at him coldly. "Sorting is the least of our priorities unless you can find one to address our personnel shortages."

"How dare you!" Eor sputtered. "The Mzodi would be nothing without sorters."

A look of delight crossed Shelton's face, probably because he thought Tahlee was about to smack Eor across the deck. The fiery first mate visibly checked her obvious desire to bitch slap Eor and turned to the rest of the crew standing nearby. "The parting ceremonies begin in one hour. I will see you then."

"It'll be a miracle if we survive this trip," Shelton muttered as the crew filtered away.

Adam leaned back on the railing and watched Eor vent his frustration to a fellow sorter. "I wonder if the problem of the manpower shortage could be solved by gems."

That drew curious looks from the rest of us.

Shelton shrugged. "Gems seem to be the answer to everything around here."

Elyssa's question beat mine to the punch. "How so?"

Adam took out his phone and projected the blueprint of the *Falcheen*. "This ship conforms with the configuration I've seen on every Mzodi ship—excepting, of course, the *Evadora*."

"Yeah, because it wasn't built by the Mzodi," Shelton said. "Do you think there's a better design?"

"Think of the navigators as rowers," Adam said. "Each one powers an oar independently which means that if one person is stronger than another, they're not using all available strength whereas the weaker ones are rowing with all their might."

"I think I see where you're going with this," Shelton said. "Centralized power?"

Adam waggled a hand. "Not quite. Think of it as linked power distribution."

Shelton snapped his fingers. "We link the levitation gems so they share power."

Elyssa frowned. "If you link the foils, that might also link the control commands so the foils can't be independently steered."

"That won't be an issue." Adam turned off the holographic image and lowered his voice. "Since we figured out how to hack the door gems, I dug into other gem enchantments to see how similar they are to Arcane enchantments."

"Holy ball sacks in a nut cracking factory," Shelton murmured. "Why didn't I think of that?"

Adam snorted. "Where the hell do you come up with these sayings?"

I winced at the imagery Shelton's exclamation evoked and steered Adam back on target. "So, do they?"

"Short answer, yeah." Adam pointed to the control rods for the levitation gems. "Those, for example are charmed to amplify magical power and direct it. If I programmed the control rods differently, I could tell them to ignore steering commands and only pass through power."

It seemed my analogy of gem sorters to nerds was even more spot-on than I'd realized. "Do the sorters program the gems with these commands?"

"Exactly," Adam said. "Plain aetherium without an enchantment basically does nothing."

"Even bloodstones?" Shelton asked.

Adam shook his head. "No, there are exceptions, and bloodstones are one of those strange gems that work even without an enchantment." He projected the image of the *Falcheen* again and drew marks between the levitation foils. "Using aethids as power distribution nodes, the levitation foils will share the power from all the navigators and take the strain off the weaker ones."

"And give us a much better chance of making it through this trip alive," Elyssa said. "I like it."

"This seems like an obvious enhancement the Mzodi could've made to their ships a long time ago," I said. "Why do you think they haven't?"

Adam shrugged. "Tradition, maybe? We'll find out when we talk to Illaena."

"I'll bet she doesn't like the idea one bit," Shelton said.

Something Adam had said a moment ago stuck in my mind. "Since aetherium is highly condensed aether, does that mean it could be used for energy?"

Elyssa's eyes brightened. "Like batteries?"

Adam pursed his lips. "That's a really good idea."

"The problem," Shelton said, "is how do you release the energy in a controlled manner?"

"True," Adam said. "Aetherium doesn't emanate magical energy."

"Well, it's something to think about," I said. "In the meantime, I think we should talk to Illaena about your linked power distribution idea."

Adam looked toward the bow where the ramp led to Illaena's cabin. "Yeah. I hope she doesn't bite off my head."

Shelton clapped him on the back. "I'm sure she'll only take off an arm if you jump back fast enough."

We made our way down to the captain's quarters and rang the gem. The wall misted away to reveal Illaena on the other side, confused wrinkles in her forehead. "What is it now?" She stepped outside the door.

Adam swallowed hard and delivered his sales pitch about the power sharing gems.

Illaena's expression never wavered during the explanation, her eyes tired and haunted.

"Overall," Adam said in conclusion, "I think this minor modification will keep the navigators from growing tired too quickly and optimize their efficiency."

"Make it so," Illaena said in a calm voice. "Tell Eor what you want and he will prepare the gems."

Adam blinked a couple of times, probably as confused as the rest of us about her quick agreement. "Uh, okay." He backed away slowly from the door. "I'm on it."

"You go ahead," I told the others. "I'll be there in a minute."

Elyssa raised an eyebrow but nodded and left with Shelton and Adam.

Illaena also raised an eyebrow. "Is there something else?"

"How did you lose your first ship?"

She flinched and her face tightened with apprehension. "I am surprised Eor has not told you. He enjoys pointing out the shortcomings of others." Her lips tightened. "In any case, it is no secret."

"I know you probably don't like talking about it," I said, "but I would like to know."

"Do you question my judgement?" She spread her hands. "Even after I have brought you this far?"

"At this point, it doesn't matter whether I trust your judgement or not." I shrugged. "We're stuck with each other for better or worse. I need to know how you'll react if we encounter a similar situation."

"In that case you have little to fear." Illaena folded her arms. "For many decades, I was the first mate on the *Asta*. When Captain Celissa decided to retire her command, she told Xalara I was an excellent first mate, but was too headstrong to make a good captain."

I grimaced. "Ouch."

"Yes, it was painful to hear, but I would not rest until I gained my own command." Illaena's eye twitched. "Xalara believed Celissa was too harsh and promoted me to captain. After several successful expeditions, I grew overconfident in my abilities and ordered the ship deep into the core of the Great Barrier Vortex." She shuddered. "We were caught in a violent downdraft. It tore apart the ship and dragged it into the ocean."

Illaena squeezed her eyes shut and exhaled. "Even to this day I don't know how I survived. I awoke in one of the escape skiffs, alone and in the middle of the ocean. I searched for survivors, but I had no food or water and had to abandon the search." Her eyes blinked open.

"That's why you resisted taking this mission." I kept my tone neutral, non-judgmental. "Taking on Voltis is like reliving your worst nightmare."

Vulnerability flickered through Illaena's eyes, quickly replaced by resolve. "I will not let overconfidence be my downfall again."

I opted not to put a friendly hand on her shoulder, because Illaena just didn't seem the type to appreciate that. I still gave her a pep talk. "If there's anything I've learned about being a leader, it's that you have to have faith in the people you serve with." I shrugged. "A captain is only as good as her crew, and I think you have a great crew."

Illaena's gaze seemed to shift from past to present as she met my eyes. "You are right, but sometimes I wish Cora was still here. She was no Mzodi, but I have never seen a person with such a connection to nature."

"Cora had an unfair advantage," I said. "In her home realm, she commanded the forces of nature."

"If only we had that unfair advantage for what lies ahead." Illaena backed into her cabin. "Let me know when Adam has prepared his linked gems. I must rest."

Before I could open my mouth to say, "Later tomater!" the wall misted back into place.

I went below and found the others in the main hold with the sorters. Eor's grumpy demeanor was nowhere to be found as he oversaw the enchantment of the power-linking gems.

"This should have been done to our ships long ago," Eor said. "I've suggested many retrofits, but the ship builders aren't interested in progress." He huffed. "They value tradition over progress."

"What about using aethids for energy?" Shelton asked.

Eor looked at him as one might a child who'd asked why water is wet. "Yes, you can use some for that purpose with the proper enchantment, but to power an entire ship would eat through every aethid in the hold in a few days."

Adam frowned. "I thought the aethids were so highly concentrated they'd last longer."

"Oh, it depends, of course." Eor motioned to a brown gem the size of a pumpkin. "Usually, the darker a gem the more highly concentrated the aether. A brown one would release—" He looked up and appeared to be running calculations by drawing invisible equations in the air with his finger. Finally, he blinked and focused on us again. "That gem would power just the levitation foils for three days."

Adam pursed his lips. "In other words, we could use it for emergency backup power."

"Yes, yes, but there's no apparatus to connect it to the foils." Eor threw up his hands. "Linking the levitation foils to share power is already enough work."

"What about linking each foil to its own emergency backup?" Shelton said.

"Easier, but since aethids are seldom used this way, I'd have to construct a new enchantment." Eor muttered something unintelligible. "It would only trigger when needed. That would mean…" He trailed off and once again seemed to go to the drawing board in his mind.

Shelton nudged Adam. "He's worse than you."

Adam snorted. "I map out everything with holograms."

I regarded the brown gem and my mind shifted back to the black stones Shelton and Adam had brought from the mountain earlier. "If darker aethids hold more energy, what about those black ones you found?"

Adam's eyes lit up. "Yeah, you're right!"

"Man, those things are so dense, they'd probably power the ship for a week." Shelton clapped his hands together.

"I cannot disagree," Eor said. "But for now, we must dedicate all our attention to the power distribution modifications."

Shelton and Adam went back to studying the black gems while Eor and the sorters worked on the new power design. Elyssa and I took a seat nearby since there wasn't much else to do. The ship crew had suffered so much loss and we still had far to go. I didn't want to put more pressure on Adam, but his ship improvements might be the only thing that got us out of here alive.

Chapter 19

By mid-morning the next day, the linking gems were in place. The experienced navigators ran several tests and seemed delighted with the new power-sharing layout. Even the new recruits noticed the difference.

"It gave me a headache yesterday," one of them said. "Today it is much easier."

Once the experienced navigators were confident the new design had no flaws, they gave the green light to Illaena.

Illaena looked supremely proud of her crew, even sparing a nod of acknowledgement to Eor. "You have done well." She turned to her first mate and issued an order.

"Onward to the core," Tahlee shouted, and the navigators thrust the *Falcheen* forward.

The rift between the elemental eruptions to port and the aether storm to starboard grew narrower during our progress until it felt as though the layers were pressing close enough to suffocate us.

A chain of skylets appeared ahead in the mist and Illaena directed the ship toward the one in the center, a hovering chunk of land about the size of Kdosh. It looked like an asteroid, pockmarked and ravaged with hundreds of impact craters. Unlike the mountain, this skylet wasn't comprised of aetherium.

A crater hosted a lake, but there was no vegetation or life to feed off its waters. The land beyond the water vanished into the aether nebula. Lightning arced against the skylet, blasting holes in the rock and leaving molten lava.

"Man, that place doesn't look too inviting." Shelton tugged on the brim of his hat as if it might ward off the elements.

Adam leaned over the railing. "Wow, those aether discharges are intense."

"You mean the lightning?" Elyssa said.

He nodded. "Regular lightning is electrical. This is raw unguided magical energy."

"It'll all kill you just the same," Shelton said. "Which begs the question, why in the hell are we headed toward it?"

I observed the grim set of Illaena's mouth and eyes and hoped the route Xalara had given her would get us through safely. "I'm sure the captain knows what she's doing."

Adam flinched as another bolt of aether exploded against the skylet. "This is gonna be tricky."

"We made it through that lightning hole," Shelton said.

"Because the discharges were concentrated at the lip of the hole," Adam said. "These strikes are so random we'll be dead before we even know we were hit."

Shelton pressed his hands over his ears. "Shut up, man! You're giving me a panic attack."

Elyssa squeezed my hand. "At least the rest of the crew looks confident."

Judging from the business-as-usual demeanors of the seasoned navigators and Tahlee, either they had confidence in Illaena's abilities, or they were totally fine with being obliterated by aether lightning.

The *Falcheen* swooped down toward the lake, and for a moment, I wondered if we were about to submerge. Instead, we parked right over the water, the bow facing what looked like the mother of all thunderstorms. Bolts of aether lashed out and pummeled the land not fifty yards from the tip of the ship's nose, revving my pulse and making me jump back.

Shelton took out his staff and clenched it.

"You look like you're ready to abandon ship," Adam noted dryly.

"Darned tootin'!" Shelton tapped the end of the staff nervously on the deck, the reflections of aether lightning playing back and forth across his eyes. "I might as well throw myself in a meat grinder if we're planning to go through that."

Illaena frowned and consulted the holographic map. Tahlee traced her finger along a line—presumably the route—and shook her head.

I walked over to them. "What's wrong?"

"These skylets have moved," Illaena said. "According to the map, they should be just inside the storm." She showed me the chain of floating land masses. "By flying the ship beneath them, the skylets would have sheltered us from the lightning."

"There must be another way," I said, though I couldn't think of anything except moving laterally through the rift between the outer and inner layer.

Adam had apparently been listening and spoke. "I have an idea."

Shelton poked his head in the group. "What's wrong?"

"The route is gone," I said.

"So we make our own," Adam said. He turned to Illaena. "Do you have more of those spiky aethids you used to disperse the lightning in the tunnel?"

"Yes, but we will be flying blind," Illaena said.

"Not if we modify the charms on the stones." He held his hands out as if holding a ball. "The stones are charmed to soak up energy and hold it in. If we charm the stones to unleash it all at once, it should give us what we need."

"Do you know how much energy one of those aether discharges produces?" Shelton said incredulously. "You're turning those stones into massive bombs."

"That's the idea," Adam said. "Think of them as depth charges, but in the sky."

Shelton frowned. "That's the worst analogy I've ever heard."

"What do you expect these sky charges to do?" Illaena said.

"The stones will temporarily neutralize the aether." Adam made a circle with his hands and expanded them. "With any luck, it'll clear a path."

Illaena nodded at Tahlee who gave the order.

A few minutes later, two sorters hauled a net filled with large spiky aethids to the deck and set them next to the ballista mounted on the bow.

"The enchantments have been modified," one of the sorters said. "Be sure to launch them far from the ship, or they'll do more damage than good."

"Understood," Tahlee said.

Soldiers installed another ballista next to the first and loaded each with the sky charges.

"Hope this works," Adam said nervously.

Shelton grunted. "I just hope you don't blow up the ship."

Adam sidled closer to the crossbow and inspected the charges. "We'll need to fire them about five degrees to port and starboard."

Tahlee angled the trajectory of each ballista. "Like so?"

He nodded. "The moment they explode, we'll need to go as fast as possible through the opening and fire two more charges every thirty seconds."

"Uh, how thick is the aether storm?" I looked uneasily at the ceaseless arcs of lightning in the gray nebula. "What if we run out of charges?"

"According to the map, the storm layer is ten miles thick," Adam said. "Travelling at top velocity, the *Falcheen* could close that distance in five minutes. I think we can make it through with just enough charges to make the return trip."

"Fine, you did the math," Shelton said, "but can the ballistas shoot the charges far enough ahead while we're moving at top speed, and how long will the explosion keep the clouds open?"

"Those are really good questions," Adam said. "Unfortunately, I don't know the mass of the aether or the power of the ballistas to calculate those variables."

Shelton face-palmed. "Just freaking great."

"On the other hand, we'll be taking a huge shortcut." Adam produced the map and traced the skylet route. "It would've taken us two days to wind our way through the storm instead of minutes. If we angle the trajectory this way, we'll end up where the mapped trail ends."

"Probably a shortcut to our doom." Shelton sighed. "Can we at least test two charges and measure the velocity?"

Adam shook his head. "We need every charge we have if we're coming back the same way." He turned to me. "What do you think, Justin?"

After all we'd been through to get this far, the thought of turning back made me sick to my stomach. "We need to try, but that's not my call." I shifted toward Illaena and waited for an answer.

She didn't take long. "Prepare to enter the storm."

"Energize foils!" Tahlee roared.

Shelton jumped back. "Christ Almighty, that woman doesn't waste time."

The levitation foils hummed with power.

She raised her arm and chopped the air. "Fire charges!"

The soldiers aimed the two ballistas as Adam had indicated and fired. Aether lightning arced out and consumed the stones the moment they made contact with the nebula. Several seconds passed in silence and then a deep boom sounded, like someone had just pounded the largest timpani drum in existence and let the sound reverberate.

Wind rushed forward, sucking at my clothes and tearing Shelton's hat from its perch. It smacked into the back of a soldier's head where the strap caught hold.

Shelton snatched back his hat and hung onto it as the vacuum tried to suck it from his hands. The ship shook violently beneath our feet and droplets of water from the lake coated the deck like dew.

Another boom shattered the air. A crimson glow lit the nebula and gale force winds roared past in the opposite direction. The roiling aether parted, the explosion ripping a tunnel through the gray mass. Our path was ready.

"All speed forward!" Tahlee cried, and the *Falcheen* lurched into the foreboding tunnel.

"I hope your math is right!" Shelton shouted at Adam. He grabbed the railing and hung on.

I tethered myself and the others to the deck with strands of Murk and gripped the railing to keep myself upright as the ship bucked and shuddered through the turbulence while a lightshow played all along the tunnel edges.

"Hey, Shelton," Adam shouted.

Shelton turned his terrified eyes on his friend. "What?"

"I just measured the last two constants." Adam tapped quickly on his smartphone. "Looks like I was off on the rate of collapse."

"Justin, look." Elyssa pointed toward the walls of the tunnel. The kinetic force holding it open was already collapsing, and the deadly forces were rushing in to fill the void.

Shelton scowled. "You picked the worst possible time to be wrong!"

Adam turned to Tahlee. "Slow to one hundred knots, and fire every twenty-five seconds."

The first mate cried out the new instructions and the ship slowed.

Adam counted down on his phone. "Three, two, one."

"Fire!" Tahlee cried again.

The soldiers launched two more charges dead ahead. The ballistas launched them at enough velocity to carry them safely ahead of the ship and into the storm, but the rift was quickly collapsing in on us.

Once again, a vacuum sucked at us before a massive explosion tore another tunnel through the boiling gray clouds.

"Full speed!" Adam said.

Tahlee shouted the command and the *Falcheen* slipped into the new opening seconds before the old one collapsed back in upon itself.

A new countdown started on Adam's arcphone as the ship bucked and surged through the violent turbulence left in the wake of the explosion. Elyssa's violet eyes lit with excitement, hand tightening around mine.

"It's so beautiful and terrifying," she shouted over the rush of wind.

"We'll be snuffed out like farts in a hurricane if this tunnel collapses," I shouted back.

She laughed.

Shelton cast an angry glare my way. "Next time you go on an adventure, I'm staying home!"

Adam and Tahlee coordinated another salvo and a new hole formed in the storm. The *Falcheen* carried us from one fleeting haven to the next, the hull shaking violently every time we hit an invisible pocket of turbulence. Minutes ticked past, and the supply of charges dwindled.

"I don't understand," Adam said. "We should've been through by now."

"Five minutes ago by your calculation," Shelton hollered over the roaring wind.

I was about to throw in my two cents when a rod of lightning arced across the rift and clipped the back end of the ship. The stern spun sideways and the *Falcheen* careened out of control.

Shelton's eyes went wide. "Oh shi—"

There was no way to fire the charges ahead of us, no way for the navigators to wrestle the ship back under control in time. I channeled a dome shield over as much of the deck as I could an instant before the dark clouds swallowed us.

Adam grabbed my arm. "Don't channel Murk or Brilliance, Justin!"

Before I could open my mouth to ask why, aether lightning pummeled my shield, as if drawn to it, like electricity to a ground.

"Release the shield!" Adam shouted.

Instead of letting it go, I tied off the weave and sent the shield hurtling off the ship. The lightning followed it, arcing across it like a plasma globe before I lost sight in the thick gloom.

"What about the foils?" Shelton said. "Those things are full of energy."

The words were hardly out of his mouth when magical energy crackled across the hull. The navigators cried out and leapt back from their stations. The *Falcheen* listed slowly as the energy faded from the levitation foils. We were at the mercy of the storm.

Illaena turned to me, eyes filling with acceptance. "We have failed."

As if that was the cue, the levitations foils burned through the last bit of energy and the ship began to fall.

Tahlee didn't seem the least bit fazed. "Deploy emergency wings!"

Soldiers and navigators rushed to large levers set nearly flush into the deck near the control rods and began pulling on them with all their might.

"Help them!" I shouted to the others and ran to assist two soldiers with a lever. We hauled back and the lever ratcheted into place. A wing the size of something you'd see on a jumbo jet sprang from the hull and locked into place. The rest of the emergency foils clicked into place and the *Falcheen*'s downward momentum settled into a shuddering glide.

Lightning struck a fore section of the deck, leaving a hole behind. Another bolt crashed into the deck only feet away. The aftershock knocked me across the deck, momentarily blinded and deaf.

Another nearby explosion thudded dully in my ringing ears. Cries rose up all around me and the ship tilted crazily beneath my prone form. *This is it. We're dead.* I hated not being able to see in the last seconds before my death. Raising a fist in a last act of defiance, I shouted, "Screw you, lightning!"

Apparently, the timing of my death wasn't quite as fast as I'd imagined, because my hearing slowly came back and the spots in my vision faded until I could make out the deck beneath me. Strong hands gripped my arm and pulled me upright. Elyssa looked more beautiful than ever, probably because I thought I'd never see her again.

"Are you okay?" she asked.

I blinked rapidly and dug a finger in my ear as if that would help anything. "Yeah." Another bright light blinded me and I prepared for more lightning. That was when I realized the sky overhead was blue, and the blinding light was the sun. "What the hell?"

"Don't ask me how, but we made it through," Elyssa said in a wondering tone. "We must have been close to the end when the ship went out of control."

I looked around and saw the healer on deck tending to the wounded. Adam sat with his back to the railing, a relieved look on his face while Shelton puked over the side. The navigators had resumed their stations and it seemed the levitation foils were once again holding us aloft. The aether storm roiled a hundred yards to port, angry arcs of lightning threading its surface while overhead, the sun shined down from clear skies.

Holding tight to Elyssa's hand, I walked to the starboard side and looked out across endless blue sea. "This is the center of Voltis?" I hadn't known what to expect. A part of me had thought there might be an eye to the storm, but certainly not a place like this. On the other hand, where was the secret weapon? Unless it was underwater, there didn't seem to be much here.

"It's bizarre." Elyssa looked back at the wall of gray behind us and followed its curve. "Is this what it's like in the middle of a hurricane?"

"I have no idea." I zoomed my vision on the horizon, but there was nothing but more and more water. A terrible suspicion welled up in me. What if Kaelissa was wrong? What if we'd just sacrificed dozens of lives to reach the eye of the storm where nothing existed? Even worse, what if this had been a clever lure crafted by Arturo or Kaelissa to keep me away from Pjurna?

If Voltis held no secrets behind its deadly walls, we had just endured everything for nothing.

Chapter 20

"How could I have been so stupid?" I felt sick to my stomach.

Elyssa looked confused. "What are you talking about?"

"We've come all this way for nothing." I jabbed a finger toward the aether storm behind us. "Now we're trapped inside Voltis while Kaelissa and Arturo have their way with the nation we left undefended."

Her forehead wrinkled. "Except they're not undefended. Our army is in Tarissa and they're plenty capable of defending her without us."

Elyssa's argument cast a blanket of doubt on my logic. I was so used to being in the middle of the fight that I hadn't stopped to think about the real scope of my importance in the army.

She continued. "If anything, there's more danger of civil war from the Darkling legions than invasion from Brightlings."

It was a depressing thought, but also the truth. "So you think there's actually something out here?"

"There's a lot of ocean out here." Elyssa waved a hand at the vast area. "There's still plenty of exploring to do."

I hoped she was right.

Though the crew was tired, Illaena ordered the *Falcheen* forward. I switched to demon vision and found an aether stream a hundred feet off the surface of the water and pointed it out. The ship glided into position and the navigators were finally able to park it and get some rest.

"The *Znosh* never made it this far?" I asked the captain.

She shook her head. "They simply marked this area with an X." Illaena displayed the map and scrolled to the end of the trail forged by the *Znosh*. It appeared to end inside the storm several miles from our current position.

"Great," Shelton grumbled. "Maybe we'll find buried treasure."

Holding his arcphone out at arm's length, Adam turned in place, a curious wrinkle in his brow. "That's odd."

I blew out a breath. "That sums up just about everything on this trip."

"No, I mean the readings are odd." Adam projected a holographic graph showing several jagged lines in hues of red, green, and yellow. "I ran a series of tests on the atmosphere in Eden and compared them to Seraphina. Basic elements like oxygen, nitrogen, and so forth are nearly identical, though the O-two content here is slightly elevated."

"That's great, Einstein." Shelton folded his arms. "Why don't you skip the science part before you make everyone's eyes glaze over?"

"I think it's interesting," I admitted.

Elyssa elbowed me. "Because you're still a nerd at heart."

Adam swiped away all but three lines on the graph. He pointed to the lowest one. "These are the atmospheric aether levels in Eden." He highlighted the line that was far above the other two. "This is Seraphina."

I frowned. "So, what's the middle one?"

Adam pointed down. "Right here in Voltis."

"Not surprising," Shelton said. "I'll bet the maelstrom sucks up most of the aether in the air."

"Possibly." Adam displayed two other lines. "The problem is, oxygen is closer to Eden levels, and the sun here is fractionally brighter than on Seraphina."

I reflexively looked up and immediately regretted it as an intense white sun nearly blinded me. Others winced as they repeated my mistake and blinked tears from their eyes. It didn't take me long to realize where Adam was headed with his analysis. "We're not in Seraphina anymore, are we?"

He shook his head. "I don't think so."

"Well, ain't that peachy?" Shelton took out his arcphone and began running scans of his own. "Guess that means Voltis is like the pocket dimensions back in Eden."

"Does that mean we're in the Glimmer?" Elyssa asked.

I shook my head. "No, the Glimmer is nothing but shattered land and stars. Unless this is a pocket dimension, we must be in one of the other realms."

Shelton blew out a breath. "Too bad it ain't Eden." He looked at Adam. "Any guesses as to where we are?"

"No." Adam put his hands on his hips and looked around. "There's only one way to find out, and that's to do some exploring."

"Brilliant," Shelton said. "Maybe we can find the natives and ask them."

Illaena stepped over to the railing and looked out at the ocean. Tahlee stepped by her side, her flaming red hair dancing in the breeze. When I joined them, I noticed a spark in Illaena's eyes I hadn't seen before. She looked excited.

My sense of adventure crawled out from beneath the fear, doubt, and other emotions dominating the journey here, and I felt a spark of wonder fan into flame. *We're in another realm!* After everything I'd been through, I sometimes forgot there was more to life than endless war.

"Are we truly no longer on Seraphina?" Illaena asked me.

"If Adam thinks so, then yeah, I'd have to agree with him." I leaned over the edge and looked at the azure water.

"You did the impossible," Tahlee said. "You did what even the *Znosh* could not do."

Illaena shook her head. "We all did."

Shelton and Adam's voices rose in debate.

"What I'm asking is, if we go out another way, do we end up in the main part of whatever realm this is?" Shelton said.

"I don't know if the other realm is confined to Voltis or not," Adam replied. "Maybe Voltis acts like an Alabaster Arch, transporting from one realm to another."

"Or maybe the two realms touch here," Elyssa suggested.

"Yeah, or that," Adam said.

I opened my mouth to toss in my two cents when a huge dorsal fin broke the surface of the ocean. Two more fins soon joined it, all swimming in a perfect line.

"Holy pork-fried pants," Shelton said. "Are those sharks?"

"Anyone bring a fishing pole?" Adam said dryly.

Three aquamarine creatures leapt from the water. With long lean muzzles, and scales that shimmered like polished metal, it only took me a split second to properly classify what I was seeing.

"Sea dragons!" I shouted.

But that wasn't what had everyone's attention. Mounted on each dragon was a female rider.

The dragons spread webbed wings and glided up toward us, their riders staring serenely at us as if this was just another day in their lives.

Elyssa's eyes flared wide. "Do you think we're on Draxadis?"

I was too stunned to answer.

Illaena issued orders, and Tahlee's shouts rose above the bellows of the encroaching dragons.

"Ready foils, adjust heading a hundred-eighty degrees!" Tahlee grabbed one of the dragon spears from the soldiers as they prepared to repel any invaders.

I'd seen enough dragon attacks to know that we were no match for three of them. Our only hope was a fast retreat. The only problem was, where would we go? We couldn't go back into the maelstrom, and unless we stuck to the aether stream, the navigators would tire rapidly without rest.

Before the *Falcheen* could take flight, the dragons were upon us. I channeled a sphere of Brilliance in one hand, and Murk in the other, prepared to unleash everything I had on the riders.

"You will come with us," one of the women said in melodious voice that was more song than speech. The words were Cyrinthian, but heavily accented, almost another dialect. Her inhumanly large eyes made her alluring and horribly creepy all at the same time.

Only one other person I'd met spoke that way and had the same huge eyes that these women had. Though I'd only spoken with Melea once, she'd also creeped me out like these women—these Sirens.

The dragons glided in circles around the ship, none making an attempt to land on the deck. Illaena looked like a trapped animal, eyes darting all around the ship.

"We wish you no harm," the Siren sang softly. "Come."

I felt a sudden yearning to do exactly what she said. Judging from the glazed looks on the faces of the others, it seemed obvious we all did.

Illaena shook her head as if resisting a waking dream. "What sorcery is this?"

"Stop compelling us," I said in a stern voice.

The Sirens exchanged knowing looks, and their presumed leader, a woman with flowing green hair and deep blue eyes, nodded. "It was not our intent. We have not seen outsiders in some time and forgot the effect our voices have on others."

A cold knife of fear buried itself in my guts. Could these Sirens make us do anything they wanted by singing? I didn't want to find out, but right now, we had no choice but to accompany them.

Illaena seemed to reach the same conclusion. "Lead the way, and we will follow."

The Sirens guided their mounts into a loose formation and turned away from the ship, apparently unconcerned that we might turn tail and flee. They also had to know it wouldn't do us any good, because there was nowhere to run.

If there's nowhere to go, where are we going?

It took a while to answer that question because after twenty minutes of travel, I still didn't see anything except water.

Elyssa gripped my arm and pointed dead ahead. At first I saw only the sparkling reflection of the sun off the water, but as we drew closer, I realized something was strange about the water. It wasn't until we were within a mile of the anomaly that I realized what I was seeing wasn't endless ocean, but a reflection of endless ocean—as if someone had mounted a huge mirror in the water.

It was like looking at one of those drawings with a second image hidden inside, seen once you shifted your perspective. One second it was all ocean, the next it was a huge reflective dome of mist. The dragons flew through it as if it wasn't even there. I had to resist throwing up my arms and bracing for impact when the *Falcheen*'s prow pierced the bubble.

Cool, salty mist brushed my face and lips and a mountainous island appeared a half mile ahead. The dragons swooped low, and Illaena directed the *Falcheen* to follow. We glided twenty feet off water so calm, it reflected everything like a mirror.

A dozen dolphins burst from the water, squeaking excitedly and leaping in graceful arcs off the starboard bow. Creatures that resembled manta rays glided up into the air and hovered next to the vessel before veering off and diving back into the water.

Amazing as the sea life was, I could hardly take my eyes off the island. Marble towers rose high, ending in tall spires with statues holding heroic action poses. A huge citadel rose at the top of the mountain, its many marble columns supporting the monumental statue of a thickly muscled, bearded man. A fierce expression gleaming in his marble eyes, the man was frozen in the act of casting a trident toward the water while his lower half was caught in the act of transforming from scales and fins to legs.

The impressive architecture reminded me of ancient Greece, but with a modern twist. It didn't take a mythology specialist to realize that the statues were those of gods. In this place, Poseidon was a bigger fish than Zeus.

"Son of a gun, are those ships?" Shelton jabbed a finger toward the harbor.

Long piers crafted from coral reefs and sea shells radiated from the curving shore. Some of the ships nearly defied description. The largest resembled a huge floating conch shell with windows and terraces all along the surface, like a seashell houseboat.

Next to it floated a huge starfish with the shell of a horseshoe crab mounted on top. I couldn't even imagine what made it float, much less propelled it in the water. Mingled with the fantastical ships were a few mundane sea-going vessels with wooden hulls and sails.

"I've never seen the like," Illaena said. "Why would you purposefully float a ship on the water when you can fly?"

"Maybe their ships can't fly," I said.

Shelton nodded toward our Siren guides. "Yeah, but they have freaking dragons!"

"Can't argue with that logic," Adam said. "On the other hand, did anyone notice the statue on the mountain?"

"You'd have to be blind to miss it," Shelton said. "This place looks like ancient Greece, gods and all."

"Except the architecture is too advanced," Adam said. "I couldn't even make a guess as to what era this represents."

"How could it be related to Greece when it's out in the middle of the Pacific Ocean?" I said.

"Voltis may be in the equivalent area of the Pacific Ocean, but it's not in Eden." Adam paused and then shrugged. "Geographical location doesn't mean much when we're talking interdimensional shifts."

"Wherever we are, it's beautiful." Elyssa had a dreamy look in her eyes that reminded me of the first time we'd gone to Venice, Italy.

"Yeah, too bad we're not on vacation." Shelton blew out a breath. "Let's hope the natives don't plan to eat us."

Adam blew out a breath. "Man, Zagg would probably give his two left nuts to be here right now."

Zagg, an Arcane history professor at Arcane University, was one of the most knowledgeable people in the Overworld when it came to Eden, but after meeting me, he'd learned more about ancient history in months than in all his previous years. Primarily because I attracted the sort of crowd that had been involved in world domination at some point of their careers.

"I almost wish it was Zagg here and not me," Shelton muttered. He looked at me out of the corner of his eye. "Answer me this. If the Sundering happened before ancient Greece even existed, then what in the hell is a statue of Poseidon doing here?"

I shrugged. "Maybe this is where the idea for the Greek gods came from."

Thousands of years even before the First Seraphim War, all the different supernatural races lived together on Earth. Cora had told me the story of how the Seraphim ruled the skies, the Sirens, the sea, and the Lyrolai, the land. There had been other supernatural creatures like dragons and, hell, maybe even unicorns back in those days. An ancient race of god-like beings, the Apocryphan, had taken over and, at some point, gone to war with each other.

This had the unfortunate effect of shattering Earth into separate realms—Eden, Seraphina, Haedaemos, Aquilis, Draxadis, Sturg, and so forth and so on. It had isolated the Apocryphan from each other along with their kingdoms. Eventually, the Sirens had trapped these gods in a prison of their own making—the Abyss.

I'd learned in my adventures that the Sirens were also responsible for making the Alabaster Arches, the Obsidian Arches, and had been the architects for the Apocryphan. If they didn't plan to kill us, it seemed like a grand opportunity to find out a lot more about the universe.

Maybe I should be a history professor.

"The Apocryphan who ruled the Sirens was named Posthanied." Adam said.

His statement snapped me from my thoughts. "Uh, I think you're right."

"Sounds close to Poseidon," Elyssa said. "Who knows? Maybe the entire Greek pantheon came from the Apocryphan."

"I ain't too sure how you get Zeus and Ares from Kathazal and Xanomiel," Shelton said, naming two of the other ancient beings, "but knock yourselves out."

The Sirens guided us toward a wide stone pier shaped like a sea turtle with a shell a hundred yards in diameter. Their green-haired leader pointed down and Illaena gave Tahlee the command to land.

Scores of seagulls burst into flight as the *Falcheen* settled in for a landing, swirling overhead like a white funnel designed to crap on everything anybody ever loved.

Shelton looked suspiciously up at the birds and pressed his hat firmly on his head. "The Sirens are paying my dry cleaning bill if those birds poop on my duster."

Tahlee charged a gem on the starboard side and a gangway of Murk projected from the side of the ship. The Mzodi soldiers lined up, weapons at the ready, but Illaena held up a hand and shook her head.

"I will go alone."

Tahlee's eyes flared. "Not without me."

Illaena offered a curt nod and the pair walked down the gangway to the turtle shell pier.

My guts knotted as I watched them descend. If the Sirens meant us harm, there wasn't anything we could do to stop them.

Chapter 21

Shelton and Adam leaned on the railing, watching with interest as the Sirens dismounted their dragons and glided toward their guests, their dresses flowing like water along with them. The sea dragons didn't wait around long, sliding off the end of the pier and into the water.

"I don't trust these Sirens one little bit," Shelton said. "Those tales about them luring sailors to their deaths against the rocks weren't just fairy tales."

"I'm sure it had some basis in fact," Adam said, "but the reality seems different."

"On the surface," Shelton said. "Dive deep enough you'll find out the truth."

"Or it might be smooth sailing," Adam said with a smirk.

I groaned. "I hate to dampen your enthusiasm by throwing cold water on this conversation, but there's not much we can do if the Sirens decide to sing us lullabies."

Elyssa shook her head. "I think I just heard more water metaphors in thirty seconds than I want to hear for the rest of this trip."

"Might be a short trip, sweetheart." Shelton unholstered a short wooden rod and flicked it out to a full-length staff. "We need to protect ourselves against the song of the Sirens or we'll never get out of here."

"I'm not walking around with cotton in my ears," Elyssa said.

"Wouldn't work anyway," Shelton said. "You need something denser like beeswax. Speaking of which—" he dug around inside his duster and removed a small pink coin purse from an inside pocket.

Adam leaned over his shoulder. "Aww, did Bella pack your toothbrush in there?"

Shelton gave him a dirty look. "Shut it, smartass." He twisted open the metal latch and removed a pair of foam earplugs. "Sometimes I have trouble sleeping when there's a lot of noise." He stuffed them in his ears where the pink tips designed to aid removal poked out like bug antennae. "There. Problem solved."

Elyssa's nose wrinked. "They look stupid."

Shelton cupped a hand to his ear. "What?"

Adam spoke loudly, speaking each word with exaggerated precision. "They. Look. Stupid."

"What?" Shelton pulled one out. "Can't hear a thing with those earplugs in."

"I'm about to backhand you across the deck," Adam said.

I ignored the banter and watched Illaena converse with the green-haired Siren. Judging from their facial expressions, the exchange seemed calm and polite, and neither of the Mzodi had the glazed look of someone under the spell of a song.

"If Adam is right about this being another realm," I told Elyssa, "we must be in Aquilis."

"Makes sense." She looked out at the city. "If that's the case, the secret weapon must be here somewhere."

I frowned and looked at the peaceful city. "Doesn't seem like the place to have a secret weapon."

"No, it doesn't," Elyssa said. "None of those vessels in the harbor look like warships, and I don't see soldiers or troops anywhere."

"They do have dragons," I reminded her.

She nodded. "True, but they didn't seem hostile."

A shout from Tahlee ended our conversation. At first I thought there was trouble, but quickly realized the first mate was ordering the soldiers to disarm and come down the gangway. I took it upon myself to head down and face the music.

Shelton swallowed hard and shoved the earplugs back in place, much to the amusement of Adam. Elyssa gripped my hand and we walked down the ramp toward the group at the bottom.

The green-haired Siren wore a long shimmering dress that hid her legs and made it look as though she glided instead of walked. She nodded at my group. "I am Narine." Her arm swept to include her other companions, one a female with soft features and turquoise hair, and the other with a round face and blue-gray locks. "This is Balaena and Dolpha."

She didn't extend a hand to shake it and I didn't feel like pressing my luck so I simply nodded back and introduced the others. "I'm Justin and these are my friends, Elyssa, Adam, and Shelton."

Vertically slit pupils regarded me curiously. Narine tucked a flowing lock of hair behind small smooth ears and glided her eyes across the others. "Some of you are mortals."

I didn't want to show all our cards so I answered with a shrug. "Are we in Aquilis?"

Her very thin eyebrow raised slightly. "The ancient kingdom of the Sirens vanished long ago."

"How would you know of it?" Dolpha asked. Her voice was unusually high pitched, but no less sing-song than Narine's.

I exchanged a confused frown with Elyssa then turned back to our hosts. "Aquilis is the Siren realm, right?"

Narine nodded. "Yes, it was once so, but our kingdom vanished into legend along with the rest of the world eons ago."

Tahlee and Illaena shared confused glances of their own. "We are from Seraphina," Illaena said.

Dolpha's head reared back as if struck. "The angel kingdom was destroyed with everything else."

Illaena's forehead scrunched. "Where else could we have come from?"

The Sirens took a turn looking flummoxed. "Are you not from Heval?" Narine pointed up and away.

"The more we talk, the more confused I get," Adam said. "Maybe it would be better if we didn't assume anything and just said where we're all from."

"What game is this?" Dolpha said in a harsh song. "We have left your kingdom alone for millennia. The mortals are free to do as they wish, so what cause have you to intrude on our sovereign territory?"

I held up my hands. "I assure you, we're not from these parts at all. We really are from Seraphina—well, not originally." I flicked my hand to indicate my friends. "We're from Eden."

"Ha!" Dolpha scoffed. "Now we know they lie."

Narine's eyes lit with wonder. "Or perhaps the legends are true."

"Could it be?" Balaena said. "Perhaps there are survivors beyond the storm."

I didn't know what to think, but I figured a brief history lesson of the Sundering might help jog their memories. It was possible that they'd suffered some sort of memory loss, or maybe they'd been isolated from everyone else.

"Do you remember the Apocryphan?" I asked.

"Indeed." Narine tilted her head slightly, as if remembering. "I was not alive during those dark days, but we still sing the legends."

"Our ancestors fled when the Apocryphan War started and founded this city in a place untouched by man." Balaena raised her chin proudly. "Many Lyrolai fled the war as well and joined us on the island, which for some reason, was invisible to the Apocryphan."

"So the legend says." Narine's huge eyes widened. "The great war wiped the kingdoms from the face of the Earth."

"Centuries later, the mortals appeared." Dolpha scowled, as if this was an unpleasant thought.

"Many moved to the island, and together, we built a great civilization," Balaena said, chin lifting even higher. "We showed them how to create magnificent, efficient structures, and educated them with ancient knowledge."

"The mortals in the other nearby lands were not so pleasant." Dolpha's scowl deepened. "For a time, we traded with them, but then they grew to fear us, claiming we were cannibals who feasted on their sailors, luring their ships to their doom."

"We cut off contact with the outsiders and they stayed far from us." Narine shook her head sadly. "It was then that another great evil appeared, and songs of a new war reached our ears. Whatever made our island invisible to the Apocryphan kept us undetected by this new evil. But then something terrible happened, and a great darkness swept the land."

Elyssa gave me a knowing look. "Sounds like the Desecration."

She was right. When stories had timelines spanning thousands of years, it was hard to keep things straight, but the Desecration was one of those worldwide events so huge, that it placed a big old frownie-face on the calendar.

Narine raised an eyebrow at Elyssa's remark but continued the story. "The storm that destroyed the world, swept in from all sides and soon we were all that remained. Now there are only the three of us, a few Lyrolai and perhaps two-hundred mortals."

Adam's eyes flared as if a lightbulb just blinked on inside his head. "What, exactly, is the name of this city?"

Dolpha scowled, apparently unconvinced that we weren't from Heval. "Your game is not amusing."

"Ah, yes," Narine said. "I apologize for my lack of manners." She spread her arms as if to present the city. "Welcome to Atlantis."

Adam might have expected that answer but I thought my jaw was going to hit my belly button. "This is the lost city of Atlantis?"

Illaena and Tahlee didn't seem to know what to make of our confusion. For that matter, neither did the Sirens.

"We are not lost," Dolpha said.

"You've got to be kidding me!" I pressed a hand to my heart. "We're in Atlantis? Do you know how freaking cool that is?"

"Totally explains the architecture," Adam said. "I knew it was inspired by ancient Greece architecture, but it was too advanced."

"Do they have flying chariots and laser beams?" I asked.

Elyssa frowned. "I thought Atlantis was underwater."

"What nonsense is that?" Dolpha said.

"Laser beams?" Narine spoke the words haltingly.

Shelton's eyes darted back and forth as he tried to read our lips. Little did he know his earplugs were making him miss all the juicy info.

Adam switched gears with his next question. "Who lives in Heval? More Sirens?"

Narine blinked. Up close it was really unsettling since she had a clear eyelid that closed before her outer one did. "Heval is a mountain that reaches far into the sky. Its slopes are rocky and steep—unsuitable for living since there is no easy access to the water. We did not realize there are people living at the top until only about a thousand years ago."

"*Only* a thousand years?" Adam said incredulously. "Who are these people?"

Balaena rolled her shoulders in what I took for a shrug. "They did not offer much information, and seemed just as surprised as us to discover there were other survivors of the world's end."

"What are their names?" I asked.

"They were very secretive," Narine said. "While they did not offer their names or background, one of them addressed the male by name—Gallifer."

A cold chill tip-toed down my back. "How many people were there?" I asked.

"Only three," Balaena replied.

"It's the Seraphim who tried to control Thussor," Elyssa said. "Gallifer, Sithain, and Purah."

"I told you these intruders are from Heval!" Dolpha said.

I shook my head. "No, we're not. You have no idea how dangerous those people are."

"They are not dangerous." Dolpha huffed—but in a musical way, of course. "Many mortals live in Heval, and they have been perfectly happy there."

"We don't actually go to Heval." Narine said. "Those Atlanteans who moved there sometimes return to visit family and say they are treated very well."

"None of them know the names of their hosts?" Adam asked.

"I wouldn't know," Narine said. "I do not interfere in their personal affairs."

"The mortals and Lyrolai are free to do as they choose," Dolpha said. "Our domain is the sea."

With a loud sigh, Shelton tugged the earplugs out and said, "Are you guys talking about hamburgers? Do they have meat on this island?"

That brought a stunned silence to the conversation until Adam burst into laughter. "Dude, you are awful at reading lips!"

"What did he have in his ears?" Narine asked.

Dolpha huffed. "I thought them peculiar decorations for a male."

"Earplugs." I rolled my eyes. "He didn't want you mind controlling him with your singing."

Dolpha narrowed her eyes at him. "We would never intentionally do such a thing."

"Fine, I get it." Shelton held up his hands in surrender. "Mind control me all you want, but I gotta know—are there hamburgers on this island? Pancakes? Bacon?"

Adam snorted. "Well, we know what's been on Shelton's mind all this time."

Admittedly, I was pretty hungry, so I phrased Shelton's question into something the others would understand. "Do you have food here?"

"Of course," Narine said. "Shall I prepare you a shell of krill?"

Shelton gagged. "Please, no."

Adam clamped a hand over his mouth and went red in the face trying to suppress his laughter.

"We request the hospitality of your land," Illaena said. "We have many tales to tell, but our journey has wearied us."

"If the others have no objections"—Narine looked at her companions—"I am happy to extend our hospitality."

Dolpha narrowed her eyes. "I do not trust these newcomers. They appear in a flying ship and claim no knowledge of our lands—yet what else exists outside of this?"

"The world." I let that sink in. "We'll tell you more later, but I assure you, everything still exists outside of your domain."

Balaena's eyes grew hopeful. "The ocean still sings beyond the ends of our earth?"

"It does." I waved a hand at the amazing city behind her. "If anything, we thought Atlantis had been lost forever. If we could have food and rest, we'll gladly catch you up on events."

"Then you are welcome," Balaena said.

Dolpha scowled and offered a begrudging nod. "Very well, but do not think we will abide any treachery."

"We're not pirates," I assured her.

"I am!" Shelton looked hurt. "You're breaking my heart here."

"Fine." I threw up my hands. "We're sky pirates, but not the bad kind."

Narine and her companions looked at each with scrunched foreheads, probably because pirate didn't exactly translate into Cyrinthian.

"I will introduce you to the mortal archon," Narine said. "I am certain the mortals will be most pleased to have visitors since very little ever changes around here."

"I thought you ruled Atlantis," Illaena said.

"We do not see a reason to rule anything," Narine said. "Life is simple. The mortals require structure, for their lives are short and even their adults are still as children to us, but they are capable of tending to their own affairs."

Nearly a dozen people burst from the water below, performed graceful flips, and executed perfect three-point hero landings, splattering water everywhere. They had bluish skin and scales, and their feet were webbed, but before anyone could comment, the scales and feet morphed into normal human feet and skin, though the bluish cast of their skin remained.

A tall male wearing only a tight pair of shorts stepped forward. He was hairless aside from the wet blue locks on his head. "Who are these people, Mother?" His inner eyelid blinked over round pupils like those of humans.

Narine remained quiet a beat, as if showing an unruly child that she was not to be questioned in that tone. "That has yet to be determined, Lash. What brings you to the shores?"

"We were swimming at the fringes when we saw the flying ship," he replied curtly.

Dolpha bared her teeth. "You're tempting fate swimming so close to the world's edge."

"*We* are brave!" a short woman shot back. "Unlike you, we know there is more than this forsaken land. If you would help us, we might find a way out."

I wanted to jump in and let her know there was something more on the other side, but Narine held up a hand.

"I will not argue with you in front of guests." The Siren folded her arms. "You may speak with the newcomers later. For now, I am taking them to meet the mortals."

"Did Sirens mate with mortals?" Adam said.

Lash burst into laughter. "In the ancient days, the Sirens began to die off. They tried to increase their numbers by pairing with mortals, but all they got was us."

The female who'd spoken earlier growled. "We are halflings—part mortal, part Siren."

"And wholly unwanted by either," Lash finished. He flashed his pearly whites. "For centuries we have sought a way out of this place."

"We saw you come from the storm," the female said. "Tell us, is there a way out?"

I nodded. "There is, but it's incredibly dangerous."

"Enough." Narine's voice made the others flinch. "We will introduce them to the mortals. If they are willing, the newcomers will speak to you later."

Lash frowned but didn't argue. "Very well, Mother." He did a back flip off the pier and vanished, his comrades close behind.

"Apologies for our children," Narine said. "We tried to make them feel welcome."

Dolpha adopted her favorite expression again, a scowl. "But they are never satisfied. It was a mistake to have children with mortals."

"The last Trident perished long ago," Balaena said in a mournful tone. "Now there are no more males."

Narine nodded, but said nothing more about it. "Come. Let us go." She turned and glided up the sloping pier toward the city, her companions at her side.

Illaena motioned for her crew to follow, and the rest of us tagged along.

Shelton tilted his head and peered under the edge of their dresses. "Do they have feet?"

Adam pushed him on the shoulder. "Stop that, you pervert."

"I ain't—well, okay maybe I am a little perverted." Shelton poked Adam in the chest. "Not like you're any different."

"They have feet." Elyssa pointed to watery footprints left behind the Sirens. "Don't ask me how they move without bobbing."

"So their males are called Tridents, huh?" Shelton's face scrunched as another thought seemed to slap him in the noggin. "Hey, do you think Tridents have three—"

Adam groaned. "Really?"

He pointed to the statue with the three-pronged trident on the peak. "Just sayin' man!"

I rolled my eyes and turned my attention back to our hosts.

The Sirens' dresses shifted and flowed as if they were floating underwater the same way their hair did, but there was no bubble of water around them from what I could tell. It was a very strange kind of magic—almost like an aura that followed them no matter where they went. I switched to demon view as we walked and nearly tripped over my own feet when I saw what was normally invisible to the naked eye.

A hazy blue nimbus glowed around each Siren, the energy rippling and swaying like ocean water. By comparison, the Seraphim had bright auras that burned like candles. Shelton and Adam had smaller, slightly dimmer halos of energy. I'd seen a lot in my short supernatural life, but the Sirens were definitely more unsettling to look at this way than most.

A group of mortals—judging by their auras—waited at the entrance to the harbor, children jostling and squeezing through the legs of adults to peer at the strangers in their land. It looked like they were dressed for a toga party, the men in short blue and red tunics, and the women in long white and beige dresses.

Shelton grunted. "Is it Halloween already?"

"Interesting," Adam said. "The clothing style hasn't advanced much from ancient Greece."

"How awful!" Elyssa grimaced. "How could clothing not change in thousands of years?"

Narine stopped nearly twenty feet from the people, and spoke in a lilting tone. "Adonis, I would introduce to you guests who claim to be from the outside."

That caused quite a stir among the crowd, some looks of alarm, and no shortage of murmurs. A rather homely man with a pot belly and a wrinkled face flourished his arms wide and bowed. "The people of Atlantis welcome you."

It was time to meet the real locals.

Chapter 22

"Archon Adonis?" Illaena asked.

"He sure ain't no Adonis," Shelton murmured, causing Adam to cackle loudly.

"I am he," he replied in accented Cyrinthian.

"I am Illaena, captain of the *Falcheen*, a vessel of the Mzodi." She thrust a finger toward the turtle pier. "We have washed upon your shores and request your hospitality."

"You shall have it!" Adonis declared. "Tell me truly, are you from Heval?"

"We are from Seraphina," Illaena said. "Her skies are beyond the walls of the storm."

Adonis's gaze wandered toward the ocean where the gray walls rose far in the distance. "By the grace of the gods, is this true?" His eyes darted to Narine.

"We cannot say," Narine replied in a slightly irritated tone. I got the impression she didn't much like dealing with the humans. "We leave them in your care."

Adonis bowed. "As you say, milady of the deeps."

Dolpha narrowed her eyes. "Very well, then. When the stories have been sung, we will hear them and determine their truth."

"You don't want to stick around?" I asked.

Narine's unsettling eyes locked onto me. "When you are ready, we will host you in our home." She dove over the side of the pier, drawing gasps from Elyssa and Shelton.

I ran to the side as Dolpha and Balaena followed and watched in horror as they plunged into the ocean some hundred feet below.

"I wonder if they ever belly flop," Shelton said.

Adam grinned. "That would be one epic smack."

"Do they always do that?" I asked Adonis.

"The Sirens do as they will," he replied.

Some citizens frowned and shook their heads as if they'd put up with enough Siren shenanigans, while others clasped their hands and bowed heads in reverence. I got the feeling the Sirens felt like they were stuck in an apartment with roommates who never cleaned their rooms or washed the dishes. Judging by the reactions of some mortals, the feeling was mutual.

"Where are the Lyrolai?" I asked.

Adonis's smile vanished. "They keep to themselves on the other side of the island."

"They take good crop land and use it for nothing," a young man spat.

"Now, now, Eris." Adonis gave the man a look of warning then turned back to us. "If you would have food and wine, please come with me."

Shelton's mouth twitched. "Do you eat pork?"

Adonis looked surprised. "Of course."

Illaena's lips curled in disgust. "Do you have something other than meat?"

"Potatoes, beets, maize, bread, and many other delights," Adonis replied. His gaze wandered back to the *Falcheen*. "Are your stores low?"

Illaena nodded. "We would trade gems for food."

"We have little use for gems," he said.

That drew sharp looks from the women in the crowd.

Adonis caught the hostile gazes and hastily amended his sentence. "But with our bountiful harvests, we have plenty to trade for gems."

Illaena offered a curt nod. "If it pleases you, we will take the food back to our ship and eat there."

Adonis looked from them to me and my friends. "I had hoped for stories of your travels."

I indicated my group. "We'll stay in town and give you all the stories you can handle."

Cheers rose from kids and adults alike as if I'd just announced free cookies.

Adonis grinned from ear to ear, revealing some teeth sorely in need of a dentist. "We have listened to the same stories so many times, it will be good to hear something new."

Shelton snorted. "That ain't gonna be a problem."

We followed Archon Adonis to large storehouses filled to overflowing with fruits, veggies, grains, and more. Even though nothing was refrigerated, the food seemed perfectly preserved.

Illaena picked up a tomato and rotated it in her hand, a perplexed look on her face. "This is glurk?"

Adonis frowned. "It's a tomato, mistress."

Illaena shook her head. "Justin, are these the mortal foods you told us about?"

Shelton rubbed his hands together and answered for me. "Yes they are!" He stared lustfully at an apple. "Can I have one of those?"

"Of course," Adonis said. He picked up a fat juicy one and gave it to Shelton. "In order to remove the preservation ward, you must mark a circle with a cross." He demonstrated on the apple. "Otherwise you will find it quite impossible to bite into."

"Thanks!" Shelton took a big bite, spilling juice down his chin, and groaned in pleasure. "I think I died and went to heaven."

"God forbid if they have donuts," Adam said. "By the time Shelton sees Bella again, he'll be ten times bigger."

Illaena spent some time testing various foods, and settled on a few bushels of pomegranates, nuts, corn, and a few dozen loafs of bread. The Seraphim seemed particularly fond of the brown Kalamata olives and took an extra basket with them back to the ship.

Adonis was perplexed by their dietary habits, particularly where it came to meat. "Animal flesh is essential for your health," he said after Illaena turned down a haunch of pork. "And it is very tasty."

"We desire none of it," she replied.

"You wouldn't be saying that if you'd tried bacon," Shelton said. "I'll bet I could whip up some bacon-wrapped grilled cheese sandwiches that'd rock your world."

Illaena and Tahlee gagged.

Eor, ever the discoverer, stepped forward. "I would be brave enough to try something that sounds so vile if only to qualify your exuberance."

"Yeah, well stick around," Shelton said.

"No, he will return to the ship with the rest of us." Illaena rounded up the rest of her crew and set out for the harbor.

Eor stayed behind for a moment and said, "Shelton, procure some bacon and bring it to me later. I assure you I am brave enough to ingest it."

Shelton gave him an approving pat on the back. "You got it."

Eor nodded and reluctantly left to follow the other Seraphim.

"What preservation spell are you using on the food?" Adam asked Adonis.

"It is something we learned from the gods of Heval," the archon replied. "Some of our family who went to live there returned with magical gifts that help us in many ways of life."

"Gods?" I said. "You mean Gallifer, Sithain, and Purah?"

He nodded. "Who else would live atop Mount Olympus?"

Shelton shrugged. "Zeus, Hera, Ares—all the Greek gods."

"I'm afraid they were lost in the destruction of the world," Adonis said, "or so the legends say."

I figured it was best not to jump straight into the story of how their supposed gods—the Fallen—had tried to mind control their king and take over Seraphina. It was best to learn about the local politics before pissing off the citizens.

"We have told and retold the old legends so often, even the young are tired of the retellings." Adonis motioned us outside. "Come, let us prepare a feast in your honor that you may tell us new stories."

Shelton paused in the middle of gorging on grapes. "A feast? Now we're talking. Can I help cook?"

Adonis frowned. "I suppose, though guests should not have to prepare their own food."

Shelton wandered to the meat aisle and sighed as if he'd died and gone to heaven. "I want to, believe me."

"Certainly, if you so desire." Adonis turned to the rest of us. "In the meantime, I can show you to your accommodations."

"That would be great," Elyssa said.

Trailed by an ever-growing crowd, Adonis led us up through the winding paths and stairs of the city. People driving donkey-drawn carts stopped in the middle of the brick-paved roads to stare when they saw our group coming toward them. Some people ran ahead of us, yelling the news that there were visitors and that there would be story time for dinner tonight.

It was an odd juxtaposition—the old-fashioned carts pulled by animals in a city where every building looked like a monument to modern architecture. Even the houses were built on a grand scale—stained glass window, soaring arches, and ornate columns. Most of them would be considered mansions back in my old neighborhood.

The yards were large, and every yard had fruit trees of some sort—oranges and lemons hanging heavy from limbs, while other yards grew other staples such as corn.

"We cannot let even the tiniest space go unused," Adonis said when he noticed me staring. "Though we have some farmland, the Lyrolai refuse to let us expand further."

"How large is this island?" I asked.

"Perhaps forty square miles," he said. "Plenty of room for the Lyrolai to allow us more land."

"Have you ever fought them?" Elyssa asked.

Adonis's eyes flared. "Goodness, no. We have not seen war here in thousands of years. The Lyrolai keep to themselves and the Sirens and their offspring do the same." He sighed. "We mortals are more dependent on the others than they are on us. I believe they would be perfectly happy if we all died off."

"How have you kept population under control?" Adam asked. "Your city seems large enough to house thousands of people, not just hundreds."

"It could house more people, but we could not feed them," Adonis said. "We live a comfortable life. There is no disease, no war,

199

and no reason to expand our numbers." He waved his arms at the grand buildings. "We have advanced medicines, but little need of doctors. We have advanced weapons left over from the days before the end of the world, but no need for them."

My heart beat a little faster. *Could those be the weapons Kaelissa wants?*

Adam's ears perked. "Advanced weapons? Can I see them?"

Adonis pursed his lips. "Perhaps. They have not been used in so long I doubt they even work, though we have schematics for making new ones."

"Do you have any flying vessels?" I asked.

"We used to have many flying chariots," Adonis said. "Unfortunately we no longer have enough raw materials to maintain them."

"Man, I'd like to see a flying chariot." Adam tapped a finger on his chin. "Do you have Arcanes here—people who practice magic?"

"Long ago, yes," he said. "The practice was banned by the gods not long after they arrived on Mount Olympus."

"Interesting." I made eye contact with Elyssa. "Sounds like the gods want to corner the market on magic."

"Good luck with that," Elyssa said. "The Sirens probably use magic all the time."

About two-thirds of the way up the mountain, Adonis stopped in front of a tall mansion with soaring columns and domes. What had once been brightly painted murals on the outer walls had faded with age, though not as much as one might expect from thousands of years of weathering.

"This is where you will be staying." Adonis motioned us inside and held up his hands to keep the crowd from following.

The foyer and most of the rooms on the first floor were empty aside from some marble tables and bronze chairs, and aside from murals on the walls, there were no other decorations.

As Adonis explained, "We have comfortable furniture, but there is no need for it in uninhabited abodes." He then led us into a bath house that could have easily accommodated twenty people, though I didn't relish the thought of bathing with Shelton or Adam around.

Elyssa was thinking the same thing. "Is this the only place to take a bath?"

"Each bedroom has a small bathroom," Adonis said. "You will find the toilets in there as well."

"Regular toilets?" Shelton sighed. "Guess I gotta start wiping again."

Elyssa's mouth dropped open. "TMI, Shelton!"

Adonis showed us the upstairs bedrooms which contained the bottom half of giant clam shells instead of beds.

Shelton ran his hand along the edge. "Are we supposed to sleep in these things?"

Adonis pulled a bronze lever and the shell filled with water. "Now you may sleep in it."

"I ain't sleeping in water!" Shelton looked at him as if he were crazy. "What do I look like, a mermaid?"

Adam hopped right in. Instead of splashing into water, it sank down like a cushion and supported him. "Wow—it's like a water bed but without all the sloshing. Give it a try!"

I sat down on it and discovered it was nearly as comfortable as a cloud bed. "Must be Siren magic."

"Indeed," Adonis said. "Now, if you'll step this way, please." He showed us the bathroom which was marble from top to bottom and had a deep circular bath with bronze faucets and handles. There was even a hand shower. The toilet was short and squat with a thick lip instead of a seat.

"Where's the toilet paper?" Shelton asked.

Adonis frowned. "What use is paper with a toilet?"

Elyssa groaned. "He means for cleaning your backside after, you know."

"Ah." Adonis grinned and pointed to a bronze handle. "Press down to flush, and pull up for a jet of water to sanitize."

Shelton shrugged. "Not as good as mist bathroom, but it'll do."

"I should be surprised they have running water," Adam said, "but then again, this is Atlantis."

"The Sirens used their water magic to make it possible," Adonis said. "They helped our ancestors build this city with their songs of

201

creation. Their magic desalinates the ocean water and distributes it to our homes, cold or hot."

The image of two Sirens singing an Obsidian Arch into existence flashed through my mind. They'd been the builders for the Apocryphan. They'd probably sung this city into existence by growing it out of the mountain itself. *Could they sing new a new Alabaster Arch?* If the Sirens had been separated from their kin for so long, they might not have learned the magic behind it.

"This place is truly a marvel," Adam said. "I'd love to study the magic that made it."

"You mentioned mist bathrooms," Adonis said. "What are those like?"

"They use magic mist to dispose of the waste and clean you all at once," Shelton said. "Makes going potty a cinch!"

Adonis's forehead wrinkled. "This sounds very much like the bathrooms in Heval."

I caught looks from Adam and Elyssa and wondered if it might shock our host to know we came in on a ship full of people with powers like their gods. "Have you heard of Seraphim?"

He nodded. "Yes, the gods of Heval once ruled the angels before the destruction of the world."

This guy doesn't even know his gods are just angels. I decided not to broach the subject right now. "Interesting. Well, we're going to rest before supper."

Adonis bowed. "Very well. Since tonight is a special occasion, we will eat at the acropolis on the mountain summit."

"The one with the huge statue of Poseidon?" Shelton said.

Adonis nodded. "The very same."

"Isn't an acropolis a defensive structure?" Adam asked.

"Perhaps it once was," Adonis said. "Now we use it for gatherings and celebrations." He smiled. "And the view is lovely."

After he left, I went upstairs and sank into a clam bed. Elyssa curled up next to me and groaned with appreciation. "This is amazing."

I wrapped my arms around her and smiled. "Lying anywhere with you is amazing."

I jerked awake to the sound of a horn in the distance. The room was pitch black but my demonic night vision kicked in, casting a bluish glow on the surroundings. Elyssa's violet eyes glowed back at me, her dhampyric night vision granting her sight.

When I stood up, the sconces on the wall began to glow and my night vision flickered off.

"The Sirens really know how to build a house." I peered inside the sconces and saw what looked like glowing algae inside.

Elyssa rubbed her eyes. "Is it time to eat?"

The horn trumpeted again. "I think so."

"Either that or we're under attack from the Kraken." Elyssa flashed a smile.

I snorted. "You joke, but the fact that we're standing in the lost city of Atlantis proves that anything is possible." I wanted to spend a few days just sight-seeing, but unfortunately, we had a mission to complete. Even more unfortunate was the fact that I had no idea what Kaelissa might want from this place. Did she know about Atlantis? Did she think they had advanced weapons of some sort?

I need to have a conversation with Adonis. Maybe there was an ancient super weapon somewhere in the Atlantean arsenal.

A large bronze chest that hadn't been there before sat just inside the door. Elyssa opened it and oohed at the clothing inside. "Finally something besides Nightingale armor."

We left the house both wearing the local fashions—Elyssa in a dress, and me in a blue tunic.

"It's weird not having underwear," I complained as we made our way up the stairs. "My junk keeps flapping around."

Elyssa rolled her eyes. "I told you to wear the loincloth."

Bronze lamps with shimmering spheres of glowing water lit the way up the winding road. A long chariot drawn by a team of horses and loaded with people came up beside us and stopped.

"It's the guests!" a young woman shouted.

"May we offer you a ride?" the driver asked.

"Yes, thanks." Elyssa stepped onto the back of the chariot and took a seat on a bench. I sat down next to her and crossed my legs so nobody would look up my tunic.

"You're so beautiful," the woman said to Elyssa.

"Thanks," I said. "I moisturize daily."

The woman's eyes flashed with surprise and then she burst into laughter along with the others.

"He's funny," a man said. "I am looking forward to his stories."

Moments later, we reached the grand building at the summit. The acropolis towered above, and the statue of Poseidon looked as huge as the goliath stone golems we'd fought during the war against Daelissa. Thankfully, this one hadn't been enchanted to life.

Statues of Sirens and other people circled the courtyard outside the building, possibly a monument of the original builders. Tall marble obelisks bore finely etched words. I stopped at one and realized it was a history of the Siren immortalized in stone next to it.

Once upon a time, Arine, mother of Narine, Jident, and Flohn left her homeland, Aquilis, to escape the Apocryphan rule. She convinced a group of Tridents and Sirens to follow her across the world where they discovered a place untouched by mortals or immortals.

Elyssa gripped my shoulder. "Hey, let's eat. You can read their stories later."

I took in the hundreds of statues and marble slabs and realized I had a lot of reading to do. My stomach grumbled and let me know I also had a lot of eating to do to make it happy, so I took Elyssa's hand and we went inside.

Music from lutes, lyres, and harps played a fast-paced ditty that adults and children alike danced to around a huge globe of brilliantly glowing water in the middle of the acropolis. I saw a group of people with bluish skin just like Lash and his friends, but I didn't recognize any of them. They seemed comfortable mixing with the mortals, and I hoped they were a bit more polite than Lash.

Adam stood on a stone pedestal near the glowing water, a tight knot of people around him as he spoke. We walked closer and heard him telling a story about how he and Shelton had pranked someone at Arcane University. While the story was considered legendary by the participants, it certainly didn't compare to everything else he'd been through. When he reached the part about how their hapless target had lost all his hair and begun clucking like a chicken, the crowd burst into laughter. Even the first time I'd heard the story I thought it was more cruel than funny, but these poor people were absolutely starved for entertainment.

Adam looked delighted to have his crowd hooked on every word. "We finally took pity on George and gave him the antidote. The moral of the story, folks, is don't try to get someone else in trouble for something you did."

The audience burst into cheers.

"Better even than Aesop!" one woman exclaimed.

I spotted the only frowning face in the crowd, an old man on the opposite side. "If looks could kill," I murmured.

Elyssa had seen the old man as well. "He must be the local storyteller or something."

A horn sounded twice in succession and then drums began rattling a beat designed to get people excited. The dancing stopped and the people stood to the sides as a procession of people laden with trays of food marched inside, setting their goodies on tables and making way for those following while everyone cheered loudly at the procession.

Adam hopped off the table and stood next to us. "Man, I can't wait to see how they react when they hear some of our really outrageous stories."

"I'll let Justin do all the telling," Elyssa said. "He's more entertaining to watch."

I was about to respond, but the sight of Shelton and three other people carrying trays filled with bacon cheeseburgers and French fries made me lose all concentration. Suddenly, there was nothing I wanted more than to be face-first in burgers.

"Holy crap!" Adam nearly danced with glee. "Looks like Shelton has been busy in the kitchen!"

Elyssa laughed. "Leave it up to Shelton to make hamburgers in Atlantis."

I could hardly hear her over the sound of my mouth watering.

The food parade ended moments later, and Adonis stepped up onto the stone pedestal. "Today we give thanks to the gods for our guests and the stories they have to tell."

The crowd burst into cheers.

Adonis smiled. "I hope old Aesop's memory is good enough to remember them all for the retelling."

People burst into laughter and the old man looked ready to cry.

"Aww, poor man!" Elyssa said. "Maybe I should give him a new story to tell."

"You're such a softie." I kissed her cheek. "I'm sure he'd love having some pretty young thing telling him stories."

Adonis spoke again. "For now, let us enjoy the exotic foods prepared for us by the legendary Harry Shelton."

Shelton pumped a fist. "Tonight you'll learn what real food tastes like!"

The crowd roared with approval.

Adonis cleared his throat and motioned to the table. "Guests go first, please."

Adam looked flummoxed. "Since when is Shelton legendary?"

"Just ask him," Elyssa said. "I'm sure he'll tell you."

I would have stuck around and laughed, but the siren song of all beef patties, special sauce, lettuce, cheese, pickles, onions, on a sesame seed bun proved irresistible. I grabbed two burgers, some fries, and a goblet of red wine since they didn't have soda. Shelton had even made fresh catsup from ground tomatoes. Without waiting for anyone else, I sat down at a table and bit into the juiciest burger I'd ever had the pleasure of eating. The crispy bacon atop the patty practically melted in my mouth.

Shelton sat down across from me, a huge grin on his face. "You in heaven?"

"Om-nom-nom," I moaned in pleasure. "You're my hero."

He took a gulp of wine and leaned forward on the table. "Yeah, I know."

"Aren't you going to have one?" I asked.

He laughed. "Man, I ate the first three that I made."

Adam sat down next to him, three burgers on his plate. "Well, well, well. If it isn't the legendary Harry Shelton."

Shelton threw up his hands. "Guilty as charged."

Elyssa dropped into a seat with two burgers on her plate and gave Shelton a respectful nod. "I'll admit it—you really pulled off an epic mealtime."

"Guess what I'm making tomorrow?" A grin split Shelton's face.

It wasn't hard to figure out since we'd shared our culinary fantasies after being stuck with Seraphim cuisine for so long. "Pizza!"

"Can I use the word epic again?" Adam said. "Because pizza would be totally epic!"

"Dude, the food here is so fresh, it's unbelievable." Shelton sighed and looked at our burgers. "Damn, I think I'm hungry again already."

Adam grinned. "I won't tell Bella if you won't."

Shelton raced away to get another burger.

The Atlanteans, for the most part, seemed a bit unsure about the burgers until the first few bit into them and loudly exclaimed their divine nature.

"Surely, this is food from the gods," one man said between mouthfuls of French fries.

Shelton sat back down. "I think they like my cooking!"

Adam polished off his last burger and sat back, swishing wine in his goblet. "While I am tickled pink to have real food once again, I think we should talk about why we're here."

For a moment, I'd stopped thinking about our mission. Now that I'd finally tasted hamburgers again, it was time to talk business.

Shelton sighed. "Thanks for spoiling the mood."

"No, Adam's right." Elyssa wiped her mouth with a cloth napkin. "We've finally reached the middle of Voltis, but we have no idea where the secret weapon is."

"Man, these people wouldn't know war if it bit them in the ass." Shelton looked at the cavorting crowd as the music picked up once again. "Ain't no way they have a super weapon tucked away somewhere."

"Unfortunately, I think I know exactly what Kaelissa wants."
Adam's eyes looked troubled. "And if she gets it, we're screwed."

Chapter 23

Adam's statement sent a chill through me. Ever since the first time I'd met him, he'd proven himself to be a genius when it came to coding magical spells and seeing patterns where most people would only see gibberish. That was why, when he thought we were screwed, odds were pretty good that he was right.

Elyssa proved she was no slouch at evaluating danger and stole some of Adam's thunder. "It has to do with the bloodstones."

Surprise flickered through Adam's eyes. "Yeah, that's exactly right." He chuckled. "You're definitely your father's daughter."

Her cheeks flushed red and her eyelids fluttered with pleasure. "Thank you, Adam. That's the nicest thing anyone's said to me all day."

Shelton groaned. "Do you think Kaelissa wants to use the bloodstones on the Atlanteans?"

"No," Adam said. "On the gods." He jabbed a finger into the distance. "She wants to control the Fallen."

I smacked the heel of my hand on my forehead. "Of course! It's so simple."

"Do you really think Gallifer and his pals are that strong?" Shelton shook his head. "I know they're ancient and all, but what makes them more powerful than any other Seraphim?"

"They're second or third generation Seraphim," Adam said. "They're probably just as powerful with Brilliance as they are with Murk."

"Not only that," Elyssa said, "but they've had access to mortals over a thousand years."

Feeding on human soul essence amplified Seraphim magic considerably and Daelissa had proven that the feeding on humans over centuries flushed her with even more power. Unfortunately, Daelissa had limited her feeding to only light essence and driven herself insane. If the Fallen had been feeding on human soul essence all this time, there was no telling how strong they might be.

"First thing in the morning we should pay a visit to Heval." I munched on a fry and considered our approach. "At least since the Fallen tried to use a bloodstone, they'll know how serious a threat Kaelissa poses. Maybe they'll know how to counter her."

Shelton held up his hands. "Do we really want to visit the Fallen? They might just kill us."

Adam frowned. "In all the time they've been here, they don't seem to have harmed the locals."

"We can't just let Kaelissa get the drop on them," I said. "I'm sure they'll be grateful. Then we can go home."

"Speaking of which," Adam said, "that might be harder than you think."

"Son of a—"Shelton put down his half-eaten burger. "You really know how to spoil my mood."

"After Justin found out about pocket dimension, I studied Queens Gate and the Grotto." He leaned back in his chair. "The scans came back almost identical to my scans of Eden, but they also have slightly altered gravity—a side effect of touching the Glimmer."

"Does this place have the same gravity?" I asked.

Adam shook his head. "No. I think this place is not a full realm or a pocket dimension. I'm just taking a guess, but putting together the puzzle pieces from the stories Narine and the others told us, I think this might be a fragment of the original Earth."

Elyssa's mouth hung open. "You mean before the Sundering?"

"Pristine Earth?" Shelton said.

Adam nodded. "Do you remember when the Alabaster Arches weren't working?"

"Yeah, kinda hard to forget," I said.

"Remember the gray static and lightning when the portals tried to form?" Adam showed us a video of an arch sparking and roiling with gray clouds where a clear portal should be.

It looked an awful lot like—"Hang on. You're saying the aether storm in Voltis is similar to the energy in a malfunctioning arch?"

"I'm going further than that," Adam said. "I think Voltis is one huge malfunctioning portal."

"Son of a butt-munching unicorn." Shelton chomped down on a fry. "It kinda makes sense."

"The fact that it's a malfunctioning portal creates a problem." Adam gave an apologetic look. "I'm still analyzing the data, but simply reversing our course back through Voltis might not get us back to Seraphina. It might take us somewhere else."

Shelton face-palmed. "I'm gonna throw up."

I didn't like that thought either. "Let's hope you're wrong."

"If it's one huge portal, that means there must be a way to other realms," Elyssa said. "It means we might be able to get to Eden."

Shelton's face brightened. "Hey, that's right."

"There are numerous possibilities," Adam said. "We just have to narrow them down."

Before we could dig deeper into the mystery, Adonis came up behind me and politely tapped me on the shoulder. "Justin, now that dinner is concluded, would you do us the honor of telling one of your stories?"

"Uh, sure." I scooted back my chair and gave Adam a sharp look. "Give some thought to the portal theory. I need to know if there might be a way back to Eden from here."

He gave me a thumbs up. "You got it."

I walked across the spacious citadel and hopped onto the central pedestal. It was time to educate these people on how they'd ended up here at the end of the universe. Seconds later, the crowd surrounded me, faces lit up like kids about to hear a fairy tale for the first time.

"Once upon a time, the world was whole." I channeled a sphere of Murk and traced the continents onto the globe.

Oohs and aahs filled the room.

211

"The Seraphim ruled the skies, the Sirens the sea, and the Lyrolai lived in the forest, the glade, and the glen." I continued the story Cora had told me about how the Apocryphan had conquered the kingdoms and how their war had split the Earth into realms, making the globe of Murk shatter into pieces and reform into their own globes, much to the amazement of my audience.

"It wasn't until thousands of years later that the Sirens anchored the worlds together by creating the Glimmer." I shattered one of the globes and did my best to recreate the shattered realm of the Glimmer. "It seems no corner of the world was untouched by the Sundering and the Anchoring except for Atlantis."

"But why?" asked a child. "Did the gods protect us?"

"I don't know." I shrugged. "If there's one thing I've learned about magic, it's that sometimes you just have to accept certain things and move on."

That drew a chorus of laughter and knowing looks.

I continued with the story of the First Seraphim War, leading up to a Siren named Melea who removed the Chalon from the Grand Nexus without properly attuning it for removal. "The magic within the arch exploded!" I channeled a globe to represent Eden and simulated a dark wave of Murk racing across it. "This Desecration drained the light from anyone near the arches, turning Seraphim into husks, and mortals into shadow creatures that hungered only for the light of the living." I formed the globe of Murk into the image of an infantile creature with skin like tar. It held up its arms as if grasping, and I made the dreaded cry I'd heard so many times before. "Da-nah!"

A woman screamed and the kids shrank back from the monstrous apparition.

I released the channel and let the image fade away. "It was at that time that Atlantis was cast adrift from the world," I said, using all my best words for poetic points. "For thousands of years, nobody knew what had happened to the lost city. Now, we have finally found you."

Anyone sitting down leapt to their feet and joined the others in a raucous round of cheers.

"We are reunited!" someone shouted. And then the chant started—"*Reunification! Reunification!*"

I felt a bit guilty, because I sure as hell didn't know how to actually reunify this fragment of a realm with Eden or any other realm for that matter. There were plenty of more stories to tell, but I decided this was enough for now. I caught a glare from Aesop who was busily scribbling on a sheaf of rough parchment. I imagined they didn't have much in the way of paper here, but given the critical shortage of stories in these parts, the old man probably figured it was worth writing down what he heard.

Adonis and the others bowed deep when I stepped down. "Surely, you are one of the gods," Adonis said. "We have never seen such magic."

"No, I'm not a god, and don't call me Shirley."

Shelton snorted and Elyssa rolled her eyes.

Adonis's forehead wrinkled. "I apologize if I offended you."

I waved off his apology. "No, it was a bad joke on my part." During my story, I'd only skimmed the surface of Seraphim powers, and barely mentioned Daemos and other supernatural types. It seemed only right I let him and the other mortals know the Seraphim weren't gods, but beings with magical powers.

"Your people can learn magic," I said.

Adonis flinched. "We can only use that which the gods have gifted us. To do otherwise is blasphemy."

"Like the food preservation spell?" I asked.

He nodded. "Yes. The gods give us what we need."

"Interesting." It sounded like oppression to me, but I wasn't here to start a rebellion.

"How did you do your magic?" Adonis asked, and the weight of a hundred stares settled on me.

"I'm part Seraphim," I explained.

That rocked the crowd back on their heels.

"He is god!" someone shouted.

Many sank to their knees, soon joined by their neighbors. I held up my hands. "Hey, enough of this! I'm not a god."

Adonis looked up at me. "Many apologies, Almighty Justin, but if you are not a god, what are you?"

Elyssa's groaning sigh penetrated the silence that followed.

I barely kept myself from laughing. "I'm just a guy with super powers."

Judging from the murmur of conversation, it seemed that the Atlanteans had a great topic of conversation to keep them occupied for a while.

We excused ourselves and headed back down the road. Shelton stared up at the moon as we walked. "Do you think the moon used to be blue instead of gray like it is in Eden?"

"If this is really a preserved slice of old Earth, then yeah," Adam said. "This place is fascinating. I wish we didn't have to hurry back."

Shelton groaned. "If I have to eat another glurk, I'm gonna puke."

I just hoped Shelton's gripes were the least of our worries.

Bright and early the next morning, the four of us walked to the *Falcheen* and convinced Illaena to fly us over to Heval. Narine and her besties didn't make an appearance, but I figured when we got back I'd have to give them the same history lesson I'd given the mortals.

Mortals. It was damned strange to be labeling humans like that, especially since I'd grown up believing I was human. Since Daemos were part human and part demon, I had a slice of humanity lurking in me, but I definitely wasn't one of them.

As the *Falcheen* cast off and headed north toward Heval, I began to have doubts about our unannounced visit. "It seems like the Fallen enjoy being gods around these parts."

"Maybe," Elyssa said. "On the other hand, they might just want to be left alone. We should assess the situation by asking the locals for information."

"Good idea," Adam said. "Walking into a den of malicious vipers like Daelissa would be pretty bad."

Shelton snorted. "Understatement of the day."

A towering black silhouette appeared in the mists on the horizon when we were about twenty miles out to sea. Mount Olympus rose so high its peak was lost above the clouds, making the mountain in Atlantis look like a molehill. The town of Heval was packed onto a wide plateau on the southern side of the mountain where some strange act of geology had created a square mile of land with grass and trees.

Though it was plenty of room for people to live, it wasn't arable, which meant they most likely traded for food with Atlantis.

"How do you figure they get down off the mountain?" Shelton said.

As we drew closer, Adam pointed to a series of stairs and bridges built into the side of the cliffs that went all the way down to a small harbor. "I'd guess they have to take the long way down."

Shelton grimaced. "Holy pant-crapping cliffs! Ain't no way in hell I'd walk that route."

The buildings in Heval looked markedly different from those in Atlantis. Built mostly of polished black rock and gray granite, they were tall and square, without much of the architectural flair of Atlantis. A few buildings near the city center bore the spires of Atlantis, leading me to believe the Sirens might have constructed some of the buildings, but not the rest.

Since there was no space to land the ship, the *Falcheen* sidled up to the cliff where a round courtyard offered space for the gangway. Three large statues of winged Seraphim stood in the center, their stone gazes fixed upon the sea. A man with a rough brush perched on the shoulder of one the statues, busily scrubbing bird poop from its shoulders.

"Let me guess," Shelton said. "Those are the Fallen."

Adam gave him a thumbs-up. "Gold star for you."

Domiciles crowded the edges of the courtyard, their windows looking straight down at the thousand-foot drop.

"Talk about the Cliffs of Insanity," Elyssa murmured. "I hope they don't get earthquakes here."

Before the gangway had reached the shore, dozens of people spilled into the courtyard, mouths agape and eyes wide at the sight of the flying vessel.

Illaena stepped to my side. "I do not like the idea of you seeking out the Fallen. I will take the ship out to an aether eddy where we will wait." She tapped the communication gem on her collar. "You know how to reach me when you're ready."

I'd kind of hoped her crew might come with us just in case we needed an assist, but the look in her eyes told me that wasn't going to happen. *She's scared.* I couldn't blame her. The idea of ancient Seraphim who'd ruled like gods in a lost land for thousands of years was enough to make anyone a little hesitant of dropping in and visiting.

I just hoped the gods of Mount Olympus didn't kill us on sight.

Chapter 24

By now, the crowds were all the way up to the cliff where a stone railing prevented them from slipping over the ledge to their doom. Like the Atlanteans, the Hevaleans wore tunics and togas though, with the chillier weather at this altitude, these people covered their shoulders and heads with robes.

A young man with a gold wreath on his head stepped forward. "I am Archon Hippias," he said in the same heavily accented Cyrinthian spoken by the humans in Atlantis. "Did the gods gift our brethren with a flying ship?" Hippias sounded a bit miffed that we'd get a fancy gift before them.

"We are not from Atlantis," I said, and was not disappointed when my declaration brought forth a chorus of confused sounds. When the noise died down, I continued. "We spent the night as guests of Atlantis and have come to visit your city."

Hippias looked comically confused. "If you are not from Atlantis, then where could you possibly have come from?"

"Oh, brother." Shelton groaned. "Here we go again."

I smiled reassuringly. "If we could have private audience, Archon Hippias, I will explain everything."

"Very well." Hippias waved his arms. "Make room for our guests!"

The crowd parted right down the center. I tried not to look down as I crossed the narrow gap between the ship and the cliff, and stepped into the courtyard. Elyssa and the others soon joined me. Illaena wasted no time and the *Falcheen* swooped out over the ocean.

Hippias led us down narrow streets of smooth polished basalt and the other citizens followed at a respectful distance, expressions wary of the new strangers. Where Atlantis was shining and beautiful, the buildings here were square and dark, casting a pall over the city. It wasn't until we reached the central section that we entered a neighborhood of white marble mansions on wide plots of grassy land dotted with trees and gardens. Unsurprisingly, Hippias led us into the largest, a great domed house that looked like it could have been a church. The inside was finished in marble with gold-trimmed tiles and murals in the floors and walls. Ornate statues of the Fallen greeted us in the main foyer, and past them was a hall filled with busts of people bearing imperious expressions.

"This is the hall of Archons," Hippias explained. "My forefathers."

"Being archon is a birthright?" Elyssa asked.

He nodded. "I am of the royal bloodline bequeathed by the gods."

"Ain't no better way to get it," Shelton said in a voice dripping with sarcasm.

Hippias entered a round room with a polished stone table in the center. Columns reached up to the domed ceiling, and behind them were shadowy alcoves with more statues. He rang a bell and a man with the universal bearing of a butler stepped inside.

"Refreshments for our guests," Hippias told the man. He motioned us into the heavy wooden chairs around the table and then took a seat for himself. "Before we commence, might I ask your names?"

I took the lead. "I'm Justin." My finger pointed out the others in turn. "Elyssa, Adam, Shelton."

Shelton tipped his hat, but didn't remove it, and I noticed he had his compressed staff at the ready in one hand. Shelton, as a general rule, didn't trust anyone he didn't know, so for him it was normal behavior. Elyssa's eyes wandered warily around the room, and I could tell she was evaluating escape routes and battle plans.

Adam was taking selfies with his phone.

"Interesting names," Hippias said. "I would ask where you are from, but I suspect that information is forthcoming."

"My story will probably upset some of your long-held truths about Atlantis and Heval," I said, "but I must assure you it's all the truth."

He nodded. "I have an open mind."

I sure hope so.

The butler returned with wine, cheese and bread. Shelton looked at it suspiciously and scanned it with a program on his phone before taking a bite. The rest of us poured ourselves glasses of white wine that tasted surprisingly sweet.

I launched into the story about the Sundering, the Desecration, and our theory of how this realm fragment came to be. Hippias remained calm and sipped on his wine until I'd finished explaining how we'd come from Seraphina and into his neck of the woods.

Hippias took a long gulp of wine after I'd finished. Despite his outward calm, he was obviously a bit shaken by the revelations. He poured himself another goblet and spoke. "You have undertaken a journey worthy of Odysseus himself to reach this place, but there is something that puzzles me."

"What's that?" I asked.

His question was simple. "Why did you come *here*?"

Elyssa's eyes met mine. She nodded. Adam nodded, and Shelton shrugged. It seemed that it was time to divulge our suspicions.

"What do you know of the gods who live on Olympus?" I asked.

"I have personally spoken to them," he said. "As Archon it is my duty to inform them from time to time of the state of our city."

I wasn't really sure how to phrase the next question. "Um, are they nice people?"

"They are gods, not people," he said sternly. "They have always treated me with respect."

"Any evil vibes?" Shelton asked.

Hippias almost spilled his wine. "What sort of question is that? Why do you ask such things about the gods?"

"We think they might be in danger," I said.

Hippias narrowed his eyes. "Though they warned me and every Archon before to be vigilant of danger, I doubt any could harm the gods."

219

I heard the sound of air through a hollow tube. Shelton was two steps ahead of me, probably forewarned by the change of tone in Hippias's voice. His staff snapped out and he shouted a word. Elyssa flipped over the table and knocked Adam over backwards. I channeled a shield just an instant before several darts bounced off of it.

Hippias scrambled backwards, but Elyssa had him in a chokehold before he could move another inch. Armed men burst from the alcoves, swords in hands, and tried to attack us. Thanks to my shield and Shelton's, they ran headfirst into the invisible barriers and bounced off like kids slamming into freshly cleaned sliding glass doors.

"Sound the alarm!" Hippias cried. "The god killers are here!"

"Son of a—" Shelton flicked away his shield and aimed his staff. A bolt of blue energy slammed one soldier in the chest, knocking him across the room. Shelton whirled his staff and spun, his leather duster flying out like a cape, and blasted another attacker in the face.

Adam took out his wand and picked off two more soldiers with precisely aimed spheres of energy that coalesced around the attackers' heads and knocked them out like gas bombs. Elyssa fought three soldiers, her body and fists a blur. Unable to even draw a sword or fend her off with fists, the men grunted, doubled over, and fell into a heap.

Elyssa stood over them and smoothed out a lock of mussed hair—the only indication she'd just taken out three armed men.

The scene resembled the day after a raucous fraternity party—a bunch of dudes in togas unconscious on the floor in puddles of their own piss and vomit. Only Hippias remained awake, and he looked absolutely terrified.

"I knew this day might come," he said hoarsely. "You will be the end of us all."

"How did you know?" I picked him up off the floor and planted his ass back in the chair. "Tell me!"

He looked up at me with tortured eyes. "The gods told us if anyone ever came from the outside, they were here to kill them."

I blew out a long sigh. "Well, today is your luck day, Hippias. We're not here to kill anyone."

Hippias looked at the men on the floor. "But your powers—who else could you be but the evil gods from beyond?"

"I hate to break it to you, buddy," Shelton said with a sympathetic pat on the shoulder, "but your gods ain't gods at all. They're just a bunch of posers."

"When was the last time you spoke to them?" I asked.

Hippias swallowed hard. "I should not say."

I squeezed his shoulder a little too tight for his comfort. "You should definitely say."

He winced. "Never," he said quickly. "I have never directly spoken with the gods."

I let him go. "But you said—"

"I have to keep up appearances," Hippias said. "How could I let the people know that the gods have not spoken to an archon for two centuries?"

I exchanged concerned looks with the others. "Where do the gods live?"

"At the top of Olympus." He rubbed his shoulder. "There is only one way up, but it does not work unless the gods will it so."

Elyssa adopted a gentler tone and offered him a smile. "Where is it?"

"How do I know you are not the evil ones from beyond?" he asked plaintively.

"Did we kill your men?" I asked. "Have we threatened to torture you for information?"

Hippias looked uncertainly around at us. "No, but I have heard the evil ones are cunning."

"We have a flying ship that could take us to the top," Shelton said impatiently. "One way or the other, we're gonna visit your gods."

The archon squeezed shut his eyes. "I am the youngest archon to ever serve. I do not wish to be known as the one who betrayed our gods."

Elyssa crouched in front of him. "The evil your gods spoke of is trying to penetrate the wall separating this place from beyond. We're here to warn them."

"Scout's honor." I held up my fingers in what I vaguely remembered being the proper sign.

"Holding your fingers like that isn't scout's honor," Adam said. "That's live long and prosper."

Shelton leaned closer to Hippias. "Like I said, you can take us, or we'll get our ship to take us. We only swung by here first so someone could introduce us properly."

Hippias took a moment to consider the offer and finally nodded. "Please follow me." He led us down a hall and to a smaller statue of the Fallen at the end. He pressed the right butt cheek of one of the statues and something clicked. The wall grated outward, revealing a hidden passage.

"Typical," Shelton muttered. "Next thing you know, we'll find the original Declaration of Independence down here."

Adam snorted. "I give them points for putting the hidden pressure point on the butt."

Hippias gave them an uncertain look before grabbing a rod with a glowing sphere on the end and leading us into a rocky tunnel that snaked back and forth for quite a distance. A dark alcove loomed at the end of the tunnel, but the glowing globe revealed what it actually was.

"That's a levitator shaft like what they use on Seraphina," Shelton said.

I charged the blue gem on the wall and was rewarded with a glowing white light from within the shaft.

Hippias gasped and would have tripped over his own feet, but Elyssa caught him.

"Only the gods should be able to do that," he said.

"Your gods are Seraphim just like me," I told him. "They have powers, but that doesn't make them gods."

"Here's hoping they don't blast us the second they see us," Shelton said.

"I say we let Hippias go first." Adam motioned the nervous archon into the shaft. "I doubt they'll blast him."

"But I have not been summoned," Hippias said. "They might strike me down on sight!"

"Nobody's going first," I said, and herded everyone into the shaft. *Take us to the top*, I commanded the levitator. It responded just like the ones in Tarissa, and an invisible platform beneath our feet shot upward at incredible velocity.

Smoothly bored rock blurred past in the glowing light of the shaft. Hippias looked up and screamed, throwing up his arms as we approached the roof with enough velocity to smash us flat as pancakes. The levitator slowed and stopped at an opening in the rock.

I stepped out into a freezing cold room. A fireplace black with ash and soot gaped emptily across the room. Three thrones of pure gold were covered in snow and dust. Golden sconces lined the walls, and what had once been magnificent tapestries hung from the ceiling, their threads rotting and colors dulled.

Hippias looked around with wide eyes. "It is just as was written in the *Book of Archons*." He dropped to his knees on the rotting red carpet that lined the floor nearly to the thrones. "That is where the gods held an audience with the archons of Heval."

"Something ain't right," Shelton said. "Did they have servants up here to take care of the facilities?"

Hippias nodded. "The gods sometimes chose from among our citizens whenever they needed new servants, but that has not happened for centuries."

"Let's have a look around." I spotted a gem in the wall behind the thrones and pointed it out to the others. "Probably a door there." A charge of Murk did indeed reveal an opening.

We stepped through and into a wonderland that drew gasps of amazement.

A carpet of sunlit clouds spread into the distance to our left and right as far as the eye could see. From this high vantage, I could see the gray walls of Voltis towering so high they seemed to go into outer space. Even though we seemed to be out in the open, there was no wind.

Shelton picked up a discarded gold wine goblet and tossed it at the clouds. It clanged off an invisible window and fell to the floor.

"Amazing," Adam said. He walked over and ran his hand along the wall. "It feels like crystal or glass."

"We are in the very heavens themselves," Hippias breathed. He got on his knees and bowed. "I am not worthy! I am not worthy!"

I pulled him upright. "You're every bit as worthy as the rest of us."

He averted his eyes. "I will surely be struck down for this blasphemy!"

"I'm gonna strike you on the head if you don't shut up about getting struck down," Shelton said.

Elyssa approached the back wall and traced a finger along an intricate painting that looked as though the Seraphim with blazing red wings might leap from it at any moment. "These are so beautiful."

Shelton didn't seem as impressed with the statues or busts of other angels and headed for the other door. "Let's find the owners and get this over with."

"Surely the Fallen must know we're here by now," Adam said.

Hippias perked up at that. "The Fallen? What do you mean?"

"Uh, nothing," Adam said.

Hippias opened his mouth to say more, but the rest of us moved on. The walls in the next room were angled to form a large octagon. Hardly a section of wall wasn't covered with book shelves. Many of the closest were written in Cyrinthian, though I found several that bore strange symbols and were made from material other than paper.

Adam fingered one of the tomes. "I think this book is made of leather."

"Even the pages are leather," Shelton said.

"If I'm not mistaken, I think this is written in Spanish." Elyssa held up another book.

"Hey, this is *The Adventures of Tom Sawyer*," Shelton said. "I love this book."

I found what looked like a large clamshell. "What in the world is that?"

Elyssa clicked a small clasp, and the shells opened to reveal pages of light green seaweed covered in Cyrinthian symbols. It read: *Songs of the Sea – Flagella Learns to Sing.*

"I'd be willing to bet this came from Aquilis," Adam said. "All of these books came from different realms."

My heart leapt for joy. "You know what that means?"

Elyssa's eyes lit with hope. "They must have an arch!"

"Holy farting fairies." Shelton leaned on the bookshelf for support. "We can go home."

Chapter 25

We spent the next few hours combing through the palace. Many of the rooms were empty aside from statues, paintings, and countless forms of art from dozens of different realms. I nearly had a heart attack when we ran into one room only to find a hulking Nazdal, its mouth gaping wide, staring out at us from within a crystal case.

"Ah!" I stumbled back into Elyssa before I realized the creature was frozen in place. Large rusty chains hung from manacles on its neck, arms, and legs—a sign of leadership among the strange creatures. Its size indicated it had drained the life force of many dying creatures.

Though Nazdal were humanoid, their backs were too malformed to allow them to walk upright, so they crawled on all fours like animals. They also had grotesquely jagged teeth that no army of dentists could ever hope to fix. I'd fought these monsters in the war and prayed I never had to fight them again. They were magic resistant, and could spew out a bloody mist that weakened their prey while they drained its life.

Hippias stared open-mouthed at the creature. "Surely it is an evil one from beyond!"

"Plenty more where he came from," Shelton said. He walked around the case and whistled. "Man, this place reminds me of the Grand Nexus."

I joined him and saw what he meant. Dozens of cases, each one with specimens gathered from other realms, filled the room.

Adam peered closely at a family of Neanderthals. "I think they're under a preservation spell."

"You mean they're alive?" Elyssa said.

He nodded. "These gems are probably enchanted with preservation spells, but they're nearing the end of life."

"Like this one?" Shelton pointed to a case filled with bones and desiccated flesh. It looked like other ancient humans had once been kept inside, but the aethid keeping the preservation spell active had apparently worn out and they'd awakened in an inescapable prison.

"Awful!" Elyssa said. "We can't just leave these people in here to die."

"Agreed." I inspected the other cases. "We'll have to come back and figure this out later."

"Please don't tell me we're releasing that Nazdal." Shelton shuddered. "Man, they must've had a fight on their hands to trap that one."

"I think I found the servants." Adam peered inside a large case filled with plushy cushions and a harem of scantily clad men and women. Every last male was chiseled with muscle, faces angular and handsome, the women curvy and beautiful.

"Pretty sure they didn't choose their servants for regular chores," Shelton said with a wink.

Adam nudged him. "Wishing you weren't married?"

Shelton pshawed. "I'd rather be with Bella any day."

Elyssa grinned. "Brownie point earned. I'll be sure to tell Bella."

He laughed. "I need all I can get."

"Let's keep looking for the Fall—uh—gods," I said.

"I have a feeling they aren't here anymore," Adam said. "Wherever they went, they haven't been back in a very long time."

I had little doubt he was right.

We searched out the rest of the sprawling palace, discovering all sorts of collectibles from other realms, but there were no Fallen to be found.

Another levitator took us to the top of a tall spire and into a room with invisible walls. By now, we were used to finding the unexpected and only Hippias freaked out—dropping to his knees and hiding his eyes.

"I could stay here for days." Elyssa spun in a circle, arms wide and took in the breathtaking view of the clouds far below.

"I think we're nearly in the stratosphere." Adam looked up where the darkness of space peeked in. "I'll bet the view at night is stunning."

"This is amazeballs and all," Shelton said, "but we haven't found a single living soul in this place and I ain't seen a single Alabaster Arch."

Hippias peeked between fingers, opened his mouth, and closed it, apparently thinking better of asking a question.

"I think we should wake the servants," Adam said. "Maybe there are secret rooms we don't know about."

I was thinking the same thing. "Wish we'd done it sooner."

We took the levitator back down and walked to the room with the cases. I charged the gem on the case with the servants. The front of the case misted away and a few seconds later, they began to stir.

The first person to fully awaken was a woman with long curly hair and dark skin. She blinked and looked at us for several minutes, obviously unsure who we were. "Did they bring you from Eden?" she asked in passable Cyrinthian.

I nodded. "Yes, from Eden. What part are you from?"

"Constantinople," she said. "Though others have said it no longer exists."

Shelton chuckled. "Istanbul was Constantinople. Now it's Istanbul, not Constantinople."

"The Turks destroy it?" The woman burst into tears.

Shelton grimaced. "Guess it wasn't as funny as I thought."

Other servants stretched awake and straggled out of the box, many of them lining up calmly as if they'd done this a thousand times before though there was no shortage of curious looks our way.

When the last yawns died away, I spoke. "Your masters are not here, so I am in charge." I figured a clear statement of authority was the best way to start.

The servants broke into panicked screams and attacked. "The god killers are here!" they shouted over and over again.

I was so shocked that I barely got up a barrier in time to hold them at bay. Hippias used me as a meat shield and ducked behind me.

The servants banged ineffectually against the shield while I formulated something else to say.

Elyssa huffed and loosed a piercing whistle. "Shut up!"

By now the servants realized they weren't able to get to us and backed off, fearful looks contorting their faces.

"We're not god killers," she said. "The gods have vanished and we're trying to find out where they went."

Hippias came out from hiding. "It is true. I am Archon Hippias of Heval and we cannot find the gods."

"Where is Archon Pithias?" a beefy male asked.

"He died nearly two-hundred years ago," Hippias said. "Much time has passed since the gods made you slumber."

Jaws dropped and eyes went wide as trashcan lids.

"Two hundred years?" one female shouted in heavily accented Cyrinthian. "They rarely leave for more than ten years at a time."

"Our masters are missing!" another woman screeched. "They are gone!"

Several servants burst into tears, ripping apart what little clothing they had on. Those who weren't crying looked pleased, some of them going so far as to smile.

"Might I once more set eyes on that faraway home?" asked a man in a hopeful voice. Silky brown hair hung to his shoulders and a neatly groomed goatee framed pouty lips. Bulky shoulder and pectoral muscles bulged against his tight silk shirt. He looked like he hadn't missed a gym day ever. "Immortality hath wrought great sadness upon my soul. My wondrous career as playwright squandered upon so few ears that I might as well have died."

Shelton made a face like he'd just bitten into a lemon. "The way you talk gives me a headache. Who do you think you are, Shakespeare?"

The man's eyes widened. "How is it my name comes to thine lips?"

Shelton flinched as if he'd seen a ghost. "You're supposed to be dead." He looked him up and down. "Damn if you don't look like a male model too!"

Shakespeare scowled. "Verily did they approach me and promise an eternity of composition should I come hither and thither in their company. But age-dulled and decrepit of mind, was I but a fool."

"They rejuvenated you?" I waved a hand up and down to indicate his muscular form. "I mean, it looks like they gave you super steroids or something."

"They promised each of us everlasting life," a woman said. "We just had to accept their terms."

Elyssa shook her head as if she couldn't believe it. "Are you all human?"

That drew scores of frowns.

"Mortals, dust to flesh, flesh to dust," Shakespeare said. "Only the false promise of divinity holds still the reaper's hand."

"Can you please stop talking like that?" Shelton said. "It's driving me crazy!"

"He insists," another woman said. "And everyone in his stupid plays talks the same way."

"It is Old English!" Shakespeare cried. "I will not deflower my native tongue just because it is in Cyrinthian."

I formed a sphere of sizzling Brilliance in my palm. "Verily shouldst thy words lose the flowers, lest your tongue suffer the wrath of my powers."

Shakespeare cringed. "Very well, but I will lodge a complaint about this treatment."

Most of the crying had died away so I lowered the shield and hoped the idiots didn't attack again. "Are there any secret rooms in this palace? Has anyone here seen an arch or magical gateways used by the gods?"

The confused looks on their faces told me not a one knew what I was talking about. I groaned and ran a hand down my face. *We're so close!* But so far, no banana.

"As a writer, verily must I be observant," Shakespeare said in a condescending tone. "From what I gathered, these beings have been alive so long they suffer from acute boredom."

"No doubt," Adam said. "It must be a struggle to keep meaning in life after so long."

"Absolutely." Shakespeare sighed. "I could pen such an amazing tragedy about the lives of these divine creatures. I interviewed each of them in the hopes I could discover more about their backgrounds." He blew out a breath. "Unfortunately, they were not very forthcoming."

The woman from Constantinople nodded in agreement. "They took long trips, vanishing for years at a time."

Shakespeare 's lip curled into a snarl. "It is as Mara said, but they always packed us in our cage before such journeys. They would show us prizes on their return—bizarre creatures and art presumably liberated from other places."

"Did they ever leave you out of your cage before taking one of these trips?" I asked.

Mara narrowed her eyes in concentration. "Yes, they sometimes grew desperate to satisfy a whim. Like the time they wanted something called pizza, but could not get it from here or Atlantis."

Shelton moaned. "Mmm, pizza!"

"They departed and returned days later," Shakespeare said. "It was the only time I watched them go because they had just finished watching a performance of *Romeo and Juliet Part Two*."

Adam scratched his head. "Part Two? But I thought there was just the one."

Shakespeare's eyes lit up. "Despite the centuries separating our births, you know of my works?"

"Man, who doesn't?" Shelton groaned. "Reading those thing was a friggin chore in school."

"Literature is not for the weak-minded or the unimaginative," Shakespeare said. "Gallifer demanded I write a sequel where the lovers came back to life. He despises tragedies."

I waved off further literary discussion. "Where did the gods go when they left?"

Mara pointed straight up. "We performed the play in the observatory. Once it was over, Purah grew very irritable because she was tired of the food. They settled on pizza and told us they would return within a few days."

"There was some discussion about locking us up," Shakespeare said, "but Purah insisted they go immediately. They boarded one of their magic clouds and flew away into the storm that is always on the horizon."

"Is the observatory the fishbowl room way up in the sky?" I asked.

Mara nodded. "Yes."

"So they just flew away into the storm on nothing but a cloudlet?" Adam asked.

"I overheard them speaking of the storm a few times," Shakespeare said. "They constantly talked of exploring different nodes, whatever that means."

Adam's eyes bugged.

"What is it?" Elyssa said.

Shelton clapped him on the back. "Spit out what you're thinking."

"The Fallen don't use an arch." Adam whistled. "Remember when I said the entire maelstrom is one huge malfunctioning portal?"

"Holy monkey balls." Shelton grinned from ear to ear. "You mean the nodes might be like portals?"

"Yes, but there's one huge problem," Adam said. "We'd have to know exactly which node leads to Eden and figure out how to get back."

"The maelstrom is massive," I said. "How are we supposed to find a node or even know what one looks like?"

"Why do you call them the Fallen?" Shakespeare asked.

Adam ignored the question. "Did the gods have any diaries or books detailing their adventures?"

"They had a magic gem," Mara said. "I once saw them looking at images of pure light coming from inside it."

"I saw it too," Shakespeare said. "I believe they had maps on it, and I once saw them marking the great storm with red dots."

"As did I," said another of the servants.

Several more chimed in agreement.

"I'll bet they take it with them on their trips," Adam said. "Unless they kept a backup here, we're out of luck."

Luckily, we had a ready-made workforce on our hands. "I'm going to tell you a few things about the world that may seem crazy, but I think it's important you're caught up on events." I gave the servants a moment to process what I'd said and then launched into more story-telling, including the origins of the Fallen. I was getting really tired of repeating myself, but there wasn't much to do but spit it out again.

Shakespeare practically salivated at all the raw material I handed him, and kept begging for something to write with.

After I caught them up on the Apocryphan War, the two Seraphim wars, and our predicament here in Seraphina, I gave them a choice.

"I don't know what happened to the Fallen." Adding a shrug to emphasize the point, I continued. "They are long-lived but they can die. It's possible they met something in another realm that killed them, or maybe they accidentally went into the Void."

Mara shuddered. "The Beast sounds absolutely horrific."

"It is," I assured her. "Now, if any of you ever want to return to Eden, we need to find the key to getting home."

"You want us to search this place for the gem," Shakespeare said. "In exchange you'll take us back."

"But Constantinople is Istanbul," Mara exclaimed. "Whatever life I had in Constantinople is now in Istanbul."

Shelton giggled.

Elyssa gave him a dirty look, squeezed Mara's shoulder sympathetically. "Fitting back in with the noms would be hard, but there's plenty to enjoy in the Overworld."

"It sounds fascinating," Shakespeare said. "I will turn this place upside down if it means escaping the drudgery of this god-forsaken palace."

Shelton snorted. "Pun intended?"

Shakespeare rolled his eyes.

Sitting alone in the corner of the room, Hippias finally spoke again. "I cannot believe the gods may be dead, and that there is an entire realm of them beyond the great storm in Seraphina."

"What we need now is for Atlantis and Heval to work together to solve the mystery of the maelstrom," Adam said. "I have a feeling that there's huge significance to this place."

"It's a fragment of the original Earth," Elyssa said. "Maybe the explosion of the Grand Nexus couldn't affect it, so it somehow created the maelstrom portal around it."

Adam pursed his lips and nodded. "I think you're right. The original geographical location of Atlantis and Olympus put it somewhere near Spain—"

"I thought it was near Greece," Shelton said.

"The theories vary wildly," Adam said, apparently used to Shelton's interruptions, "but from what Narine said, it sounds as though it might have been somewhere near the coast of Spain and possibly Morocco, which puts it in the vicinity of an Alabaster Arch. The same thing that kept the Apocryphan from seeing this chunk of land must also be what caused it to remain whole while everything else was torn into different realms."

"Whatever the case, I think we just found our way home." I couldn't keep from grinning at the prospect of returning to Eden, making sure Ivy was okay, and kicking Victus's ass. Then we could return rested and in full force to do what needed doing in Seraphina.

"Verily canst thou rely on us," Shakespeare said.

Shelton groaned.

"Let's get back to Atlantis," I told the others. "I want to tell the Sirens what we found."

We headed back toward the levitator shaft leading to Heval, Hippias shuffling along sadly behind us. His entire world had been shattered in the space of a few hours, and I wasn't sure if he'd be able to hold up beneath the burden.

My gem crackled with static several times as we walked. I tried contacting the *Falcheen*, but couldn't get a response. When we stepped into the throne room, the gem finally burst to life with chatter.

"Justin, are you there?" It was Illaena.

234

"I'm here, what's up?"

"We traveled along the storm wall and discovered something very alarming." Anger filled her voice. "I think you will want to see it for yourself."

Judging from her tone, whatever she'd seen wasn't good for our immediate future.

Chapter 26

"We're on our way back down," I said.

"I take it you're atop the mountain?" she asked.

"I'll tell you all about it." I gave the others a worried look and then charged the gem to the levitator.

We dropped at an alarming rate, but Hippias looked too preoccupied to care. When we reached the bottom, he grabbed my arm. "Are there no gods, Justin? Do our souls perish when we die?"

I felt awful for the poor guy, but I didn't want to lie to him. "I honestly don't know, Hippias. With all the magic and wonders in the world, it wouldn't surprise me if there is an afterlife."

He wiped away tears. "I pray my forefathers were not lost to oblivion."

Having come close to being eaten by oblivion incarnate as the Beast, I could totally agree. "If you help us, we can answer the mysteries of the universe together."

Hippias managed a smile. "I would like that very much."

Elyssa squeezed his hand, and Shelton patted him on the back.

"Stick with us and you'll be okay," Shelton reassured him.

I wasn't entirely sure that was true.

The crowds made way as my party raced back to the waiting *Falcheen* where a grim-faced Illaena waited on deck. She turned to Tahlee, and the first mate shouted the order to get underway before the gangway had even vanished.

"What did you find?" I asked.

Illaena's jaw tightened and her body trembled with rage. "The Brightlings have outdone themselves this time."

My senses went on red alert. "What happened? Did you get a communication from outside?"

"No." She leaned on the railing and gripped it tightly. "We spotted the *Xanda* entering this realm, but it is not controlled by Mzodi."

My heart went cold. "Brightlings control an Mzodi ship?"

"Cursed land dwellers," she hissed. "They were just inside the storm and appeared to be waiting on something."

"Did they see you?" I asked.

She shook her head. "We were flying much higher, and they did not look up."

After several tense moments, Illaena ordered the *Falcheen* to a stop and looked over the railing. She handed me a scope with gems in the ends and I peered through it.

Far below, a ship twice the size of the *Falcheen* hovered a few hundred yards from the maelstrom. The shimmering silver hull of the *Xanda* bore the outline of a hawk, wings tight against its body. Weaponized gems studded the hull, and it had double the aether foils to keep the ship aloft. Soldiers in shiny white armor manned the foils and the weapons, and an entire platoon stood in neat rows along the center of the wide deck.

A blond woman stood near the helm and I realized it had to be Kaelissa.

I noticed something odd about a section of the maelstrom directly aft of the *Xanda* and zoomed the scope in further. It was as if someone had sliced a neat hole through the roiling gray clouds. "Oh god," I breathed. "There's a tunnel through the maelstrom."

Adam stepped close to me. "Can I look?"

I handed him the scope and met the shocked looks from Elyssa and Shelton.

Several minutes later, Adam grunted. "That's crazy!"

"What is?" Shelton snatched the scope and looked through it. "Holy jumping frijoles. They've got some kind of gem rigged to make a passage through the maelstrom."

Adam shook his head. "Not just a gem." He took out his arcphone and scrolled through dozens of images until he found a picture of a small obsidian orb laced with intricate white patterns.

It wasn't a fancy striped gumball we were looking at, but a Chalon—the master key to opening portals in Alabaster Arches from one realm to another. I stared at the image. "They have a Chalon?"

Adam nodded grimly. "They mounted a large gem on the front of the ship and put the Chalon in front of it." He rubbed his chin. "I don't understand how it works, but channeling through the gem and into the Chalon seems to have created a safe tunnel through the aether storm."

"If Voltis is one big cluster of portals, it makes perfect sense." Shelton sketched something on the screen of his arcphone and then projected a rough drawing of a gem focusing magic through the small orb. "The Chalon usually has to be musically attuned to a specific realm or else it won't work with an Alabaster Arch."

Adam nodded. "Right, but how does that create a tunnel through the maelstrom?"

"It's not a tunnel," Shelton said. "It's a single portal. The Chalon can single out the magical frequency needed to open a portal to a specific realm."

"Like when my mom had to sing to the Chalon to open a portal to Seraphina?" I asked.

Shelton nodded. "Exactly. Except in this case, they're not aiming to open a specific portal, but to separate all the frequencies."

Adam's eyes widened. "Of course! The storm is like white noise caused by too much interference. They're running the interference through a filter and cleaning it."

"Yep, they just created a portal from the outside of Voltis directly to the inside." Shelton blew out a breath. "That ship is probably only the beginning."

Illaena's face glowed crimson with anger. "I will not tolerate the theft of an Mzodi ship. We must attack."

I shook my head. "There must be a hundred soldiers on the *Xanda*. We can't possibly fight them."

"We sure as hell can't let them bring through more soldiers," Shelton said. "Maybe we can cripple their portal."

Adam snapped his fingers. "Damage the gem."

Illaena made a fist. "We attack the gem and retreat."

"The *Xanda* is too large outrun or outmaneuver us," Tahlee said. "We should stand and fight."

"Yeah, but they've got about ten times the firepower." Adam shook his head. "We need to play this smart."

"Land dwellers cannot hope to defeat Mzodi in their native element," Illaena said. "We will strike and dart away."

"Um—" Adam waved a hand. "I have a better idea. Since the land dwellers don't see us up here, why don't we simply bomb them?"

Laughter boomed from Shelton. "They'll never see what hit 'em!"

"Bomb them?" Illaena looked at the two men. "We have no such weapons."

"Then thank your lucky stars you've got us around." Shelton tapped a finger on his lips and squinted. "Maybe we could rig some gems to explode like we did with the depth charge ones."

Adam looked at Illaena. "Do you have any gems suitable for something like that?"

The captain turned to Tahlee. "Fetch Eor."

Tahlee promptly shouted the command at another nearby soldier who hustled away and returned moments later herding an annoyed Eor in front of him. The gem sorter's rumpled uniform looked as if he'd slept in it, though his red eyes and mussed hair suggested he'd partied all night. "What do you want now? I am very busy cataloguing gems!"

Illaena simply handed him the scope and pointed down.

Eor frowned but looked over the railing. His face turned bright red and his hands shook with rage. "How dare they! Those land dwelling scum have gone too far this time."

Shelton chuckled softy. "That sure got him in the mood."

"We need to make gems that will explode on impact," I said. "Do you have any that will work like that?"

Eor handed the scope to Tahlee and shook his head. "Gems can be charmed to emit pulses of magical energy, but they will not simply explode."

"There must be a way," Adam said. "Maybe we could use Arcane enchantments on one."

"Need I remind you that aetherium is extremely stable?" Eor said in a lecturing tone. "It would be like making a normal rock explode."

"We need gems that work like the depth charges we used," Shelton said.

"Those aethids are highly specific," Eor said. "There's simply—" He trailed off, eyes lost in the distance.

"I think his brain just got run over by a train of thought," Adam said.

Shelton grunted. "Let's hope he didn't have a stroke."

Eor snapped his fingers, proving he most likely hadn't suffered brain damage, and focused back on the group. "I believe I have the answer!" His eyes flashed wide and he hurried off toward the down ramp without another word.

The rest of us jogged along behind him, eager eyes and hopeful hearts praying he knew what to do.

Eor reached a wall and charmed the gem to open the doorway. We crowded inside and found huge piles of rainbow-colored dust.

"What the hell is this?" Shelton said. "Looks like someone emptied out a thousand pixie sticks on the floor."

"Or a unicorn farted." Adam knelt and rubbed the dust between his fingers. "Feels like fine sand."

"This is the dust that results from cutting and polishing gems," Eor said. "We usually dispose of it, but perhaps it can be put to better use."

Shelton picked up a handful and let it drain from his fist. "What are we supposed to do? Throw it in their eyes?"

Eor stuck his nose in the air. "Ignorant as always." He put about a teaspoon of dust in his palm, led us out into the hallway and down several doors to an empty room where he placed the dust on the floor. "Would someone be so kind as to strike the powder first with Brilliance and then with Murk?"

I wasn't sure what to expect so I backed away from the dust and zapped it with Brilliance. A puff of powder rose in the air, but otherwise nothing happened. As instructed, I followed up with a burst of Murk. Once again, the dust poofed as if someone had sneezed into it, but whatever Eor had expected to happen, didn't happen.

"Amazing," Shelton said. "What was that about ignorance?"

Eor ignored him. "This time, I would like you to strike the powder with Murk and Brilliance at the same time."

"You want me to hit it with Stasis?" I asked, since blending the two elements created the third.

He regarded me as a teacher might look at a particularly dense student. "No. Separate charges of Murk and Brilliance, but at the same time."

My face flushed with heat and it took some effort not to zap Eor in the face. I extended my middle fingers in a sign Eor probably didn't recognize, then channeled a bolt of creation from one finger and destruction from the other at the target. With a loud whoosh, the dust combusted in a flurry of rainbow sparks and gray smoke.

"Jumping Jesus on a pogo stick!" Shelton said. "Now that was a unicorn fart!"

His analogy probably wasn't far off, provided unicorns really did poop rainbows.

"Ah, it requires positive and negative polarities to ignite." Adam inspected the charred spot on the floor, using his arcphone to scan it. "What we have here, folks, is akin to magical gunpowder. We could fill a vessel with the stuff and set a charm to detonate it."

"What if there are Mzodi prisoners onboard?" I asked. "We don't want to harm them."

"The Murk hull will protect anyone below deck," Eor said.

Adam stood and turned to Eor. "What can we use for a casing?"

"It needs to be tight for maximum explosion," Shelton said.

"Perhaps food storage containers would work," Illaena said. "We have dozens of empty ones in the cargo hold."

"It will take at least ten minutes to properly charm a gem to detonate the powder," Eor said.

Adam nodded. "Let's get to it then."

A worried looking soldier appeared in the doorway. "Captain, there are more vessels entering our airspace."

Illaena pounded a fist on the wall. "Zhuka!" She hurried from the room.

"Get to work on the bombs," I said. "I'm gonna see what we're up against."

Elyssa and I raced up to the deck and joined Illaena and Tahlee at the railing. What I saw made my heart freeze. Two slightly smaller Mzodi ships also crewed by Brightlings hovered near the *Xanda*.

"They took the *Akata* and the *Ptarn*," Illaena said. "How is this possible?"

"Trickery," Tahlee hissed. "Just as they held our gem sorters hostage, so they must have done to the other ships."

"They could have had them for months," Illaena said. "During my last conversation with Xalara, she mentioned several ships that had not contacted the *Uorion* in some time."

I peered at the other ships with the scope. The *Akata* and *Ptarn* looked nearly identical, their sleek black hulls shining in the sunlight, a sharp contrast to the silvery *Xanda*. Like most Mzodi ships, each prow resembled the head and beak of a bird. The sharp-tipped wings curved forward, filigreed with silver to make the ship look scaled like a dragon instead of feathered.

Where the *Xanda* was an eagle, the other ships were ravens—possibly nimbler and easier to maneuver. It was hard to tell from this distance, but the smaller ships still looked larger than the *Falcheen*.

"We can do nothing," Illaena said. "Even the land dwellers can defeat us with three ships."

"How many soldiers can those ships hold?" I asked.

"Two hundred crew on the *Xanda*, and half that on each of the other ships," Illaena said.

Elyssa's lips peeled back. "More than enough to take Heval."

"It doesn't matter if they take Heval, not with the Fallen gone." I wondered if maybe we could talk to Kaelissa and tell her that her targets were no longer here. On the other hand, she'd probably be more likely to take us prisoner. Hell, she'd hijacked two Mzodi ships already.

"I don't get it," Elyssa muttered. "How did Kaelissa know how to enter Voltis? How did she know the Chalon would create a portal? How did she know where to find the Fallen?"

"We can't exactly ask her." I ran a hand down my face. "Maybe once she finds out the Fallen are gone, she'll just leave."

"Doubtful," Elyssa said.

I squeezed my eyes shut and racked my brain for an answer. The image of Kaelissa's smug face filled my mind and I remembered what she'd told me only a few days ago. "There is little hope you could win a war. If you refuse, I will soon sing a song none can resist."

Kaelissa didn't intend to challenge us to a rap battle or a karaoke faceoff. She also hadn't come here looking for the Fallen. What she wanted had been right in front of our eyes from day one, and her secret weapons would be far more devastating, provided she had the bloodstones to pull it off.

"Oh, crap," I murmured. "We have to get back to Atlantis now."

"What about Heval?" Elyssa asked.

I gripped the rail and watched as the three ships began to glide toward their true destination—toward Atlantis. "Kaelissa doesn't want the Fallen. She wants the Sirens."

Chapter 27

The Fallen were powerful Seraphim, but even their power paled in comparison to the song of the Sirens. "Kaelissa said she would return within two weeks with a song none could resist."

Elyssa's eyes flared. "If the Sirens are that powerful, they could seduce our entire army. Nothing in Pjurna could resist them!"

Illaena spun to Tahlee. "Back to Atlantis, all speed."

We shot up above the clouds so the other ships wouldn't see us and streaked toward the island. I looked down but was unable to see the other ships. Hopefully, Illaena's assessment of the Brightling crews would prove true. As I'd learned, there was a lot more to piloting a sky ship than simply channeling into control rods, and the inexperienced Brightling navigators might not be able to coax top speed from their stolen vessels.

Adam and Shelton raced above decks eyes wide with confusion.

"Where are we going?" Shelton said. "Did something happen?"

"More ships," Elyssa said, and told them what we'd figured out. "Kaelissa probably hoped they could take the Sirens by surprise. If we warn Narine and the others, there's no way her plan will work."

"Holy crapola." Shelton ran a hand down his face. "We are so screwed if Kaelissa brainwashes a Siren."

"It'll never work if the Sirens know," Adam said. "In fact, maybe we can flip this situation on Kaelissa."

"Hell yeah," Shelton said. "Let's get the Sirens to put her army to sleep."

I grinned. "That would deprive the Brightlings of several hundred soldiers." I grinned. "Maybe we'll capture Kaelissa and end the war before it begins."

"You're telling me Kaelissa is onboard?" Adam asked.

I nodded. "She has to brainwash the Sirens herself if she wants to control them."

"Yeah, I hadn't thought of that."

We angled down through the clouds and reached the shores of Atlantis moments later. The *Falcheen* slid in for a graceful landing on the turtle pier. There was just one other problem—how in the world could we contact the Sirens if they were underwater?

I raced to the end of the pier and started waving my arms and shouting. "Narine! We need to speak with you. It's an emergency!"

Adam, Shelton, and Elyssa jumped up and down beside me, shouting and flailing their arms like a bunch of lunatics. I didn't care. The Brightling ships weren't more than ten minutes behind us.

Adonis hurried down the pier, face screwed up with confusion. "What is wrong?"

"Do you know how to contact the Sirens?" I asked.

"Yes, of course," he replied. "They gave us a conch shell we use to call them in times of need, though we rarely use it."

"We need it right now," I said. "There are enemies on their way."

"More newcomers in Atlantis?" Adonis gasped. "That would explain where the Sirens were going."

"What do you mean by that?" Shelton said.

"I saw them on their sea dragons heading east just before they submerged in the ocean," Adonis said. "They have an uncanny ability to know where everything is in this place, the same way they knew you were here."

Shelton face palmed. "You've got to be kidding me."

I circled a finger in the air to round up everyone. "Back on the ship. We've got to stop them."

Illaena had already rushed up the gang plank and I heard Tahlee shouting orders. The second the last of us boarded the ship, the *Falcheen* took flight, skimming just above the water and throwing a rooster tail of spray behind.

245

Adonis gasped and held on. "Oh my, this is frightening!"

I hadn't even realized he'd followed us onboard.

The ocean blurred past beneath us and small dots on the horizon grew larger. I grabbed the scope and zoomed in. Three sea dragons sat on the deck of the *Xanda*. A lone figure appeared from a ramp way and leapt atop one of the dragons. An angry, frightened face briefly looked my way—it was Dolpha! Her sea dragon leapt into the air and glided our way.

Soldiers appeared and the weaponized gems on the hull began firing wildly after the fleeing sea dragon. Kaelissa emerged from the ramp way, Narine and Balaena at her flank. I zoomed in on their faces. Their eyes were red as blood, faces devoid of emotion.

A lance of white energy pierced a wing and Dolpha's dragon screamed in pain. Kaelissa's eyes widened as her eyes took in the sight of the *Falcheen* cruising her way. She waved an arm and the three ships rotated to take on the new threat.

We didn't intend to fight her—not now. Illaena was already giving orders faster than I could keep up. At first I thought she meant to turn the ship around. Instead, the *Falcheen* swooped low and caught Dolpha and her injured sea dragon before they crashed into the water. The sea dragon skidded across the deck and the Siren was flung from the creature's back.

I leapt into the air and caught Dolpha before she unceremoniously face-planted on the deck, and landed back on my feet. The ship tilted hard and centrifugal force pressed everyone onto the deck as the *Falcheen* made a sharp turn starboard. Before the unskilled Brightling sailors could get close, we were already flitting away across the ocean.

Adonis clung for dear life to a railing, his face greener than a moldy potato. "This is more excitement than I can handle!"

Dolpha squirmed in my arms. "I can stand, thank you."

I set the Siren on her feet. "Why did you go out to those ships? I warned you there were bad people trying to get in here."

Dolpha leaned heavily against me. "They were in ships like yours. We thought they were more of your people."

"Those ships were hijacked," Elyssa said. "What happened?"

A tear trickled down Dolpha's face. "We were invited aboard. Narine accepted, even though I told her to use caution." She looked behind us, large eyes pools of green. "We were greeted by a woman and a man. Then everything happened so quickly. Narine and Balaena were rendered unconscious. I saw red stones and beams of crimson energy entering their foreheads. I immediately knew what was happening, but before I could do anything, soldiers attacked me."

"Here's the real question," Shelton said. "If they start singing, how in the heck are we supposed to resist?"

"Earplugs?" Adam said.

"You cannot close your ears to the song," Dolpha said. "You hear with your entire body."

I didn't like the sound of that. "In other words, Kaelissa can just swoop in and put us all to sleep?"

"The song can compel, but those who are strong-willed can fight it." Dolpha glided over to her injured sea dragon and inspected its wing. "I can grant some protection with my own song, but there is no guarantee."

Elyssa took the scope and looked behind us. "They're still coming. Kaelissa probably doesn't want us to escape so we can warn our forces."

"Even if we escaped through the tunnel they made in the maelstrom, what good would it do?" Shelton's face blanched. "How are we supposed to fight mass brain washing?"

"Let's not get hysterical." Elyssa knelt next to Dolpha. "Everyone has limits. Do Sirens have to continuously sing to keep us compelled?"

The Siren nodded. "The effects might linger for several minutes afterward."

Elyssa nodded. "Can other loud sounds counteract the song?"

"No, only the song of another Siren," Dolpha said. "There is more to the song than simple sound."

"An underlying current of enchantment," Adam said. "It probably acts on several levels."

"Does the song affect everyone close enough to hear it?" Elyssa said.

Dolpha shook her head. "No, it can be modulated to affect only those you wish to affect."

"You keep saying song as in singular," I said. "Is there only one song?"

Dolpha seemed confused. "The song is what you make it. The song is life."

"That makes so much sense," Shelton said sarcastically. "Want me to sing out of my ass for you?"

Elyssa narrowed her eyes. "That's not productive, Shelton."

He threw up his hands. "Excuse me, but I'm terrified of losing my mind while Kaelissa has her way with us."

Adam smirked and tried to adjust his non-existent glasses. "You afraid she'll diddle your bum hole?"

"I'm a good-looking man," Shelton shot back. "Ain't no telling what she'll do."

Elyssa bit her lower lip and gave me a hopeless look. "I don't know what to do. We can't possibly evacuate the island, though I doubt Kaelissa will care much about Atlantis."

"I have never known war," Adonis said. "My people only know the tales of old. We are not equipped to stop an invasion."

"What about those big ships in the harbor?" I asked.

"They are not large enough to move our entire population," Adonis replied. "Even so, how would they make it through the storm wall?"

Our choices were boiling down to nothing. We couldn't stand and fight, but running away would leave Atlantis wide open to Kaelissa. Thomas had taught me that retreat was sometimes the only option, even if it meant giving up ground. We also had a responsibility to the people in Seraphina to make it out of here with news of Kaelissa's master plan.

I steeled my resolve and told the others what we had to do. "We have no way of defending Atlantis. Our only choice is to leave using the portal Kaelissa created to get in here and warn our people about the Siren threat."

"You mean to leave us undefended?" Adonis said.

"There's nothing we can do," I told him. "I suggest you surrender to her. Odds are she won't even care about Atlantis right now since she has her eyes set on a bigger goal."

"Yeah, world domination," Shelton grumbled.

Fingers mentally crossed, I turned to Dolpha. "We desperately need you. There's no way for us to stand against your sisters if you're not with us."

The Siren whispered in the ear of the sea dragon, and the great scaly beast whimpered. She made a sweeping motion with her hand. The dragon groaned and refused to move. Dolpha sighed and turned. "It appears Galla and I will be coming with you."

"Thank you," I said.

Shelton raised his hands. "Praise the lord!"

Dolpha frowned. "It is the only way I may save my sisters."

Adonis looked back and forth between me and the Siren. "I pray you are right about Kaelissa. For all I know she will slaughter us."

"Can you evacuate into the woods?" I said. "Maybe the Lyrolai can protect you."

"I have a better idea," Elyssa said. "Let's lead Kaelissa back through the portal to Seraphina. She has what she wants, so there's no reason for her to stick around."

It was risky, but at least it provided some safety for Atlantis. "Let's do it."

The island faded into view through the misty bubble around it. Dropping off Adonis with the Brightling ships so close behind would make for a tight window of escape. Even though the odds were three to one, I had faith the Mzodi were skilled enough to outmaneuver our pursuers.

Adam frowned at something on his phone and flicked the screen. "Whatcha looking at?" Shelton asked him.

"Bloodstones," Adam said. "Even if we escape Voltis, we need to disable the bloodstones controlling the Sirens."

"It's too bad the Fallen weren't home," Shelton said. "I'll bet they know a thing or two about bloodstones."

"What if we use the bloodstone we have on Kaelissa?" I said.

Adam shook his head. "We don't even know how to do that yet."

In other words, we were hella screwed. The only option left to us would be killing Narine and Balaena—a solution Dolpha wouldn't accept.

"You look like you're having second thoughts," Elyssa said.

I bit my lower lip and tried to think of alternatives, but if we left, trying to get back inside Voltis would be almost impossible with this new Brightling fleet in the air. Buried somewhere inside their palace, the Fallen probably had a gem or diary filled with their secrets about the bloodstones. Even better, they might have information about the nodes they used to access Eden.

All our answers were here, but we had to beat back Kaelissa to buy the time needed to find them. The alternative was leading her back to Tarissa and trying to fight her with our army. Even with one Siren on our side, it would be extremely difficult to win that battle.

Shelton groaned. "We're not going back are we?"

"The Fallen have the answers to bloodstones and getting home." I met his eyes. "We have to beat Kaelissa here."

"I can tell you right now we won't win a direct confrontation." Elyssa tapped her chin and stared at Atlantis. "We need to resort to trickery."

I rubbed my hands together. "Ninja mode."

"There's another issue," Adam said. "That portal through Voltis won't last long without the device on the *Xanda*. We need to make sure we get our hands on it somehow."

Elyssa took out her arcphone and began tapping on the screen. "We still have three functional brooms, right?"

Shelton's forehead pinched. "Yeah."

"I might have a wheelbarrow around here too," I quipped.

Elyssa's lips spread into a wide smile. "I have an idea that could get us the portal generator, the Sirens, and get Kaelissa off our backs."

"Don't play with my heart," Shelton said. "I'm feeling really vulnerable right now."

Elyssa turned to Dolpha. "We need protection from the Siren song."

The Siren's inner eyelid flicked across her eye and retracted, almost like a nervous tic. "There is a way, but I must return to Pacifis."

Elyssa blinked. "Where?"

"The Siren city beneath the ocean." She touched the wing of her sea dragon. "Galla is well enough to take me there."

"How long will it take?" Elyssa asked.

"Not long." Dolpha slid easily onto Galla's back. "I will return and meet you in the harbor." The sea dragon dove gracefully over the railing and vanished into the waters with hardly a splash.

Elyssa grabbed my arm and headed for the ramp way. "Let's get the brooms. We have to be fast if this is going to work."

"I need to feed," I told her as we jogged down the ramp. "How are you feeling?"

"Bursting with energy," she said. "Take what you need."

"When we have a minute." I dashed into the cabin and grabbed the brooms and stopped Elyssa before she bolted away. "You seem awfully confident about our chances for success."

"That's because there's one major thing Kaelissa didn't consider when she captured the Sirens." Elyssa's lovely lips spread into a smile. "Hopefully we can use that to our advantage."

As she explained the plan to me on the way back above decks, I couldn't help but share some of her confidence. We had to have perfect timing, a lot of luck, and a rookie mistake by Kaelissa.

There was one huge "if" hanging on our gambit. *If* Elyssa's assumption about the Sirens was wrong, then Kaelissa would easily capture us, I'd probably lose my mind, and Seraphina would be doomed.

Saving the world really stressed me out.

Chapter 28

I finished feeding my inner demon and angel by the time the *Falcheen* reached the harbor and swooped in for a quick landing.

Adonis raced down the gangway toward the turtle pier. "We'll be ready," he shouted over his shoulder. "May the gods be with you."

"Which gods is he talking about?" Shelton said. "The Fallen? The old Greek gods?" He threw up his hands. "I just need to know who to pray to for this insane plan to work."

Elyssa handed each of us a broom. "Make sure they're working. We can't afford any glitches."

I flicked the runes on my broom and tested it out, taking a few practice circles around the ship while Elyssa and Shelton did the same.

Shelton got off his and frowned. "This one has some cracks in the handle." He tested the polished wood with his hands. "I think it'll be okay, but I can't get too crazy on it."

Adam appeared with a bulging satchel over his shoulder. He reached inside and withdrew several nets filled with small cylindrical casks the Mzodi used to keep food preserved. "There are three gem bombs for everyone."

I took one of the nets and slung it across my back like a paperboy satchel. "How do these things work?"

Adam took one and tapped on the gem sealed into the lid of a cask. "Twist the lid and the gem will start to glow. You have ten seconds to get rid of it before Kaboom!" He spread his hands like a mushroom cloud.

Galla burst from the ocean, salt water foaming and running from his scaly blue hide. Naked atop his back, Dolpha's skin looked smooth and gray like that of a dolphin's. Two long tail fins morphed back to human legs, and her diaphanous dress reappeared to cover her naked form.

"Whoa." Shelton's jaw hung open. "Man, these mermaids got it going on."

"These are Sirens," Adam said.

"Don't split hairs with me." Shelton backed up as the sea dragon alighted on the deck. Dolpha slid off and glided across to us without missing a beat.

She handed each of us necklaces of seaweed with intricately curved shells strung on them. I heard a faint sound emanating from within the shell on mine and held it up to my ear. An eerie but lovely melody of clashing disharmonies and a chorus of voices sent a calming warmth through my body.

"I have trapped the song of protection within these shells," Dolpha said. "Take care, for they will not last long."

"How long specifically?" Shelton asked. "Five minutes—an hour?"

"Perhaps an hour," she said, "though measures of mortal time often elude me."

"We'll be long dead or long gone by then," Elyssa said.

I spotted two black specks flanking a shimmering silver dot on the horizon. Kaelissa was nearly here. Dolpha raised her hands and sang out a single piercing note. Massive dorsal fins broke the surface of the sea about a hundred yards out. A tartha broke the surface and bellowed out a note in response.

Another great chorus sang out and thousands of seagulls funneled into the sky, swirling higher and spreading out above. More creatures rose from the deeps. Three smaller sea dragons, flocks of flying manta rays, and dolphins by the hundreds, leaping far into the air before diving back into the ocean.

Shelton's eyes grew wide at the massing armada of sea life. "Uh, can't the ships just keep out of range of them?"

"Not if they wish to see the island," Dolpha said. "The mist shield allows us to see out though they cannot see in."

The huge gong at the acropolis atop the mountain rang out and the ever-present mist around Atlantis thickened, a shimmering translucent bubble from the inside.

Adonis jogged down the dock followed by fifty men dressed in strange shiny cloth armor that looked like something out of a black and white sci-fi movie. They held silver tridents with aquamarine energy pulsating up the prongs and wore bizarre three-pronged helmets also glowing with energy.

"That armor doesn't look like it could stop a rusty spork," Shelton shouted at them.

Adonis slid a dagger from his sheath and stabbed himself in the stomach. The armor pulsated and rippled like water in a pond from the point of impact. "It is more than it seems."

Adam pushed up his imaginary glasses and whistled. "Water magic is really cool."

"I just hope they remember how to fight," Elyssa said.

I hopped on my broom. "Let's get into position."

Elyssa climbed into the saddle on her broom. "That's my line."

Shelton clapped Adam on the back. "If I die, tell Bella I looked like a total badass doing it, ok?"

Adam chuckled. "You'll be a legend by the time I finish the story."

Shelton secured the net with the bombs to his back and the three off us jetted off high into the sky. The seagulls gliding overhead spread apart to allow us through and then closed back up to conceal us.

"I hope bloodstones don't allow Kaelissa to read minds," Shelton said. "If she figures out what Sirens are capable of, we're screwed."

I shared his concerns, but there wasn't much else we could do. The deep basso of the great horn in the harbor rumbled once, twice, three times. Elyssa reached across the gap between our brooms and squeezed my hand three times. *I love you.*

I leaned over and kissed her long and hard. "I love you too."

"Where's my kiss?" Shelton said.

I blew him a kiss. "We love you too, Shelton."

He pretended to catch it and tucked it under his wide-brimmed hat. "I'm saving that for later."

We shared a laugh, and then the horn blew the fourth and final note. Our smiles faded with the somber realization that it was time. The plan was simple, but anything could go wrong. It all began with simply letting go.

We turned off our brooms and began to fall.

The seagulls screeched and dove before us, leaving just enough space between their collective body to see the decks of the three ships below. Shelton took out a gem bomb and the rest of us followed his lead.

Elyssa angled for the *Akata*, Shelton the *Ptarn*, and I aimed for the mothership herself, the *Xanda*. I spotted Narine and Balaena near the bridge, their dragons curled around the portal generator in the front. Golden blond locks blew in the wind—a beacon to Kaelissa where she stood between the two Sirens.

I could end it all right now. One bomb would kill the Sirens and Kaelissa. Leaderless and without their secret weapon, the Brightlings would have to retreat. But I would kill two innocents to secure the peace.

Dolpha would never forgive me, but what if we failed? What if Kaelissa won this fight and took her prizes to Pjurna? Bloodstones were one thing, but the Sirens seemed capable of mind-control on a massive scale. I couldn't let her escape.

The cry of the gulls and the rush of the wind merged to a dull roar in my ears as my conscience wavered between decisions of life and death. Strategically, it made the most sense to cut off the head of the snake even if the collateral damage was awful. Deep down, I knew I couldn't do it because there was one thing that had seen me through the darkest days during the war against Daelissa.

Hope.

We can save the Sirens.

I just knew it. All we had to do was execute the plan. I pulled my broom back on target.

Kaelissa looked up at the funnel of birds swooping toward her deck and pointed. The Brightling soldiers drew swords and began firing bolts of Brilliance. Gulls screeched and burned all around me, bodies twisting and tumbling as the barrage of deadly energy took its toll on the outer layer.

I felt horribly guilty using these poor animals as a meat shield, but the enemy was about to get a taste of what they were dishing. About a hundred feet off the deck, I twisted the gem in the canister and let it go. The birds unleashed their little bowels and veered away, keeping me safely hidden inside their funnel.

The Brightlings soldiers shouted and desperately tried to leap away as dead birds and several gallons of bird crap landed on their heads. They were so desperate to get out of the slime that they didn't even notice the bomb.

Three closely timed explosions thundered.

Bodies flew across the *Xanda* and the ship veered out of control as Brightling navigators were thrown from their positions. The *Akata* went into a steep nosedive and splashed into the ocean a hundred feet below. Brightlings spilled over the railing and into the water though the ship itself stayed afloat.

The explosion on the *Ptarn* hit too far aft, knocking out the rear navigators, but not dealing enough damage to keep it from flying. I twisted the gem on another canister and flung it toward the rear of the *Xanda* to take out more navigators. A shimmering ray of Brilliance slammed into the bomb.

I had just enough time to throw up a shield before the explosion ripped through the seagulls and knocked me into a violent tailspin. Before I could stop the spin, my broom hit the deck of the *Xanda*. The impact threw me across the surface. I skidded to a stop paces away from Kaelissa.

Her eyes glowed an angry white. The two Sirens turned to me, their hair undulating in that eerie underwater way, their eyes glazed over, as if they saw nothing.

"You dare attack me," the Brightling Empress hissed. She waved a hand and Arturo appeared at her side. "Bring me the other attackers."

"At once." The archangel raised a fist. Wings blazed to life on his back and the backs of over a dozen other soldiers. They leapt into the air and flew after the flocks of gulls protecting Elyssa and Shelton.

Another canister fell toward the *Ptarn*, but the archangels blasted it from the sky before it could land.

I spotted my broom thirty paces away. There were also a dozen Brightlings standing between me and escape. *Yeah, not gonna happen.*

"You're damned right I dare attack you," I said, desperately trying to buy time so I could think of a way out. "I can't let you use the Sirens to take over Pjurna."

Kaelissa smiled. "I'm afraid that is out of your hands, boy." She waved an arm toward the mist surrounding Atlantis. "I knew of this place long ago. My dear Sithain spoke of it during one of her visits. It took me quite some time to discover how to get inside."

My jaw went slack. "You knew Sithain?"

"Oh, yes," she replied. "You see, Sithain's birth name was Saeissa."

It didn't take long for me to make the connection. "She's from the bloodline of Issa."

"Indeed." Kaelissa preened her hair as if she were awfully proud of herself. "She is my sister."

"Son of a biscuit!" It didn't take much reasoning to see that the daughters and granddaughters of Issa had cornered the market on crazy in Seraphina.

"Sithain vanished after the failed attempt on King Thussor." Her forehead pinched with sadness. "For centuries, I thought her dead."

It seemed I was buying plenty of time, and a quick glance at the skies showed me that Shelton and Elyssa were racing away from the pursuing archangels. The seagulls had turned and attacked Arturo and his people, preventing them from catching up. With my friends safe, it meant I was only responsible for myself.

Kaelissa plucked a red gem from within a pouch at her side and her lips spread into a rather pleased smile. "I had thought to save this for the last Siren, but it somehow seems more fitting to use it on the hero of Eden instead."

My chest went cold and my knees wobbled. Boots stomped the deck behind me and I saw the Brightlings moving in to hold me. I couldn't let that happen. I opened the cage to my inner demon and let it all out.

Freedom! The demon half of my soul shouted in elation.

Muscles coiled around my arms like snakes, bulging and stretching my clothes until they tore. Pain stabbed my forehead, long twisting horns erupting while my fingernails blackened and turned into claws. A forked tail sprouted from my backside, lashing back and forth like a whip. My body swelled higher and wider until I towered over the angels around me. Blue flames flickered in my vision.

The instant before my demon half consumed my conscious mind, I slammed on the brakes and kept it at bay. The Brightlings drew swords and channeled shields.

I stomped a foot and glared at Kaelissa. "Back off, bitch."

Her eyes flashed with surprise, but she didn't back off. "Secure him!"

Brightlings swarmed me.

I lashed out with my tail and upended a handful of soldiers. My fist sent another flying over the railing and my foot sent a heap of them to the ground. It was a good show, but there were simply too many of them for me to keep this up. Unfortunately, I was now too huge and heavy for my broom.

Another squad of soldiers came at me. With a guttural roar, I leapt over them, using their heads as a walkway for my monstrous feet. I channeled a barrier of Murk as a pathway and raced for the railing.

Heat blasted me in the side and sent me skidding across the deck. Kaelissa leapt high, her dress flowing around her like a super cape, and landed nearby. Her eyes glowed with joy and twin spheres of Brilliance blossomed in her palms. "You are more powerful than I thought, Justin Slade. Perhaps your seed would break the curse of the Schism and give me immortal children."

I nearly threw up in my mouth, and not because of the blistered skin on my ribs. "You're sick, lady! I'm like, uh"—I didn't know how to do the math on this one, but she was thousands of years old, and I was only twenty—"one-thousandth your age, or maybe even less!" I pushed up, nursing the wound on my ribs and raced for the railing.

Kaelissa flung another volley. I intercepted with a shield. Twenty feet to the railing. Ten feet. Soldiers leapt on me, grabbing my legs, my neck, my arms. I threw two of them off. Kicked one in the face and sent him tumbling. Kaelissa fired a beam of destruction at me. I twisted and the white-hot bolt caught one of her soldiers instead.

Two big brutes slammed their shoulders into me and I stumbled backward over the bodies of fallen soldiers and slammed onto my back. Before I could push to my feet, a dozen angels pinned my limbs to the deck while several more sat on my horns and forced my head back. I roared and struggled, but they held me fast.

Kaelissa straddled my chest, her eyes alight with pure joy. "I had forgotten what it was to live. Now I know why my sweet Daelissa reveled in battle. It is so sweet to claim victory."

"Then I guess you've never had a chance to eat a tub of ice cream while vegging out to reality television," I shot back. "War has the unfortunate side effect of killing people."

"I see my destiny clearly now," Kaelissa said, eyes growing distant. "My daughter was but a lesson to me. Now I control the Sirens and the great hero of Eden. I will finish the conquest she began so long ago."

She held the bloodstone lengthwise between thumb and forefinger. "Rest easy, hero. You will be my champion henceforth."

Chapter 29

I hated to say it, but Elyssa's plan hadn't worked quite as well as we'd hoped and now it looked to completely backfire on us. I really wished I knew of some way to stop what was about to happen, but in moments, I'd be one of Kaelissa's brainwashed minions. I didn't know how to shield myself from the magic of the bloodstone. Hell, I didn't even know how it worked.

On the other hand, I had a little brainwashing magic of my own. It wasn't super effective against Seraphim, but it might be enough to distract the crazy sera on my chest. She released the bloodstone and let it hover in the air. I tried to see what she was doing, but for some reason, the flow of magical energy between her and the stone was invisible.

I switched to incubus vision and saw the intricate weave wending its way from Kaelissa's fingers and the bloodstone. It appeared she was channeling three threads of energy, Murk, Brilliance, and Stasis through the crimson rock, but at such a low level, it was invisible to the naked eye.

The liquid aether inside began to bubble and I knew my time as a free-thinking individual was quickly dwindling to nothing.

Kaelissa's soul halo glowed like white fire laced with dark smoke. I didn't have time to be subtle, so I lashed out with a tendril of psychic energy and wrapped it around her halo. Her soul fought back, bucking like a horse that didn't want to be ridden, and her eyes flashed wide.

I redoubled my efforts, grasping at her with more of my own essence, and Kaelissa gasped. The magic between her and the bloodstone faltered. Her face flushed with lust as the demon magic amped up the sexual heat by a thousand degrees.

Just when I thought I had her, she burst into laughter. "You will make a worthy mate." My attempt at incubus magic had caused her to stop channeling into the bloodstone, but it was only a brief respite.

I'm screwed. And there was no good way of getting screwed by Kaelissa. One last desperate thought hit me. What if I mimicked her channeling? At this point it couldn't hurt to try. I didn't have any fingers free, but Seraphim magic could be channeled through any part of the body.

Careful to keep the energy level low and the threads invisible, I channeled a stream of Murk from my left eye and Brilliance from my right, then wiggled my nose so I could focus on the tip, and generated a stream of Stasis. I usually had to weave creation and destruction into Stasis, so channeling it straight was difficult.

My concentration wavered and the first two threads lost cohesion. *I'm losing it!* I saw the liquid in the bloodstone begin to slowly bubble as Kaelissa's magic began to affect it. *Concentrate, damn it!*

Being frightened out of your mind while trying to channel something you've never done before isn't easy. I'd trained to overcome these challenges, but this weave was so new to me that I couldn't maintain it. Any second now the mind-controlling magic would emerge from the bloodstone and consume me.

In a few seconds, I won't be me anymore. I'll be Kaelissa's puppet. She could make me kill Elyssa.

The thought of hurting the woman I loved was all it took to firm my resolve. I gritted my teeth and gave it everything I had. My aether streams entered the bloodstone and the liquid began to boil. I tried to push out of the other side, but it felt as though Kaelissa's threads were blocking my own.

Her brow furrowed, and it appeared she was having the same difficulty as me. It wouldn't take her long to realize it was due to my interference. I couldn't push back at her, but there was no resistance to the other sides of the stone. I let the energy flow to the side and saw a single red thread emerge.

Bearing down with my willpower, I directed it at one of the big brutes holding down my arms. His eyes flashed red and his jaw clenched tight. Kaelissa didn't seem to notice, and neither did anyone around him. Several seconds passed, and the liquid in the bloodstone seemed to boil away to nothing.

Kaelissa's face screwed up into comical confusion. I didn't know how she hadn't figured out that I'd counter channeled her, until I realized she suffered from the same character flaw that had brought down Daelissa—her arrogance. She'd underestimated me.

I felt a tingling sensation in my brain and realized with horror that I was linked with the soldier on my right arm. I couldn't sense his thoughts, but I felt the strings that bound his will to mine. I sent a command: *cross your eyes and open your mouth.*

The soldier did as commanded, looking hilarious in the process.

Kaelissa stared at me, seemingly unaware of the comic relief going on at her side. "You," she hissed. "You did someth—oof!"

My new buddy punched Kaelissa in the face. He stood and kicked her in the ribs hard enough to send her sprawling across the deck. Then he drew his sword and ran at her.

As you could imagine, that caused a panicked reaction from the other soldiers. One of their own had suddenly gone crazy and attacked their empress. Since they didn't realize I was controlling him, they rushed him to take him down. I still had soldiers pinning me to the deck, so I did something else unexpected.

I slammed my demon soul back into its cage and my body began to rapidly shrink to normal size. My horns detached and my tail retracted. The soldiers at my head suddenly found themselves grasping nothing but air and some spare horns that might make interesting hood ornaments for a car.

Grabbing one of the horns from the grasp of a surprised soldier, I twisted upright and smacked him in the face, reversed my grip, and knocked the other soldier senseless. Before the Brightlings who'd run after their traitorous comrade could react, I raced for the railing.

A terrible scream filled with frustration shattered the air. "You will not escape me!" Kaelissa roared. "Sing to him, my Sirens!"

Narine and Balaena glided toward me at an angle to prevent me from leaving the ship. Their lips parted and the sweetest song I had ever heard filled my ears. I felt a stirring in my heart, a great yearning to answer the call of that song. Ecstasy awaited if only I turned and ran into the light.

But another song whispered from the shell on the seaweed around my neck. Its countermelody soured the sweet wine and filled my mouth with bitterness. I regained control and looked back. The soldiers turned as one toward the Sirens, eyes filled with great longing and began shuffling toward them like mindless zombies. The navigators manning the levitation foils left their positions and the ship slowly began to sink as the foils used the last remaining energy.

Kaelissa was so intent on me that she hardly noticed the effect the song had on the others. I was surprised that it didn't affect her—a side effect of her link through the bloodstone? I looked for the soldier I'd controlled earlier but he lay in a pool of blood, apparently executed by his fellows to protect their empress.

It's working! Sure, it had taken a while, but Kaelissa had finally made the mistake we'd been waiting for. I held out my arms and made zombie noises, shuffling toward the Sirens along with the other soldiers even as the ship began to plunge toward the water.

Kaelissa suddenly realized the mess she'd gotten herself in, but before she could command the Sirens, I picked up a nearby sword and flung it at her. The hilt smacked her in the shoulder and she tumbled backwards with a scream of pain. I saw my broom lying a few yards away and ran for it as the wind from the fast descent whistled in my ears.

I scooped up the broom and lifted off an instant before the massive ship belly-flopped into the ocean with a thunderous splash. Brightling soldiers crashed into the deck, bodies bouncing once and going still. Those that weren't knocked out from the impact dragged themselves toward the Sirens. The ones that had already reached them, gazed adoringly up at their mistresses.

Apparently, the Mzodi had planned for emergency water landings because like the *Akata*, the *Xanda* remained afloat. The Brightlings might be our enemies, but watching them drown as their minds were caught in the Siren song would have been sickening.

I swooped down toward the deck just as Shelton and Elyssa zipped back into sight on their brooms. The *Falcheen* burst into view from out of the mist and barreled toward us. The massive tartha bellowed and swam full steam ahead for the ship while seagulls hovered overhead. The Sirens continued to sing mindlessly while their puppeteer struggled to recover from face-planting into the deck.

At Kaelissa's waist hung the pouch from which she'd taken the bloodstone intended for me. I leapt off the broom, leapt over sprawled bodies, and tore the pouch from the strap. Inside were the bloodstones controlling the Sirens. I'd hoped that taking them would allow me to assume control, but the connection didn't work that way.

Somehow, I had to destroy the bloodstones to sever the link.

Kaelissa whirled and flung an orb of Murk at me. I dodged it and hit her chest with a battering ram of energy. She grunted and slid on her backside.

She shrieked like a banshee and climbed to her feet. The Sirens stopped singing and a hundred dazed and confused Brightling soldiers began to gather their wits. We didn't have long.

Thankfully, Shelton and Elyssa were on point.

Elyssa knocked out the Sirens with lancer darts. Dolpha soared in on Galla, and the sea dragon grabbed the two sirens, one in each claw then circled back out to sea. I lunged for Kaelissa, but a squad of soldiers threw themselves in my way. Explosions thundered, and the entire deck shook as two gem bombs went off behind me.

Dozens of soldiers lay stunned, dead, and dying, but there was no way I could take Kaelissa alive. I hopped on my broom and rose above the fray. Blood trailed down her face, soaking her white gown, and her lovely blond hair was singed on the right side.

I tried one last time to reason with her. "Stop this madness, Kaelissa! We can make peace and end the bloodshed. There's no need for you to die."

She looked up at me, pure rage boiling in her eyes, and screamed. "There will never be peace so long as you live, boy! I will see you and your friends burned by the light, and my Daelissa will be avenged!"

"That's not the answer I was hoping for," I said in a chiding voice. I'd given her a choice and she'd taken the wrong one. Elyssa and Shelton came up beside me.

Shelton held out his last gem bomb. "You want the honors?"

I didn't like the idea of killing Kaelissa like this. She was tired, frazzled, and nearly defenseless. My hesitation nearly cost me my head. A beam of energy speared past close enough to give me a sunburn. I twisted the broom around and saw the *Ptarn* closing the gap, all forward weapons firing. Arturo and the archangels flew ahead of the ship, clearing a path through the seagulls trying to hinder their progress.

"Don't go soft on me, man!" Shelton twisted the gem and dropped the bomb. "Get out of here!"

We darted in different directions as beams of Brilliance and Murk sprayed the area where we'd been. The magical bomb exploded and bodies flew. I was too busy dodging death beams to see if Kaelissa had made it out alive.

The giant tartha bellowed as the ship fired on it, but the attacks did little damage and only made it angrier. With the singing of the Sirens silenced, the *Falcheen* closed in and engaged the *Ptarn*. Magical energy sizzled through the air as the gems charged and fired.

Though there were far fewer crew on the *Falcheen*, her firepower gouged the tough Murk hull of the enemy ship while enemy return fire left only blackened marks. The Mzodi obviously knew what they were doing.

Arturo seemed to realize this and dove for the deck of the *Xanda*. I circled around, but a squadron of archangels veered toward me. Elyssa and Shelton pulled into formation next to me, but I waved them off.

"We can't take them," I said. I could probably injure a few, but their concentrated firepower would be too much.

Arturo pulled a body from beneath a pile of soldiers. Two archangels alighted next to him and lifted Kaelissa by her arms. Burdened by the extra weight, they struggled, but managed to gain altitude.

"Is she alive?" Shelton said.

265

I zoomed my vision, but with all the blood covering Kaelissa, I couldn't tell.

The *Falcheen* blasted one of the weapon gems on the *Ptarn*. The explosion left a hole in the enemy hull and rocked the ship hard. Arturo slashed a hand and two squadrons of archangels flew at the Mzodi ship. The *Falcheen* fired, but the skilled fliers dodged the beams and homed in on the crew with their lightning lances.

"We've got to help them!" I throttled my broom to full speed and zipped toward the enemy. White hot energy blossomed around my fist and I fired deadly beams at the backs of the attackers. Shelton whirled his staff and unleashed torrents of brilliant orange.

The archangels tried to dodge, but Shelton's magic homed in on them, wrapping around their wings and rendering them helpless. Two archangels cried out and fell, unable to keep aloft. Four of their comrades came to their aid while the others turned and fired on us.

Shelton disabled another flier before we had to take evasive action and dodge the return fire. Beset on both sides by us and the *Falcheen*, the archangels carried their disabled companions back toward the retreating *Ptarn*.

With the imminent danger over, we landed on the *Falcheen*.

Tahlee cried out the command to pursue and we lurched forward after the enemy ship. Smoke trailed from the hull of the *Ptarn* where the weapon gem had exploded, but it didn't seem to affect the levitation foils. We gained slowly on the larger ship, the half mile separating us narrowing to a quarter mile while the great gray wall of the vortex grew larger on the horizon.

"They've got nowhere to run," Shelton said. "Are they just gonna commit suicide in the maelstrom?"

Elyssa looked through Illaena's scope and shook her head. "The portal is still open, but it's a lot smaller than before."

"Holy farting fairies," Shelton said. "They're gonna try to make it back through before it closes."

We closed the gap to a hundred yards and the Mzodi soldiers fired the front weapon gems. Beams of destruction left black marks on the back of the *Ptarn*, but it was too late.

The enemy ship reached the portal and flew inside, its reverse wings barely clearing the sides. By the time we reached it, the *Falcheen* was too big to fit, and we were going way too fast. Tahlee cried out a command but there was no way we'd stop from smashing ourselves into the deadly storm ahead.

Chapter 30

The *Falcheen* veered hard to starboard and the entire ship tilted sideways. Navigators held tight to their stations and gave it everything they had. The levitation foils thrummed with effort and the ship screeched to a halt just at the edge of the lightning-laced storm.

The ship tilted back to center and hung still, thunder rumbling and shaking us down to our bones.

"We did it," Shelton said, as if he could hardly believe it.

Adam walked over to us on unsteady legs, eyes wide. "Did we actually win?"

Elyssa nodded slowly. "We somehow just beat an entire army and sent them packing back to Seraphina."

"And saved the Sirens," I added.

"And liberated two Mzodi ships," Illaena said proudly. She shook a fist at the storm. "The Brightling Empire will pay for this outrage!"

Tahlee pumped her hand in the air and shouted, "*Falcheen! Falcheen!*"

The crew joined the cry, soon catching us in the infectious mood of victory.

I don't know how we did it. Somehow, we'd survived.

We returned to the *Xanda*. One of the ships from the harbor in Atlantis floated next to it, several gangways securing the ships together, and the Atlantean soldiers had already boarded the ship and started rounding up prisoners. The *Akata* was also boarded. In all, nearly a hundred Brightling soldiers were taken into custody, while the bodies of the dead were arranged for funerals.

Adonis and his people looked horrified at the carnage, but grimly went about their tasks.

"I have never seen such fighting in all my lifetime," Adonis said. "I would rather never see it again."

"Boy and how," Shelton agreed. "Too bad there's always another asshole out there who wants to be top dog."

The Archon scrunched his forehead, obviously confused by the literal translation. "Will more like Kaelissa come?"

Elyssa and I looked at each other and shrugged.

"It's doubtful." Elyssa tapped a finger on her chin. "We kept her from taking the Sirens, and we took two of their hijacked ships. The next step is to leave Voltis and warn the other Mzodi that Kaelissa has broken the peace."

"Gotta figure out how to work that portal generator first," Shelton said.

Adam shrugged. "Won't be too hard. I'm more worried about releasing the Sirens from the influence of the bloodstones."

We'd won the day, but there was a lot of road in front of us.

The Atlanteans towed the *Akata* and *Xanda* back to their harbor where Illaena and Tahlee inspected them for damage. Adonis and his troops secured the Brightling prisoners in a dungeon that the Sirens assured us would hold them until we decided their fates. Adonis promised there was enough food to keep them fed but he didn't seem too keen on having long-term prisoners to worry about.

It looked like life for the Atlanteans was going to get more complicated.

Adam and Shelton studied the portal apparatus and made plans to move it to the *Falcheen*. Meanwhile, Eor worked on destroying the bloodstones so Narine and Balaena could be free of their influence. Without orders from Kaelissa, they stood passively, apparently possessing no free will to do anything.

I shuddered to think of what might have happened to my consciousness if Kaelissa had worked the bloodstone magic on me. Would my real self be trapped and screaming somewhere in the back of my head, or would it have gone to oblivion?

Shelton made pizza for the four of us that night. Topped with sausage, tomatoes, olives, and cheese very similar to mozzarella, the first bite was like going to heaven.

Shelton held up a glass of wine. "Here's to the Four Horsemen of the Apocalypse!"

I snorted. "Maybe as far as Kaelissa is concerned."

"What is it with the women of Issa?" Elyssa said. "They're nuts."

Shelton raised an eyebrow. "You realize the end of your first name sounds an awful lot like Issa. How do we know you're not a long-lost sibling?"

Elyssa narrowed her eyes and scowled. "You calling me crazy, Shelton?"

He nearly choked on his pizza. "Nah, just kidding."

The rest of us burst into laughter.

"Here I was, just about to give you a medal of courage," Adam said.

Shelton huffed. "Hey, I'm brave, not stupid."

Much as I enjoyed the break from being all serious, I steered the conversation back to the future. "What did you find out about the portal apparatus on the *Xanda*?"

"The short answer is we can have it transferred to the *Falcheen* within a few hours." Adam waggled a hand. "Probably have it up and running by the afternoon."

"We'll need to test it as soon as possible," Elyssa said. "I have to send a message to my father and let him know what happened."

"I hope Pjurna isn't embroiled in civil war." I grabbed another slice of pizza. "With Kaelissa off our back for the time being, we might have a chance to unify the Darklings again."

"Do really think she survived the explosion?" Adam said.

I shrugged. "Doesn't really matter. Arturo will just pick back up where he left off."

"Speaking of which," Shelton said, "I think it's pretty obvious she didn't use a bloodstone on him so she could take power."

"He sees her as the second coming of Daelissa." Elyssa sighed. "Either way, we've got a fight on our hands in the near future."

"What's to stop us from using the Sirens?" Shelton said. "Maybe that'll be enough to keep the Brightlings off our backs."

I pressed my lips together and nodded. "I've given it a lot of thought, but we have to wait for Narine and Balaena to wake up. Dolpha was helpful, but she's the Negative Nancy of the group, and I don't want to leave the decision in her hands."

Adam held up a hand. "Amen to that!"

"If it comes down to a fight, I'm concerned we won't have the military might to win," Elyssa said. "Maybe there's a way to change this on a smaller scale."

"Assassination?" I said.

She gave me an apologetic look. "We have to consider all options."

Picking off Kaelissa or Arturo felt dirty, but they hadn't exactly kept their hands sparkly clean. I sighed. "We'll do what we have to."

"In the meantime, we can keep looking for a way home," Adam said. "All we have to do is find the nodes the Fallen were using."

Shelton polished off another slice of pizza. "I'd say we're sitting pretty right now, and not just because we can eat like humans again."

He was right. This journey had brought us one step closer to home and possibly given us new allies. But there was still a lot to do.

The next afternoon, Shelton and Adam finished the portal apparatus, and Illaena ordered the *Falcheen* out to the Voltis Maelstrom so we could test it. We told Adonis that if everything went as planned, we would briefly visit Seraphina and return to Atlantis.

Once we reached the roiling gray storm, I stood in front of the Chalon and channeled Brilliance through it. The orb levitated off its platform, the intricate designs on its surface catching fire. It spun faster and faster, but nothing else happened.

Adam stepped beside me. "I think you have to will it to focus energy through the gem."

I'd only used Chalons to open portals in Alabaster Arches—a process that required little more than willing it to happen. Maybe Adam was right and all the thing needed was a little direction. I imagined the Chalon sending energy through the large gem mounted in front of it and without further ado, beams of magic speared out, using the gem like a giant focusing lens.

The energy spread into the clouds ahead. Slowly but surely, static and destructive energy filtered away, leaving only a crystalline portal behind. Minutes later, the beginnings of a tunnel lay before us. Illaena ordered the ship inside. It took the better part of an hour, building the portal tunnel in front of us as we went, but before we knew it, clear skies and blue waters extended before us.

Adam took out his arcphone and scanned the environment. After a time, he nodded. "We're back in Seraphina."

"You think there's a way to attune the Chalon to do the same thing, but take us back to Eden?" Shelton said hopefully.

Adam shrugged. "Maybe. We'd have to test it."

Illaena stood next to us and drew in a deep breath. "It is good to be home."

"I need to speak with my father," Elyssa said. "Can I use your communication gem?"

Illaena nodded and took me and Elyssa to her cabin. Thomas's holographic image appeared almost immediately, and relief swept across his face when he saw his daughter.

Elyssa smiled. "Hello, Dad."

"I'm glad to see you're okay," Thomas said. "We've been very concerned."

"A lot has happened." Elyssa tucked her hair behind an ear. She quickly summarized our perilous journey, the existence of Atlantis, and Kaelissa's mission to kidnap the Sirens, her secret weapon.

"Amazing," Thomas said, his usual stony mask slipping. "If you hadn't stopped her, she could have strolled into Pjurna and worked her way across the continent, taking every city without spilling a drop of blood."

"I doubt it would have been bloodless," I said. "There's no telling what she had planned."

"I could use Sirens here in Tarissa." Thomas leaned on the table in front of him. "Legiaros Kohval marched his troops from the north and controls the northern part of the capitol." He flicked his hand and his image vanished, replaced by a map of Pjurna. A red line traveled south from Kohvalla and down to Tarissa where it pooled in the northern sections of the city.

Thomas continued with the troubling news. "Legiaros Meera led Gallix Legion into the city and assumed control of the south." An orange line highlighted the route from the western side of Pjurna and into Tarissa. "As of now, the Eden army is trapped between the two forces. Civil war could break out at any moment."

Illaena remained quiet, but her eyes flared in alarm.

"Are you safe?" Elyssa asked.

The map vanished and Thomas reappeared. He nodded grimly. "We're safe, but we're in no position to intervene between two full legions."

"What do our faction leaders have to say about it?" I asked.

"McCloud says the lycans will do whatever I request, but he already told me in no uncertain terms that if I can't force peace, we should let Kohval and Meera fight it out." Thomas folded his arms, a façade of steely resolve covering his frown. "Saber said the felycans will follow whatever the lycans propose, while the Blue Cloaks want to try to force peace talks."

Elyssa bit her lower lip. "What about the vampires?"

"They want to abandon Tarissa and wait it out." Thomas looked down at something. "Flava and her people have recruited nearly two hundred Seraphim for their new Tarissan Legion, but they still have to heal hundreds of the citizens Cephus mutated into his flying soldiers."

My stomach knotted. "I take it she wants to stay and fight?"

"She won't leave Tarissa," Thomas said. "If we relocate, we'd have to leave her behind."

"What about other citizens?" Elyssa asked.

"I don't know." Thomas sighed. "It's not an easy decision, but it's one we need to make soon."

I pounded a fist on the table. "We need to make Kohval and Meera realize that the Brightlings are the real enemy!"

Elyssa squeezed her eyes shut and shook her head. "What if we relocated our troops to Atlantis?" Her eyelids blinked open, revealing the sadness behind that question.

"We'll consider it if the logistics work," Thomas said. "It would mean asking a lot of the Mzodi."

Illaena, who'd remained quiet until now, spoke. "We will help you however we can."

"Is Atlantis big enough to support so many people?" I said. "Vampires, werewolves, felycans—it would be a tremendous change for everyone."

"We'll have to ask Adonis." Elyssa's lips formed a tight line. "If we allow Kohval and Meera to fight each other, the Brightlings will sweep in and take over what's left. All our sacrifice, all our hard work will have been for nothing." The sadness and uncertainty in her voice vanished, replaced by resolve. "I say we move the injured and non-essential personnel to Atlantis, and rouse every able body to help us fight for the future of Seraphina."

I felt a fierce grin stretch my lips, and a surge of pride warmed my heart. "I'm with Elyssa. We've lost too many good people to give up now." *We'll do this for Nightliss.*

A smile broke Thomas's mask. "Agreed. I'll work on the logistics from this end. Find out what the Atlanteans are willing to put up with. The more civilians we can evacuate, the easier it will be to fight."

Elyssa pressed a hand to her chest in a Templar salute. "Yes, Commander."

Pride shone in Thomas's eyes. "As you were, Templar." The holographic image vanished.

Illaena took Elyssa's hand. "I will consult with Xalara. Together, we can prevail."

Elyssa pressed her other hand over Illaena's. "Together we can do anything."

Illaena nodded. "I will join you outside after I've contacted the Muhala Kajeen."

"We'll let the others know what's going on," I said.

Elyssa and I returned above deck and told the others about our plans.

"Well ain't this just a ray of fairy-farting sunshine!" Shelton grumbled when we finished. "Do you really think the Atlanteans are gonna want to put up with a refugee crisis?"

"The Lyrolai won't like it either," Adam said. "The island is plenty big, but most of it is controlled by them."

Elyssa didn't look a bit deterred. "Atlantis is the safest place to keep those who can't fight out of harm's way."

"We've been in more difficult situations," I said, not entirely sure if that was true. "We'll get through this."

"And I'll be there to save your bacon." Shelton flashed a grin. "No rest for the weary."

Adam snorted. "Or the wicked."'

Illaena returned to the top deck and spoke with her first mate. Tahlee shouted orders and the *Falcheen* set course back through the portal and toward Atlantis. I hoped the denizens of the island would be willing to help us.

Once we arrived back in Atlantis, I spoke with Adonis and told him that we'd need to speak with the Lyrolai once Narine and Balaena were freed from the grasp of the bloodstones. He agreed to make the arrangements.

It took a few days, but Eor finally destroyed the bloodstones, restoring free will to Narine and Balaena. Dolpha took them back to the underwater city of Pacifis with her to help them recover, but they promised to return the next day to hear the requests we had of them, the mortals, and the Lyrolai. I hated the extra waiting, especially with Pjurna teetering on the brink of civil war. Unfortunately, it couldn't be helped.

The next morning, we met the others on the turtle pier. Narine, Balaena and Dolpha were all present, the first two looking no worse for the wear after their brief bloodstone captivity. Kalume, the Lyrolai representative watched us approach. The tall man looked apprehensive, but the way his eyes darted toward the ship and us, he was probably curious about these newcomers.

Adonis stood between the other parties, shifting nervously foot-to-foot. This was probably the most important meeting he'd attended in a long while. He cleared his throat and made introductions. "Kalume, this is Justin, Elyssa, Shelton, and Adam."

Kalume looked at us, green, almond-shaped eyes regarding us suspiciously. His long silver hair hung in small braids, and his skin held an almost bluish hue. Otherwise, he looked mostly human. I wondered if he had any powers over nature like the ones Cora exhibited.

"A pleasure to meet you." I didn't offer him a handshake, figuring he wouldn't know what it meant.

"I am pleased to hear you prevented an attack on the island," Kalume said in a sonorous voice that commanded respect. "The people of the wood are grateful."

Narine smiled inhumanly wide. "Your brave actions have also returned us to our sister," she said to us. "We owe you a debt."

"Would you consider helping us defeat Kaelissa once and for all?" I asked.

Her smiled faded. "We swore long ago never to use our abilities for harm. Fighting a war would go against everything we believe."

"But Dolpha helped us fight for you," Elyssa said. "Isn't that the same thing?"

"Dolpha requested the aid of our brethren in the sea," Balaena said. "She gave you a counter spell to our song. She did not use the song to fight."

"That's kind of a fine line," I said. "With your song, we could reunite Seraphina without bloodshed."

"You cannot force harmony among enemies," Narine said. "Powerful as the song might be, it grants only temporary unity. Hearts must be changed from within, not without."

Balaena nodded her agreement. "We will help you in other ways, but we will not use the song as a weapon."

Elyssa's shoulders slumped.

"War is an evil we left behind long ago," Kalume said. "For millennia we have lived here in peace and the wood, the glade, the glen, have prospered."

Adonis rolled his eyes, but didn't offer comment.

I'd expected things to go this way which was why I'd baited the hook with talk of war. Now they'd hopefully talked their way into a corner. "If you will not help us fight, then may we request asylum for those of our people who cannot fight? We have civilians and others injured from previous battles that need refuge. The citizens of Pjurna may soon face a civil war that we have to stop."

Narine's eyebrows rose sharply. "How many people?"

"Several hundred," Elyssa said. "Most of them will be Seraphim—citizens from the capitol city of Tarissa."

Adonis's eyes grew wide.

Kalume frowned, but he didn't dismiss the request outright. After all, he and Narine had just talked a big game about peace and gratitude. Turning down peaceful asylum would make them look like jackasses.

"We can certainly accommodate more people," Adonis said. "Thousands once lived in this city, so there are plenty of empty homes that can be used. We may need additional farmland for the food supply, if the Lyrolai are willing."

Kalume's frown deepened, but he nodded. "There may be room, but we would need assurances that they would not intrude on our domain."

"We approve," Narine said. "But request that you not base your army here."

"We'd like to have some defenses," Elyssa said. "Would that be acceptable?"

"Yes," Narine said.

Kalume nodded. "So long as they remain in the city."

Adonis rubbed his hands together. "Goodness, this is exciting! I can only imagine the stories your people will bring with them."

It was a good start, but there was a lot more to talk about, so I let Elyssa get down to the nitty gritty details.

That night, Elyssa and I sat on the hill next to our temporary home in Atlantis and looked at the dazzling sky and huge moon overhead.

"When I spoke with my father earlier," Elyssa said, "he told me something I didn't want to repeat in front of the others."

A knot formed in my gut. "What is it?"

"Issana isn't Nightliss's daughter." She let that sink in before continuing. "When Cephus took Nightliss captive, he tried to copy her."

I gasped. "He cloned her?"

Elyssa shook her head. "Issana is a golem."

The knot in my gut turned to ice. "The only person who can make such lifelike golems is Fjoeruss."

"Cephus and Serena were working on perfecting his technique," Elyssa said. "Thomas said that our people found plans to replace high-ranking officials with golems."

"Why make someone like Issana?" I said. "It doesn't make any sense even by their sick, twisted standards."

"Maybe they thought she'd make a good heir, or maybe their attempts to make a golem clone of Nightliss failed." Elyssa stroked my neck. "I just thought you should know."

I gripped her hand and kissed it, tear burning my eyes. "I'd almost hoped…"

She smiled through tears of her own. "I know. It would have been nice if Issana was Nightliss's daughter even if she's not that pleasant."

I took a deep breath and let the grief melt back into numbness. "It makes me happy that we're not abandoning Seraphina. I know Nightliss wouldn't have given up on her people even if they're acting like idiots."

"She would be very proud of us right now." Elyssa wiped tears from her face. "I know it feels like all of Seraphina is against us. We might have to fight Kohval, Meera, and Kaelissa."

"God, I hope not," I said.

She leaned her head on my shoulder. "It doesn't matter."

I stroked her hair and kissed her forehead. "Because we have each other?"

Elyssa looked up at me with big violet eyes. "Because you never give up on your friends and you always find that one ray of hope in the worst situations."

"That's not what gets me through my worst times." I pressed my hands to her cheeks and drank in the most beautiful sight in the universe. "When Kaelissa was about to steal my mind with the bloodstone, all I could think about was how much I love you and how awful it would be to lose you. Whenever I feel lost, I just think about you, Elyssa. You're my center."

Fresh tears welled in her eyes, but her accompanying smile was like the sun on a rainy day. "Justin, you are so cheesy, but I love you."

I planted a kiss on her soft lips and sighed. "And that, my dear, is why we will win."

She laughed. "Is it really that simple?"

"As simple as this: One ass-kicking at a time, we're gonna bring Seraphina together." I looked up at the stars, swallowing the lump in my throat. "And on that day, I just know Nightliss will be smiling down on us."

Elyssa held out her fist. "One ass-kicking at a time." We bumped fists and made explosion noises before bursting into laughter.

I had a feeling Nightliss was already smiling.

###

I hope you enjoyed reading this book. Reviews are very important in helping other readers decide what to read next. Would you please take a few seconds to rate this book?

For the latest on new releases, free ebooks, and more, join my VIP Club at www.johncorwin.net!

Books by John Corwin:

The Overworld Chronicles:
Sweet Blood of Mine
Dark Light of Mine
Fallen Angel of Mine
Dread Nemesis of Mine
Twisted Sister of Mine
Dearest Mother of Mine
Infernal Father of Mine
Sinister Seraphim of Mine
Wicked War of Mine
Dire Destiny of Ours
Aetherial Annihilation
Baleful Betrayal
Ominous Odyssey

Overworld Underground:
Possessed By You
Demonicus

Overworld Arcanum:
Conrad Edison and the Living Curse
Conrad Edison and the Anchored World
Conrad Edison and the Broken Relic

Stand Alone Novels:
No Darker Fate
The Next Thing I Knew
Outsourced
Seventh
Mars Rising

Meet the Author

John Corwin is the bestselling author of the Overworld Chronicles. He enjoys long walks on the beach and is a firm believer in puppies and kittens.

After years of getting into trouble thanks to his overactive imagination, John abandoned his male modeling career to write books.

He resides in Atlanta.

Connect with John Corwin online:
Facebook: http://www.facebook.com/johnhcorwinauthor
Website: http://www.johncorwin.net
Twitter: http://twitter.com/#!/John_Corwin